Editor: Bill Buford
Deputy Editor: Tim Adams
Managing Editor: Ursula Doyle
Editorial Assistant: Cressida Leyshon
Contributing Editor: Rose Kernochan

Managing Director: Catherine Eccles
US Publisher: Anne Kinard
US Financial Comptroller: Margarette Devlin
US Deputy Publisher: Louise Tyson
General Assistant: Harley Malter

Picture Editor: Alice Rose George
Executive Editor: Pete de Bolla

Subscription and Advertising Correspondence in the United States and Canada: Anne Kinard, Granta, 250 West 57th Street, Suite 1316, New York, NY 10107. Editorial Correspondence: Granta 2–3 Hanover Yard, Noel Road, Islington, London N1 8BE, England. All manuscripts are welcome but must be accompanied by a self-addressed envelope and international postal money order for return postage from England or they cannot be returned.

Granta, ISSN 0017-3231, is published quarterly for $29.95 by Granta USA Ltd, a Delaware corporation. Second class postage paid at New York, NY and additional mailing offices. POSTMASTER: send address changes to GRANTA, 250 West 57th Street, Suite 1316, New York NY 10107.

Granta is printed in the United States of America. The paper used in this publication meets the minimum requirements of American National Standard for Information Sciences—Permanence of Paper for Printed Library Materials, ANSI Z39.48-1984. ♾

Granta is available on microfilm and microfiche through UMI, 300 North Zeeb Road, Ann Arbor, MI 48106-1346, USA.

Granta is published by Granta Publications Ltd and distributed by Penguin Books Ltd, Harmondsworth, Middlesex, England; Viking Penguin, a division of Penguin Books USA Inc, 375 Hudson Street, New York, NY 10014, USA; Penguin Books Australia Ltd, Ringwood, Victoria, Australia; Penguin Books Canada Ltd, 2801 John Street, Markham, Ontario, Canada L3R 1BR; Penguin Books (NZ) Ltd, 182–190 Wairau Road, Auckland 10, New Zealand. This selection copyright © 1993 by Granta Publications Ltd.

Cover by Senate.

Granta 43, Spring 1993
ISBN 014 014059 X

# BEST OF YOUNG
# BRITISH NOVELISTS

43

# CONTENTS

# It's not homework.

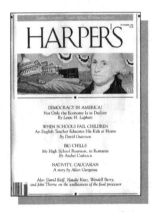

# Editorial

I thought there should be three judges—that seemed the right number for this sort of task—and I wanted to be one. Was I entitled to be? Probably not. Although I edit this magazine, a literary one, I had read few new novelists—Helen Simpson, Robert McLiam Wilson, Lawrence Norfolk, Adam Lively, Rose Boyt: I had their books but they were stacked in a corner of my house, unread. It was, I could see, evidence enough of the charge made against *Granta* that it was not publishing younger, 'unknown' writers—not all that surprising if the editor wasn't reading them. So, no, I was not qualified to be a judge. But I wanted to be: I wanted to earn my qualifications. It would make me, I felt, a better editor.

The other judges were eminently qualified. I was relieved, after my first conversation with A. S. Byatt—the first of many long phone calls, an hour in length, sometimes an hour and a half—to hear someone who took fiction seriously; it wasn't a career, like being an editor or *merely* a writer; it was much more, involved a commitment of such an absolute kind that few other enterprises could be compared to it: it was, in that wonderful phrase applied to jazz musicians, as serious as your life. Antonia was concerned especially for women writers who, for reasons of marriage or childbirth or social conditioning, tended to come in to their own later than their male counterparts. It had been true, she said, of herself—she wouldn't necessarily have qualified for a list of promising writers under the age of forty—and of others like Hilary Mantel or Jane Rogers: their situation was different from that of men; it was harder.

Salman Rushdie was no better read than I was, but driven by a refreshing curiosity: Just who were these young novelists? He wanted to know. He was the perfect judge. While he is a great, contentious cultural critic—full of fight and argument and aggression when the occasion demands it—he is, once introduced to a young novelist, capable of magnanimous displays of generosity (maybe you have to be a great novelist not to feel threatened by a younger generation). Like Antonia, he understands the novelist's plight, and the vulnerability

9

and fragility surrounding the task of sitting in a room, day after day, sometimes for years, 'making up' a book. All writing is difficult, but no writing is more difficult than writing of the imagination. Naturally enough, perhaps, I find the refrain from *Haroun and the Sea of Stories* knocking round my head, the same refrain that every novelist hears at some point: 'What's the use of stories that aren't even true?' Salman and Antonia understand the use of stories that aren't even true, believe in the duty and hardship of inventing them.

There would be a fourth judge—at the insistence of a consortium of five literary publishers who held a clandestine evening meeting to boycott the whole affair. ('Our authors are certainly not participating,' said one, huffily; 'Nor ours,' said another, 'who are mainly women and it's well known that *Granta* never publishes women.') In fact, their principle concern was that the enterprise—Rushdie? Byatt?—had become a touch too literary (just the objection you'd expect from literary publishers), and, in a spirit of compromise, I offered to invite John Mitchinson to join us: the marketing director of Waterstone's and, as such, a representative of the *trade*. In fact, John Mitchinson is as 'literary' as the novelist-judges, if not more so, having actually read many of the books that were about to be submitted (and I had always thought it wasn't such a bad idea to have someone along who had read the books). This mollified the literary publishers, although not entirely: the judge who really made them unhappy was me (after all, one publisher observed, you're just like us; you're an editor—a remark that has perplexed me ever since: isn't that what editors are meant to do—*judge* books?). Literary publishing, I've come to conclude, is a deeply mysterious process.

I should point out, especially for the foreign readers of this magazine, the reason for the proprietorial concern: 'The Best of Young British Novelists' is not only a special issue of *Granta*; it is a marketing campaign: at its most elementary level, nothing more than a gimmick to get people to buy literary novels. It was originally the idea of Desmond Clarke who, ten years ago, ran the Book Marketing Council, created in the characteristically eighties' belief that books should be treated like any other commodity, and that just as there was a Meat Marketing Council, urging everyone to go out and eat a British cow, so it followed there should be a comparable institution urging everyone to buy good, honest British novels. Desmond Clarke organized several campaigns, including, in 1983, his most successful: the twenty 'best' young British novelists under forty, which in turn inspired a special issue of *Granta*. But the campaign's greatest value was this: it became, despite itself, a serious statement about British literary culture.

But which came first—the writing or the campaign? I'm convinced that, had it been organized even three years before, it would have flopped: there was too little to promote. At the end of the seventies, there were only two young novelists whom anyone was making a fuss over: Ian McEwan and Martin Amis (I know this because, editing the first issues of *Granta*, I had no young British writers to put in them). The novel belonged not to the young author, who was writing a play or a television drama or a poem or nothing, but to another, older generation: Iris Murdoch, Angus Wilson, Kingsley Amis, Barbara Pym, Paul Scott, Stanley Middleton. It was easy, I recall Ian McEwan observing in 1985 with the rueful irony of someone now having to share the limelight, to be a young celebrity writer at the end of the seventies, because there was no one else around. I remember the metaphor he used: the horizon was uncluttered.

But not for long. In January of 1980, the beginning of the decade, I read a short story that was good, but, for reasons that must have been persuasive at the time, not good enough to publish, although *apparently* good enough for me to want to contact the writer and urge him to send us something else, resulting in a series of phone calls—to Norwich, London, Guildford—until finally I reached an unknown Kazuo Ishiguro in a bed-sit in Cardiff; the pay-phone was in the hall. Three months later, Adam Mars-Jones published his first story; two months later, Salman Rushdie completed *Midnight's Children*. The shortlist for the Booker Prize is an arbitrary literary chronicle at best, but it is revealing to compare the names that appear on it up to October of that same year, when William Golding's *Rites of Passage* won, and the names that emerge over the next five years: Salman Rushdie, D. M. Thomas, Ian McEwan, William Boyd, Timothy Mo, John Fuller, Graham Swift, Julian Barnes, Peter Carey, Kazuo Ishiguro. The last ten years have been good to readers—they represent a renaissance in the novel—so good that it's easy to forget just how bad they were before.

At our first meeting as judges, we established informal guidelines. After all, however contrived the task—why twenty? why under forty?—it was a daunting business: publishers were proving unreliable—both Polygon, a small press in Edinburgh, and Penguin, a larger one in London, took

seven weeks to deliver books that we'd asked for at the beginning
—and there was the persistent anxiety that authors would be excluded
simply because we never saw their work. (With what horror we greeted
the parcel of Iain Banks's novels that arrived two days before we made
our final decision. How could we have forgotten him?) Each session
began with the question: who have we left out? Each one ended with:
who can we eliminate? Antonia proposed that every book be read by
at least two people (you could tell that, unlike the rest of us, she had
done this sort of thing before) so as to ensure that no hidden prejudice
was governing someone's judgement. The system proved efficient, but I
remain uneasy that there are authors whose work I haven't read. After
our list was announced, I was challenged (twice) for excluding Janice
Galloway and went through my notes to confirm that she had been
read, and rejected, by two of us (Antonia and Salman); but it still
makes me uncomfortable

There wasn't much argument, which disappointed me: after all,
why gather such colourful people in one room (a series of different
rooms, in fact, because one judge, arriving with armed guards, could
not be seen in the same place twice), if you don't have the occasional
row. There was disagreement, but, in general, we followed the principle
that if three judges favoured one view, the fourth, after some squealing,
eventually deferred: thus Antonia, eventually, deferred to the decision
to leave out D. J. Taylor; thus John Mitchinson, after expressing
considerable astonishment, deferred to the decision to leave out Adam
Thorpe; and thus I likewise deferred to the decision to leave out
Richard Rayner, whose writing I seemed to have pushed so aggressively
that it led to one of the few times that Antonia became angry, snapping
that I was behaving just as the publishers had warned her that I would
(her other angry moment was when she rebuked John Mitchinson as
'chauvinist' for referring to Esther Freud as 'quite a babe.')

When our first session ended—each of us departing with a big box
of books—we all felt a little unsure about what was in store. We had
established a shortlist of the writers whom we knew deserved a place in
the final selection, but it consisted of only seven—Alan Hollinghurst,
Kazuo Ishiguro, Hanif Kureishi, Adam Mars-Jones, Ben Okri, Caryl
Phillips and Jeanette Winterson—and two of those had been on the list
ten years ago. In fact that list of ten years ago was never far from our
thoughts, and we regularly looked back to it to see how we were
faring: I pointed out, in an act of anticipatory defensiveness, that the

overall standard hadn't necessarily been that high, but the reality was that more than half of the selected writers had gone on to write exceptional books. Was the next generation as good? John Mitchinson advanced the view that it was not; Antonia argued again for extending the age limit, that we would be misrepresenting the achievement of women writers if we didn't; Salman pointed out that you couldn't extend the age limit past forty and still call any of them young, and suggested, instead, that if we didn't find twenty writers we liked, we should announce a shorter list. I tried to come up with a way of working Irish novelists into the campaign, although on the whole I was optimistic: after all, there were 196 more books to read.

A week later, a message from Antonia: she was depressed.

'They're so awful,' she said, when I phoned. 'There is no thought or history or interest except the miseries of the world we've made. They're full of the horror of the horrid eighties, but they are themselves that horror: they are what the eighties produced. It's as if a diet of video nasties has ruined a generation.' She lashed out at Martin Amis—not for being a bad writer, but for engendering so many bad imitations: 'He has had a baleful influence on a whole generation.'

I wasn't doing much better. I had got through twenty-five books and selected the worst (twenty-four) to send on to John Mitchinson: not for a second opinion, but so that John would read himself the junk that publishers were peddling as literary fiction. I entertained the hope that he'd send a note round to the Waterstone's branch managers, with these titles listed on it and instructions to do whatever possible to ensure that no one purchased the books.

Salman, however, had the luck to leave with a better box of books. He was happily halfway through Robert Erdric's *In the Days of the American Museum* and confidently advocated two further additions to our shortlist: Candia McWilliam and Nicholas Shakespeare. I reminded him that Shakespeare had written so rudely about *The Satanic Verses* that Salman had vowed revenge; and Salman said, yes, he remembered, but what could he do? Nicholas Shakespeare had written a good novel.

Our next meeting was two days before Christmas: London traffic was impenetrable, clogged up by last-minute shoppers and IRA bombers. I had just finished editing our winter issue and was exhausted; John Mitchinson had just been left by his wife and didn't know where he'd be sleeping that night; Antonia had just come down with the 'flu and was bundled up in jumpers; and Salman had just finished reading fifty novels. We protested—it's because he's got protectors looking after him that he gets so much time—but in fact he had been spurred on by the reading. His excitement was contagious.

By the end of the session, it was evident that our perception of this generation was different from the one we had even two weeks before, and that our anxieties were unjustified. Will Self's *The Quantity Theory of Insanity* was one of the best short story collections that any of us had read in a long time—full of originality and bite and surprise—rivalled only by Helen Simpson's *Four Bare Legs in a Bed*. Lawrence Norfolk's *Lemprière's Dictionary* was so ambitious and successful that I couldn't understand why he hadn't been on the Booker Prize shortlist (or, for that matter, hadn't won the prize itself). Why hadn't I read him before? Since then I've learned the depressing statistic that in the last eighteen months Lawrence Norfolk has been asked by more than eighty journalists for an interview—but hasn't been asked once in Britain (his book sales have a comparable home-abroad ratio).

Our shortlist was now seventeen.

A new year's eve fax from Salman Rushdie:
Bill:
A. L. Kennedy: Enjoying.
D. L. Flusfeder: No.
Philip Kerr: Excellent.
Adam Lively: *Very* good.
Carl MacDougall: Likewise, I think.
Sean French: Very surprising and enjoyable.
Anne Billson: Antonia digs her, too.
Alexander Stuart: Second thoughts—out?
See you—
Salman

We had intended to announce our selection on 2 January, but had to delay: there were too many books (more than three times the number that our predecessors considered ten years ago). Polygon, however, had still not responded to our letters or our phone calls or our faxes, and we were desperate to get hold of Tibor Fischer's *Under the Frog*. John Mitchinson said there were copies at the Charing Cross Waterstone's, only to learn later that twelve had sold that very afternoon: there was none left. If we didn't get a copy, would we have to delay our announcement again?

Our shortlist, in the meanwhile, had become a long list, and seven writers were going to have to be eliminated. And then John Mitchinson disappeared again: his father was in hospital, having had a heart attack (which, fortunately, turned out to be untrue, but not before John struck out for Yorkshire, with a parcel of late submissions under his arm, including the fugitive Fischer novel).

Until finally, five weeks and 211 novels after we began, we reached our decision: there was some discussion—one name was replaced by another—but, on the whole, the session was irritatingly amicable. Why did we all get along so well? I think it was because we were animated by the belief that, in coming up with this list, we had something important to say—that people didn't know—about this generation of writers.

And yet wasn't something wrong: why didn't they know already? Why didn't we?

And in conclusion?

No conclusion, merely observations, many trivial: that, in our post-Aids culture, the authors writing playfully about sex are gay—old-fashioned sex between boys and girls no longer, it seems, being of much interest; that this generation confirms, as if confirmation were needed, that the Empire has now fully and properly struck back; that the women novelists, with the exception of Jeanette Winterson, are writing too cautiously, too unambitiously (or perhaps their novels illustrate Antonia's point: that, as writers, they need more time to develop). I found myself growing increasingly irritated with the notion of a British novel, which was really an irritation with the word British, a grey, unsatisfactory, bad-weather kind of word, a piece of linguistic compromise. I still don't believe I know anyone who is British; I know people who are English or Scottish or Northern Irish (not to mention born-in-Nigeria-but-living-here or born-in-London-of-Pakistani-parents-and-living-here) and who sometimes, especially if they're English, make a point of calling themselves British so as not to offend the Scottish or the Northern Irish or the born-in-Nigeria-but-living-here-Nigerian-English. But it's a milky porridge kind of word, which to me says: everyone except the Irish (and is it possible to have a discussion of the novel *in* English *on* this side of the Atlantic and exclude the Irish?)

But, otherwise, while I believe that, overall, these authors are,

15

sentence by sentence, writing at a higher, more accomplished level than their predecessors ten years ago, I couldn't tell you if they are dirty realists or neo-gothics or baggy monsters or anything but themselves. In fact, my thoughts tend heavily towards inconclusiveness. I continue to be haunted by the first half of *Rose* by Rose Boyt and her menacing evocation of Hans and the atmosphere of sexual threat created around him. Shouldn't she be on our list of twenty, after all? Does Antonia share my regrets? She defended Rose Boyt's talents as she did Tim Pears's, whose *In the Place of Fallen Leaves* has already won the *Publishing News* award for the best first novel—a not inconsiderable achievement, given that, at the time, the book hadn't been published. My own doubts surrounding Robert McLiam Wilson are so strong as to amount to full-blown anger—with myself, with the others, with our failure: how could he have been left off? Salman is re-reading Deborah Levy's novels: Remind me again, he asked when we spoke on the phone, why she's not on the list?

Five weeks and 211 novels taught us that our preconceptions about what is being written today were dead wrong. And far from having to settle for a list that was less than twenty, we found that twenty was too restrictive a number: that it fails to represent the talent that is there.

There are problems: of perception (how exciting can a generation following a renaissance ever be seen to be?) or volume (the glut of books being published today makes it very, very difficult to see what's good) and, finally, of critical reception (it is an ungenerous, bigoted time), culminating in the symptomatic moment when the acting literary editor of the *Sunday Times*, after revealing that he needed controversy to secure himself the permanent position, exploited our exclusive agreement to announce the list only to denounce it. He had already admitted to having read less than half the authors.

Perhaps, then, it is no wonder that we haven't heard of many of these writers. But we will. I even suspect that someone may want to interview Lawrence Norfolk.

In the meanwhile, put this issue away once you've finished it. Pull it out again in the spring—in the year 2003—and see how we did.

Bill Buford

GRANTA

# IAIN BANKS
# UNDER ICE

Andy runs out across the ice. I am five years old and he is seven. Strathspeld is everywhere white; the sky is still and shining, hiding the sun in a dazzling, brilliant haze, its light somehow distanced by the intervening layer of high cloud overlooking a chill wilderness of snow. The mountain-tops are smothered, black crags violent spattered marks against that blankness; the hills and forests are blanketed too, the trees are frosted and the loch is hard and soft together, iced over then snowed upon. Here, beyond the gardens of the lodge and the woods and ornamental ponds, the loch narrows and becomes a river again, bending and funnelling and quickening as it heads towards the rocks and falls and the shallow gorge beyond. Usually from here you can hear the thunder of the falls in the distance but today there is only silence.

I watch Andy run out. I shout after him but I don't follow him. The bank on this side is low, only half a metre above the white plain of the snow-covered river. The grass and reeds around me are flattened under the sudden, overnight fall of snow. On the far side, where Andy is heading, the bank is tall and steep where the water has cut into the hill, removing sand and gravel and stones and leaving an overhang of earth and exposed, dangling tree roots; the dark gravel space under that ragged overhang is the only place I can see where there is no snow.

Andy is yelling as he runs, coat-tails flapping out behind him, gloved hands outspread, his head thrown back, the ear-flaps on his hat snapping and clapping like wings. He's almost half-way across and suddenly I go from being terrified and annoyed to being exhilarated, intoxicated; overjoyed. We were told not to do this, told not to come here, told to sledge and

**Iain Banks** was born in Dunfermline in 1954. His father was an Admiralty officer and his mother an ex-professional ice-skater. He was educated at Stirling University. His first novel, *The Wasp Factory*, was published in 1984. He has written eight further novels including three works of science fiction. 'Under Ice' is taken from a work-in-progress, *Complicity*, which Little, Brown will publish in September.

Photo: Barry Lewis

throw snowballs and make snowmen all we wanted, but not even to come near the loch and the river, in case we fell through the ice; and yet Andy came here after we'd sledged for a while on the slope near the farm, walked down here through the woods despite my protests, and then when we got here to the river bank I said well, as long as we only looked, but then Andy just whooped and jumped down onto the boulder-lumped white slope of shore and sprinted out across the pure flat snow towards the far bank. At first I'm angry at him, frightened for him, but now suddenly I get this rush of joy, watching him race out there into the cold level space of the stilled river, free and warm and vivacious in that smoothed and frozen silence.

I think he's done it, I think he's across the river and safe and there's a warm glow of vicarious accomplishment starting to well up within me, but then there's a cracking noise and he falls; I think he's tripped and fallen forward but he isn't lying flat on the snow, he's sunk up to his waist in it and there's a pool of darkness spreading on the whiteness around him as he struggles, trying to lever himself out, and I can't believe this is happening, can't believe Andy isn't going to jump free; I'm yelling in fear now, shouting his name, screaming out to him.

He struggles, turning round as he sinks deeper, chunks and edges of ice rearing into the air and making little puffs and fountains of snow as he tries to find purchase and push himself out. He's calling out to me now but I can hardly hear him because I'm screaming so hard, wetting my pants as I squeeze the screams out. He's holding his hand out to me, yelling at me, but I'm stuck there, terrified, screaming and I don't know what to do, can't think what to do, even while he's yelling at me to help him, come out to him, *get a branch*, but I'm petrified at the thought of setting foot on that white, treacherous surface and I can't imagine finding a branch, can't think what to do as I look one way towards the tall trees above the hidden gorge and the other along the shore of the loch towards the boat-house but there are no branches, there's only snow everywhere, and then Andy stops struggling and slips under the whiteness.

I stand still, quietened and numbed. I wait for him to come

back up, but he doesn't. I step back, then turn and run, the clinging wetness round my thighs going from warm to cold as I race beneath the snow-shrouded trees towards the house.

I run into the arms of Andy's parents walking with the dogs near the ornamental ponds and it seems like an age before I can tell them what's happened because my voice won't work and I can see the fear in their eyes and they're asking, Where is Andrew? Where is Andrew? and eventually I can tell them and Mrs Gould gives a strange little shuddering cry and Mr Gould tells her to get the people in the house and phone for an ambulance and runs away down the path towards the river with the four Golden Labradors barking excitedly behind him.

I run to the house with Mrs Gould and we get everybody —my mum and dad and the other guests—to come down to the river. My father carries me in his arms. At the riverside we can see Mr Gould on his stomach out on the ice, pushing himself back from the hole in the river; people are shouting and running around; we head down the river towards the narrows and the gorge and my father slips and almost drops me and his breath smells of whisky and food. Then somebody calls out and they find Andy, round the bend in the river, down where the water reappears from a crust of ice and snow and swirls, lowered and reduced, round the rocks and wedged tree-trunks before the lip of the falls, which sound muted and distant today, even this close.

Andy's there, caught between a snow-covered tree trunk and an iced-over rock, his face blue-white and quite still. His father splashes deep into the water and pulls him out.

I start crying and bury my face in my father's shoulder.

The village doctor was one of the house guests; he and Andy's father hold the boy up, letting water drain from his mouth, then lay him down on a coat on the snow. The doctor presses on Andy's chest while his wife breathes into the boy's mouth. They look more surprised than anybody when his heart restarts and then he makes a gurgling noise in his throat. Andy is wrapped in the coat and rushed to the house, submerged to the neck in a warm bath and given oxygen when the ambulance arrives.

He'd been under the ice, under the water, for ten minutes or more. The doctor had heard about children, usually younger than Andy, surviving without air in cold water, but never seen anything like it.

Andy recovered quickly, sucking on the oxygen, coughing and spluttering in the warm bath, then being dried and taken to a warmed bed and watched over by his parents. The doctor was worried about brain damage, but Andy seemed just as bright and intelligent afterwards as he'd been before, remembering details from earlier in his childhood and performing above average in the memory tests the doctor gave him and even doing well in school when that started again after the winter break.

It was a miracle, his mother said, and the local newspaper agreed. Andy and I never did get properly told off for what happened, and he hardly ever mentioned that day to me unless he had to. His father didn't like talking about it much either and used to be slightly dismissive and jokey about it all. Mrs Gould gradually talked less about it.

Eventually it seemed it was only I who ever thought about that still, cold morning, recalling in my dreams that cry and that hand held out to me for help I could not, would not give, and the silence that followed Andy disappearing under the ice.

And sometimes I felt he was different, and had changed, even though I knew people changed all the time and people our age changed faster than most.

Even so, I thought on occasion there had been a loss; nothing necessarily to do with oxygen starvation but just as a result of the experience, the shock of his cold journey, slipping away beneath the grey lid of ice (and perhaps, I told myself in later years, it was only a loss of ignorance, a loss of folly and so no bad thing). But I could never again imagine him doing something as spontaneously crazy, as aggressively, contemptuously fate-tempting and *unleashed* as running out across the frozen ice, arms out, laughing.

GRANTA

# LOUIS DE BERNIÈRES
# THE BRASS BAR

In the late seventies I was desperately attempting to avoid having a career by doing what I supposed were 'real' jobs. It was a depressing time. Utopia was failing to emerge from the revolutions of the sixties, and those natural drop-outs who remained found themselves with nothing to drop out into and nowhere to go. I had been keeping my life together by gardening in the daytime and teaching philosophy classes in the evenings. My idea of hell was, and still is, to have to put on a tie and go to an office, and I believed that I was a part of the new world where everybody would wear faded jeans and work would be less important than 'finding yourself' and seeking nirvana in the arms of gentle long-haired girls. I had also swallowed heavy draughts of the kind of left-wing thinking that implies that only working-class people are worth while. Being impeccably middle class myself, I threw aside all my advantages and privileges and took only those kinds of occupation that 'real' people take. Having become used to the idea that working-class people were the repository of all that is authentic and good, it took me a great many years to disembarrass myself of it.

My notions about the dignity of labour were shattered when I discovered that very little of it was ever done. I once worked in a hospital garden where my workmate skived off every day with 'backache' and disappeared to work on his car at home. This attitude being infectious, I passed an entire summer making love to a tall and neurotic skivvy in a very large wheelbarrow in the greenhouse, when I should have been mowing the lawns and

**Louis de Bernières**, born in 1954, was determined never to have a career. After four disastrous months in the British army, he left for a village in Colombia, where he worked as a teacher in the morning and as a cowboy in the afternoon. Since his return to England he has been employed as a mechanic, a landscape gardener and a groundsman at a mental hospital. He currently teaches truants in London.

'I don't do granny novels, or novels about sex and shopping,' he says. He does write comic novels with baroque titles: *Señor Vivo and the Coca Lord*, *The Troublesome Offspring of Cardinal Guzmán* and *The War of Don Emmanuel's Nether Parts*. He is hoping to call his next novel simply *Corelli's Mandolin*.

tending the chrysanthemums. When the head gardener became hopelessly depressed about the state of the hospital gardens, he tried to drown himself in a rain barrel and was discovered with his legs poking up from it. Somebody hauled him out and said, 'What are you doing, George?' to which he replied, 'I'm trying to kill myself.'

Of course, at university I came to believe that the working classes were in the forefront of progressive thought, which caused me to be ever more stunned by the slow discovery that the opposite is true. In working mens' clubs I was amazed and disillusioned by the opinions that passed unchallenged around the tables laden with watery beer, whisky chasers and barley wine. No Colonel Blimp could have been more nationalistic, more money-fixated, more hang-'em-and-flog-'em, more unreasoningly racist.

By this time I was working at a garage in the East End of London. My boss, who was a cockney Italian, once refused to call an ambulance for a little black boy who had been run over outside. He backed off when he saw that I was about to abandon my ideal of non-violence, but afterwards I only avoided the sack because of the intervention of the foreman, Vic, who told him that I was the only one of the mechanics who understood how an engine worked. This was actually true.

I had arrived at this garage one morning, looking for a job that was authentically working class. Vic said, 'Got any qualifications?' and I pointed to my Morris Minor and said, 'I built that from two old ones.'

'Eighty quid a week,' he said. 'Start on Monday and do alternate Saturdays.' His cash-in-hand tax-avoidance approach was to land me with considerable difficulties later on from the Department of Health and Social Security.

The garage was a tiny establishment in a back street. It had a pit but no real equipment, so we had to work under unpropped jacks with metric spanners, regardless of whether cars were fitted with American or imperial bolts. It was like doing the most strenuous yoga all day every day, and my pursuit of nirvana in the arms of long-haired girls was reduced to falling asleep as soon as I went to bed, too embarrassed to touch them in any case on account of the ineradicable grime on my hands.

Everything about the garage was dishonest. They sold second-hand engines as 'reconditioned' (we labelled old engines as either 'OK' or 'F' for 'fucked'); they charged for elaborate work, using technical language, that had not been done, and did work that was unnecessary. My boss always got us to change rubber bushes on the suspension and in fact my very first job was to change brake-shoes that were perfectly serviceable. When I pointed this out to him he looked at me as though I were utterly mad. He made a particular point of conning women, on the grounds that they did not know anything about cars anyway. In the end I used to try to work at the entrance of the garage so that I could warn them on their way in.

In this garage we had two guard dogs who had the same attitude as the workers. There was an Alsatian and a spaniel. They would steal anything that could be moved, eating it even if it were inedible. They were filthy from oil, and they would shit on the back seats of the cars in the night, so we would have to clean them up before the customers arrived. One day we missed some, and the customer became hysterical, thinking that we had insulted her deliberately. The two dogs used to welcome burglars with enthusiasm, and the boss had to install an alarm to compensate for their deficiencies. The dogs were also racist, having been trained to bite blacks.

We did have a black welder for a little while, but he was obsessed with the smartness of his white clothes. He eventually stopped turning up because he preferred unemployment to getting muck on his garments, and his gold chains kept getting caught up in suspensions and exhaust clips. The boss said, 'I'm never employing a fucking wog again.' Having been in that company for a while, 'fucking' became the only adjective that I ever used, and it took me many years to get out of the habit. It was the kind of place where the answer to a question like, 'What's fucking wrong with the fucker?' would be, 'The fucking fucker's fucking fucked, fuck it.' I was later to learn at university that working-class speech was as rich and varied as Standard English. The research was done in New York, however.

Louis de Bernières

My boss always dressed in black and had a gold chain around his neck. He had a very pretty wife and a ten-year-old daughter who was dressed in Gloria Vanderbilt clothes and attended a private Catholic school. The inevitable result of this was that she would grow up to despise her father. The boss had two Mercedes, and used to flee to the United States in shame every time that he beat up his wife. He worked out a scam for shipping all the cars over there that would normally be scrapped. He sold them to the Americans as 'Classics'. He thought that he was very strong and macho and once challenged me to an arm-wrestle, as I was the garage champion. When he started losing he pulled away, saying that he had a customer to attend to. After that, Vic had to save me from being fired again.

Vic was in fact a carpenter who was technically unemployed. He earned a very large wage at the garage, claimed social security and also creamed off the takings when he delivered them to the boss at the end of the day. We used to call him 'Wic' for reasons that shall be explained, and he only had one sentence in his repertoire. He would look at something he had just finished and say,'That is so fucking pukka I could fucking spunk myself.' His eyes would go wide with pleasure, and I would say that he was the only one there who found genuine joy in his work.

He was called 'Wic' because we had a Turk there called Tommy. Tommy the Turk could not say his 'V's, and he always called Vic 'Wic'. This caught on, and by extension I became 'Wouis', Neil became 'Wheel', Trevor became 'Revver' and he himself became 'Wommy'.

Wommy's favourite tool was a large hammer. He used it upon even the most delicate tasks, frequently with startling success. His ambition was to spend his life playing 'wolleyball', and he had married an English girl just so that he could stay in England and play it. He was always deeply depressed about his marriage because he could no longer stand having to sleep with a wife whom he had not even liked in the first place. His life was a long reverie about finding true love and playing wolleyball. One day he was cutting a rusted piece off the back of a customer's car with a welding torch, and caught the fuel tank. The resultant explosion destroyed the car completely and left him black from head to foot. The boss looked at him and at the wreck of the car and said, 'I'm not employing no more fucking wogs.' Wommy ended up selling ice-creams from a van in Stoke Newington.

Wheel was a young lad, tall, blond and silly. He was in love with his Cortina, which he had juiced up so much that he had had to cut a hole in the bonnet to accommodate the enormous twin carburettors. It had a special megaphone that relayed wolf-whistles at pretty girls at the touch of a button, and it had furry seats. Wheel used to race it with other cars in the streets, and once he came into work ashen-faced because a car he had been racing with had just killed three pedestrians. He had fled from the scene unscathed and shaking. He used to work in the paintshop, and after spraying a car he would come out, covered with paint except for the area of his face that had been masked, and collapse in the yard. He would lie there giggling like a lunatic, completely and irretrievably stoned on the thinners. He became very good at bodywork, after some disastrous experiments on various customers' cars, and eventually he fell in love with a woman and sold his Cortina.

Trevor, or Revver, was already a supposed lunatic when he arrived. I thought that his illness was that he was too natural and too kind. He was bald except for black wisps at the side of his head that stuck out horizontally, he had perpetually surprised brown eyes and he was very thin. He loved his girlfriend deeply, was crazy about sex and quickly realized that the appearance of work was more important than its actual accomplishment. He used to do a delightfully gross impression of cunnilingus by touching the tips of his forefingers together and the tips of his thumbs and waggling his tongue through the resultant impression of a vulva. He referred to oral sex as 'plating' and would come into work with his eyes gleaming. I would say, 'Alright Rev?' and he would reply, 'Fucking plated me girlfriend for breakfast. Fucking lovely.'

Because Trevor was so joyful he was referred to a psychiatrist by his doctor. Trevor himself was convinced that he was mad, because he believed that the fumes of welding always caused welders to become demented. When the psychiatrist questioned Trevor about his sex life, Trevor told him to 'fucking mind your own fucking business,' whereupon the psychiatrist was also persuaded of Trevor's madness. Not wishing to disappoint anyone,

Trevor himself began to act up to the label, mainly in his work.

I used to help him under the cars by holding the metal plates in position, and at first he was very conscientious; his welding was as careful as needlework. But when fate conspired to declare that he was crazy, he became disillusioned. Metal sheet was replaced by newspaper, body-filler and heavy coats of underseal. His craftsmanship in this novel form of laminate was immaculate, though his perfect mock-ups of welding actually took twice as long to execute as the real thing. However, nemesis inevitably arrived one day when a customer got into his car and the whole of the new floor fell out beneath him, revealing itself to be made of the *Sun* and wrappers from the kebab shop that we raided every lunch-time. I told him that he should have used *The Times*.

Trevor got the sack on the same day as he was allocated a place in the mental home. He came out of the boss's office looking depressed for the first time and gave me a brass bar. It was his favourite tool. It was very heavy, very golden, and he had always kept it carefully chamfered at the business end. 'This is fucking high-class metal,' he told me. 'Every bodyworker would give his fucking life for a bar like this. It won't never break nor wear fucking out, and I want you to have it.'

It was the bar that he used to knock metal straight when it was in awkward corners. It was exactly the right hardness to do the job without damaging the target metal and without itself bending or fracturing. 'My dad passed it on to me,' he said. 'He was a welder 'n' all.'

'Did he go potty?' I asked, and Trevor replied, 'Always fucking was.'

After poor Trevor had left for the last time I showed the brass bar to Wic, and he exclaimed, 'Fucking pukka. You should fucking spunk yourself, having that.'

After Trevor we got a new welder who came from Newcastle. At first I couldn't understand anything he said except 'fucking'. He told us that he was in the SAS and that he worked as a deep-sea welder on the North Sea oil rigs. He never forgave me for beating him at arm-wrestling, his attendance was desultory and he disappeared after a fight with the boss, which he lost despite being in the SAS. He was even more vilely racist and reactionary than the others, and he sincerely believed that he was a hero or a demigod simply because he came from Newcastle.

I left to do teacher training. At the polytechnic the middle-class students, who flattened their vowels and said 'fucking' a lot, granted me tremendous street cred for having had such authentic working-class jobs, at exactly the time when I was beginning to understand what a fraud that street cred was. Ten years of teaching was to be enough to disillusion me about all classes whatsoever, and persuade me that the Great British Public was uniformly allergic to culture of any kind. But that is another story.

At teacher training college I sometimes repaired the tutors' cars, and I still use Trevor's indestructible brass bar when I do the bodywork on the same Morris Minor as I had then. The more I use it, the more I realize how much Trevor was giving up when he gave it to me, and the more I understand that for him it was a farewell to happiness, purpose and his natural self, and to the trade that had made him what he was. Where I come from you can be madder than Trevor and simply be a 'character', without being shunted off to a mental home. You know not to tell psychiatrists to mind their own business, you know not to celebrate oral sex in public (I remember his shining eyes as he slopped his tongue around in lascivious imitation of oral sex, his thick stubble glistening with tiny drops of saliva) and you don't do the kind of jobs where the terror of white heat and the jagged edges of steel make you prefer to do botch-ups. I cannot help but hope that his girlfriend had the sense to diagnose him sane and take him out of hospital, and I wish I could find him and thank him for the gift of the brass bar.

Every other drift that I have had since then has bent, peeled back from the point or splintered. Only Trevor's has survived, pristine, still bearing the marks of his careful chamfering. It lies gleaming in my toolbox, heavy, solid and waiting imperturbably for the clubhammer blows that will never defeat it. Trevor's best possession is now one of mine, a fucking pukka brass bar that makes you want to spunk yourself.

GRANTA

ANNE BILLSON
BORN AGAIN

I had no time for vices. Sex, drugs, cigarettes—I'd kicked them all long ago. I had a vague notion that I could take them up again one day, once I'd got everything under control, but not yet. The only weakness I allowed myself was wine. So when I awoke that morning with a thumping great hangover, I put it down to the bottle I'd finished off the night before.

My stomach was playing up. It rejected everything I poured into it: orange juice, camomile tea, soluble aspirin. Muesli was out of the question. Dry toast didn't appeal. It was only when I was in the cab on my way into work that I realized what I wanted. I'd thought junk food had been consigned to the scrap heap of vices, but my digestive system had other ideas. None of that freshly squeezed nonsense; it was crying out for a Fudge Tub. I'd never had a Fudge Tub before, but the desire was so overwhelming that I had to get out of the cab at Marble Arch and go in search of one. I was supposed to be getting down to business with the Belgians, and yet here I was, looking for a sweet-shop while the seconds ticked away.

I was going against the morning rush-hour tide; everyone seemed to be headed in the opposite direction. I wasn't used to walking in such crowds. But suddenly they started giving me space. I could see pedestrians veering away as I approached, pressing into the doorways of shops or stepping off the pavement, and they were all staring at me. Or rather, staring at something just behind me. One or two of them giggled, but most of them

---

**Anne Billson** was born in Southport in 1954 and grew up in Exeter and Croydon. She saw her first horror film—*Bambi*—at the age of five. After leaving art college in 1976, she became a freelance photographer and journalist, reviewing films for *Time Out* and the *Sunday Correspondent*. Her first novel, about bloodthirsty yuppies in the heart of London's Docklands, is called *Suckers: Bleeding London Dry* and is published by Pan.

She currently lives in Cambridge and is working on her next novel—'It's a ghost story, and I can only write during the day; I scare myself too much if I try and do anything at night.' Her favourite pastime is reading medical textbooks; she recently fainted in a bookshop while examining colour photographs of psoriasis.

35

looked slightly alarmed. One passer-by began to say something, then shook his head and moved on.

I glanced over my shoulder. What I saw made me stop dead. There was a man right behind me. When I stopped, he stopped too. Ordinarily he wouldn't have attracted much attention, though his grey suit was creased and he was looking a bit wild-eyed. But the reason everyone was looking at him was that round about waist height he was clutching a Kitchen Devil. The knife was so big it was absurd. This was not a concealed weapon; you could have spotted it from a passing 747. I dismissed it. No. If some maniac was going to attack you, he didn't creep up like a look-behind-you villain, not with a weapon like that. Not in broad daylight. Not in front of hundreds of witnesses. Not in *Oxford Street*.

Then I saw his chin was wet with saliva. It was this, more than the knife, that made me uneasy.

We stood and stared at each other. He mumbled something. I checked my watch and told him the time. One of the onlookers tittered. The man frowned and mumbled again.

I thought maybe he was lost and asking directions. 'I'm sorry,' I said. 'You'll have to speak up. I'm afraid I'm not really with it this morning.'

He seemed to make up his mind and opened his mouth and yelled. 'Abomination! Queen of the Bitches! Whore of Babylon!'

I said, 'I think you must be mistaking me for someone else.'

He shook his head, adjusted his grip on the handle of the knife and ran at me.

My life didn't exactly flash in front of me, but I felt just the tiniest pang of regret for all those things I had given up because they were bad for my health. All that self-denial, and for nothing. Then the regret was replaced by a rather sluggish survival instinct. I thought about diving into the crowd, but it was too late. No one was going to step forward and help; I was on my own here.

The blade was very big, and the steel looked very sharp and it was coming closer. It was no longer six feet away. Now it was five feet. Four feet. Three.

The man emptied his lungs in a saliva-splattering yell and lunged forward. I didn't see how he could possibly miss, but miss he did. He let out a sort of surprised grunt and froze like a mime artist encountering an invisible wall.

And then he did a sort of back-flip. It should have been an impossible manoeuvre, but he did it as lightly and as gracefully as any Olympic gymnast. You could tell from the look on his face that he hadn't intended to do it, and at some point in mid-air all the lightness and grace left him and he bungled the landing. He stuck out a hand to save himself, but unfortunately for him it was the hand with the Kitchen Devil in it, and he fell straight on to the blade.

It turned out to be every bit as sharp as it looked. It sliced through most of his neck. There was a pause, and then it was as though someone had turned on a tap somewhere. The blood fanned out like fine spray from a garden sprinkler, and everyone said *ooooh*. Not quite everyone. Someone was screaming. Imagine my embarrassment when I realized that someone was me.

'How are you feeling?' asked the man in the tweed jacket. I told him I was feeling groggy.

I was lying on a bed, fully dressed, but my clothes felt as though someone had been interfering with them. I tried to sit up, but it wasn't easy.

'I wouldn't get up if I were you, not just yet,' said the man in the tweed jacket, peering over the top of his spectacles at the clipboard he was holding. 'You can relax. You've had a bit of a shock, but there is absolutely *nothing* to worry about.'

'What's going on?'

'You're feeling a bit woozy because we gave you a sedative. A perfectly safe one.'

'What about the Fudge Tub?' I asked, and then I remembered. 'There was a man with a knife . . . '

'It's all right,' the man said. 'You're in a hospital. You've been checked over and everything's fine. I'm Doctor Webster by the way.'

'Is he—dead?'

'Afraid so.' He jotted something down. 'Who was he, have you any idea?'

I shook my head. 'Never seen him before in my life. He must have been nuts.'

37

Doctor Webster nodded. 'It certainly looks that way. Well, it's for us to find that out. Now, would you like us to phone your husband?'

'I'm not married,' I said.

'Boyfriend, then?'

'I don't have a boyfriend,' I said. 'But I should phone the office. Good Lord, is that the time? Jesus, I was supposed to be having lunch with the Belgians.'

I tried to get up again. This time, I got as far as a sitting position. The doctor frowned.

'Father, then. We can phone the father, let him know everything's fine.'

'You can't phone my father,' I said, feeling slightly miffed at his insistence on bringing men back into my life. They were another of those vices I'd given up. 'My father died.'

The doctor frowned again. 'I'm sorry,' he said. 'Miss—it is Miss, isn't it? Miss—'

'Oh, it was seven years ago,' I said. 'Loughlin, Nancy Loughlin.' The attack had dwindled into a distant dream-memory, but I was getting a bad feeling about the here and now. 'Why do you have to phone *anyone*? I'm OK, aren't I?'

Dr Webster shrugged. 'I thought you might want the father to know that the baby's fine.'

My attention wandered off. It wandered all the way past his left shoulder and fixed on an anti-smoking poster on the wall behind him. Suddenly that poster seemed fascinating.

I heard myself saying, 'Excuse me?'

'The baby's fine.'

Soon after I'd recovered from a second dose of perfectly safe sedative, Dr Webster and I had a long chat. I learned fast. I learned it was useless to protest that I couldn't possibly be pregnant. There was no way at all I could be having a baby, because I was a born-again virgin; I hadn't had sex for years. I told Dr Webster, but he didn't believe me. He thought my refusal to acknowledge the situation was due to moral confusion and deep-seated guilt.

I began to question my sanity. Had I been living an illusion all these years? Maybe I'd got the facts of life muddled. I'd always assumed it was intercourse that made you pregnant, but what if I'd been wrong? What if it was kissing or sneezing or shaking hands? Maybe I'd never really known what sex *was*. Maybe I'd been having it all along without realizing. Or maybe I was suffering from some rare disease which mimicked all the symptoms of pregnancy.

I couldn't even remember having missed a period, though I'd never bothered to keep track. But I was definitely pregnant. Dr Webster showed me the results of the scan. I demanded a second opinion, and he rolled his eyes and sent for a nurse and she double-checked and told me yes, I was definitely pregnant and congratulations, how happy I must be. I burst into tears but it didn't change a thing.

'I can't possibly have a baby,' I said. 'What about my career?'

Dr Webster got bored and drifted away. I said I couldn't wait, I was quite happy to go private, and the nurse gave me some telephone numbers and I slipped her a tenner and we phoned up and made an appointment for the next morning. Then I rang the office and told Jamie I'd be taking a couple of days off. This was unheard-of, but I let it slip that I'd been attacked, and then he suddenly came over all concerned and tried to persuade me to take the next fortnight off. I said no, that wouldn't be necessary, I would be in at the end of the week, and Susie was to take over with the Belgians for the time being, but she should call me at home if something came up.

The nurse was smiling sadly as I replaced the receiver. 'It's a big decision,' she said. 'Wouldn't you like to think it over?'

I thought about the embryo that was growing inside me, and wondered whether it had tiny arms and legs and fingers and toes. I wondered if it had a face yet and whether it would take after me or its non-existent father. I wondered if it was some sort of miracle and I couldn't wait to get rid of it.

I told her I didn't need to think it over; I'd been thinking about it all my life. She looked taken aback at this, so I added something about how bad I felt about it all, and she nodded sympathetically.

Therewere no taxis. I was going to have to take the tube to the clinic and it was pelting with rain. On my way to the station I had the feeling I was being followed. While I waited for the train I kept glancing along the platform. There were a couple of dozen people waiting with me, but as far as I could see none of them had a knife. I decided I was being paranoid. Being paranoid, after what had happened, was perfectly natural.

The indicator board announced there was a train approaching. There was a distant rumble and a rush of air. As I took a step towards the edge of the platform, I felt myself being *pushed*. I clutched at empty air but there was nothing to grab. The word *unfair* flashed through my brain.

Then the man who had been doing the pushing sailed past me. He did a double somersault and landed on his back across the rails. As he tried to sit up, I caught a glimpse of his shiny white face staring at me. His mouth moved but I didn't get a chance to work out what he was saying because the train was suddenly there and it was making such a noise that I must have imagined the *squelch* as it mashed into him.

Doors slid open and people got off, unaware that anything had happened. I wondered whether I should be screaming but I didn't because I didn't want any more fuss. There was no way I was going to talk to the police again. I knew they would give me a hard time. The man with the knife had been bad luck. But now this—it was starting to look suspicious.

Further up the platform, the driver leant out of his cabin and was violently sick. There was a certain amount of scurrying and shouting but no one took any notice as I lurched towards the exit. One or two people had seen some poor sod lose his balance, but none of them had seen what he'd been doing to me just before he'd lost it.

The collector shot me a quizzical glance as I handed in my unused ticket. 'Someone fell under the train,' I gasped. Outside, I propped myself against a wall and took big deep breaths. I stood there feeling queasy until the thought of a Fudge Tub floated into my head and made me feel a whole lot better.

It didn't stop there but I was beginning to grow blasé. I'd always been good at adapting to suit the circumstance, which was why my business had thrived while so many others had gone under. I bought a Fudge Tub from the confectionery kiosk, barged in front of a couple of tourists who had just managed to hail a cab, waved cheerio as they stood there gawping and settled down in the back.

I felt I was ready for anything now and I didn't have to wait long. Around Knightsbridge, I watched with interest as a Ford Fiesta came screeching through the red lights and tried to ram us. The cab driver swerved sharply, but I knew the Fiesta wouldn't hit us and it didn't. One moment we were on a collision course, the next it was careering across the road and straight through the window of Harvey Nichols. My driver took it in his stride. 'Guy must've had a coronary,' he growled as we drove on. I finished my Fudge Tub and twisted round to watch through the rear window as the wrecked Fiesta went up in flames.

Nothing else happened on the way to the clinic. I was sifting through my memory trying to come up with clues. Maybe I'd inherited a fortune without knowing it, or inadvertently rubbed up against the Cosa Nostra on that last Italian account. Maybe the local council had tipped toxic waste into the water supply. Maybe people were wigging out all across town.

But I doubted it. I was starting to think I was a special case.

The appointment went smoothly. I watched Dr Madison carefully, half expecting him to whip out a scalpel and launch himself at my throat at any second, but he was polite and professional. He didn't waste time on ethics. I filled out some forms and wrote out a cheque and agreed to come back in two days' time. I would book in before noon, have the op shortly afterwards and then my best friend Belinda would come along to see me home. With any luck I would be back in time for the Nine O'Clock News.

'I had no idea abortions were this easy,' I said.

'It's a woman's right to choose,' said Dr Madison, and neither of us mentioned the fat fee I'd just coughed up.

The body count mounted steadily. My journey home was like a Roadrunner cartoon with my assailants in the Coyote role. They tried, how they tried, but none of them came close. The next man was carrying a syringe, but no sooner had I spotted it than he did a clever little pirouette and keeled sideways into the path of a number 88. Ten minutes later and another man was striding towards me, tugging something metallic out of an inside pocket, when there was an almighty yell from up above and an ornamental clock which some workmen had been cleaning sort of toppled off its perch and came plummeting down on to his head with a sickening crunch. I was just beginning to think I was mistaken about the next man when two pit bull terriers came barrelling out of a shoe shop. They hurtled straight past me and I didn't bother to look round, not even when the snarling stopped and the screaming began.

There may have been other attempts, but I didn't notice them. I spotted a cab on Brook Street and went straight home. As soon as I was inside the flat, I double-locked the door and turned to find myself staring down both barrels of a shotgun.

'Whore of Babylon!' spat the man. 'You shall die!'

'Oh, for God's sake,' I said. '*Why*? Why *me*?'

His suit was crumpled but had it not been for the saliva and the bloodshot eyes and the hair that needed combing he might have passed for a perfectly respectable businessman. He lowered the gun, seemingly taken aback that I wasn't on my knees begging for mercy. But I felt quite safe, even now. *Especially* now.

'Nothing personal,' he said.

'You just called me the Whore of Babylon,' I said. 'If that's not personal, I don't know what is.'

I could see doubt creeping into his face. 'I'm sorry,' he said. 'Really I am. We know you can't help what happened.'

'We?'

'Brothers of the Divine Order of the Dead Saints.'

'So what *did* happen, exactly?'

'You mean you don't know?'

'All I know is, I've been walking around all day with a "please kill me" sign pinned to my back.'

'You're carrying something . . . '

'*Now* you're telling me.'

'You're carrying something that must be destroyed.'

'Listen,' I said, 'I have no problem with that.'

'You have no idea,' he said and began to cry. I almost felt sorry for him. 'You don't know what it *means.*'

'Try me,' I said.

His head jerked up and he started getting all wild-eyed again. 'The end of *everything*,' he babbled. 'The end of life itself. The trumpets will sound and *no one* is saved.'

A thought suddenly occurred to me. 'But whose side are you on? And what about me? Are we talking about the Second Coming, or is this a *Rosemary's Baby* situation?'

'The blood of the Lamb!' he blurted, which didn't leave me any the wiser. He was pointing the shotgun again but his hands weren't terribly steady. I offered to make him a cup of tea. He shook his head, tears running down his cheeks. 'I'm sorry,' he said, 'Really sorry. I've got to do this, it's the only way.'

'No it's not,' I said, reaching into my bag. 'Here, take a look.' I handed him the forms I'd filled in at the clinic.

'What's this?'

'Day after tomorrow,' I said. 'I don't want it any more than you do. You have absolutely nothing to worry about.'

At first he couldn't see what I was getting at. Then he lit up. 'You mean—?'

'No problem,' I said. 'Whoever it was, they made a big mistake picking me. I'm just not the maternal type, never have been. I mean, I have my career to think of.'

I made him a cup of tea and we had a long chat, and then, at last, he went away.

There were no more attempts on my life, not for the rest of that day, nor the day after that. The man with the shotgun had been as good as his word and called his Brothers off. They knew I was on their side, maybe for secular reasons, but working towards the same end. It had been an extraordinary adventure while it had lasted but now it was over and all that remained was for me to get shut of whatever it was that had been planted inside me and get back to work.

On the morning of the appointment I woke feeling refreshed

and optimistic. I travelled to the clinic with a light heart, changed into a nightdress and settled down in my small private room to flick through the latest magazines, though they were so dull and trivial I ended up going through one of the reports I'd brought along with me instead.

Just after noon the nurse popped in to take my temperature and blood pressure. 'Feeling nervous?'

'Not in the slightest.'

'Of course not,' she said. 'It's just a routine procedure.'

Half an hour later they trundled me into the tiny operating theatre, arranged a sheet over the bottom half of my torso and stuck my feet into some straps. Dr Madison peered down at me and smiled. I hadn't noticed his teeth before. They were very shiny and white, like the theatre walls. 'All right Miss Loughlin?'

'Fine,' I said.

'This is Arthur. He's our anaesthetist.'

'Hello Arthur.'

Arthur stuck a needle into my arm and told me to start counting. 'One,' I said. 'Two. You will make sure I'm unconscious, won't you?'

'Of course we will,' he said. 'Just keep counting and before you know it . . . '

'Three,' I counted. 'Four . . . Five . . . '

I was feeling groggy again. I knew there was something I had to remember but I couldn't work out what it was. I opened my eyes. The light was too bright and I was cold in all the wrong places. Where was my Fudge Tub?

'Nancy? Nance? Are you OK?'

Someone was leaning over me. I blinked rapidly, trying to see who it was.'

'Belinda? Here already?' I felt a rush of relief. It was all over.

'Oh Nancy,' she said.

I blinked again. I'd never seen Belinda look like this before. Someone had drained all the blood from her face and replaced it with porridge. 'You look awful,' I said.

'Hey, let's get you out of these straps.' There was a wobble in her voice.

I tried to disentangle myself but my limbs weighed a ton and I couldn't make them move. 'Where's the nurse?' I asked, and at that precise moment everything swam back into focus.

'What the—' I said, trying to sit up.

'Oh no, you mustn't look,' said Belinda, pushing me back. Then there was someone else alongside her and I was being rolled on to a stretcher and covered with a blanket and wheeled away from the bright lights, and there seemed to be an awful lot of people milling around. Some of them were in uniform.

Belinda bent over me and took one of my hands. 'Well, at least that's over,' I said and noticed her looking at me anxiously. 'It *is* all over isn't it?'

And suddenly I knew that it wasn't over at all. The operating theatre, when I'd gone into it, had been white. But now it was mostly red. Now I had one doctor, one nurse and one anaesthetist to add to the Roadrunner tally. It hadn't been their fault. They had meant well.

The police tried to give me the third degree but I told them I wasn't going to talk until someone had brought me a Fudge Tub. And even then I had no intention of telling them what was really going on. They knew I was guilty of something, they didn't know what, but they couldn't very well beat a confession out of a pregnant woman.

I had to hand it to the Brothers of the Divine Order of the Dead Saints. At least they gave me a breathing space; it was forty-eight hours before the attacks started up again. They tried, how they tried, but none of them came close. I didn't know whose side they were on and I didn't care because as far as I was concerned it didn't make much difference either way.

I was beginning to look on it as a unique opportunity. I could tackle the North Face of the Eiger or explore the bottom of the Mariana Trench. I could saunter through Central Park at night or dine on the liver of the Japanese blowfish. I could tell hulking great men with big biceps and menacing tattoos to pick up the litter they had dropped. I could do *anything*.

There were another seven months of this to come. I thought I might as well take up smoking again.

# The Magazine For Thinking People

## An unprecedented monthly publication

Written for informed, sophisticated readers like you, **The World & I** provides definitive insight on all aspects of human endeavor.

Is **The World & I** an encyclopedia? A literary review? A journal? A news magazine? Is it a picture book? Or is it a reference manual? The answer is ... It's all of these, and scholarly and readable at the same time.

Each issue carries **more than 100** interesting, authoritative articles - all beautifully illustrated - reflecting a truly global spectrum of interests, ideas, and points of view.

If you demand excellence, insist on staying informed, want the best return on your reading time investment, or simply enjoy owning the best, then **The World & I** is for you.

Truly one magazine in a million, **The World & I** belongs on the coffee tables and bookshelves of all who have a serious interest in what's happening in the world.

## Here's what our readers say:

*"The World & I is an extraordinary assemblage of scholarly and cultural articles that is interesting, readable, and very well illustrated. ... This great publication must ... play a leading role in creating our future."*
**Sir John Eccles,** Nobel Laureate in Physiology and Medicine, 1963

*"The World & I is one of the most original concepts in American journalistic history."*
**Robert Nisbet,** Historian, Albert Schweitzer Professor of Humanities emeritus, Columbia University

*"Serious magazines are judged first and foremost ... on their intellectual range and originality. By this standard, The World & I has in recent years had no equal."*
**Everett C. Ladd,** Director, Roper Center for Opinion Research

### FREE Trial !

Just call toll-free **1-800-822-2822** or mail in the order form provided and we will send you the next issue totally risk-free. If you are not totally satisfied with it, simply write "cancel" on the invoice and owe nothing.

(The trial issue will be yours to keep.)

*You're Invited, to Order Your Free Trial Issue Today!*

---

GRANTA

# TIBOR FISCHER
# LISTED FOR TRIAL

He didn't like attending County Hall. Too far from the railway station, especially when it was raining. Tutty didn't make it any more attractive. Going to County Hall for Tutty. Now that was something Guy could live without. He had tried to get out of it, but there had been no one else. He had had Tutty all the way, probably precisely because he had said to Gareth something such as, 'Try and keep me away from Tutty, will you?'

It was money. Money he really did need, since although he had made a point of sleeping with his landlady on the last two slow Sunday afternoons (when there wasn't anything good on television), she had remarked pointedly afterwards: 'Guy, don't think this changes a thing.' Still, she was already going easy on him.

If a landlady had never rented to an actor, it could get you some indulgence. Actors were sometimes considered interesting by people who hadn't had much to do with them. Mother Art's kids. Naturally, if a landperson had had an actor on the premises before, you weren't getting in anyhow. They could be very vindictive. There was one still chasing him from four years ago over a question of a collapsed roof.

It was quarter-past ten, that was cutting it fine. But Tutty, if he had arrived, could wait for once. Guy shoved his reflection in the glass door out of the way. He really did look like a lawyer. Amazing.

Admittedly, he didn't have an ironed shirt. Suit and tie yes, but he hadn't bothered to iron the shirt. Because he had been

---

**Tibor Fischer**'s parents, both professional basketball players for Hungary's national team, emigrated to England in 1956. He was born in Stockport three years later, and grew up in Bromley. After graduating from Cambridge he became a freelance journalist and was briefly Budapest correspondent for the *Daily Telegraph*. The title of his first novel, *Under the Frog* (for which he won a Betty Trask Award), is shorthand for a Hungarian expression— being 'under the frog's arse down a coal mine' means living at the lowest point of existence. Tibor Fischer is working on his second novel, which he describes as 'a short book about all human knowledge and experience.'

hoping to get out of it and because, well, some people weren't worth ironing shirts for. Cf. Tutty. He had to wear the suit and tie because otherwise the judge might fuss. But even at Kingston the judges couldn't be eagle-eyed enough to spot the rumples in his collar.   ґ`

He looked round. Since there were only two courts at County Hall, you couldn't miss anyone. No Tutty.

He would have been surprised if he had been there. Tutty's only reliable quality was his infallibility in irritating. He was the Pope of wrong-way-rubbing. He should have been there at ten. Guy should have as well, but then he wasn't looking at five years. It was a pity you couldn't go down to your nearest turf accountant to load a tenner on Tutty not showing. In a way he was pleased Tutty was absent—the only drawback was that if Tutty didn't show it was down to him to do something about it. Not that there was much he could do.

When he had started as an outdoor clerk, Guy had been apprehensive, as what he knew about the law was, well, it existed. He'd never been to court. However minor his part, he'd been anxious about being involved in deciding someone's freedom or imprisonment. He'd been worried that if he wasn't looking properly, if his writing wasn't legible or he mislaid a paper, whoops, someone could go down for twenty years. Now he found himself praying that clients *would* disappear for twenty years. Take Tutty.

But in practice being an outdoor clerk required next to no knowledge. The only real qualification you needed was owning a suit. The suit did the work of suggesting professional competence. Otherwise you didn't do much. You carried the file to court. Wrote down the gist of what was going on. You could chase things, make phone calls. You saved counsel the use of his feet by shuttling back and forth between him and the client. You obtained cigarettes for the def if he was on remand.

The clients expected some knowledge of course. But this was where the suit earned its money. And you quickly picked up enough to keep the clients spinning, to camouflage yourself. They asked two questions. Number One: 'Am I going to get off?'

Number Two: 'How long will I get if I go down?'

The answer to the first was to point to the evidence the prosecution had and watch the client wince, and then say something like 'We've got a chance,' even if you hadn't any rational grounds for saying so. The answer to the second was to say, 'It's not a science,' explain that the judge's diet was an important factor and then give the client the maximum sentence and watch him wince—because if he got off he might even go as far as thanking you, and if he didn't he felt he'd had fair warning.

Guy had only taken the work because he thought it would nicely cover a month till he got a beer commercial. That had been eighteen months ago. As his agent had repeatedly assured him 'You've got beer-drinker's face.' Guy had looked forward to complaining to his chums about having to drink beer for thirty takes and getting thousands of quid for it. But the commercial had kept on treading water a month away as the seasons seasoned. His agent had kept saying, 'They're coming. The hops are on the hop,' until finally Guy had said to him: 'Look I don't care what you tell me. Tell me I'll never work again, but don't ever tell me that the hops are on the hop.'

Guy flipped through the file, making sure everything was in its right place. He glanced through the medical report. They had sent Tutty to a head-doctor. The report was double spaced, covering four sheets. The doctor hadn't called Tutty a lying shitbag because that wasn't a recognized medical term and because if you actually spelt something like that out you were unlikely to be consulted again by solicitors bearing fees that would help put down some more paving stones outside your villa in Tuscany. For anyone who had seen reports before the judgement was clear. But the doc had earned his money by helpfully saying that just because there was no evidence that Tutty was epileptic, that didn't mean he wasn't. And as Xavier had pointed out when he had advised getting the report: 'We don't like it, we don't use it.' Checking his watch, Guy went to look for counsel.

He went into the robing room, an unheated space that had all the atmosphere of a shoebox. Wigs were being broken out.

Collars were done up with a dreamy expression, minds wallowing in fantasies of big fraud trials with endless refreshers. The thing about everyday criminal work was hardly anybody really wanted to be there.

Xavier was seated, looking relaxed, the papers all bound up crimsonly. He knew it all by heart since this was the fourth occasion the matter had risked coming to trial. Xavier was wearing a suit that was certainly worth more than Tutty's accumulated wealth, worth probably more than everything Guy owned. It had to be one of the ten most expensive suits in the country. You just wanted to go up and stroke it. And it fitted him perfectly, spiritually as well as girthily.

It wasn't that Xavier was so well-off; he just liked to invest his money in clothes. To Xavier it didn't make any difference that it was Tuesday morning, that it was Kingston; you could hear the halves of air hit the ground as he cut through. The other barristers felt and looked dowdy compared with Xavier. At six-two, he could probably walk into a job as a male model if the briefs ran out. Though he had doubtless been out a.m.-ing in a casino or club, he was fresh.

'Have you got our man?' Xavier asked.

'No sign.'

'I really am going to have a word with him this time,' he said testily. This was surely the greatest indictment for Tutty. Xavier never lost his good humour. People whom you could happily describe as scum, scorbutic armed robbers, child-murderers, stinky drug-addicts who raped old-age pensioners, he greeted them all with a chuckle like long-lost friends. Everyone wanted to work with Xavier. While the prosecution or judge was summing up, he'd be entertaining you. Judge to jury: 'While I direct you on the law, you, and you alone, are the judges of the evidence . . . ' Xavier to Guy: 'The doctor says to him, there's good news and bad news. "What's the bad news?" "You've got AIDS." "And the good news?" "You've also got Alzheimer's so you'll have forgotten all about this by the time you leave the room."' But he missed nothing, he was as quick on the draw with an appeal as anyone. People, you felt, almost went out to commit offences to be represented by Xavier.

'I'll go and have another sweep,' Guy offered.

Tutty didn't know how lucky he was to have Xavier.

Certainly word spread among the more alert offenders. 'I want that Mr Rawlings,' would be the request of sweaty individuals in police cells. Chambers cruised him up because having a black brief got you Hampstead points and was supposed to soothe the black clients. But Xavier was big all round with everyone from skinheads to Yardies. Skins up on race charges wanted Xavier because it was like having a living testimony to their tolerance, an endorsement on two legs. And he got them off. The British National Party sent him Christmas cards which he showed everybody before wiping his feet on them and tearing them up.

And the Jamaicans all forgave him for coming from St Lucia. They liked him because he spoke bad bwoy. And he got them off. Nearly always. And if he didn't, well, a trial with Xavier was fun, and you knew you'd had a good roll of the dice.

'Are you effective?' inquired the court usher, peering round the door. Xavier took her to one side to recount their difficulty.

It was twenty-five past ten. Tutty could, of course, just be a little late. But he had been told to be there for ten and his previous attempts at punctuality didn't encourage optimism. He could be a little late, Guy repeated to himself, but found it impossible to sound convincing.

This was after all one of the barcodes of those that ended up in the system. Time-blindness. Date-deafness. Appointment-deficiency. It was as if policemen walked up to people in the street and asked them: 'Do you know what time it is?' If the answer was 'No idea,' they'd be taken in.

The other common feature was guilt. Either amoralists with beer-guts of culpability, or unfortunates splashed with misdemeanour. But uninnocent. The plods weren't much cop at doing their job, but it had to be said that the bodies that ended up at the cop shop were usually the right bodies.

There had been only one client whom Guy had felt was innocent: Yusuf, the Somalian paratrooper who had got political asylum because he hadn't felt like killing women and children and had ended up on a housing estate in Peckham no less civil-wary. He had been coming home from his night shift at a yoghurt factory when someone twice his size (unemployed, history of assault) who had been waiting for him (convinced that Yusuf had been molesting his sister) smashed him in the face. Yusuf burst his assailant like a bubble with a couple of stabs from a pointed screwdriver. If you don't get beaten up, you get charged. Yusuf was charged with malicious wounding, despite the sister giving evidence making it clear Yusuf hadn't been bothering her. Yusuf went down. Too nice, that was probably his mistake. He was begging for it. He turned up for his appointments and said things like thank you.

There had been a few other cases where Guy hadn't been sure, until the clients had gone for a guilty on a deal. James, for instance, one of the Frontline's leading sinsemillia retailers, had been picked up on a smash and grab on a corner shop in the early hours of the morning. The haul was three teddy bears.

Bearing in mind James could buy as many corner shops as he wanted, and his usual legal problems were mysterious strangers leaving Uzis in his car boot, it didn't look right. James had been arrested urinating against a wall, with the three bears next to him.

At the nick, James had been total in his denial. However when the Crown hinted at handling rather than burglary, he dived with both hands. Even distinguished businessmen went out, got newted and did stupid things on Saturday night.

Guy walked outside to see if Tutty was wandering there, unable to work out how to cross the road. Back inside he found another brief complaining to Xavier about the failures of his clients to appear for conferences. 'We might as well start double-booking them.'

Tutty had missed his first appointment with Xavier. That wasn't unusual. He had also missed his second. You might think that looking at a few years inside would be an incentive to filling in your counsel as to why you are innocent. Especially as it didn't cost you anything. Legal Aid. But even missing two wasn't unique. Guy wouldn't have minded that much normally but he had had to sit in the office for forty minutes assessing Tutty's non-appearance and dwelling on the lift from two Australian girls to a party in Ipswich he was missing. 'Who're you waiting for?' Gareth had asked.

'Tutty.'

'Ah,' he had said walking off, 'arsehole.' Confirmation from the boss. Gareth had developed a sort of shorthand for his firm's clients, which rather dismayed his fellow solicitors who felt he was letting the side down by being so brusque, though he noticed most of them couldn't argue very forcefully he was wrong. Most solicitors liked to look concerned, solicitous about their clients' welfare. They talked a lot about justice, deprivation and stuff like that. Gareth just filed them away: 'Charge it up. Charge it up.' His thoughts always got airtime and he was always developing systems of classification.

'The Baddies. The Maddies. The Saddies . . . Plus the Paddies.' He'd pick up some files from the enormous stacks on his desk, and would shuffle them like a deck of cards, commenting as he went. 'Toe-rag.' 'Nutter.' 'Arch toe-rag.' 'Chancer.' Etc. Guy had worked for another firm where the earnestness had been like air freshener. Saving the planet expressions. Whether it was his Welsh voice that made him seem more relaxed and detached than he was, Gareth might be caustic but never tired. He had come from the Welsh valleys to Brixton in the mid-seventies to ceaselessly mine the deep seams of iniquity in the inner city, arriving in the quiet days before it had been colonized by gays, hacks and slightly successful rock stars, and before they had even had any interesting riots. His card was carried all over South London. He got them off.

And Gareth never fizzled. Guy admired him for that and wished he could borrow some of his poise. Tutty really wore you down. Tutty was the original inert client. He never replied to letters. He never phoned in despite being strongly urged to do so, since staying in contact with your solicitors might help prolong your liberty. It would probably be simpler to follow him around all week, dress him in the morning and have a taxi standing by to take him to court.

Then Tutty got upset when he was picked up on a warrant not backed for bail. He saw his arrest as your failure. 'I give you good business, you're getting your money,' he said when Guy had gone to deal with him at the police station, 'and I don't get anything. I'm jacking you next time.' He had been hoping Tutty would jack them then, but he hadn't. Generally the ones that talked about it most didn't. They saw this as a brilliant tactic to get service, they saw the bloated lawyers fearing for their piles of gold bullion. Gareth only made money because he had arrived when you could buy a street in Brixton for a couple of cartons of cigarettes. But a lot of the clients thought you'd be down a Swiss chalet if they switched to another company, not appreciating that one file more or less would make no difference to Jones & Keita. What was one less turd in the sewer?

Moreover Tutty had threatened him (just before asking him if he'd care to stand surety for him and trying to ponce some bus fare—doubtless some ovum was waiting): 'Yeah, maybe see you on your own walking down the road one day, you know.' It had taken Guy a moment to realize this was Tuttyspeak for promise of violence. This was infuriating because it was rather outrageous going to a lot of trouble for someone who was threatening you and who had been stupid, and not just once or twice—someone who had never unclenched his stupid-muscle.

Tutty's warning was also insulting because Tutty didn't have the mandate to threaten him. Plenty of clients were frightening, but not Tutty. He was disgusting, and the idea of physical contact with him was alarming in that sense, but he was too runty.

His skill in carving up pregnant women shouldn't let him think he could try his hand at outdoor clerks. It was the suit, of course. The suit marked you out as belonging to a docile, drone caste that was there to be robbed, begged from, taxed, burgled and hit. It would be unprofessional, but Guy had promised himself—since he fancied a new job—that if Tutty tried getting menacey again, he would give a big smile, adjust his tie and kick him in the balls. He had promised himself that.

He phoned the office from the one payphone. It was a curious thing how in courts they seemed to go to great lengths not to provide phones. Gareth answered. 'Any news from Tutty?' Guy asked.

'Tutty? Any news from Tutty? A man who is in the running for arsehole of the year? Do you think he'd blow it by contacting us? No, the wise money's on our Mr Tutty. No, Mr Tutty is a man who knows how to make the taxpayer pay. I can hear the jingle of paying taxpayers behind you.'

He certainly could. They were there. The jury. The witnesses. The police officers. The barristers. The court staff. As before. Though to be fair to Tutty, the previous failures had not been his fault. He had been late for the first trial but that hadn't gone ahead because the arresting police officer had been hospitalized. The victim herself, Ms Grant, had gone immaterial on the next two occasions. It was clear she wasn't happy about giving evidence, but once the system got hold of you, well . . .

There she was, flanked by concerned individuals from the Domestic Violence Unit, Guy presumed. That was the problem for both Ms Grant and Tutty—theirs was fashionable stuff. And however much they wanted to forget about it, the Unit wanted a result. Ms Grant had been unhappy about giving evidence against Tutty, they knew, because she had written to them as well as to the Crown Prosecution Service explaining that she would like to carry on with Tutty because she was carrying Tutty's child, and their domestic bliss was being marred by legal proceedings.

He had heard that Ms Grant had had a credit-card fraud outstanding which had somehow quietly ended up in the shredder. Whether this was the main motivation for her attendance, or whether it was the discovery that Tutty now had another blastula on the go in another young lady, they weren't going to find out.

Xavier appeared bewigged. Guy shook his head. 'They're going to stick in some pleas. He had better have something inventive and interesting to say if he turns up. But he'll probably go for some rubbish about the trains.'

'So what do we do?'

'You carry on waiting. You're a natural, you know that? You wait better than anyone I know. I'll be having a coffee.'

Of course they never said they forgot. They never said they couldn't be bothered to get out of bed. And it was never their fault. Amidst all the tardiness, Guy had never heard once the simple, 'Sorry I'm late.' If he ever heard that he'd buy the utterer a drink. Usually it was Jones & Keita's fault.

Tutty had been very vexed about the letter they had sent to his address, the address he had given them. The address he was bailed to. He had been in fact on the other side of London busy on an impregnation. It seemed to be that those who had the least reason for reproducing themselves went to the greatest trouble to do so. Tutty procreated like other people doodled. 'I've moved,' Tutty had said, as if somehow that was their fault too. 'And our team of psychic monitors didn't spot that? I can't understand what went wrong.' Guy had been hoping this would offend Tutty or annoy him, but sarcasm didn't seem to get through to him any more than anything else they said.

Perhaps Tutty had some work. He was a plasterer. Few clients had a trade, but when you pondered how builders disregarded the clock, you realized their intrinsically criminal nature. And it had to be said the building profession was always well-represented in matters of violence, notably vicious domestics, as in the case of Mr Tutty.

Guy was realizing more and more that it wasn't just hard to put yourself in another's mind, but nearly impossible, although that was supposedly part of the acting profession. The truth was that you absorbed traits rather than mentality. In plays and scripts you always had the tracks of cause and effect. But in life if you were dealing with people who didn't come from your own patch you weren't going to get it right. The answers came haphazardly, from the spinning wheel of a roulette table.

Take Ms Grant. He really couldn't understand how she could have ended up in such proximity to Tutty, living with him. You could understand how in life you might have to pass someone like Tutty in the street, but the healthy reaction to the prospect of further intimacy was to reach for an automatic weapon with a full magazine.

You very rarely got to escort a client all the way through the legal process, but Guy had been with Tutty from the first evening in Battersea police station. When Guy had started outdoor clerking, he had thought he might get some useful material to act with, but it was no use trying to trade places. The things they came out with, you couldn't concoct.

Tutty was up on GBH and assault on one of the officers who had wanted to arrest him when the blood-drenched Ms Grant had been found huddled up, clutching her young daughter. Tutty wasn't worried about the GBH. 'She won't give evidence,' he had said, the expert's assessment. And the assault on the policeman? 'A technicality,' he had said. A technicality?

Tutty had been wrong. It was the assault on the policeman that had been dropped. It hadn't been much of an assault, even the police surgeon's report had only spoken of slight swelling. Guy heard from the CPS that the police officer had got a place on an advanced driving course he had been waiting for for six years, and couldn't be bothered to hang around court to nail Tutty. They didn't usually drop stuff like that, but the plods obviously reckoned they had Tutty bang to rights for GBH anyway, and that he would be spending many a night sniffing his own shit, H.M.P.-ing somewhere.

So Tutty had been wrong about Ms Grant. Which was odd because you would have thought that Tutty was the sort of client you could count on to have Ms Grant tied up, whimpering in a basement somewhere. If she hadn't shown, the case would have folded. He was vicious, but he couldn't even be vicious in his own interest. If you said to Tutty, you push this button, all your problems will be over and you'll get a million quid to boot, he wouldn't make it.

Perhaps he had gone on the run. That was sound. Let the witnesses move, disappear, die. The Crown offers no evidence. And nothing much happened if you were caught—but you probably wouldn't be if you could be bothered to move three miles from where you had lived. Police investigations consisted of ringing the doorbell at your last known address; if you had someone to answer the door and say you weren't there you could even carry on watching television.

Having phoned the office again for word of Tutty, they had gone in to explain to the judge they were having client trouble. Judge Foxx didn't look too happy. He had been told by the usher what was going on, but judges like to get counsel up on their feet to hear it from them. If they were going to have a difficult morning, so could counsel.

Tutty, B. Trial, KCC, 11.05 a.m. Court 6. Judge Foxx. Counsel: X. Rawlings. Clerk: G. Gavett, he wrote on his pad. Foxx wasn't really vicious, but he didn't see his job as making life easier for counsel. He liked to ask questions and watch them squirm. Foxx wasn't tolerant of the shortcomings of the system, in the way that some others were. The shrug of the shoulders was becoming a common sight on the bench. He could be quite a turn too.

When Potts had gone down for threats to kill and breach of probation, he had been standing quietly in a boozy haze (he had sneaked out at lunchtime for a session at the pub) when the dock officer had wanted to take him down to the cells. Suddenly, as if he had just noticed he was in a courtroom and going down for the two-year count, he started bawling at Foxx; 'You cunt! You fucking cunt!' They bundled Potts below, but Foxx indicated he should be brought back when he had cooled. Everyone was anticipating that he was going to top up Potts's sentence.

'Mr Potts, let me tell you a few things. I'm going home in a few minutes. Then I'll out my feet up, read a paper. Have a nice hot bath. Chat with my wife while she makes supper. Then I'll relax. Watch television. Have a brandy. Maybe not. Phone a friend or two. Maybe not. But it's up to me. You on the other hand are going to Brixton prison. Now, Mr Potts, on reflection, you tell me who's the cunt?'

Foxx suggested a review in three quarters of an hour. There was no doubt that if Tutty was going down, he was really going all the way.

Guy re-examined his newspaper, but he had consumed all the interest on the train. Returning the paper to his bag, he got up and strolled over to the staircase.

Tutty. He could see him on the ground floor approaching the staircase, slowly, like he'd never seen a staircase before. You couldn't be seen doing anything like concern. It was eleven-forty.

But he looked a bit twitchy. That was Tutty. Arsehole with just a hint of nuttiness. Not the sort of solid, twenty-four hour insanity that would get you stamped padded-cell fodder, or the sort of sad obsessional behaviour that could earn some sympathy. Just the jumps every now and then. And bad luck if Tutty had the carving knife and you didn't.

Tutty was carrying a beery force field. You got clients who were double-barrelled trouble: nuts and drunk. Out of their head anyway and eager to erect another barricade to the return of good sense. 'Whoa, Mr Tutty,' you felt like saying, 'don't have another drink, you're disgusting enough already.' If the police could manage to arrest everyone who didn't know what time it was and who drank Tennent's, the crime figures would really slump.

'You do know you're late?' Guy opened. Tutty looked quizzical.

'It was eleven-fifteen last time,' he replied stonily.

'Didn't you get the lexigram?'

'It was eleven-fifteen last time,' he repeated, which obviously in Tuttyland counted as a clear explanation. And he was right. It had been eleven-fifteen last time. Tutty was dressed as if auditioning for the part of a felon. You gave advice to clients about how to dress from time to time; there was no need to overdo it and get a cummerbund, but there was no doubt that clothes acted as ambassadors and Tutty's were succinctly saying up yours. He had a pair of headphones around his neck which was broadcasting the message: I had to bring some music because you're all boring me so much.

Despite his sunglasses, Tutty was visibly tense. A tension which rapidly gained ground when he saw Ms Grant across the hall. For whatever reason, he obviously hadn't been counting on her appearance. He must have been hoping, as Guy had been, for a no Ms Grant, no trial morning.

They all got sweaty. Some could stay loose until the verdict, but then, no matter how hard they were, they all got gulpy. Because that was the moment you realized that the silly looking sod in a wig opposite you, who had probably spent his youth train-spotting, could drop you into a place where you'd be eating cold mashed potato, where brushing your teeth would be huge excitement and where you'd be sharing a cell with someone so reeky it would take an entire perfume department to swamp it. And it didn't matter how unlikely that was. Even Guy got nervous when the verdict came.

Xavier appeared, shook hands with Tutty and moved off after minimum courtesy to inform the court that Tutty was ready. Child molesters even got more than that, a slap on the back.

He sat with Tutty going through the file as if he were looking for something important, doing his job. Any measure to dissuade conversation. He flicked through the transcript of the interview Tutty had given at the police station. Tutty had done the selective memory number. He had talked co-operatively with the police. He had talked so freely that the interviewing officer had had to break in repeatedly to try and steer him back to the chargey bit. Your real vet never veered from no comment. Right to silence. An interesting one the lawyers had smuggled through.

Normally officers liked them to ramble on because they nearly always blotted themselves; the more they talked the more chance there was of them tripping. But after fifteen minutes of Tutty's intro on the history of his domestic relations with Ms Grant, Guy had been itching to say, yeah but what about the stabbing? Just tell us about that so we can go home. But there was more about how they liked to go out and look for carpets together and how they had been discussing what colour the kitchen should be painted. Tutty went through the afternoon of that day in real-time detail.

He skilfully related how the argument had started because Ms Grant had been angry about the behaviour of Tutty's son by a previous liaison. Tutty had been angry about the behaviour of Ms Grant's daughter by a previous relationship. Various observations were traded on the brattiness of the offspring. Cases cited. Tutty was lavish on that. The detective had to change tape. Observations were exchanged on the likely behaviour patterns of the unborn child Ms Grant was carrying depending on which parent it might most resemble. Ms Grant decided that their relationship had reached the end of the road and announced her intention to leave.

Here Tutty owned up to hitting her. Nice touch. An admission of veniality. Man under pressure after carpet-hunting and smears on his son. But Mr Memory ran out of steam.

No, he didn't remember stabbing her seven times. That's it, Guy had thought, when it comes to explaining something tricky, wholesale denial or just go for the blank. Don't wobble. The detective tried to elicit something from him, fished around in Tutty's mnemonic black hole. Yes, Ms Grant had obviously been stabbed, he remembered the ambulance coming, the police arriving, but not the stabbing.

The tapes were a great help to the police. Apparently they hadn't been very keen on their introduction, but they were very useful for dealing with people who couldn't make their minds up about their guilt. They loved it now. They taped everyone. Of course, just because you confessed on tape to something didn't mean you couldn't deny it later when you had considered (on remand) that putting your hands up wasn't in your best interests. It was uphill work for counsel, but it could be done: They said if I told them I did that they'd let me go home/give me some cigarettes/wouldn't charge me with a rape.

Guy glanced over at Tutty who had that preoccupied look that people have when they begin to imagine a five-year sentence. Even some of the arseholes you could feel sorry for, but not Tutty. Some you felt really sorry for. Because while it was true that many of the clients were people whose imprisonment made you sleep better at night, there were also a lot who had had no chance. Like Tutty's kids. Clients in the making.

Tutty was wilting now. He had his head in his hands. Clearly Ms Grant's presence had had a cataclysmic effect on his morale.

'Don't want to go to jail,' he said, which was fair enough.

Guy felt professionally bound to try and be encouraging. 'You've got no form for GBH,' (Tutty had form for plenty else); 'You won't necessarily get a custodial.'

More head-holding from Tutty. 'It wasn't no GBH.'

Guy nodded sympathetically because he was paid to. Not enough, but it was his job. Although it was hard to see what else it could be apart from GBH? Had Ms Grant mutilated herself to frame Tutty? Had passing Martians beamed her up for a spot of vivisection, leaving Tutty to take the can?

'Wasn't GBH,' Tutty reiterated. Another sympathetic nod. Across the hall, it had to be said, Ms Grant too didn't look happy.

Tutty glanced over. 'She knows it wasn't GBH. At least not me.' Guy felt Tutty had received his portion of sympathetic nods. Tutty shook his head powerfully as if trying to shake off his irritation. 'You know all I want is a wife and kids. Just to be left in peace to get on with my life.' It was a reasonable request. 'She's pregnant, you know. Tell the judge that.'

'If it comes to that we will,' Guy said, thinking that for so many of the clients children stood for mitigation.

He looked at his watch. No one else was around him and the woeful Tutty. No one in earshot.

'I've got to tell you something,' said Tutty, 'on a private basis. This ain't how it looks.' Guy tried to appear attentive.

'I didn't attack her. Three guys came round. Drug-dealers. They tried to rob us. One of them cut Hilary up.' Yes, when you needed walk-on villains, drug-dealers were your men. For on-tap scum, you can't beat drug-dealers. Their union should do something about it.

'I killed one of them,' this was said quietly, but unfortunately audibly.

'I don't want to know,' came out of Guy faster than he thought possible, because actually he didn't want to know. 'I didn't hear that.' He didn't really know what to do, a client confessing to a killing. Be professional.

'Do you want to change your instructions? Do you want to change your instructions to us?' he asked. Tutty looked really tortured. If this was a put on, Tutty should consider a career change from plastering to acting. As a dissimulation technician Guy couldn't fault it. Tutty breathed heavily.

'Nah,' he said finally. But just as he was calming down, Tutty continued: 'I buried the body. I'm sure they're going to find it. I listen to the news all the time. I keep listening cause I'm sure they'll find it.'

Guy got up and walked hurriedly to the phone. He misdialled the number twice, before forcing himself to do it so slowly he couldn't get it wrong. The thing was, ostensibly, the story fitted. Knowing what was on file, there was nothing which prevented the idea of three men coming in, having a go at Grant, one getting killed and Tutty just having time to dispose of the body before the police turned up, alerted by neighbours. The call had been made earlier, forty minutes before the police turned up. Had he stuck the body out back? Would the police have checked? Called to a domestic, finding a gory woman, why check the garden, or anywhere else where Tutty might have stashed the corpse? And in her statement Ms Grant had been rather unremembering about the knifings.

'Gareth, look, Tutty's just told me he's killed someone.'

'What, just one? We could really do with a serial killer.' Guy repeated Tutty's revelations.

'Well, I think he's making it up,' Gareth pronounced.

'Shouldn't we tell someone?'

'No. We can't. It's the confessional—we have to respect the confidence. Get him to endorse the instructions in writing. Otherwise, if he sticks with them, there's nothing else we can do.' Who was he to care? Probably Tutty was inventing the whole business out of some rogue logic—in the belief his smiting the drug-dealer would win him a round of applause instead of some bird. Nevertheless, Guy found his guts looping the loop as he went upstairs and saw the usher emerging from the court to call: 'Mr. Tutty?'

In they all went.

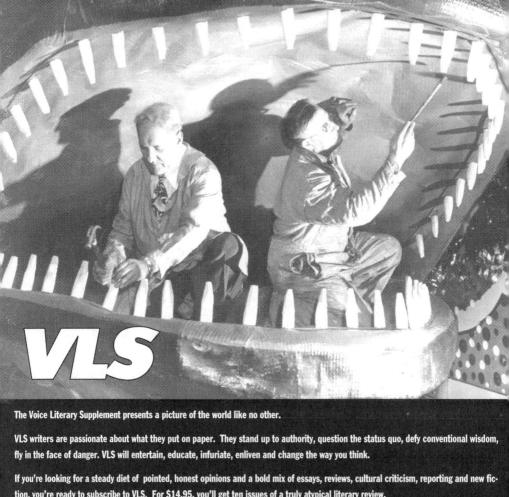

GRANTA

# ESTHER FREUD
# LESSONS IN INHALING

Lisa was meeting her father for supper. She was glad to have an excuse for going out and she took the tube into the West End. Lisa rarely saw her father without her sister Ruby. Secretly she thought of him as Ruby's father and felt uncomfortable about seeing him alone, even a little treacherous. After all, it was really only Ruby's tenuous link that bound them together.

They were having dinner in a fish restaurant. Lisa arrived to find her father sitting drinking Pernod with a girl she knew. 'Hello, Dad. Hello, Sarah.' She stood awkwardly at the end of the table.

'Oh, has it been raining?' her father asked, and Lisa looked down at her bedraggled coat and the boats of her shoes and wished she had washed her hair.

The waiter pulled out a chair and tucked Lisa in with a thick white napkin opposite her father. Sarah crinkled up the eye nearest her in a smile. Lisa ordered a Pernod too and picked at the radishes and bread sticks that adorned the table.

'I was just walking along and I saw your father leap out of a taxi.' Sarah laughed, and then added, 'I hope you don't mind, I'm starving.'

Lisa didn't mind. In fact it was nice to have a buffer between her and her father and the inevitable pauses.

Sarah was a year older than Lisa and she had known her on and off since she was seven. They had met at an Easter egg hunt in Scotland in the garden of Sarah's family home. Lisa had had the great luck to meet up with the owner of a telescope—a man who led her to various eggs nestling in the low branches of trees, on window ledges and scattered in the grasses of the outer lawn. Lisa had collected so many eggs she couldn't hold them all in her arms and a bag had to be found to carry them.

'Are you living in London now?' Lisa asked Sarah, and

**Esther Freud** was born in London in 1963, and grew up mostly in Sussex. After studying acting at the Drama Centre, she co-founded a women's theatre company called the Norfolk Broads. Her first novel, *Hideous Kinky*, was published last year. 'Lessons in Inhaling' is taken from her second, *Peerless Flats*, which is published by Hamish Hamilton.

Sarah said she was working in a clothes shop on the Fulham Road. She stood up to show Lisa a pair of maroon corduroy jodhpurs she had bought there at a discount.

'And how about you?' Sarah asked. 'How long have you been in London?'

'Three weeks.' Lisa felt anxious about having a conversation that didn't include her father. She looked at him from time to time and smiled expansively. 'I'm doing a drama course. At a college in King's Cross. I'm about to start any moment.'

The waiter arrived to take their orders. Lisa's father ordered oysters and so did Sarah, but Lisa couldn't quite bring herself to the challenge and asked for a prawn cocktail. She knew it was a childish and unsophisticated starter but she loved the sweet pink mayonnaise of the dressing, and in a defiant mood she followed it with fish cakes.

Lisa sat at the table and blushed to think how she had suggested only the year before they meet for supper at the Wimpy, Notting Hill Gate. She had seen its red and glass exterior from the top deck of a bus on several visits to London and her longing to go there was overpowering. Brought up in the country on a diet of brown rice and grated carrot, a cheeseburger and chips were her idea of gourmet delight. The Wimpy had in fact turned out to be a success and Lisa even heard her father exclaim over the deliciousness of the hot apple pie spiced with cinnamon, served in little cardboard packets.

Sarah and Lisa's father were discussing the people on the next table. Sarah giggled and pointed out the sharp line of the man's curling, auburn wig. The woman, Lisa's father said, looked as if she had been recently discovered under a large rock. He said it was enough to put him off his oyster. Lisa sweated for them.

'Ruby sends her love,' she attempted to pull the conversation around.

'Oh, how is Ruby? I haven't been able to get hold of her.'

Lisa explained about the flat, and Ruby's boyfriend's father getting out of jail, but it turned out that Ruby hadn't mentioned Jimmy to their father and he was under the impression she was living with a girlfriend.

'Oh, well maybe she is . . . ' Lisa didn't want to betray Ruby's confidence, let alone disagree with her father. 'Well, she probably is by now.'

Lisa drained her Pernod.

'What's Ruby up to, anyway?' Sarah asked.

'Music.' Lisa jumped at the question. 'She's going to be a singer. she's got a friend who says when he can find a band talented enough to play with her . . . ' Lisa broke off. She was only repeating what she'd been told. It was strange how much more convincing things sounded in other people's mouths.

'I think I bought her a guitar last Christmas,' her father was saying, and Lisa nodded, knowing he had, and knowing also that it had been stolen or swapped or lent to someone glamorous like Mick Jagger's brother or a roadie from The Clash.

Lisa's father insisted she try an oyster. 'Just swallow it, with a passing bite,' he said.

Lisa swallowed it so fast that she didn't even get a chance to graze it with her teeth and she was left with the sensation of having sea water in her mouth and a pebble on her heart.

'Not quite sure about that,' she said with a grim smile.

Sarah slurped her oysters joyously. 'It's an acquired taste.'

Lisa braced herself for news of Sarah's brother Tom. Lisa had been in love with Tom, among others, ever since she could remember. Once, on a holiday in Wales they had lain together on a tartan blanket, Tom, Sarah and herself, and she and Tom had held hands and talked about how many children they would have when they were married and what they would call them. She couldn't remember the names they had chosen now, but there were to be three and they had been in complete agreement over every last detail of their upbringing. Lisa could almost see the stars in the black sky, how they had looked that night. Clear and calm and full of promise.

'You know when you stick your finger up your bum?' Tom had asked.

'Yes . . . ' Sarah spoke as if she were waiting and eager for him to continue.

'Lisa?'

'What?' She unclasped her hand.

71

'What I just said.'

Lisa refused to be drawn. She stood up and wandered off across the lawn to lean against a box hedge as high as the first floor of the house. Lisa hated conversations like that. She couldn't help herself.

'So how's your brother?' she asked, when the waiter had cleared away the plates. 'How's Tom?'

'He's fine.' Sarah looked at her with a sly expression that made her wish she'd kept the question to herself. 'He's learning about farm management in East Anglia. He's living in a cottage on the estate with Lenny. In domestic bliss.'

'Who's Lenny?' Lisa's father asked for her.

'Lenny is a man Tom met at the Marquee. He's black and incredibly good-looking and Tom thought it would be fun to have someone around to keep him company.'

'So what does Lenny do all day when Tom's at work?'

'It's hard to tell,' Sarah laughed. 'The last time I went down there I arrived at four in the afternoon and they were both still asleep. I can't help feeling that Tom probably isn't cut out to be a farmer.'

It was only once they were out in the street that Lisa realized how drunk she was. Her head felt as though it was full of cotton wool, and her ears wouldn't pop.

'Which way are you heading?' her father asked her, hailing a taxi.

'Old Street,' she said.

The cab stopped and Lisa's father kissed her very lightly on the forehead. 'Do you mind if I take this? I'm meant to be somewhere.' And he glanced at his watch. He pressed a twenty-pound note into Lisa's hand. 'Will you take the next one?'

Lisa nodded.

'Goodbye. Goodbye, Sarah,' he said and he jumped in.

'Thank you . . . and thank you for supper,' Lisa shouted through the closing door of the cab and she waved at his back in the low back window as he sped away.

Lisa and Sarah walked towards Leicester Square. Lisa weighed up in her mind the quandary of the journey home. If she took the tube, she could avoid breaking into her twenty-pound note. A taxi might be three or four pounds, whereas the tube, especially if she got a half ticket, would only cost her ten pence. Lisa was small anyway and if she bent her knees and looked with wide eyes into the little window, 'Half to Old Street please,' she found it never failed. 'If I were to buy some trousers like yours, how much would they be?' she asked Sarah.

'About nineteen pounds.'

'You wouldn't mind, would you? I'd get a different colour.'

'Listen,' Sarah said when they reached the station. 'I'm going to stay with Tom at the weekend. Why don't you come?'

Lisa's heart began to pound. 'All right,' and they kissed each other on both cheeks and said goodbye, separately bracing themselves for the last tube home.

Sarah's shop was a boutique not far from the Fulham Road cinema. Lisa had managed to keep her twenty-pound note intact by travelling half fare to college and back, and using the luncheon vouchers they handed out to each student to buy her midday meal.

Sarah's trousers were undoubtedly the highlight of the shop's collection. They came in three colours: maroon, mustard or a grey-green which reminded Lisa of lichen.

'You've got to have the green ones,' Sarah said. 'To bring out your eyes.'

Lisa kept them on, packing her skirt into her bag with her nightie and her copy of Stanislavsky's *My Life in Art*. They caught the train from Liverpool Street. Sarah had some grass, which she rolled into a joint under the train table. She suggested they smoke it in the Ladies so they'd be in a good mood when they arrived. Lisa crouched up on the lid of the toilet seat and Sarah leant against the basin.

'Can I ask you a question?' Sarah said, the smoke billowing out of her mouth. Lisa's stomach tightened. Her head began to click with the first bitter inhalation of smoke. 'It's a question from Tom.'

'All right.'

'Tom wants to know . . . ' And Sarah began to giggle.

'What?'

But Sarah couldn't bring herself to tell her. 'He can ask you himself,' she said.

Instead Sarah told her about her cousin Tanya who was still a virgin and ashamed of it and was coming down next weekend in the hope that Lenny would deflower her.

Lisa hated that word, 'deflower'. It made her squirm. Sarah looked hard at Lisa through the smoke and Lisa knew what she was wondering. She pulled on the joint and kept the smoke inside her lungs as long as she was able.

L isa hadn't seen Tom for over a year and he was taller than ever and thinner. His long, grey eyes drooped at the corners. Lisa and Sarah climbed into the front seat of the Land Rover, Sarah shuffling behind so that Lisa had to climb in first and squeeze right in next to Tom. Their legs pressed against each other and the musty oilskin smell of him tingled in her nose. Sarah leant over the seat to talk to Lenny, who was lying stretched out in the back.

'How's it going, Len?' she asked him.

'Not so bad, and you?' Lenny said. Lenny was smoking, and every bit of energy in his body was concentrated in the hand that lowered and raised the cigarette to his mouth.

'Tanya sends her love,' Sarah said, and Tom sent out a peal of cruel laughter that made Sarah twist round to hide the blush that spread over her face.

They were driving out of the small town through flat, green fields dotted with barns and farmhouses and wispy autumn trees.

'So, when are you going to be a famous actress?' Tom jerked his leg against Lisa's.

'I don't know. Never, I expect,' Lisa stammered. Secretly she hoped that she *was* going to be a famous actress, or even an actress of any kind, but after one week of Full Time Speech and Drama she couldn't imagine it.

'Don't be all floppy,' Tom broke in. 'You've got to play the part. You've got to sleep with important people and say "Darling" if you want to get anywhere. Have you got an agent?'

'No,' Lisa said.

'Do you hear that, Lenny?' Tom shouted over his shoulder,

and Lenny said, 'Yes, sir.'

Tom's cottage was on a road that led past the gaunt family house of the estate. It was beyond the farm buildings and was surrounded by fields. For Lisa, an air of glamour hung over Tom's house like mist.

It was dark when they arrived. Tom opened the door and flicked on a light. The sitting-room was barely furnished but the floor was so littered with moulding cups of coffee and dirty plates that it gave the impression of clutter. A stale smell of fried food hung in the air.

Sarah showed Lisa round the house. The kitchen was a bomb-site with every piece of cutlery caked in butter or jam, and each surface supporting a toppling tower of plates and pans and half-empty cans of baked beans and rice pudding. The cupboards hung open, and proudly empty.

Upstairs there were two bedrooms. An unmade bed in each. Lisa refused to catch Sarah's eye and looked instead into the bathroom, noticing a spray of blood on the wall beside the sink that made her duck back on to the stairs.

'It's great,' Lisa said, as she came back into the sitting-room.

Tom was making a fire with half a packet of fire-lighters and what looked like the remains of a chair.

'How's Ruby?' he asked.

'She's fine . . . she's . . . '

'What?' Tom watched her suspiciously and Lisa wondered whether or not to tell him how Ruby had arrived at Bunny's the night before they moved out with her arm slashed and dripping blood. She had knocked on Lisa's window and, under strict orders not to wake their mother, Lisa had walked with her to the Whittington Hospital where she received a tetanus injection and five stitches. Ruby had made her swear not to tell anyone. At the time Lisa had interpreted 'anyone' as Marguerite and their father, but that was because she didn't know anyone else in London she could tell. Tom, she felt, could only be impressed by the news.

'She got into a bit of a fight last week,' Lisa told him, lighting up a cigarette.

'With who?'

'With a bread knife.' She felt proud of that remark.

At first Ruby told her how she'd been slicing bread when the knife slipped and caught the side of her arm, but later, worn down by painkillers and the long wait in casualty, she had confessed that during an argument with Jimmy she had stabbed at herself in a moment of despair.

'Seven stitches,' Lisa told Tom, and Tom looked suitably impressed.

'You should tell her to come and stay,' he said, and his eyes softened. For a moment Lisa remembered what she had suspected since they were children, that really Tom was in love with Ruby. Something heavy pulled inside her chest and she pushed the thought away. She inhaled deeply. She could feel Tom watching her out of the corner of his eye. It was Tom who had taught her how to smoke. Or at least how to inhale. Before Tom took her in hand, shortly after her thirteenth birthday, she just used to swallow the smoke, gulping it down like a drink and then waiting for a respectable length of time to elapse before letting it out again. This method of smoking invariably resulted in draining the blood from her face and making her feel sick.

'It's interesting how you inhale,' Tom had said to her. She was on holiday with Sarah and Tom's father on the Isle of Man, where all there was to do was smoke cigarettes and read aloud to each other from the *Thirteenth Pan Book of Horror*. 'You see, whereas you swallow the smoke, I breathe it in.' He hadn't said it in a sneering way and he demonstrated 'inhaling' to Lisa with all the gentleness of an elder brother. They sat by the side of the sea experimenting with smoking styles until Lisa felt so dizzy she almost fell into the waves. Tom had to hold her steady with his hand. It was the summer after that they had named their children on the tartan blanket.

L isa waited until the last possible moment before going to bed. Sarah had gone up first with a cheerful goodnight and Lenny had followed shortly after. Eventually Tom drained his can of beer. 'I think you're staying in my room,' he said and with that he disappeared up the stairs.

Lisa changed into her nightie in the bathroom. She brushed her teeth and, as there was no sign of a towel, shook her hands until they were dry. She noticed the blood had been wiped from the wall.

Tom was lying in bed, a long thin shape under the blankets. Lisa slipped in beside him. The moment she touched the sheets she began to shiver.

'Are you cold?' Tom asked, his voice unfriendly from the other side of the bed, and she had to stop her teeth chattering to answer.

There was nothing comfortable about Tom's embrace. When he put his arm around her, the bones and sinews of his long limbs bit into her flesh. They lay still, Lisa's neck resting in the crook of his arm, his hand icy on her shoulder. Lisa stared up at the ceiling. Her mind raced with the beginnings of a conversation. Any conversation. Tom twisted on his side and reached his long arm swiftly down to the hem of her nightdress. Lisa doubled up and clamped her legs together and gripped his wrist with both hands. She strained with every muscle to pull his hand up above the covers. She turned on his trapped arm and faced him and dragged at his free hand with gritted teeth. Finally his resistance went and she raised his arm up like a trophy and rested it on her shoulder. Lisa's chill had left her. She could feel Tom's hot breath on her face. She folded her arms in front of her, holding them out like breakers against her breasts. Tom kept his hand where she had placed it.

Words Lisa could not get a grasp on burnt in her throat and dissolved. She leant forward and kissed Tom on the side of his mouth. She wanted him to know that she loved him whatever he did. She wanted to tell him that she didn't really care about the sex except she couldn't stand it all being over, as she assumed it would be, and then they weren't due to get the train back to London until Sunday. Lisa released one of her hands and stroked the hair back from his face. His breath came hot and fast, and with no warning his free hand slipped off her shoulder and lunged down the front of her nightdress.

Wordlessly they fought, Lisa tugging at his iron wrists and all the while rolling away from him with her knees bent up to jab him in the stomach. As she struggled, she caught his smile in the filtered light from the window. 'It's me,' he seemed to be saying, and she relaxed in his arms and grinned stupidly back at him.

'Couldn't we just go to sleep?' She turned and pressed herself warmly into the curve of his body.

'You should have said,' he whispered, touching her ear with his lips and they lay awake until morning, on guard for each other in the tangle of the bed.

L isa and Sarah walked aimlessly along the fenced edges of one field after another.

'Did you sleep well?' Sarah asked. 'Last night?'

Lisa ignored the light in her eye and the stress of her words. 'Yes,' she said. She knew she was treading close to the edge of Sarah's patience.

They walked on in silence.

Tom had had a meeting at midday with the farm manager. He got up at five to twelve, pulled on his clothes and roared away in the Land Rover. Lenny was on a day-trip to London and wasn't due back until the evening.

'Do you think Lenny likes me?' Sarah asked when they'd walked so far in a circle that they could see the back of Tom's cottage three fields away. She sounded as if she had reason to believe he didn't.

'Of course he does,' Lisa said automatically. 'Why shouldn't he?'

Encouraged, Sarah linked her arm. 'And Tom, I know he likes you. He told me.'

Lisa decided against believing her. She couldn't imagine Tom coming that close to a declaration of love. His conversation was almost entirely made up of little cryptic phrases. 'Really?' she said.

L enny arrived shortly after dark with a gram of heroin. 'H' he called it. Tom shovelled it into four lines with a razor-blade and snorted his share into his nose with a rolled-up pound note. The insides of Lisa's head began to shrink and crack and the burning ice that had lifted seeped back into her skull.

Tom smiled at her with his elder-brother eyes. 'It's all right,' he said.

Lisa didn't know you could snort heroin as if it were cocaine. Ruby, she knew, injected it into the veins in her arms. She had tried to get Lisa to share a needle with her but Lisa had lost her nerve at the last minute. Ruby was like Tom. They hated anyone to be left out.

'Come on, Lisa Lu.' Tom crawled across the floor to where she was leaning against the legs of the sofa. 'You won't regret it.'

Lisa's stomach turned bitter and she needed to go to the toilet. 'Is it like . . . like . . . ' She could hardly say the word. Tom bent his head down to hers. She lowered her voice. 'It's not at all like . . . ' she whispered what was on her mind, 'acid?'

'My God, not at all. It's literally the opposite,' Tom reassured her, pressing the rolled-up note into her hand.

'So you don't hallucinate or anything?' she persisted faintly.

Tom shook his head.

Lisa gave in and sucked the powder up into her nose, using one nostril and then the other in an imitation of Tom. Tom took the magazine off her lap and patted her leg like a schoolteacher. He pulled a blanket from the sofa and spread it over the four of them as they lay in a circle in front of the electric fire.

'So when did you take acid?' Tom wanted to know. He sounded annoyed. Tom liked the idea of having introduced Lisa to everything illegal she had ever done.

'About a year ago.'

'What was it like?' Sarah asked.

'All right . . . ' and then, admitting a fragment of the truth, she added, 'A bit scary.'

The heroin was beginning to take its effect. Lenny, whose line had been fatter than the others, lay back with his eyelids heavy and a dark smile on his lips. Tom sank his head on to his chest and was silent. As far as Lisa could tell, it wasn't affecting her, but then the thumping of her heart had subsided and, apart from the occasional click, the inside of her head was as soft and safe as history.

'I had an aunt,' Sarah said, 'who took acid. Someone put it in her drink.'

'Really?' Lisa asked. 'What happened?' A pinpoint of fear was fighting with the milk in her veins.

'She went crazy. She tried to eat a biscuit tin and then she walked to the nearest station and boarded a train. She jumped off just outside Audley End.'

'Was she all right? I mean, did she ever recover?'

'Never, not as far as I know. Tom, did Aunt Bird ever recover?'

'What?'

'From whoever spiked her drink with acid.'

Tom raised his head and looked at her with cat's eyes.

'Never,' he said, and he smiled a thin smile as if he were in some way responsible.

When Lisa woke the next morning she was lying on the floor, her head under the crook of Tom's arm. She scrambled free and stood up. She thought for a minute about what she would do if the others all turned out to have died in the night, but the very fact of having survived made her feel so cheerful that without even checking on their pulses she went upstairs to the bathroom.

Lisa locked the door and ran herself a bath. She felt thin and white, and when she lay face down in the water the bones in her hips pressed against the bath's bottom and her empty stomach lifted away like the curve of a bowl. She washed her hair and brushed her teeth and put on a clean shirt with her green trousers. She sat outside in the sun. A sense of calm spread over her body. She knew what it was. She had taken heroin and survived and now she would never have to take it again. She had proved herself. Like a Red Indian coming of age and scarring his face with warlike marks. She was sixteen and she had tried every drug she had heard of. She was free to begin her own life.

ALAN HOLLINGHURST
SHARPS AND FLATS

The first person I was in love with was called Mark Lyle. I was ten, and a day-boy at a pious little prep-school I could walk to on the edge of town. Mark Lyle was perhaps three years older—too old to be a friend to kids like me but equally too young to be acknowledged by my sixteen-year-old brother Charlie and his set. He occupied a fascinating limbo; his voice had broken, in my eyes he was a man already, but clearly not a man in the full self-important way that Charlie was. When he left my school, his parents couldn't afford to send him on to Stonewell, and he became a kind of outlaw figure in my mind, whom one might expect to find living under canvas in a dell on the Common. In fact his father was an epileptic who had lost his job, but to me it seemed that some dark, perhaps ancestral secret had exerted its pull. Ancestry was much in my mind at the time; I was at work on my first book, *The Manners Family of Kent*, fed with boastful anecdotes by my great-aunt Connie and rather more disillusioned sidelights from my Uncle Wilfred, sometimes quite hard to understand. I described how the glory of a family grew, until it was crowned with genius like my father's, who sang on the wireless and was likely to get a knighthood. Seen in this perspective Mark Lyle's family clearly suffered from some critical defect. It even seemed possible that Mark Lyle was a dropout, something of which there was a lot of talk at the time.

One or two of the older boys heard from him after he'd moved to the comprehensive, and bragged discreetly about the contact. Occasionally I would see him myself in the town and watch him with the considerate pretence of indifference that one accords to the

**Alan Hollinghurst** was born in 1954 and grew up in Gloucestershire and Berkshire. He read English at Oxford and subsequently taught there and at University College London. He was appointed deputy editor of the *Times Literary Supplement* in 1988 and his first novel, *The Swimming Pool Library*, was published the same year. 'Sharps and Flats' is taken from his second novel, *The Folding Star*, which will be published by Chatto & Windus in the spring of 1994. 'The writers whom I revere are grand and shadowy—Nabokov, Proust, James,' Hollinghurst remarks. 'I like things to reverberate, to be suggestive.'

Photo: Barry Lewis

truly famous. I was anxious about his new friends, giants of fourteen or fifteen with fluffy upper lips, waiting at the bus-stop with ties undone and shirts bagging out and a No.6 on the go; like them Mark Lyle was growing his hair in thick dirty bunches swept behind the ears, and this seemed to me both wrong and beautiful.

Late one afternoon I saw him walking past our house, and ran out and followed him. I had shorts and sandals on—one didn't go into long trousers till the sixth form—and he had his black blazer hooked on a finger over his shoulder. I wasn't close to him, but still as I walked along I found myself in a heady slipstream of Old Spice. He must have been drenched in it, perhaps he was addicted to it in some way. Ours was a dourly Palmolive household, in which none of the males used talcs or colognes, and I found it intoxicating that Mark Lyle should be so sweetly and knowingly scented. I trailed him down the hill, having to stop and dawdle from time to time to prevent myself from excitedly catching up with him. He was clearly in no hurry to get home, wherever that might be. I wanted him to do something definite—meet a friend, enter a shop or a house—so that I would have something on him, and could go back home and ponder it in the context of my other, patchy, research.

I'd imagined he would turn left into one of the residential streets lined with flowering cherries where some of my schoolfriends lived, but he ambled odorously on until we had come in view of the Flats and I began to get worried. The front range of the Flats was built above a row of shops—a ladies' hairdressers, a newsagent, the dry-cleaners where I took my father's concert tails, the Indian grocers that stayed open till eight o'clock—and overlooked a broad oily forecourt, where residents worked sporadically on cars with long-expired tax-discs. But beyond that it was unknown territory to me. The Sharps and Flats my father called the place, as if we lived in the cloudless naturals of life. I don't think I was actually forbidden to pass through into the grassy courtyard or even to enter those long white buildings with corroding metal windows. It must have been a self-imposed prohibition, a social fear that was activated again when I understood that Mark Lyle's parents had now been reduced to a council flat.

That summer holidays I got serious about Mark Lyle. In my fantasy he became my protector, and introduced me into the thieves' kitchen of the Flats as someone to be respected or they'd have to answer to him. At the same time I was to have a redemptive effect on him, leading him back to the life of virtue and culture from which fate had deflected him. I would often ask insouciant questions about him, and my brother would say, 'What are you always going on about Mark Lyle for, stupid?' and my mother would say, 'That poor family, I don't know . . . ' She was inclined to charity work, but they seemed not quite to qualify. I imagined going down there with her, taking blankets, and meals under tinfoil.

A lot of the day I was out on the Common. It was harmless and healthy, and though I'd overheard remarks about leathery old Colonel Palgrave, who sunbathed up by the woods with nothing on, I never had a sense of danger. Sometimes I tagged along unwelcomely with Charlie and his friends as they stumbled round complaining and calling things bummers; often I played out complex romantic games on my own, or dared myself to clamber up trees, giving instructions to imaginary followers. Once or twice I stumped round on the edge of a group that included Mark Lyle, ready to drift off if they got threatening. We had a huge, friendly dog at the time, who ran away at once if I let him off the lead, but who was a useful means of meeting people. I was embarrassed to tell boys from the Flats that he was called Sibelius, and pretended ingeniously that his name was Bach, which led to one or two jokes but by no means eased the problems of discipline. I became increasingly excited when I saw Mark Lyle, and my early troubles of manhood about that time took him as their object and even as their cause.

One day he was up by the pond with some other boys and a couple of girls. They were trying to fly a kite in the intermittent breeze, but after a few dips and a few spoolings-out of the thread it would smack to earth. Then the thread got snagged in a sapling pine, and the others suddenly lost interest in the whole idea of kite-flying and sloped off. With heart thumping, and not knowing what to say, I came forward and started to disentangle the cotton line from the little tree. Mark Lyle looked at me and didn't say

85

anything either. We worked it clumsily free, managing to ravel up the rest of it in a series of loops that tugged into knots as we tried to pull them straight. Still not speaking except in grunts of concentration and annoyance we bundled the whole lot up and went off to the bench to work on it.

'This is a fucking game,' said Mark Lyle after a bit. It was fantastic to be spoken to like that. I perched there in the swirl of his swear-word and his Old Spice, looking into a new life of almost frightening pleasure. I glanced at him shyly; his shirt was half-unbuttoned and I could see a brown nipple as he leant forward. Sometimes our hands touched as we rolled the cleared thread on to the plastic reel.

'That Dave Dobbs is a fucking cunt,' he said.

'He *is* a fucking cunt,' I agreed, and Mark Lyle gave a big bright laugh. He had a wide sun-browned face and a large mouth with one or two spots by it that he should have left alone. When we'd more or less finished, he patted his thigh and asked me if I wanted a cigarette. I blushed and said no.

'Mind if I do?' he said, with surely unnecessary courtesy. Actually I was terribly worried about him meeting an early death from lung cancer; but I was overcome by the glamour and intimacy of the occasion. I watched him raptly as he smoked an Embassy to the filter. Each frown, each wincing inhalation, the way he balanced the smoke between his open lips and then as it escaped drew it back up his nose, the two or three different fingerings he essayed, all were written on my mind like a first exercise in sexual attraction. I thought Mark Lyle was the most handsome man I had ever seen.

Later that summer I saw him again. The friendship I had envisaged had not blossomed. Indeed, he'd vanished altogether for about three weeks, leaving me full of forlorn agitation. Then one evening I was rambling homewards from the far side of the Common through the long dry grass when I saw his unmistakable mane of fair hair. He was sitting on a seat with his back to me, and I dithered for several minutes just a few yards behind him. He wasn't aware there was anyone there. Occasionally he lifted what looked like a beer-can to his lips. I looped round and came back in front, pretending to notice him at the last moment. Following our convention I said nothing but sat down beside him and waited.

He can only have been fourteen, but he was managing to grow real side-burns, a more gingery colour than the rest of his hair. He was wearing a Cream on Tour T-shirt and tight, high-waisted shiny brown trousers with generous flares. You could see the stub of his cock very clearly.

'I wondered if you'd been flying that kite again?' I said at length. 'I should think it's a jolly good one.'

Mark Lyle tilted the last of the beer into his mouth, swilled it round and swallowed it, then belched so that I could smell it. He seemed to have forgotten about the Old Spice. 'I'm fucking pissed, man,' he said, and dropping the can on the ground stamped on it violently two or three times. Again the conflict of excitement and distress. In a way this was the opportunity I needed to put my redemptive impulse into operation, but when it came to it I wasn't at all sure of myself.

It was one of my mother's phrases I used: 'There can't be any need for that.'

He looked ahead and laughed mirthlessly. 'Yeah, fuck off now, there's a good little fucker.'

Tears came to my eyes; I wanted to blurt out, 'No, no, I love you, I love you, I didn't mean that, don't say that.' But he got up and stumbled away. I couldn't watch him. I sat picking at the edge of the bench with a thumbnail. I let ten minutes go past, calming myself only to be shot through again with the awful words of rejection. I tried to sound out the note of merely friendly exasperation in them, but it was soured every time by the fierceness of the rest. I thought, no one should be spoken to like that.

Then I leapt up and ran the last few hundred yards to home.

# Bastard out of Carolina

"Simply stunning...
as flawless as any reader
could ask for."
—*New York Times Book Review*

"Tough, plain-spoken, and
thoroughly unsenti-
mental... a coming-of-age
novel like no other."
—*Los Angeles Times Book Review*

"*Bastard*'s success is in its
emotional precision and
irrepressible lyricism,
forcefully combined."
—*San Francisco Review of Books*

*A Selection of The Quality
Paperback Book Club*

# Jazz

"A brilliant daring novel...
Every voice amazes...It
has all the ingredients
of wonderful."
—*Chicago Tribune*

"A thrillingly well-writ-
ten book...passionate...
seductive."
—*Chicago Sun-Times*

"Mesmerizing...a sensu-
ous, haunting story...a
masterpiece."
—*Cosmopolitan*

*A Main Selection of The Book-
of-the-Month Club*

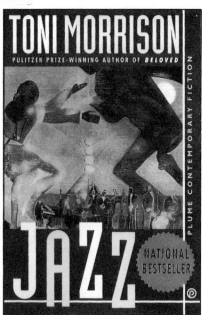

 PLUME
Penguin USA

GRANTA

# Kazuo Ishiguro
# The Gourmet

1. A CHURCH IN A LONDON STREET. 1904. NIGHT.
   A large church set back from the street. A horse-drawn
   carriage stands outside.
   *Close shot*: a wooden plaque on church gate reading:

   I was hungered and ye gave me meat
   I was thirsty and ye gave me drink
   I was a stranger and ye took me in.

   Matthew 25:35

2. CHURCH CRYPT. NIGHT.
   *Point of view*: unseen protagonists as they search around the
   darkened crypt with a lantern. The lantern reveals ragged men
   heaped one on another, sleeping in whatever posture the
   conditions allow. A chorus of snores.

3. CHURCH. NIGHT.
   Viewed from the pulpit. Shadows. We see the empty pews by
   the moonlight coming through the windows.
   Breathing is heard. At first barely discernible, it grows
   clearer: the sounds of two men in physical exertion. Their
   shapes emerge from the shadows, coming slowly towards us

**Kazuo Ishiguro** was born in Nagasaki, Japan, in 1954 and
emigrated to Britain with his family in 1960. He was educated at
the University of Kent at Canterbury and received an M.A. in
creative writing at the University of East Anglia. He became a
British citizen in 1982—just in time to be included the following
year in the original 'Best of Young British Novelists'. His second
novel, *An Artist of the Floating World*, was the Whitbread Book of
the Year in 1986. In 1989, he won the Booker Prize (picture
opposite) for his third novel, *The Remains of the Day*.

Why publish a film script? Mainly, owing to its author's
narrative skills, because it reads so effectively on the page—like a
long short story or a novella. Kazuo Ishiguro's three novels have
all been characterized by their strong use of image and scene, and it
isn't surprising that he has been asked on two occasions to write
film scripts for Channel Four. *The Gourmet* was shown in 1987
—produced by Ann Skinner and directed by Michael Whyte—and
is published here for the first time courtesy of Screbe Productions.

down a side aisle: two men dressed in cloaks and hats. They are carrying something heavy between them.

We hear whispering again, sinister, the words barely discernible.

WHISPER 1: Perhaps over there. [*Heavy breath.*] Over towards that door.
WHISPER 2: Yes, yes. [*Heavy breath.*] We'll take it through to the vestry.
WHISPER 1: Just a little further now. As you say, the vestry.

4. VESTRY. DOORWAY TO BACK ROOM.
The vestry is a small bare room, which we see by the moonlight through a window. At the moment, we are interested only in the doorway which leads through to a back room. This doorway has no door—it is black and ominous, like the gateway to another world.

Meanwhile, the whispers continue.

WHISPER 1: Yes, indeed, you're quite correct. We should cut it along this piece . . .
WHISPER 2: Yes, yes. [*Heavy breath.*] We'll take it through to the vestry.
WHISPER 1: Just a little further now. As you say, the vestry.

5. CHURCH. NIGHT.
*Long shot*: the Church. We are zooming in slowly. Sound of horse hooves in the distance.

6. VESTRY. DOORWAY TO BACK ROOM.
Still moving in on the black doorway. The whispers continue.

WHISPER 1: Yes, yes. I think that direction.
WHISPER 2: You think we should cut it along here?
WHISPER 1: Yes, indeed, along that strip there. As you say.

We have now come right up to the doorway, but there is utter blackness across the threshold.

We then move down slowly, in time to see a thin line of blood run out from the blackness towards us along the vestry floor.

7. AIRPORT RUNWAY. DAY. 1985.
Jet-liner coming into land.

8. ROOF. CAR PARK OF AIRPORT TERMINAL. DAY.
Carter stands at the edge of the roof, watching the landing.
Carter, mid-twenties, slim, dapperly dressed in chauffeur's uniform. Even if he were not wearing dark glasses and his cap pulled down low, his face would probably reveal little emotion; as it is, there is something sinister and assassin-like about him.
He looks at his watch, then back out towards the runway. Evidently, this is the plane he has been waiting for. He walks off out of shot with an almost deliberate lack of hurry.

9. CARRIAGEWAY. DAY.
Rolls Royce in motion.

10. CAR.
Carter is driving. He continues to wear his dark glasses, as he will do throughout the film.
Manley Kingston is in the back seat, preoccupied with something on his lap.
Manley is in his fifties; large, formidable British upper-class presence. He wears a habitual expression of disdain and boredom, but there is also a maverick streak in his face—a hint of the decadent or criminal.
*Close up*: photograph of church in Manley's hand. The church is the one we saw in scene one. The photograph has emerged from an attaché case on Manley's lap.
*On Manley*: studying the photograph as though to commit its details to memory.
*Close up*: open attaché case into which Manley returns the photograph amid other documents. Evidently, he only happened across it while searching for something else, and he now continues through the contents of his case. We glimpse two sketch plans (of the church) and three mortis keys on a ring. Each has a large tag; one is marked 'vestry'. Manley's hand moves these aside as he continues to search. Carter continues to drive silently, while Manley remains preoccupied with the attaché case.

In the ensuing exchange, there is just a hint of malice and sarcasm in Carter's voice—but no more than a hint, and Manley is too preoccupied to notice. Carter has a London working-class accent.

CARTER: Weather nice in Brazil, was it, Sir?
MANLEY: [*Not looking up from his case.*] Paraguay. [*Pause.*]
CARTER: Beg your pardon, Sir?
MANLEY: Paraguay. I've just come from Paraguay.
CARTER: Sorry, sir. Madam told me you were in Brazil.
MANLEY: I suppose I was. I became tired of the place.

Manley has found what he was looking for—an address card. He leans forward and holds it out for Carter.

MANLEY: We're going to drop in at this address on our way home, if you will, Carson.

Carter takes the card without turning, glances at it and puts it on the dashboard. Manley settles back in his seat and gazes out of the window, a preoccupied look still on his face.

CARTER: Carter, Sir.
MANLEY: What?
CARTER: Name's *Carter*, Sir.
MANLEY: [*Turning back to window, impatiently.*] Oh yes, yes.

Move in on Carter's face. It is impossible to tell what is going on behind his glasses.

11. LONDON.
A series of shots of the Rolls's journey into London.

12. DR GROSVENOR'S HOUSE. DAY.
Rolls halts in front of a very expensive house. Manley gets out, studying an address card. He waves carelessly towards the car, then walks to the house.

13. DR GROSVENOR'S ENTRANCE HALL.
A hum of conversation coming from within the house. The doorbell rings.
The figure of Watkins as yet not clearly seen comes into shot

and opens the door. Manley is on the doorstep.

WATKINS: [*Off: cheerfully.*] Good afternoon, Sir.
MANLEY: Ah. My name is Manley Kingston. Dr Grosvenor is expecting me.
WATKINS: Come in, Mr Kingston. [*Following Manley's gaze.*] Oh, we're having a little reception. Eduardo Perez is in London, and he wished to premiere some of his new dishes.
MANLEY: [*Distracted*] Is that so?

Manley goes on looking through into the inner room. Watkins, who should really be leading him in, is delaying doing so to savour these few moments with a celebrity. He beams admiringly at Manley. Manley begins to move further into the house.

MANLEY: Dr Grosvenor about?
WATKINS: [*Suddenly remembering himself.*] Why yes, of course. Let me get you a drink, Mr Kingston, then I'll go and find him.

14. DR GROSVENOR'S HOUSE. RECEPTION ROOM.
An elegant, spacious room of a private house, large enough to hold comfortably the twenty or so guests present. The guests are middle-aged to elderly, formally dressed, men far outnumbering women. This could be a gathering of university professors or classical music critics. They stand conversing in groups of three and four, holding wine glasses.
Watkins is leading Manley across the room towards the wine. Two male guests break off talking as Watkins and Manley come past them. They steal interested glances at Manley, looking him up and down, then stare after him, somewhat disapprovingly. We can hear amid the general hubbub the following exchange, taking place elsewhere in the room:

MALE VOICE 1: But I do think I agree with you on the whole. You have a genuine point there. That whole generation, their central themes were far too centred on protein. Far too centred on protein . . . [*Then in lowered voice.*] I say, look, I believe that's Manley Kingston. That fellow there . . .

15. RECEPTION ROOM. ONE CORNER.
Watkins and Manley have reached the table with the wine.

Watkins hands Manley a glass.

WATKINS: I'll go and find Dr Grosvenor. Won't be a moment, Mr Kingston.

Watkins goes out of shot. Manley turns to the table with a preoccupied air. His back is to the camera and the rest of the room.

Meanwhile, amid the general hubbub, we hear:

MALE VOICE 2: Not at all, not at all, don't get me wrong. I'm very fond of de Montière's work. He does have a splendid sensitivity towards textures. But don't you find his soufflés in particular a little—incoherent?

Two guests we have not yet seen have come up to Manley. These are Proterston, a grey distinguished-looking man, and a Japanese, Takeda. Initially, it is not clear if they have come simply to replenish drinks, or if their interest is in Manley.

Manley remains with his back turned. Proterston attempts to catch Manley's attention. Meanwhile, Takeda is staring at Manley as though he is an exhibit in a museum.

FEMALE VOICE: But I suppose one can't help getting the feeling de Montière achieved his best work in the mid-sixties. I suppose there I do have to agree with you . . . [*Fades into general hum of conversation.*]

PROTERSTON: [*Finally deciding on the direct approach.*] Excuse me, it's Mr Manley Kingston, isn't it?

Manley turns, startled out of his thoughts. He has not touched his wine. Proterston smiles genially. Takeda continues to stare.

MANLEY: Er—yes. Indeed.

PROTERSTON: This is a genuine pleasure. My name is Proterston.

Proterston clearly hopes Manley will recognize the name.

MANLEY: [*No sense of recognition.*] Oh really?

PROTERSTON: [*Gives small self-conscious laugh.*] As a matter of fact, I published an article about you quite recently, Mr

Kingston. In *Gourmet Academica*, the spring issue. I thought perhaps you might have come across it.

MANLEY: [*With little interest.*] I'm afraid I didn't.

Manley now becomes aware of Takeda staring up at him. Manley looks down at him with distaste.

PROTERSTON: Oh—er—this is Mr Takeda.

TAKEDA: [*Heavy accent.*] Great honour. [*He continues to stare at Manley without offering his hand.*] Great honour. Manley Kingston. Great great honour.

PROTERSTON: I should point out, Mr Kingston, my article was entirely in support of your—er—approach. I'd been an admirer of yours for some time and thought, well, in my own small way, I should add my voice to the ranks of your supporters.

Manley is searching the room for Watkins.

MANLEY: Very grateful. I'll keep a look out for it.

Takeda now speaks a great torrent of words in his native tongue. He addresses Proterston while gesturing dramatically towards Manley. Proterston nods throughout. Manley continues to look over at some point behind the camera.

PROTERSTON: Mr Takeda was wondering what had brought you over to London. He was wondering if in fact you had a specific project in mind—here in London?

Clearly, Proterston is himself very eager to know the answer. But Manley has been signalled to from across the room. He puts down his glass and starts to move off. He remembers Proterston and Takeda at the last moment.

MANLEY: Oh, excuse me. Delighted.

16. RECEPTION ROOM.

Manley moves through the guests towards Watkins, who is standing near some double doors. Watkins, smiling eagerly, has his arm raised in preparation for ushering Manley through the doors.

17. DR GROSVENOR'S HOUSE. HALLWAY.

Manley comes through doors held open by Watkins and they move towards the stairs.

18. DR GROSVENOR'S STUDY. EARLY EVENING.

Dr Grosvenor likes to work in a darkened atmosphere. Perhaps this is why he has drawn the blinds, although it is not yet dark outside. The source of light is a powerful desk lamp.

The room is used for consultative purposes as well as for its owner's private study. A client's chair faces Dr Grosvenor's desk. Behind the desk, bookshelves. The books we can see are about food; not cookery books, but serious studies with titles like *Eating Rituals of the Aborigines in the Nineteenth Century*, *Protein and Culture*, *The Evolution of the Carnivore*.

Dr Grosvenor, fifty-five, elegant, assured, but also with an air of depravity; he may be a wealthy doctor in private practice who performs shady operations.

MANLEY: You mentioned in your letter, Doctor, you were having difficulty obtaining one of the solutions I requested . . .
DR GROSVENOR: [*Cutting in.*] Oh no, no. A very minor problem. I have everything you asked for.
MANLEY: Ah.
DR GROSVENOR: And may I say, Mr Kingston, I'm very happy to be of assistance to you. An honour.
MANLEY: Mmm.
DR GROSVENOR: [*A small laugh.*] Forgive me, I suppose you must be getting rather impatient.

He opens a drawer in his desk. Before removing anything, he looks teasingly at Manley.

DR GROSVENOR: [*Continuing.*] You look rather like a hunter, Mr Kingston, just before his big kill.

He smiles and produces an attaché case. He puts it on the desk, opens the lid, then turns it towards Manley.

DR GROSVENOR: [*Continuing.*] I think you'll find everything in order.
MANLEY: Ah.

Manley leans forward hungrily.

Over the shoulder: the attaché case contains papers and documents packed in an orderly manner, uppermost of which is a large photograph of the church we saw in scene one. The case also contains a small metal box.

Manley adjusts the desk-lamp and begins to examine the contents. Dr Grosvenor leans back and smiles.

DR GROSVENOR: Would I be correct in supposing, Mr Kingston, that tonight's adventure, if successful, would even by your standards constitute something of a remarkable feat? A—shall we say—crowning achievement?

MANLEY: [*Absorbed with the attaché case.*] Indeed, indeed.

Dr Grosvenor watches Manley for a few beats, smiling.

DR GROSVENOR: Your career has interested me for some time, Mr Kingston.

Pause. Manley remains absorbed and does not respond.

DR GROSVENOR: I've come to love and enjoy dishes which the average European would feel nauseous just to look at. But let me say, Mr Kingston, I have no hesitation in admitting I have not come anywhere near your level of er—enterprise.

MANLEY: [*Not listening; still absorbed.*] Mmmm.

Dr Grosvenor goes on watching Manley, smiling silently, for another beat or two.

DR GROSVENOR: You know, Mr Kingston, I have little time for those who attempt to denigrate your name . . .

*Close up*: attaché case. As Dr Grosvenor continues, we watch Manley's hands sorting through the contents.

Manley's hands move to the metal box. Inside, the box is antiseptically packed with test-tubes, packets and containers. Meanwhile, Dr Grosvenor is enjoying his own lecture.

DR GROSVENOR: [*Continuing.*] You see, I've always found something noble about your career. Noble in the most fundamental sense. In the primitive world, man was obliged to go out into an unknown wilderness and discover food. He was unbound then by prejudices about what did and did not comprise the edible. He tried anything he could get his hands on. You, Mr Kingston, are one of the few in modern times worthy of our great pioneers in taste. The rest of us, even someone like myself, we're akin to the womenfolk who waited in the caves worrying about how to cook what the hunters brought back . . .

Dr Grosvenor is interrupted by Manley snapping shut the lid of the attaché case.

MANLEY: I am most indebted to you, Dr Grosvenor.
DR GROSVENOR: Not at all. A pleasure.

Manley gets to his feet, holding the case. He moves towards the door.

MANLEY: I'll be on my way.

Dr Grosvenor rises to show Manley out.

DR GROSVENOR: You're extremely welcome, Mr Kingston, to remain a while and sample Señor Perez's new offerings. He'll be presenting his dishes in twenty minutes.
MANLEY: [With haughty disdain.] So kind, no thank you.
DR GROSVENOR: You're familiar with Señor Perez's work?
MANLEY: [Shaking his head; he has long been above such things.] Mmmm.
DR GROSVENOR: A very interesting talent. Personally, I find his preparations suffer from certain unnecessarily romantic effects. But really, overall, a very interesting talent. In his native Central America, he's regarded as something of a revolutionary. You're sure you won't stay? [But he laughs before Manley has time to respond.] But of course, you have other plans.
MANLEY: Quite.

19. CAR. DAY.
Carter is in the front seat of the stationary Rolls, eating a take-away hamburger. He chews slowly and deliberately, as though

he is chewing over some deep plot. He glances outside, and something makes him stop chewing. Then he puts away his unfinished burger, carefully re-packing it in its napkins and cardboard.

20. DR GROSVENOR'S HOUSE. DAY.
The Rolls has remained where we last saw it.
What Carter has seen is Manley emerging from the house and coming towards the car, attaché case in hand. Carter gets out of the car and opens the back door for Manley. Manley gets in. Rolls drives off.

21. BEDROOM. DAY.
Manley is sitting on the edge of a double bed, dressed in a safari jacket. What resembles items of kitchenware dangle from his belt. He is examining something on the bed, which means his back is turned to his wife, Winnie, kneeling on the carpet by the bed. She is fastening a small saucepan to Manley's belt.

Winnie, forty-seven, is a small, stay-at-home woman; not the type to have affairs during her husband's prolonged absences. Her nervous manner in the ensuing scene arises not from any fear of Manley, but because she is in awe of him. Her bedroom would normally be tidy, comfortable and conservative. But for the moment, spread all over the bed are 'tools' which look vaguely surgical, vaguely like more kitchenware; also, an open suitcase from which the 'tools' have originated, a small camping stove, a bulky net. On the floor nearby—though we need not see this for the moment—is a large empty duffle bag.

Throughout the ensuing dialogue, Manley remains preoccupied with these items—concerned there is nothing omitted and that all is in working order.

Winnie finishes fastening the saucepan. She now begins to tie a wok on to Manley's back. Her task is not facilitated by Manley, who—oblivious to Winnie—is constantly moving. This infuriating charade continues throughout the following dialogue. But Winnie, for her part, displays not a hint of impatience.

WINNIE: Was the trip to Iceland useful at all?

MANLEY: Mmm? Oh . . . I didn't go. Nothing very interesting up there any more.
WINNIE: What a pity. Mr Knutsen would have been so disappointed.
MANLEY: Knutsen? Oh yes.

Then Manley turns slightly towards Winnie, thus sabotaging her wok-tying.

WINNIE: [*An embarrassed smile.*] You wrote to me last time you were in Iceland. You told me all about Mr Knutsen. And about his most interesting oven.
MANLEY: [*Preoccupied again.*] Mmm.
WINNIE: [*Fondly.*] Two years ago now. 1984.
MANLEY: Mmm.

Manley begins to load the various items into his duffle bag, giving each item a final check before packing it. Meanwhile, Winnie continues her attempts to secure the wok on to Manley's back.

MANLEY: I suppose . . . [*He turns slightly, again sabotaging the wok-tying.*] you're curious as to where I'm going tonight.
WINNIE: [*Laughs.*] I know you don't like me to pry.
MANLEY: [*Preoccupied with packing again.*] Mmm.

Winnie finally succeeds in securing the wok.

WINNIE: There!

*Another angle*: Manley stands up and surveys the room to check he has not forgotten anything. He picks up his duffle bag, which is now very full.

MANLEY: [*Looking around the room a last time.*] Hmm. Should be everything.

Winnie, too, glances concernedly around the room. Manley turns to exit.

22. MANLEY'S MANSION BLOCK.
Carter is waiting, leaning against the Rolls, eating his hamburger in the slow deliberate manner we saw before. As he

does so he is looking at the front of the Kingstons' mansion block.

*Point of view*: Carter. Move slowly up and across the obviously expensive and ornate archway around the Kingstons' front door. Resume on Carter: chewing his hamburger slowly as though chewing over the details of the archway. His face, as usual, gives little away.

23. HALL.

Manley begins to put his coat on. This presents difficulties on account of the dangling objects about his person. As he moves to the door Winnie comes into the hall. She moves to follow him and we hear the front door slam off screen. Hold on Winnie, devoid of expression.

24. MANLEY'S MANSION BLOCK.

Manley comes down the front path towards the Rolls, still parked as we last saw it. He is carrying his duffle bag and is still struggling a little with his coat. Carter holds the door open for Manley.

25. A STREET. NORTH OF WEST END.

Rolls Royce moving through the street.

26. CAR.

Carter is at the wheel. Manley is in the back seat, looking out of the side window, deep in thought.

27. ANTE-ROOM IN SOUTH AMERICA. NIGHT.

*Close shot*: Rossi.

28. CAR. DAY.

*On Manley*: deep in thought.

MANLEY: You know, Carson, I've been working on this project now for nine years.

*On Carter.*

CARTER: Carter, Sir. [*Pause.*] Name's Carter, Sir.

*On Manley*: still lost in thought, no sign of his having heard Carter. Move in on Manley's face—car drives into a tunnel.

29. ANTE-ROOM IN SOUTH AMERICA. NIGHT.
    *Close shot*: Rossi.
    MANLEY: [*Voice over.*] Mmm. Three times before, I've tried and failed. But this time, I've covered every eventuality.

30. CAR.
    *Close shot*: Manley still lost in thought.

    MANLEY: Trial and error, Carson. Persevere and it's bound to come right in the end.

    *On Carter*: who does not react at all.

    MANLEY: Nine years . . .

31. ROOM IN SOUTH AMERICA. NIGHT.

    MANLEY: Nine years since I met Rossi.

    Background music begins. A room with four men and two beautiful women.
    Background music gets louder and continues through the following series of shots. The shots are silent—we hear no sound other than the music.
    *The door*: which is chained and bolted. This is the object of the men's stares; evidently, someone has knocked. A servant in breeches, about forty, comes into shot. He looks through a peep-hole, says something through the door and waits apprehensively. Then, satisfied, he unchains and unbolts the door, lets in Rossi, and quickly shuts the door again. Rossi is over seventy, a white-haired man in a white suit. He could be a scientist. He surveys the room with a calm, amused expression.
    *Point of view*: Rossi. The room suggests money and decadence—like a back room of a brothel or casino. Five male guests are sitting around the room. Four of these—all aged forty-five or over—are of Latin origin. They look like men accustomed to power, but at the moment, they are smoking as though to relieve nervousness. They look furtively towards the camera. A guilty thrill hovers around them, as though a drug- or sex-orgy is about to take place.
    Rossi's gaze settles on a fifth guest: this is Manley sitting

apart, looking bored. Manley is fanning himself with a hat.
*An electric fan*: in motion on a chest of drawers.
*A large joint of meat*: being brought in on a platter and placed at a low table at the centre of the guests. The meat is not readily identifiable.
*Latin man*: looks at the meat like a Catholic boy looking at his first naked woman—shock, fascination, fear, embarrassment.
*Faces around the table*: display unconvincing attempts to conceal nervousness and excitement. Grins exchanged as though for reassurance. Manley, by contrast, is eating without the least self-consciousness. Again, he looks over to Rossi. Rossi too is an old hand. He wears a similar bored look.
*The joint*: being carved. Soft, pinkish, bloody.
Faces eating the meat, chewing and tasting with fascinated deliberation. Guilt, pleasure, nervousness.
Manley eats without the least self-consciousness. He looks over to Rossi, who returns a look as though to say: 'What a bore.'

32. ANTE-CHAMBER. NIGHT.
Background music fades. Sound of insects and birds fade in.
Manley is looking out of the window, smoking a cigar. He looks sulky. Rossi is standing in the room behind him, also smoking. He has just been trying to make some point to Manley. The door into the next room is ajar, through which can be heard sounds of merry-making—tension-relieving after the eating of the meat. Laughter and shouting continue in the background throughout the ensuing dialogue, but never so loud as to interrupt the speakers.

ROSSI: [*With an Italian accent.*] You look offended, Mr Kingston. [*He smiles reconcilingly.*] Please. I didn't mean to imply you are not a man of great achievements. Of course you are. And I am very sincere, when I ask you to see me as your father-figure. You see, Mr Kingston . . . [*Lowers voice.*] I am now old. I have a bad heart. I will not live much longer.

Manley turns to Rossi. He looks vaguely interested, but not at all sympathetic. He says nothing.

105

ROSSI: No need for sympathies, Mr Kingston. I have no desire to live much longer. I have done everything there is to do. My tongue has tasted everything on this earth. [*Pauses. Then with meaning.*] Even once, something that was *not* of this earth.

Rossi smiles conceitedly. Manley's curiosity has been aroused. He takes the cigar from his mouth and turns to Rossi.

MANLEY: Not of this earth?
ROSSI: You see, Mr Kingston, I am your true father. And you are my true son. I wish you to be the heir to my greatest accomplishment. This is why I tell you this. Yes. I have tasted that which is not of this earth. I have eaten a ghost.

Manley is stunned. He is at once inspired and humiliated. He asks the following question despite himself.

MANLEY: What—er—did it taste like?
ROSSI: [*Laughs triumphantly.*] I wonder how many in the world have had the privilege of hearing such a question from your lips, Mr Kingston.

Manley is now really put out. He turns to leave.

MANLEY: Quite, quite.

ROSSI: [*Becoming suddenly serious.*] Mr Kingston, please.

Rossi ushers Manley to come back. Manley hesitates.

ROSSI: Don't mix with those nonentities. I wish to help you. You are my natural heir.

Manley comes back and stares again out of the window. He puts his cigar in his mouth and avoids looking at Rossi. Rossi too looks out at the view. He draws deeply on his cigar.

ROSSI: The process by which one consumes a ghost is not a simple one. I devoted many years research to the task. I am willing, Mr Kingston, to pass to you—and you only—the fruits of my labour. I ask only in return that you acknowledge me, in the years to come—in your *great* years—as your mentor. You are interested, are you not, Mr Kingston?

A confident glint is in Rossi's eye. He has Manley hooked.

ROSSI: Good. Come to my apartment tomorrow and we will discuss this further. [*With a smile, Rossi starts to leave. Then turns.*] As for your—er—question, the taste is exquisite. [*He gestures with his hands.*] Like nothing on earth.

33. CENTRAL LONDON. NIGHT.
Rolls Royce in motion. Background music ends.

34. CAR. NIGHT.
On Manley: now very alert, leaning forward to see up ahead.

MANLEY: That's it there, Carson. Slow down.

35. STREET OUTSIDE CHURCH. NIGHT.
*Point of view*: Manley from car. A dingy back street. Derelict houses and graffitied walls. Up ahead is the church we first saw in 1904 (scene one). Outside it, along the church wall, is a queue of men.
*Reverse angle*: Manley through the window of the approaching car. The car has slowed right down. Manley is looking out intently.
*Point of view*: Manley from car. We are passing the church gate. At its centre is a wooden plaque. This is not the same plaque we saw in scene one—the design and translation are modern.

I was hungry and you gave me food
I was thirsty and you gave me drink
I was a stranger and you welcomed me.
                                        Matthew 25:35

36. CAR. NIGHT.
Manley is looking intently out of his window.

37. STREET OUTSIDE CHURCH. NIGHT.
*Point of view*: Manley from car. We are now moving along the queue of homeless men—about twenty in number. Some lean against the wall, some crouch, others sit on the pavement.
There are only men here, because the church takes in only men. Otherwise, a mixed crowd—multi-racial, all ages. Only a

few of them are 'traditional' tramps; most are losing a battle to maintain a conventional 'respectable' appearance. A significant number of teenagers. Their faces are bored and weary. They look towards the passing Rolls without surprise and with little interest.

MANLEY: Drive on a little, Carson. Round that corner there.

*Close shot*: Carter, whose face gives away nothing. *Another angle*: Rolls moving past queue of men.

38. CUL-DE-SAC. NIGHT.

Dingy ground covered with rubbish. The car comes into shot as it rounds the corner into the cul-de-sac. It halts.

Carter gets out and comes round to open the door for Manley, but Manley has already opened the door himself before Carter can do so.

Manley struggles out, with his big coat, holding his duffle bag. Indeed, he is not unlike a stereotype tramp.

MANLEY: Be here at five tomorrow morning, will you, Carson?

Manley turns and sets off towards the corner, hoisting his bag on his shoulder. He raises his hand without looking round.

*On Carter*: his face impassive as ever.

39. STREET OUTSIDE CHURCH. NIGHT.

Manley walks purposefully towards the queue of men.

*Another angle on a section of the queue*: Manley comes into shot. He walks past the queuing men, completely ignoring them. He goes out of shot, leaving us to favour the men in the queue. The men in shot glance neutrally after Manley. He is of no special interest to them.

*A few further angles on men in the queue*: there is little conversation; most have arrived singly and do not have the will to strike up new acquaintances. Many look exhausted—they have been walking around aimlessly all day—and some look ill. There is a self-consciousness here, such as one may find in a dole queue.

40. FRONT OF THE CHURCH GATE.
Two or three men at the head of the queue are in shot, leaning against the gate.
Manley comes striding into shot. He tries to open the gate, which is locked. He pushes at it.

MAN IN QUEUE: There *is* a queue, mate.
MANLEY: [*Turning.*] What?
MAN IN QUEUE: Queue. [*He nods in the direction of the queue.*]

Manley looks towards the queue, then again at the locked gate. He is very put out.

MANLEY: Mmm.

Grudgingly, Manley strides off towards the back of the queue and out of shot.

41. STREET OUTSIDE CHURCH. NIGHT.
Manley is walking back towards the end of the queue. He ignores the men.

42. PAVEMENT.
David, the last man in the queue, is sitting on the pavement, his back against the church wall.
David, thirty, wears a corduroy jacket and a shirt—which appear for the moment to be in reasonable condition—and ill-fitting trousers with wide flares. Like others in the queue, he looks bored and tired. To a large extent, he is affecting these looks to disguise his feeling uncomfortable and undignified.
Manley comes into shot and takes his place in the queue beside David. Manley shuffles discontentedly, then looks worriedly at the length of the queue ahead.
David observes Manley. In the ensuing dialogue, David speaks with a nonchalance which is not quite convincing.

DAVID: Don't worry, we'll be alright.
MANLEY: [*Noticing him for the first time.*] What?
DAVID: The first fifty always get in.
MANLEY: Oh. Oh yes. [*A quick glance down the queue.*] But *when* do we get in? I was given to believe the place opened at eight.

DAVID: Supposed to. Never does these days though. Not enough people to run the place any more.
MANLEY: Mmmm. I didn't reckon on standing in a queue.
DAVID: Gets longer every night. Here's a few more.

43. STREET.
*Point of view*: Manley and David. From the direction Manley originally came, two more men are coming down the street to join the queue.

44. PAVEMENT. NIGHT.
Manley and David are both sitting on the ground, gazing emptily ahead of them. During the ensuing dialogue more men join the queue and Manley keeps looking anxiously at the queue in front of him.

DAVID: Get around much, do you?
MANLEY: What?
DAVID: You travel around much.
MANLEY: Oh—yes. I suppose I do. Thousands of miles each year.
DAVID: [*Nodding in weary sympathy.*] Yeah. Same here. [*Pause.*] Just the last few weeks, I've been up to Manchester, come back down here, up to Scunthorpe. Get fed up after a while. [*Pause.*] You're *from* London, are you?
MANLEY: [*He has not been listening.*] What?
DAVID: You were born here. In London.
MANLEY: Oh—yes. Yes. I don't stay here much though. [*With disparagement.*] A city like this has little to offer someone like me.
DAVID: [*Nodding sympathetically again.*] Yeah. Hopeless. Just as bad everywhere else in the bloody country. If not worse. So what you doing back in London then?
MANLEY: [*Shrugs.*] Usual reason I go anywhere. Hunger.
DAVID: Yeah well. You got to eat.
MANLEY: [*Looking away again.*] Hunger. The lengths I've gone to satisfy it. Yet it always returns.
DAVID: I know what you mean. One point last week, I actually started looking in the bins. [*Laughs.*] Really.

MANLEY: [*A tired shrug.*] It's an old game, but always worth trying. I often recommend it.

DAVID: Surprising what you find if you bother to look.

MANLEY: An interesting process takes place inside a refuse bin. A kind of stewing pot of randomness. The chance factor often produces recipes far beyond the capabilities of ordinary imaginations.

For the first time, the thought crosses David's mind that Manley may be a little eccentric. He decides to agree anyway.

DAVID: Yeah, I suppose so. No good being proud and starving to death. Still, you'll get a decent supper tonight.

Manley turns slowly and looks at David as though for the first time.

MANLEY: How do you know that?

DAVID: Well, that's what you're waiting here for, isn't it?

MANLEY: But how the devil did *you* get to hear of it?

DAVID: [*Shrugs defensively.*] Known about it for ages.

MANLEY: You've what?

DAVID: Got it from an advice centre. Off Piccadilly Circus.

MANLEY: [*Outraged.*] Piccadilly Circus? [*Then realizing his mistake.*] Ah. Ah yes. [*Turning away again.*] No doubt, no doubt.

45. STREET OUTSIDE CHURCH.
*Long shot*: the queue along the wall.

46. IN FRONT OF THE CHURCH GATE.
Sounds of the gate being unlocked from the inside. It opens.

47. CHURCH COURTYARD.
The men are moving in line to some point around the side of the church building. The main doors of the church remain closed.

48. CHURCH. BACK LOBBY.
The men are filing in from outside, crossing the small lobby and going further inside the church through another door.

There is occasional conversation, but no more than might be expected in a bus queue. When people talk, their voices tend to be lowered self-consciously.

Manley and David go by in the procession. David shuffles along, looking only ahead of him. Manley is looking around with careful interest.

49. STAIRCASE DOWN TO THE CRYPT.

The procession files down an old stone staircase. Very much a feeling of going underground.

50. CHURCH CRYPT.

A catering trolley is being wheeled along. On the trolley are a large soup canister, a bakery tray loaded with an assortment of rolls, two ladles, a few 'towers' of polyester beakers.

We do not see clearly the surroundings through which the trolley is being pushed, but from the dim artificial light, we get an impression we are down near the basement of the building. The trolley stops momentarily. Widening, we see this is due to some double doors which are presently closed. Volunteer 1, a young woman in shirt and jeans, comes into shot to hold open one of the doors. As we follow the trolley through the doorway, Volunteer 2, a young man, comes into view. It is he who is pushing the trolley. We follow the volunteers and the trolley into the church crypt.

The crypt is the same large basement room we saw in scene two. If space alone were the criterion, this room would be adequate shelter for the fifty or so men now present. However, there is a comfortless, airless feeling about the place. There are now mattresses spread on the floor beside the walls, but otherwise there has been little visible change since 1904. Lighting is by spotlights, which create heavy shadows.

The men have been sitting on the mattresses conversing much more than they did in the queue outside. As the trolley comes in, there is an oddly quiet, but immediate response; the men rise and move towards the centre of the room where the trolley is expected to halt. No one pushes or comes rushing; there is, nevertheless, an urgency in their manner.

51. CRYPT. A CORNER.

*Over the shoulder*: a sketch plan of the church, which we

glimpsed in the attaché case.

*Another angle*: Manley is seated on a mattress, back to the wall, studying the sketch plan. He is ignoring the arrival of the trolley.

Beside him, David is crouching on his heels. He looks anxiously in the direction of the food, then hesitantly at Manley. Shadows moving around them suggest they are among the last to get up.

DAVID: I thought you were hungry.

MANLEY: What? Oh . . . No, no. I'm going to dine later.

DAVID: There won't be any left later.

But Manley is absorbed in his sketch plan. He looks at it intently, frowns, then cranes his neck trying to see something on the other side of the room.

David shrugs, gets to his feet and goes out of shot.

52. CRYPT. A CORNER.

Manley is still sitting by the wall, studying his plan.

53. CRYPT.

At the trolley, the two volunteers are as busy as ever.

Then—a series of shots around the room of the men eating.

Some of the men, not far from the trolley, are eating standing up. Others eat sitting on their mattresses, backs against a wall. Not only the environment, but the means by which they are obliged to eat makes the whole procedure appear rather disgusting. The men 'drink' the beans from the beaker, then chew, taking an occasional bite from a roll. Some eat hungrily. Others appear to be eating only because they know they should, without really caring if they do or not. Many look mentally and physically exhausted. Meanwhile, the buzz of conversation continues. Above which we hear:

VOLUNTEER 1: [*Off; calling in background.*] Don't bung your cups on the ground, please. We'll come round with a bag in a minute. Don't bung them on the ground, you've got to sleep here, remember.

One young man stares into his beaker, not eating.

113

An older man is making a particular mess of his supper. The beans are running down his chin, but he chews on regardless.

54. CRYPT.

The lights have been turned off, but there is still light coming in from somewhere, enabling us to make out the shapes of the fifty or so men huddled or lying asleep.

A grotesque chorus of snores.

55. CRYPT. IN FRONT OF THE DOUBLE DOORS.

The snores continue.

One of the double doors opens. Manley enters. He comes in backwards, preoccupied with something outside the doors. His duffle bag is on his shoulder.

He closes the door quietly and turns. He is holding his sketch-plan. He brings this close to his face in the bad light, lowers it again, then looks about him with a perturbed air.

56. CRYPT.

A slow pan across sleeping, snoring shapes.

57. CRYPT. A CORNER. NIGHT.

*Close shot*: David, asleep on his side. A hand comes into shot and shakes David's shoulder. David starts awake—the reflex of someone used to sleeping in places where he fears discovery. He looks up.

*Point of view*: David. Manley's face is looking down at him. There is something alarming about Manley's face seen in these circumstances.

MANLEY: [*Whispering; he is now more animated than we have yet seen him.*] I need your assistance.
DAVID: What's the matter?
MANLEY: [*Holding up the sketch-plan.*] My information has not proved to be as accurate as I had a right to expect. Do you know the geography of this building?
DAVID: [*Props himself up on to his elbows and looks past Manley as though for some explanation.*] What? What you up to?
MANLEY: I wish to reach the vestry. I need first to get up to the main church.

DAVID: [*Pointing.*] Well, you can go up through . . . [*He breaks off.*] Look, what you up to?

MANLEY: I am hungry. I wish to dine. Perhaps you'd be so good as to indicate to me how to get to the main church.

DAVID: Well, no wonder you're hungry. You should have ate when you had the chance. What's all this about the vestry anyhow?

MANLEY: [*Becoming impatient.*] I expect to find my dinner there.

DAVID: You reckon?

MANLEY: To *that* extent, my information should prove reliable. Now, if you'd be so good as to assist me. I'm *very* hungry.

DAVID: Should have eaten when I told you to.

David turns over to go back to sleep. But he remembers the times *he* has been hungry. Almost immediately, he looks up again at Manley, sighs and begins to get up.

DAVID: There won't be anything left anyway.

58. STAIRCASE.
David and Manley are climbing the staircase we came down earlier. We cannot see much in the darkness, but we hear Manley's heavy breathing. This may well be due to physical effort, but it also sounds like mounting excitement.

59. TOP OF STAIRCASE.
The better light shows us that Manley is still carrying his duffle bag.

DAVID: [*Low voice.*] You'll know better next time. Stomach's *always* going to catch up with you.

Manley, breathing heavily, consults his sketch map.

MANLEY: Mmmm.

Manley starts to go in one direction. David touches his arm and leads in the opposite direction.

DAVID: This way.

60. CHURCH.
Viewed from the pulpit. Many shadows. We see the pews, etc.,

by the moonlight coming through the windows.

In a shot strongly reminiscent of scene three, we first hear Manley's breathing, then gradually make out the figures of Manley and David. We hear, in lowered voices:

DAVID: [*Voice-over.*] They catch us doing this, we'll get banned from this place. [*Then a new thought.*] Anyway, it'll all be locked up.

MANLEY: [*Voice-over.*] I have all the appropriate keys.

DAVID: [*Voice-over.*] God. How d'you get those?

61. IN FRONT OF THE VESTRY DOOR.

*Close up*: Manley's hands sorting through a bunch of mortis keys. These keys all have large tags—these are the same we glimpsed in scene ten.

*Wider angle*: Manley selects a key and fits it to the vestry door. Meanwhile, David stands beside him, casting nervous glances all around the church.

MANLEY: [*As key turns.*] Ah.

Manley opens the door. David looks quickly at the doorway, then throws more furtive glances around the church.

DAVID: Well, enjoy yourself.

David begins to move off. Manley grasps his arm—but not aggressively. It could almost be an insistent hospitality.

MANLEY: You're very welcome to join me. In fact, I suspect I'll need further assistance. Please.

Manley ushers a reluctant David into the vestry.

62. VESTRY.

David looks about him. Manley comes in behind him. He shuts and *locks* the door. David does not see this. Manley also surveys the vestry.

*Point of view*: Manley and David: A small bare room as in scene four. Light from outside illuminates the doorway through to the back room. Now, as in 1904, the doorway has no door. It is black and ominous, like the gateway to another world.

DAVID: [*Trying to hide nervousness.*] Well, I can't see any food. Anyway, I've had my supper.

David turns and goes to the vestry door, and finds it locked. He tries a few more times to open it. His manner reveals how desperate he is to get out of the vestry. He turns and looks back at Manley.

Manley, all the while, has been looking around the room with interest, not bothering with David's efforts to get out.

DAVID: You've locked it.

Manley puts down his duffle bag, then takes off his coat, revealing his safari costume with dangling pans, spoons, etc. He drops the coat on the floor.

David watches for a beat, then looks towards the doorway to the back room.

DAVID: [*Sounding casual.*] Er—I'll take a look what's in here.

David sneaks past Manley towards the black doorway. Manley is too preoccupied with his unpacking to look up at David.

*On black doorway*: David hesitates at the threshold, trying to see into the blackness. He gives a quick glance towards Manley, then vanishes through the doorway.

*On Manley*: who looks up and watches the doorway as though for confirmation of something he knows will happen.

*On black doorway*: hold on the doorway for an ominously long time—long enough so that we expect a scream or something from within.

Then David appears in the doorway. He looks utterly drained.

MANLEY: [*Smiling.*] Well? What did you find in there?
DAVID: [*Shocked.*] There's nothing there. Completely black. [*He manages a nervous laugh.*] I thought for a minute I wouldn't get back out.
MANLEY: Now, my friend, why don't you help me instead of wandering around like that. There's a good fellow.

Manley is holding out his hand invitingly towards the floor.

*Another angle*: in the half-light, we make out an array of objects Manley has laid out on the floor. These are basically the objects we saw in scene twenty-two: the stove, the various metallic utensils, the net, jars and containers—and Dr Grosvenor's box.

*On David*: the experience in the back room has shaken him. He seems to have lost the will to offer any resistance. He looks meekly at the equipment. Then, as though suddenly remembering, he looks nervously back to the black doorway and takes a step away from it. *Dissolve to*:

63. VESTRY.

*Close shot*: a candle burning on a saucer on the floor.

*Another angle*: Manley is shifting about studying something on the floor around the black doorway. We cannot yet see what it is he is studying. He crouches, moves around to get another perspective, like a golfer assessing a crucial putt.

David is standing behind him, leaning against a wall. He is clutching his jacket protectively to himself.

MANLEY: Mmm.

Manley crouches again to scrutinize the unseen objects on the floor. Clearly, he is unhappy about something.

Manley straightens, then without taking his eyes from the floor, gestures towards David.

MANLEY: Your jacket. That will do.
DAVID: What?
MANLEY: [*Gesturing more impatiently; eyes still fixed on the floor.*] Give me your jacket.

David is still clutching his jacket to himself.

DAVID: Rather not, if it's all right with you. I need this jacket.
MANLEY: [*Impatient.*] You'll get it back, man. Now this is important. Your jacket.

Manley goes on studying the floor, a hand held out in full expectation of being handed the jacket.

David looks about him, then reluctantly begins to take off

his jacket. At one point, he hesitates, then continues. The reason for his hesitation is that there is a big hole in his shirt, previously hidden by the jacket. He tries to make the hole less conspicuous by hiding it under an arm.

Manley takes the jacket from David without looking at him and continues to shift and assess, holding the jacket open before him.

DAVID: Look—er—I need that jacket. It's not going to get . . .
MANLEY: [*Cutting in.*] You'll get it back. Now, kindly allow me a few moments of silence. The most *precise* calculations are essential here.

David looks on, worried for his jacket.

64. VESTRY. LATER.

*Close shot*: the rip on David's shirt. David is fingering it self-consciously, as though somehow it can be folded away.

Widen to find Manley and David sitting on the floor, backs against the wall, facing the black doorway. The candle is on the floor in front of them. Manley is not expecting the ghost to appear quite yet. Nevertheless, his eyes are fixed on the doorway. He wears a brooding look. David is also looking at the doorway. His posture suggests he is trying to maximize the distance between himself and the doorway.

*On the black doorway*: hold on the doorway for a beat. Then moving down, we see something has happened to the floor in front of the threshold. A line of what appears to be pieces of bread forms a semi-circle around the doorway. Within the semi-circle, the floor is covered with white powder, dotted with what looks like olives. In a central position, David's jacket is laid out, arms outstretched.

*On Manley and David*: David gives a start at Manley's voice, though it is not loud.

MANLEY: Very well. I will tell you.
DAVID: What's that?
MANLEY: One night in nineteen hundred and four, a pauper was murdered. In *there*.

David follows Manley's gaze.
*On the black doorway*: we close in slowly over the following exchange.

DAVID: [*Voice-over.*] Why?
MANLEY: [*Voice-over.*] What?
DAVID: [*Voice-over.*] Why was he murdered?
MANLEY: [*Voice-over: he considers this an irrelevant diversion.*] Oh . . . some human organs were needed for research purposes, some such thing. In any case, he was brought up here and killed through *there*. Eighty years ago.

MANLEY: [*Continuing; teasing David into the conclusion.*] On this very night.

DAVID: I get it. We're waiting for his ghost to appear.
MANLEY: Very good. And I am informed it is a very reliable ghost, as ghosts go. [*A pause.*]
DAVID: And you're going to . . .
MANLEY: Precisely.

*On the black doorway.*

MANLEY: [*Voice-over continuing.*] And I am now *quite* hungry.

65. VESTRY. AN HOUR LATER.
*Close shot*: the rip on David's shirt. Now, it is being allowed to hang open. Widen to reveal David, sitting as before, back against the wall. He no longer looks frightened; he seems resigned, past caring.

Pan slowly until close on Manley, sitting beside David. He now looks much more hungry and impatient. He is hunched forward, breathing heavily, his gaze fixed on the doorway. He looks lecherous.

*Another angle*: Manley suddenly lurches forward, looking intently ahead. David does not react, but goes on staring blankly in front of him. This is because Manley has lurched forward numerous times before during the past hour. Manley relaxes and settles back.

MANLEY: Hmm. I thought I saw something move again.

DAVID: [*Emotionlessly.*] I'm the ghost around here. It's me.
MANLEY: Now, you're quite clear what you are to do? It's absolutely imperative everything is timed precisely.
DAVID: [*Staring blankly ahead.*] I'm the ghost around here. Could vanish tonight, nobody would notice.
MANLEY: Sssh!

Manley lurches forward.
*On the black doorway*: hold for a few beats. Nothing happens.
*On Manley and David*: Manley is settling back again. David is still gazing blankly ahead.

MANLEY: Mmm.

66. CHURCH.
*Point of view*: unidentified presence which is moving up the side aisle of the church. It then seeks out the vestry door.

67. VESTRY.
*Close shot*: Manley's face igniting with excitement.

MANLEY: [*Hissing.*] There!

Manley rises to his feet, his eyes never leaving the doorway. We see his net is grasped in his hands. David, as though awakened from a dream, starts, then also hurries to his feet.

MANLEY: [*Off; hissing.*] This time definitely! Something moved. Prepare yourself.

*Hold on the doorway*: there is a movement amid the darkness, which we cannot identify. Then a tramp appears in the doorway. His coat and body become visible, then his face. This is an 'old-fashioned' tramp, with a big raggy coat. He is middle-aged, small, with a friendly, cheeky face. There is absolutely nothing eerie about him. The tramp rubs his eyes, as though he has just been awakened, then grins sheepishly.

TRAMP: Evening.

*On Manley and David*: both staring at the tramp in some confusion. Manley's net is poised in one hand.

121

TRAMP: What's going on here then? What's all this? [*He prods with his foot the powder on the floor.*] Spilt something here, have you?

MANLEY: Leave that alone!

TRAMP: [*Looking offended.*] Don't know who are you are, mate, but you won't catch much with that there. After butterflies, go back to Hampstead Heath.

MANLEY: [*Lowering his net, outraged.*] What are *you* doing here?

TRAMP: What am I doing here? I might ask you geezers the same question. I always sleep here. I clean the floors for the old reverend and he lets me stay in here. Can't sleep down there with all that snoring and God knows what else going on. Still, don't know how you geezers got to come up here.

MANLEY: We happen to be awaiting a highly important event. And you, my man, are *in the way*.

TRAMP: [*Shrugs.*] Pardon me, mate. But I tell you there's nothing much in there. If there is, I never noticed it.

As he says this, the tramp turns and looks into the black doorway. Hold on the tramp, his back turned to camera.

MANLEY: Well, I assure you something is very likely to materialize, and I would ask you kindly to remove yourself from that vicinity.

The tramp does not respond. His back has not moved since he turned. Hold a further beat, then zoom in quickly as the tramp begins to turn back towards camera. For a fleeting moment, we glimpse the tramp's face, which has changed. It is the face of a dead man—staring, horror-struck, blood on the lips. We only catch this fleetingly, because we immediately cut to: Manley and David, utterly shocked. Manley comes to his senses first.

MANLEY: The flame, quick! Quick, man, quick!

*Another angle*: something causes a ring of flames to burst around the doorway. The figure of the tramp remains as still as a statue, caught half-turned, looking over his shoulder. We cannot see the face through the flames.

*Point of view*: Ghost. Through the flames, David is frantically throwing some powder from a bowl towards the camera. His urgency owes more to some illogical sense of self-defence than to enthusiasm for Manley's cause.

Manley is unfurling his net. Taking deliberate aim, he throws it. The net covers the camera, and the screen goes black.

68. VESTRY/BACKROOM. A HALF-HOUR LATER.

*Fade in*: the vestry is empty. The net, and David's jacket, lie on the floor at the doorway to the back room. The flames have gone and there is no sign of fire-damage.

There is now light coming from within the back room. We move in slowly through the doorway to discover: Manley sitting on a small stool, hunched over his stove, cooking something in his wok. The flame of the stove appears to be our only source of light. It is not strong enough to show us details of the back room. However:

David is caught within the glow of the stove. He is propped against a wall. He is staring towards Manley.

*Close-up*: Manley's face. Impatient and lecherous, looking down at what he is cooking. He smiles in anticipation.

Manley puts spices into the wok. Hissing and sizzling sounds issue from the wok. We do not yet see the contents of the wok.

David, eyes blank, is still staring towards Manley.

69. CENTRAL LONDON. VERY EARLY MORNING.

Charing Cross and Trafalgar Square. The city has not yet awoken.

70. BACK ALLEY NEAR CHARING CROSS. VERY EARLY MORNING.

Garbage and old newspapers on the ground. A row of dustbins line the alley. At the far end, an old man is looking through a bin for food. He holds a plastic carrier bag into which he puts anything edible. We watch him going from bin to bin, coming towards us up the alley.

Manley appears in the foreground of our shot. He now has his overcoat on again. He is staggering. He halts and leans against a wall, turning to camera as he does so. Manley looks very ill. He is clutching his stomach and breathing heavily. Manley turns and vomits into the nearest dust-bin. Meanwhile, the old man, searching a few bins away, has his back towards Manley and is thus unaware of Manley's vomiting. Manley finishes vomiting, turns towards us and staggers away out of shot. The old man finishes with his bin and turns to the next in line. One glance tells him this is empty. His next bin is the one Manley has vomited into. The old man comes walking up the alley towards us, holding open his carrier bag expectantly. Just as he is about to peer into the bin, we cut to:

71. THE UNDERPASS OF A BRIDGE. VERY EARLY MORNING.

About fifteen men are sheltering on the pavement beneath the bridge. There are signs here of permanent encampment; empty bottles, blankets, newspapers and cardboard boxes marking out 'places'. Around half the men are in sitting positions, propped up by the wall—either because they are awake, or because they sleep in this position.

Manley's figure appears at the far end of the underpass and comes staggering towards us. The men pay little attention to him. Manley stops halfway down the underpass, leaning against the wall to regain his breath.

*Another angle*: just where Manley has halted, one homeless man is sitting on the ground. He is around forty. He wears a suit but no tie. His clothes are now stained and creased, but conceivably, in these same clothes several months ago, this man may have sold insurance. The homeless man looks up sympathetically at Manley and indicates the space next to him. There is a 'seat' of flattened cardboard.

HOMELESS MAN: Sit down. Take a rest.
MANLEY: Mmm.

Manley sits down, still short of breath. He looks broodingly into the space ahead of him. The homeless man fixes Manley with a friendly smile. Manley ignores him for a while, but the homeless man continues smiling. Manley gives the homeless man a quick glance, then looks beyond his companion, down the underpass.

*On Manley and homeless man*: Manley rubs his stomach slowly and gazes broodingly into space once more.

HOMELESS MAN: Overdid it, did we?

MANLEY: What?

HOMELESS MAN: Bit too much of the old . . . [*Makes a drinking gesture.*]

Manley looks at the homeless man with disdain. Then with dignity:

MANLEY: I was hungry. I ate. Now I am sick.

HOMELESS MAN: [*Shrugs.*] Right, right. See what you mean.

MANLEY: You see what I mean? I very much doubt that. How could *you* ever understand the kind of hunger I suffer?

HOMELESS MAN: Well. We all get hungry, don't we?

Manley gives the homeless man another disparaging look.

MANLEY: You have no idea what *real* hunger is.

Homeless man shrugs. Manley continues to look broodingly into space, slowly rubbing his stomach.

72. THE UNDERPASS. EARLY MORNING. A LITTLE LATER.
A Rolls Royce appears at the far end of the underpass and comes slowly past the homeless people.

73. CAR. EARLY MORNING.
Carter, driving, is watching the pavement. He has been searching for some time. His gaze fixes on Manley and the barest hint of a smile crosses his face. He brings the car to a halt, then for a beat or two, remains in his seat, gazing out towards Manley.

74. THE UNDERPASS.
The Rolls has stopped in front of Manley and the homeless man. Manley looks moodily up at the car, but makes no move to stand up. Carter comes out, unhurrying. He makes no move to assist Manley to his feet; instead, he opens the back door and stands holding it open. Manley rises to his feet tiredly. Carter continues to hold the door open, making no effort to

assist the struggling Manley as he climbs into the car. *On homeless man*: there is no surprise on his face. Few things surprise him. He watches with the same friendly smile.

Sounds of doors slamming.

*Another angle*: the Rolls starts up. It moves past the rest of the homeless people and out of shot.

75. A LONDON STREET.

The Rolls moves along a deserted street.

76. CAR.

During the following speech, Manley continues to look tiredly out of the window. Although he ostensibly addresses Carter, he is really just thinking aloud and thus does not notice anything amiss in Carter's silence.

MANLEY: [*Without triumph.*] You may like to know, Carson. I achieved what I set out to do last night.

Carter shows no reaction.

MANLEY: Not quite as extraordinary as one may have expected. [*Pause.*] A disappointment all in all. Perhaps I'll take a trip up to Iceland again. [*Pause.*] Mmm. So dreary, Carson. [*Pause*] Life gets so dreary once you've tasted its more obvious offerings.

Manley continues to gaze out of the window, lost in his thoughts.

77. BACK ROOM/VESTRY. VERY EARLY MORNING.

*Close shot*: David. Asleep propped up against the wall, then he starts awake. He looks around then relaxes. The back room is small and stark, a kind of storeroom for odd bits of church junk. Although we need not notice this yet, there is an old full-length mirror propped against one wall. On the floor are the remains of Manley's presence. It looks much like any untidily abandoned camp-site. The wok sits crookedly on the gas stove. Spoons, spatulas, an empty plate, jars and packets lie strewn around. Manley's stool has keeled over.

David is behaving much like someone waking after a heavy

drinking binge. He sighs heavily and rubs the back of his neck. He suddenly remembers the rip in his shirt and examines it as though in hope that it may have healed overnight. He rises to his feet tiredly. He continues to finger the rip in a preoccupied way, while his eyes search the room for something.

*Point of view*: David.

The wok with three or four pieces of meat still stuck to the edges. With a tired curiosity, he goes to the wok and crouches down by it.

David reaches down and picks off a piece of meat from the wok. He holds it gingerly, as one might a slug. He brings it cautiously to his face. The smell—powerful and awful—hits him. He grimaces and flings the piece of meat away. Then he sighs again and stares emptily in front of him. Still fingering the rip in his shirt, David goes to the doorway. He continues to glance about him in search of something. Through the doorway, we can see to the vestry door, which is now slightly ajar. We move down to the floor around the back room doorway, to discover the object of David's search—his jacket. It lies amid white powdery ash.

David picks up his jacket, brushes as much ash off as possible, then puts it on. There is a large hole burnt around the shoulder. David notices this with dismay. He fingers the hole in his jacket, then his attention is caught by something in the back room. He returns into the back room, holding the burn in his jacket as though it is a wound.

What David has seen is the full-length mirror, left abandoned against a wall. He stands in front of it, then takes his hand away from the burn in his jacket. He looks at his appearance with an empty expression. Then he sighs, shrugs and turns away, once again rubbing the back of his neck.

78. CENTRAL LONDON. EARLY MORNING.

Rolls moving through morning streets.

# A. L. KENNEDY
# FAILING TO FALL

T his is the one thing I know from the minute I lift the receiver and slip that voice inside my ear: it will happen.
'Come now.'
'What?'
'I need you. I need you to come right now.'
'I'm working.'
'And I'm not. I'm at home. Come on.'
'You don't—'
'I do. Tell them you're feeling ill. You've got to be somewhere. There's an emergency. This is an emergency.'
'I can't.'
'Will you come now. I want you to. I want you.'
'I can't.'
'I want you.'
'Really, it's impossible.'
But it happens: I walk through the crashing or silent corridors and clean out of the building without even noticing whether I've put on my coat. I'm already on the way to somewhere else.

It seems a kind of falling, and anyone can fall. I wonder if we don't all wait from time to time, ready to make a dive, to find that space where we can drop unhindered. Like an internal suicide.

So I start my fall and the door into the outside air swings snug behind me and I'm somewhere I can't go at other times. Here we all walk together; are together. Watch for our feet, see our bodies; we all of us have the same music romping inside our heads. We're moving through a big, blue waltz without a collision

**A. L. Kennedy** was born in Dundee in 1965. She studied drama at Warwick University and after she graduated began voluntary work at a community arts centre. Now she directs a creative writing programme and spends the rest of her time writing about 'death and bad weather and sex,' in her Glasgow flat. Her first collection of short stories, *Night Geometry and the Garscadden Trains,* won a Scottish Council Book Award and the Saltire Award for Best First Book. Her novel, *Looking for the Possible Dance,* was published earlier this year by Secker & Warburg.

Photo: Barry Lewis

or a slip and I have my very own personal direction, smooth ahead of me: build a wall and I will simply walk it down. Today I can do that. Look for my heart and you'll see it beating, even through my coat.

This is the only time I have when to be nothing other than me is quite enough. I love this.

It may have been raining for weeks, there may be salted snow and litter greasing together under my feet, dog shit and vomit—the usual pavements we have to use—but today I will neither notice, nor be touched. Angels have decreed it; I will be clean today. The air will shine. And if I glance to the side, the effect is disconcerting. Things are blurred, as though I were watching them from a moving car. Once I have my direction, I can get up a fair head of speed. The final corner spirals off to my right, the sun is blazing a banner in every window and there they are, the reason I came: the taxis.

I can't be sure why the taxis are always involved. I only know I have always taken taxis when I've been falling. When I could afford them and when I could not and when I had to borrow money before I climbed in. It was almost as if they had some claim on me. Sometimes I would find myself clipping that phone call short, just to get moving, to get aboard.

'Come now.'

'Yes, I'll get a taxi, I'm on my way.'

That kind of thing.

Standing there with the taxis, I pause for a wonderful moment —I enjoy that—and then I reach my hand out for the door. Inside, in the air-freshener and cigarette and boot-sole smelling cab, things change. Moving away, the fear begins.

With my face beside the window, I become acutely visible. I fill out with the feeling of being on my way and keep growing. I turn into something cinematically huge. Surely, someone I work with, someone I know, someone representative of God's wrath will take away this much pleasure before it arrives. Because this is too big for only me to have; I should be at work, I should be doing some intermediate something for someone I do not know. I shouldn't be growing this noticeably.

I am afraid of eyes that will see me this way and then not understand. I myself have no understanding, because I am falling. There are meadows and opening seas of room between working and paying and shopping and cooking and eating and sleeping and general household maintenance in which I can be me, doing what I want. I no longer have to look out of the window and wonder who has my life, and if I miss it.

Seated in the expectancy of the taxi, I can love all the halts, the lights, the flaring pigeons. My journey will take forever and no time at all. When I pay the driver I will only faintly notice how much, because money is irrelevant. It lies in my hand, defeated—just for today, we've changed places and I can pass it across with a big, careless smile before the door barks shut behind me.

There is an irregular instant when I leave the cab, a slight loss of rhythm which is no more than natural, before I push the steps away beneath me and make the slow walk to the lift. Almost there. I plummet up the storeys in a stale little scrawled-over can with a pulse in my stomach. There is the flutter of arrival, of the door sliding back, the final steps, another door. Then I feel the pressure of movement between my face and another; the touch of hands, of air, of breath within breath.

And the fall is over. I know what will happen now.

What I have described occurred perhaps once every two or three months. I would much rather let it be over with and hope it won't happen again, but I know that I am not a strong person and that I very much miss those times when I was me and that was enough. Even so, on the days when I was not falling I rarely thought of it—a particular sky, the movement of a breeze, a conjunction of word and feeling might give me a spasm of what I might call completeness, and I would pass into that other life for an instant or two—but for the most part I existed and made myself satisfied with that.

The alteration began at the taxi stance when I arrived one morning and found there were no cabs there, I would have to wait.

'We're out of luck.'

The voice was calm, soft, really very pleasant.

'I said we're out of luck. Odd for this time of day.'

'Yes.'

'I believe I've seen you here before.'

'That's possible.'

'I mean at this rank. I wait at this rank quite often because of what I do. It's my rank.'

'Well, I suppose it's mine, too. If it's anybody's.'

I am not normally this ill-tempered, but I was too far into my journey to focus on anything else and I never like speaking to people I don't know—it makes me feel stupid. I end up discussing the weather when the weather is all around us and both I and whoever the stranger might be must surely have noticed it. We would be better off asking each other if our faces are still there. Against my nature and my better judgement and possibly because this was the only way that Fate could have arranged it, I turned to the stranger and asked with a little ironic twist I was rather proud of, 'What is it that you do?'

'I beg your pardon?'

'You said you were here often because of what you do. I wondered what that was.'

'I see. What I do.' The smile was fully there now. 'I make love.'

'What?'

'That's what I do. I don't mean that's what I'm paid my wages for. I mean that's the most important thing I do. My vocation.'

I wanted to leave then—this was obviously not the kind of person I would usually speak to, not even the kind who was capable of small talk. I couldn't go, though. It was that word—vocation—I knew exactly what that meant. For a breath or two I was aware that both of us were falling together, passing and repassing, nudging briefly as we soared down our particular trajectories. I had never before met somebody so like me. There was no need for words, but my companion spoke in any case.

'I've offended you.'

'No, no.'

'Surprised you then. I only mentioned it because . . . well, because I thought we had similar reasons for being here. A fling, an affair, a fuck. I'm in the right area.'

This was all delivered with a beery smirk and of course, I was alone again at once, spiralling off in a way that no one seemed able to understand. No one knew. I wanted to explain the way things were for me. What I did wasn't about sex, wasn't about running amok and dangerous diseases, perversion, sweat. At that time, I could only have said that the only way not to feel squeezed all the time was to set off on my little journeys to someone close whenever I needed to, no matter what. I needed to be able to fall, to meet sometimes in a way that other people didn't, to be outside the average shape of the day. Now that sounds like a whim, an eccentricity, but it was the heart of my life and here was a total stranger quietly stamping all over it.

I wish I had pointed that out, instead of just saying, 'No, not the same area.'

'You can tell me, it's all right. We aren't the only ones, by any means. I know the type.'

'Uh-huh.'

'No, you don't see what I mean. We aren't the only ones who come here to catch taxis to do . . . things in that area. I know the look. You do, too, if you think about it. You know how it feels. You think that doesn't show?'

I didn't want to hear this. It was like watching my own reflection wink and walk away without me.

'I think something shows.'

'Naturally it shows. When I first realized—what we were all doing—when I looked at the taxis, smiling and creeping along . . . well, even now I can hardly keep from laughing.'

The people around me had stopped being together and the day looked the way it normally did. Nothing was special. There was a metallic feeling about where my liver would be and, more than anything, I felt angry.

'No, it's not like that.'

'Like what, exactly?'

'Like the way you make it sound—as if we all just ran about doing all that we liked. No one can do that. There are consequences, diseases, people are dying of that.'

'Pleasure isn't fatal. I've been in the same relationship for more than a decade now, we simply happen to be unconventional. I thought I'd made myself clear—this is a part of me and what I am and nobody else's hysteria will stop me from being who I am. We are careful because we care and we are happy. You have any objections to that?'

'No, no, I'm sorry.'

'Do you really not know what it's like when you want to make that call—to see him, to see her, whoever is important for you? Are you saying you'd just give it up if somebody told you to?' There was an ugly little pause. 'Surely you do that? You do call?'

'No.'

'Really?'

'I don't make calls, I just answer them.'

We didn't say anything else after that. There was a polite silence; as if something about what I said had been obscene. By the time my taxi came I didn't want it, but I took it anyway. I was going to be late and in the wrong mood and I couldn't help looking for other taxis to see who was inside and if they were happy.

That afternoon, it wasn't very good. I couldn't say what was wrong about it and we made no fuss at the time, but the atmosphere was odd. I strained somewhere in my neck.

It took several weeks before whatever difference we had developed was dispersed and for all of that time at the back of my mind there was a little fleet of taxis full of people I didn't know. They were all being special without me. Perhaps it was that slight mental disturbance which made me think it was strange that I never made the call. I was always the one that got the taxi. Never the caller, always the called. Why shouldn't the process work in reverse? There was a pleasant logic in it. The only component transferred would be the element of surprise. Who would begrudge that? There would still be an expectant journey, a tension, a reward for waiting. No problem. I made a call.

'Right now.'

'Who is this?'
'You know who it is. I have to see you. Come now.'
'I can't now.'
'I want you to.'
'I can't.'

I waited at home for three hours and nobody came. I stayed in all that evening and nobody came.

Sometime later, a matter of months, I found I was waiting at the stance for a taxi. It was going to be an innocent taxi and I felt a little embarrassed at catching it there. In fact, the whole situation was uncomfortable because I hadn't caught a taxi in hot blood since that unfortunate call. Everything was reminding me that I didn't know how to fall any more. I couldn't do it on my own.

'Hello, I thought it was you.'

It was, unmistakably, that voice. That mouth. The steady eyes.

'Here we are again. Not speaking?'
'We're not here again. I'm catching a taxi because I'm late.'
'That's a shame. Trouble at work?'
'What do you mean?'
'Excessive absenteeism?'

I didn't have to look, I knew the mouth would be smiling.

'If it's any of your business, it was trouble at home. No more taxis. Full stop. Not needed.'

'Now that is a shame. That's terrible news. Look, I'll write this down. Call me, will you?'

'What?'
'Call me. On the telephone. That's my number.'
'Why the fuck would I do that?'
'Call me and see.'

I can only say I was shocked and, because my journey was less important than those I had been used to, I walked away without saying another word. I didn't need the stance; I could flag down a cab in the street; it didn't matter.

137

A. L. Kennedy

I don't know if you are familiar with the story of the guru who told his pupil that the meditative life was simple, as long as you never, ever, once thought of a monkey. Naturally, after this, the pupil's meditations were filled with monkeys of every colour and description, arranged in a series of faintly mocking poses.

I was reading to try and improve my condition of mind and I had come across this story. Every time I walked down the street I would think of the pupil, the guru, even the monkey, and none of them would help me because my particular problem was the taxis. They were everywhere. I didn't want to wonder where they were going and why, but I did wonder. I didn't want to lie on my back in the night and hope that the phone might ring and there would be a journey and hands I could hold with my hands. I didn't want to wish for dreams of falling. Everything I did was something that wasn't wanted.

You can guess what came next. What else could I do but another thing I'd never intended? Who else did I know who had even the slightest experience in this field? I had no choice.

I hadn't thrown the stranger's number away. I had hidden it right at the back of a drawer in the hope I'd forget where I put it or that it might spontaneously combust: just disappear and go away. I took under a minute to find it—a corner of paper torn from something more important with seven numbers printed on one side. I had a coffee and called. Engaged. The next time there was no answer; an hour later, the same. I gave the number one final try on two or three other occasions, the last of them late on a Sunday afternoon.

'Hello.'

I couldn't think what to say.

'Hello.'

We had never introduced ourselves and, even if we had, I wasn't precisely certain of what I was calling for. Perhaps help.

'I beg your pardon?'

'Hm?'

'Look, I'm going to hang up now.'

'No. I mean I—Hello.'

'Well, well, well. We met at the taxi rank, isn't that right?'

'Yes. Yes. I'm sorry, we did.'

'You're sorry we did?'

'No, I'm not sorry we did, at all. I didn't mean that.'

'So why are you calling? I gave you my number for a reason—not for a casual chat. Why are you calling?'

'I . . . because I . . . am afraid.'

'Of what?'

'Of what I might do.'

'To whom?'

'I don't know. Mainly to me. I can't get this out of my head, the taxis, the journeys . . . the whole thing. I seem to have nowhere to go now. I thought, because you knew about it . . . You gave me your number.'

'All right. Don't worry. Now . . . '

I could hear a small disturbance at the other end of the line. Imagine that, the same noise, far away in a stranger's room and inside my head. Telephones are wonderful.

'Yes, here we are. Are you listening? Are you there?'

'I am, I am.'

'I want you to catch a taxi at the stance. I want you to tell it to go to the Odeon cinema. When you get there buy a ticket for the next screening in Cinema Three. Go in and take a seat in the fourth row from the back. Is that clear?'

'Yes—'

Far away in that other room, the receiver was replaced and I couldn't even say thank you, or goodbye.

Outside, the half moon risen, people were moving together again, the music was back; we were special. I stepped inside the taxi, rested my hands in my lap and let the world dip away to leave me somewhere altogether better. Even in the half dark, I knew my fingers were jumping a little with every heartbeat, and we were in hot blood again.

Cinema Three was almost empty, pleasantly cool, and I tipped back my head while the trailers reeled by, feeling my breath going all the way in and then all the way out again.

'Good film, wasn't it?'

I held the receiver in both hands to stop it from shaking.

'You never came.'

'I'd already seen it.'

139

'I thought you would be there.'

'You thought wrong. Did you enjoy the film?'

'I . . . Well, yes, I enjoyed the film, but I was waiting for you.'

'You shouldn't have been. I didn't say I would be there. You don't know what you're calling for, do you?'

'What?'

'Give me your number at home and your number at work. Are you still there?'

'Yes.'

'Then give me the numbers. You do want this to continue, don't you?'

And even if I had no idea what we were doing, I did want it to go on, so I passed over the numbers and that was that.

I don't think I lack pride; do you think I lack pride? In my position, you might have fed those numbers down the line and not considered it humiliating. I hadn't known why I was going to the Odeon and, yes, I had expected company, but at least something was happening now. I felt so much better, so much more special again. That isn't something you come by every day. Perhaps a month or two in the Seychelles would do it for you; a fridge full of vodka; a night-sighted rifle and two hundred rounds. These things would be of no interest to me, but I never would blame anybody for making the best of whatever they'd got: I had a voice on the telephone.

So I do believe I kept a little of my pride, while admitting that I waited for the next call with something less than dignity. When it came, I was invited to wait by the Sunlight Cottages in the park. Call three sent me to the sea front; call four, the necropolis, and on every outing, I met no one, spoke to no one, saw no one I recognized.

'I'm sorry, but what's going on?'

'Two o'clock, the Abbey. Be there.'

'But you won't be.'

'I know.'

'So why am I going?'

'Because I'm telling you to. Or don't you want to do this any more?'

'Please, I don't want to stop. I don't want that. I just want to understand what the fuck I'm doing. Please.'

There was a sigh. It came slipping all the way down miles of wire to me, soft but unmistakable.

'You still don't understand?'

'No.'

'Then there's no point in our continuing.'

'No. Please.'

I winced against the clatter of the receiver going down, but nothing happened.

'Please don't hang up. If you explained I would understand, I'm sure of it.'

'What do you enjoy?'

'I . . . how do you mean?'

'What do you enjoy? What makes you take the taxis? What do they do to you? You must know, it's you it happens to. Your heart fists up and quivers, doesn't it? The call starts and your blood is suddenly pushed high, round your ears. You can hear it sing. There are pulses setting up all over you, ones you can't stop, and your stomach is swinging and then convulsing and then turning into a hole punched through to your back. Right?'

'Ye—'

'Right. All your senses shine—it's as if someone pulled a carrier-bag off your head and life is very good and you feel special. Yes?'

'Mm-hmm.'

'And now you can remind me—did you enjoy that film?'

'Yes, I did.'

'You were there because you chose to go there—no one but you. You were happy. You were there and nowhere else, not even in your mind.'

'I think—'

'Don't think, we haven't got the time, just do it. Be there.'

'At the cinema again?'

'Do you still have my number?'

'I think so.'

'You'll find that I've changed it and I won't be ringing you again. This has already gone on too long. Goodbye.'

141

'No!'

'Take care of yourself. Goodbye.'

I didn't find this a very helpful conversation. I remember it very clearly, because, of course, it was the last. I imagined I might be angry, but the anger never came; there was only a numbness which would sometimes wake me in the early dawn. For a long time I thought I would just keep on that way, but the numbness faded and then I felt sad.

Particularly, I was sad because I thought I had really caught the idea of the thing. I'm not really so terribly stupid. I figured out that it didn't matter where I was going in the taxi, as long as I went. It didn't matter who made the call. It didn't matter if there was a call, I could catch a taxi anyway, decide where I was going and then take off.

I took myself back to the cinema and it didn't work. I went back to the park and it didn't work. I took a taxi to cruise past that particular block of flats I had been so used to visiting and it didn't work. I walked up and down the streets, very often in the night, looking for a way into life, a tiny space to fall through, and it didn't work.

The last thing I've done is to write this. It should be that laying out all of these words and recalling the way that it felt when I really was living will help me. I've been turning the problem around here. I have even had to put myself in the place of the stranger on the telephone and that must mean we are a little closer than we were when we knew each other. Perhaps we have knowledge in common now that we didn't have then.

I can say I feel more peaceful than I have in a while and quite tired. When I read this back, it may be that things will come clearer. I think what I hope is that the sum of all I have written will amount to a tiny piece more than I intended and that piece will be what I was looking for all this time. I think that's what I hope.

**GRANTA**

# PHILIP KERR
# REFERENCE POINTS

# Remembering Dad

It was eating oysters, four hundred of the bivalve sons-of-bitches, that finally killed my father, in a theatre-bar off St Martin's Lane. But it was advertising that was truly responsible: by endorsing a new triple-headed, retractable, swivel-headed, disposable electric razor, the old man got more money than he had in the whole of his fifty-odd years put together, not to mention a taste for the high life which, indirectly at least, brought about his untimely death.

As long as I could remember, my father had been possessed of a prodigious appetite and could eat a cart horse under the table. A strange place to eat a horse, you might say. But what seven-foot tall, 330 pound man doesn't eat a lot? For most of his bow-legged life he liked simple, home-baked dishes. Steak pies mostly. And to drink, gallons of hot sweet tea that was as strong as creosote. People said they never saw him touch alcohol and that was just as well since he was quite destructive enough when he was sober. With liquor inside of him there's no telling what he might have been capable of, for to say that he was strong is like saying that Einstein was clever: something of an understatement. With Dad we're talking Hercules, Samson and a whole jungleful of apemen. This was a man who could demolish a wall with his bare hands, carry a sick mule to the vet in town and bite his way through a half-inch thick length of wire, all in one day.

Dad's destructiveness wasn't malicious however. He honestly did not know his own strength and quite often even he was

**Philip Kerr** was born and brought up in Edinburgh and studied law at the University of Birmingham. His most recent novel is *A Philosophical Investigation*. He is also the author of three crime novels: *March Violets, The Pale Criminal* and *A German Requiem*, featuring the detective Bernie Gunter and based in Germany in the 1930s and 1940s. His new book, *Dead Meat*, set in post-Communist St Petersburg, will be published by Chatto and Windus in June and adapted for television in September. He is the editor of the *Penguin Book of Lies*.

Photo: Barry Lewis

145

surprised at just how fragile his surroundings turned out to be. A tree was never quite secure on its roots when Dad was leaning on it. If he walked into a door it was usually the door that came off worst. Once I saw him sneeze the heads off a whole bed of flowers.

The truth is that Dad was none too bright. Allowing for the fact that he was my father, he should never have been permitted to marry my mother. She died giving birth to my twin sister and me. But the real damage had been done long before that happened—to be precise, on their wedding night. The occasion of our being plucked from infinity, in short our conception, spelt curtains for mother and her insides. It goes without saying that the damage which Dad's loofah-sized cock inflicted on her vagina was quite unintentional. Even so, it was irreparable. The old man tore her apart, practically, so that nine months later my sister and I were delivered by caesarean section. But this did not help mother, and she died the very same day.

Poor dad was heartbroken and for a time they took away the .45 calibre Colt Python revolver he always carried, for fear that he might try and kill himself.

After mother's death, Dad's Aunt Agatha came to look after us. She was a thin, wizened old woman who, from her appearance, seemed no more kin to Dad than the Queen of England. Aunt Aggie was a kind, patient sort of woman who had a clear idea of Dad's simple needs, dietary and sexual: the meat pies and hand-jobs she provided him with were instrumental in keeping him out of a mental asylum. I don't think she ever thought that there might be something immoral about an ageing maiden aunt manipulating the genitals of her adult nephew. It was simply one of the many chores she felt obliged to perform in the creation of a stable home for us all; and a sexually frustrated father with the strength of a silver-backed mountain gorilla would have been a danger to the whole family, to say nothing of the local townswomen.

With his bell-shaped chest and those great hams of fists, he looked mean, real mean. This impression was exacerbated by the small pimp moustache he wore and by the fact that the rest of his big, boxing glove of a mug was invariably covered in coarse, thick stubble that was as black and spiny as a sea-urchin. Of course it was this chin that was his most celebrated feature: Dad had a five o'clock shadow before elevenses and was obliged to shave up to three or four times a day. Which is how the Gillingham Sword people and their advertising agency, Cawley, Roland, Allen and Pizzarro (CRAP) became interested in him and signed him up for a series of thirty-second television commercials. He had for a long time been enjoying a very limited kind of fame, as a character in children's literature. But in the post-Thatcher Britain of the 1990s, 'children' also included those more adult brats who are never content with the passive enjoyment of something as innocent as a childhood memory, and actively look towards its exploitation. I refer of course to advertising copywriters. Dad was their natural prey just as many others before him had been. The only wonder was that they took so long to think of using him.

A hundred thousand quid is probably an expense account lunch to the hucksters, but to Dad it was the treasure of Monte Cristo and Sierra Madre rolled into one and it turned his grizzled old head as quickly as a well-volleyed Slazenger Number One. Aggie warned him about the money. She said, 'The best things in life are free,' but Dad said he had always been willing to settle for second-best and anyway he just wanted some fun. The sort of fun he had in mind was harmless enough I guess. Dad had always been a formidable trencherman and he told me how he had half a mind to become a bit of a gourmet. Like Balzac he became devoted to eating oysters. Of course this meant more work for Aggie. None of us reckoned on the fact that oysters are an aphrodisiac. Even today she suffers from Repetitive Strain Syndrome. No matter how many he ate, Dad was never ill. It was simply bad luck that, while swallowing his 299th Colchester of an evening, he should have choked to death on that rarest of precious objects, a black pearl.

Since his untimely death, which left us even richer than before, I have come to consider the inappropriateness of his famous sobriquet (which respect for his memory forbids me from mentioning here), for he always struck me as a uniquely optimistic personality. Indeed his inherent recklessness was more a corollary of his great enthusiasm for life than of any Nabokovian sense of despair. All the same, for those who were not privileged to have known him, it is easy to see how such a misapprehension of his character could have been perpetuated. As Milton has it, 'his look denounc'd desperate revenge.'

# Manor Farm

Aubrey Frederick, the owner of neighbouring Pinchfield Farm, had made it a difficult, not to say expensive year for us. It was a boundary dispute and Frederick won it, so I'll say no more about it except that the bastard lied in his teeth which, if the talk in the taproom at the Red Lion was to be believed, were as false as he was.

I could have understood the loss of the land and even the money we were obliged to pay our solicitor to cover the costs of the action. No, it was the effect it had on Hilda that I really resented, and in truth, after the autumn of the court case, things between us were never quite the same.

Hilda was not what you would have called a typical farmer's wife—all big hands and wide faced. She was rather better looking than the usual sort of woman to be found in Willingdon. A sight more intelligent too. She had always been of an independent frame of mind and I was used to her moods, but a few months after the case was over, she started behaving strangely.

At first she took to wandering about the house naked; and then the farm itself. Now I'm no prude. I like D. H. Lawrence and a bit of community with Nature as much as the next man. Many's the time when I've taken Hilda into the hayfield to have my way with her. What's more she has a lovely body: fine breasts, a good rump and a neat, clean, deep furrow for a man to sow his seed in. So it wasn't that I was ashamed of her. I didn't even mind her going naked about the house. But I did draw the line at going around the farm like that. Especially on the day that Mr Denbeigh the vet came to call.

I had asked him out to take a look at Molly, our white mare. She was in a proper sweat, and I was never one to try and save money where the animals were concerned. So there Denbeigh was, in the stable attending Molly, when in walks Hilda as naked as a key without lock. She had snowdrops in her hand and dried flowers in her hair, and was singing like she was Ophelia herself and touching herself on the breasts and between her legs. Now this was March, mind, and snow lay thickly upon the ground. Denbeigh's jaw dropped like a hanged man's.

Eventually I said: 'I think my wife may have had a bit too much of last year's elderberry.' Then I wrapped my coat around her, took her back up to the house and locked her in the bedroom.

After Denbeigh was gone, I went into the scullery and drew myself a glass of beer from the barrel. I must have had more than one because it was dark by the time I went upstairs. Drunk I may have been and angry I certainly was because having scolded her I bent her over my knee and spanked her bare bottom. She yelled a good deal, and her behind was as red as a beetroot by the time I'd finished, but for a while at least, there was no more nonsense out of her.

There's always plenty of work to do on a farm and soon I forgot this curious incident; and Denbeigh knew better than to go telling tales in the Red Lion. Professional confidence and all that.

It was a fortnight later, when Old Major died, before she fell off the spar again. He was a fine old Middle White boar that had won many a prize at the Willingdon Show, to say nothing of the four hundred pigs he had sired. I ought to have butchered him before then, only I was sentimental about Old Major. When he died I buried him in the orchard underneath my favourite apple tree. He would have liked that. I never knew a pig that was as fond of apples as Old Major.

Naturally Hilda was upset. We'd had that pig for near enough twelve years, ever since he was a piglet and a pet to her, for she loved pigs. It was pigs that brought us together. Before she and I were married, Hilda's brother Tom used to deliver swill to my farm and sometimes she would accompany him so as she could see the little ones. I let her look after one of the runts until he was too big for hand-rearing. When she brought Major back (for so she had called him) I had to promise her never to sell him

to the butcher. In return I asked her to marry me and so she did.
A fair exchange, she said later: one pig for another. When Old
Major died I could understand her being upset. But Hilda cried
for three days and three nights.

The men I employed on the farm were mostly Poles—an idle
and dishonest lot. The fields were full of weeds and the
hedges were neglected. Again and again I had asked them
to pull their socks up, not to mention a few of those blooming
weeds, but they took no notice. They knew that farm labour was
short. There were five of these Poles and four of them looked to
the fifth, a dark, hawk-faced git whose name was Sarbiewski, to
find out what they were supposed to do, since he was the only
one who spoke English.

Now one day, in early May, they'd all gone out rabbiting
without bothering to feed the animals. So when they returned I
called them over and sacked Sarbiewski on the spot. To my
surprise he laughed and with a shrug marched down the cart-
track that led to the main road, stopping only to collect the
money that was due to him from my wife.

That same night, when I was sitting in the kitchen, feeding
crusts of bread soaked in beer to my pet raven Moses, Hilda said:
'You shouldn't have sacked him. He's a gyppo. Proper Romany.
He could understand what they were saying.'

'I'm not interested in what they've got to say,' I heard myself
snort. 'All I want is a day's work. And I reckon I can make
myself understood if they've a mind to hang on to their own
jobs.'

'Idiot,' she hissed. 'Not them Polacks. I mean the animals.'

'The animals?' I repeated dumbly.

'That Romany could understand what they were saying. I've
heard them talking myself, only I can't understand their
language. Not like Sarbiewski could.'

'What are you talking about, woman?' I said weakly.

Hilda looked at me with a mixture of triumph and contempt.

'It's true, I tell you,' she said. 'Our animals talk, just like you
or me, only in a different language. But a language nonetheless,
with names for things like "tree" and "table" and "bread", and of

course the proper names they have for each other.'

'Animals don't bloody talk,' I said. 'They lack the mental capacity. Or to put it a better way, they do not use language.' I shook my head, exasperated. 'The animals talking,' I sneered, with even greater contempt.

'Especially the pigs,' said Hilda. 'They're always talking. They're the leaders. Snowball, Squealer, Napoleon. And you sacked the only man who could have negotiated with them. Fool.'

There was no doubt about it. She was quite mad. But by now my shock was giving way to irritation and anger.

'And Moses here,' I said, nodding at the raven. 'I suppose he talks as well, does he?' This was a trick question. Moses could repeat the odd word (more often a curse) parrot fashion, when he was in the mood.

'He's the cleverest talker of them all,' she jeered. 'Only the other animals won't speak to him. Sarbiewski told me they think Moses is your spy.'

I had had enough of this. I stood up and shook my head vigorously.

'I just don't know about you,' I said. 'Whatever will you come out with next? Talking animals . . . Spies . . . Pigs are the leaders. I suppose you're going to tell me that they're all ruddy Bolsheviks as well?'

# AND ON THE EIGHTH DAY, WE BULLDOZED IT.

The oldest rainforests date back to the dinosaurs, 100 million years. Today they offer the last refuge for half of all plant and animal species on earth.

But how much time do rainforests have left? Millions of acres have been bulldozed and burned. Unless we act now, the last traces of original, irreplaceable paradise will vanish in a single human lifespan.

A miracle of creation will be wiped out, thousands of species doomed to extinction. And nobody will gain.

Rainforest soils are too shallow for agriculture, their complex ecology too fragile for humans to exploit without turning our planet's richest natural regions into eroded wastelands. Short of sustainable uses, leaving the rainforests alone would be the most promising development.

**50,000 acres a day are lost worldwide.**

**What can you do to save the rainforests?**

You can support activist organizations in a dozen nations compaigning to conserve the splendid variety of living things which depend on these endangered environments.

Elusive jaguars, rarest orchids, colorful birds of paradise. And the latest arrivals on the scene: the children of humankind.

# HANIF KUREISHI
# EIGHT ARMS TO HOLD YOU

One day at school—an all-boys comprehensive on the border between London and Kent—our music teacher told us that John Lennon and Paul McCartney didn't actually write those famous Beatles songs we loved so much.

It was 1968 and I was thirteen. For the first time in music appreciation class we were to listen to the Beatles—'She's Leaving Home', with the bass turned off. The previous week, after some Brahms, we'd been allowed to hear a Frank Zappa record, again bassless. For Mr Hogg, our music and religious instruction teacher, the bass guitar 'obscured' the music. But hearing anything by the Beatles at school was uplifting, an act so unusually liberal it was confusing.

Mr Hogg prised open the lid of the school 'stereophonic equipment', which was kept in a big, dark wooden box and wheeled around the premises by the much-abused war-wounded caretaker. Hogg put on 'She's Leaving Home' without introduction, but as soon as it began he started his Beatles analysis.

What he said was devastating, though it was put simply, as if he were stating the obvious. These were the facts: Lennon and McCartney could not possibly have written the songs ascribed to them; it was a con—we should not be taken in by the 'Beatles', they were only the front-men.

Those of us who weren't irritated by his prattling through the tune were giggling. Certainly, for a change, most of us were listening to teacher. I was perplexed. Why would anyone want to think anything so ludicrous? What was really behind this idea?

'Who did write the Beatles' songs, then, sir?' someone asked bravely. And Paul McCartney sang:

---

**Hanif Kureishi** was born in Bromley in 1954. His first full-length play, *The Mother Country*, won the Thames Television Playwright Award in 1980, and in 1982 he became writer-in-residence at the Royal Court. His first film, *My Beautiful Laundrette*, was released in 1986 and received an Oscar nomination for best screenplay. His novel, *The Buddha of Suburbia*, won the Whitbread Best First Novel Award for 1990. Kureishi's four-part adaptation of the novel will be broadcast by the BBC this year. 'Eight Arms to Hold You' was first published with the screenplay of his latest film, *London Kills Me,* by Faber & Faber.

Photo: Barry Lewis

*We struggled hard all our lives to get by,*
*She's leaving home after living alone,*
*For so many years.*

Mr Hogg told us that Brian Epstein and George Martin wrote the Lennon/McCartney songs. The Fabs only played on the records —if they did anything at all. (Hogg doubted whether their hands had actually touched the instruments.) 'Real musicians were playing on those records,' he said. Then he put the record back in its famous sleeve and changed the subject.

But I worried about Hogg's theory for days; on several occasions I was tempted to buttonhole him in the corridor and discuss it further. The more I dwelt on it alone, the more it revealed. The Mopheads couldn't even read music—how could they be geniuses?

It was unbearable to Mr Hogg that four young men without significant education could be the bearers of such talent and critical acclaim. But then Hogg had a somewhat holy attitude to culture. 'He's cultured,' he'd say of someone, the antonym of, 'He's common.' Culture, even popular culture—folk-singing, for instance —was something you put on a special face for, after years of wearisome study. Culture involved a particular twitching of the nose, a faraway look (into the sublime) and a fruity pursing of the lips. Hogg knew. There was, too, a sartorial vocabulary of knowingness, with leather patches sewn on to the elbows of shiny, rancid jackets.

Obviously this was not something the Beatles had been born into. Nor had they acquired it in any recognized academy or university. No, in their early twenties, the Fabs made culture again and again, seemingly without effort, even as they mugged and winked at the cameras like schoolboys.

Sitting in my bedroom listening to the Beatles on a Grundig reel-to-reel tape-recorder, I began to see that to admit to the Beatles' genius would devastate Hogg. It would take too much else away with it. The songs that were so perfect and about recognizable common feelings—'She Loves You', 'Please, Please Me', 'I Wanna Hold Your Hand'—were all written by Brian Epstein and George Martin because the Beatles were only boys like us: ignorant, bad-mannered and rude; boys who'd never, in a just world, do anything interesting with their lives. This implicit belief, or form of contempt, was not abstract. We felt and sometimes recognized—and Hogg's attitude towards the Beatles exemplified this—that our teachers had no respect for us as people capable of learning, of finding the world compelling and wanting to know it.

The Beatles would also be difficult for Hogg to swallow because for him there was a hierarchy among the arts. At the top were stationed classical music and poetry, beside the literary novel and great painting. In the middle would be not-so-good examples of these forms. At the bottom of the list, and scarcely considered art forms at all, were films ('the pictures'), television and, finally, the most derided—pop music.

But in that post-modern dawn—the late 1960s—I like to think that Hogg was starting to experience cultural vertigo—which was why he worried about the Beatles in the first place. He thought he knew what culture was, what counted in history, what had weight and what you needed to know to be educated. These things were not relative, not a question of taste or decision. Notions of objectivity did exist; there were criteria and Hogg knew what the criteria were. Or at least he thought he did. But that particular form of certainty, of intellectual authority, along with many other forms of authority, was shifting. People didn't know where they were any more.

Not that you could ignore the Beatles even if you wanted to. Those rockers in suits were unique in English popular music, bigger than anyone had been before. What a pleasure it was to swing past Buckingham Palace in the bus knowing the Queen was indoors, in her slippers, watching her favourite film, *Yellow Submarine*, and humming along to 'Eleanor Rigby'. (*'All the lonely people . . . '*)

The Beatles couldn't be as easily dismissed as the Rolling Stones, who often seemed like an ersatz American group, especially when Mick Jagger started to sing with an American accent. The Beatles' music was supernaturally beautiful and it was English music. In it you could hear cheeky music-hall songs and send-ups, pub ballads and, more importantly, hymns. The Fabs had the voices and looks of choirboys, and their talent was so broad they could do anything—love songs, comic songs, kids' songs and sing-alongs for football crowds (at White Hart Lane, Tottenham Hotspur's ground, we sang: 'Here, there and every-fucking-where, Jimmy Greaves, Jimmy Greaves'). They could do rock 'n' roll too, though they tended to parody it, having mastered it early on.

One lunch-time in the school library, not long after the incident with Hogg, I came across a copy of *Life* magazine which included hefty extracts from Hunter Davies's biography of the Beatles, the first major book about them and their childhoods. It was soon stolen from the library and passed around the school, a contemporary *Lives of the Saints*. (On the curriculum we were required to read Gerald Durrell and C. S. Forester, but we had our own books, which we discussed, just as we exchanged and discussed records. We liked *Candy*, *Lord of the Flies*, James Bond, Mervyn Peake and *Sex Manners for Men*, among other things.)

Finally my parents bought the biography for my birthday. It was the first hardback I possessed and, pretending to be sick, I took the day off school to read it, with long breaks between chapters to prolong the pleasure. But *The Beatles* didn't satisfy me as I'd imagined it would. It wasn't like listening to *Revolver*, for instance, after which you felt satisfied and uplifted. The book disturbed and intoxicated me; it made me feel restless and dissatisfied with my life. After reading about the Beatles' achievements I began to think I didn't expect enough of myself, that none of us at school did really. In two years we'd start work; soon after that we'd get married and buy a small house nearby. The form of life was decided before it was properly begun.

To my surprise it turned out that the Fabs were lower-middle-class provincial boys; neither rich nor poor, their music didn't come out of hardship and nor were they culturally privileged. Lennon was rough, but it wasn't poverty that made him hard-edged. The Liverpool Institute, attended by Paul and George, was a good grammar school. McCartney's father had been well enough off for Paul and his brother Michael to have piano lessons. Later, his father bought him a guitar.

We had no life guides or role models among politicians, military types or religious figures, or even film stars for that matter, as our parents did. Footballers and pop stars were the revered figures of my generation, and the Beatles, more than anyone, were exemplary for countless young people. If coming from the wrong class restricts your sense of what you can be, then none of us thought we'd become doctors, lawyers, scientists, politicians. We were scheduled to be clerks, civil servants, insurance managers and travel agents.

Not that leading some kind of creative life was entirely impossible. In the mid-1960s the media was starting to grow. There was a demand for designers, graphic artists and the like. In our art lessons we designed toothpaste boxes and record sleeves to prepare for the possibility of going to art school. Now, these were very highly regarded among the kids; they were known to be anarchic places, the sources of British pop art, numerous pop groups and the generators of such luminaries as Pete Townshend, Keith Richards, Ray Davies and John Lennon. Along with the Royal Court and the drama corridor of the BBC, the art schools were the most important post-war British cultural institution, and some lucky kids escaped into them. Once, I ran away from school to spend the day at the local art college. In the corridors where they sat cross-legged on the floor, the kids had dishevelled hair and paint-splattered clothes. A band was rehearsing in the dining-hall. They liked being there so much they stayed till midnight. Round the back entrance there were condoms in the grass.

But these kids were destined to be commercial artists, which was, at least, 'proper work'. Commercial art was OK but anything that veered too closely towards pure art caused embarrassment; it was pretentious. Even education fell into this trap. When, later, I went to college, our neighbours would turn in their furry slippers and housecoats to stare and tut-tut to each other as I walked down the street in my army-surplus greatcoat, carrying a pile of library books. I like to think it was the books rather than the coat they were objecting to—the idea that they were financing my uselessness through their taxes. Surely nurturing my brain could be of no possible benefit to the world; it would only render me more argumentative—create an intelligentsia and you're only producing criticism for the future.

(For some reason I've been long under the impression that this hatred for education is a specifically English tendency. I've never imagined the Scots, Irish or Welsh, and certainly no immigrant group, hating the idea of elevation through the mind in quite the same way. Anyhow, it would be a couple of decades before the combined neighbours of south-east England could take their revenge on education via their collective embodiment—Thatcher.)

I could, then, at least have been training to be an apprentice. But, unfortunately for the neighbours, we had seen *A Hard Day's Night* at Bromley Odeon. Along with our mothers, we screamed all through it, fingers stuck in our ears. And afterwards we didn't know what to do with ourselves, where to go, how to exorcize this passion the Beatles had stoked up. The ordinary wasn't enough; we couldn't accept only the everyday now! We desired ecstasy, the extraordinary, magnificence—today!

For most, this pleasure lasted only a few hours and then faded. But for others it opened a door to the sort of life that might, one day, be lived. And so the Beatles came to represent opportunity and possibility. They were careers officers, a myth for us to live by, a light for us to follow.

How could this be? How was it that of all the groups to emerge from that great pop period the Beatles were the most dangerous, the most threatening, the most subversive? Until they met Dylan and, later, dropped acid, the Beatles wore matching suits and wrote harmless love songs offering little ambiguity and no call to rebellion. They lacked Elvis's sexuality, Dylan's introspection and Jagger's surly danger. And yet . . . and yet—this is the thing—everything about the Beatles represented pleasure, and for the provincial and suburban young pleasure was only the outcome and justification of work. Pleasure was work's reward and it occurred only at weekends and after work.

But when you looked at *A Hard Day's Night* or *Help!*, it was clear that those four boys were having the time of their life: the films radiated freedom and good times. In them there was no sign of the long, slow accumulation of security and status, the year-after-year movement towards satisfaction, that we were expected to ask of life. Without conscience, duty or concern for the future, everything about the Beatles spoke of enjoyment, abandon and attention to the needs of the self. The Beatles became heroes to the young because they were not deferential: no authority had broken their spirit; they were confident and funny; they answered back; no one put them down. It was this independence, creativity and earning-power that worried Hogg about the Beatles. Their naïve hedonism and dazzling accomplishments were too paradoxical. For Hogg to approve of them wholeheartedly was like saying crime paid. But to dismiss the new world of the 1960s was to admit to being old and out of touch.

There was one final strategy that the defenders of the straight world developed at this time. It was a common stand-by of the neighbours. They argued that the talent of such groups was shallow. The easy money would soon be spent, squandered on objects the groups would be too jejune to appreciate. These musicians couldn't think about the future. What fools they were to forfeit the possibility of a secure job for the pleasure of having teenagers worship them for six months.

This sneering 'anyone-can-do-it' attitude to the Beatles wasn't necessarily a bad thing. Anyone could have a group—and they did. But it was obvious from early on that the Beatles were not a two-hit group like the Merseybeats or Freddie and the Dreamers. And around the time that Hogg was worrying about the authorship of 'I Saw Her Standing There' and turning down the bass on 'She's Leaving Home', just as he was getting himself used to them, the Beatles were doing something that had never been done before. They were writing songs about drugs, songs that could be fully comprehended only by people who took drugs, songs designed to be enjoyed all the more if you were stoned when you listened to them.

And Paul McCartney had admitted to using drugs, specifically LSD. This news was very shocking then. For me, the only associations that drugs conjured up were of skinny Chinese junkies in squalid opium dens and morphine addicts in B movies; there had also been the wife in *Long Day's Journey into Night*. What were the Mopheads doing to themselves? Where were they taking us?

On Peter Blake's cover for *Sergeant Pepper*, between Sir Robert Peel and Terry Southern, is an ex-Etonian novelist mentioned in *Remembrance of Things Past* and considered by Proust to be a genius—Aldous Huxley. Huxley first took mescalin in 1953, twelve years before the Beatles used LSD. He took psychedelic drugs eleven times, including on his death bed, when his wife injected him with LSD. During his first trip Huxley felt himself turning into four bamboo chair legs. As the folds of his grey flannel trousers became 'charged with is-ness', the world became a compelling, unpredictable, living and breathing organism. In this transfigured universe Huxley realized both his fear of and

161

need for the 'marvellous'; one of the soul's principal appetites was for 'transcendence'. In an alienated, routine world ruled by habit, the urge for escape, for euphoria, for heightened sensation, could not be denied.

Despite his enthusiasm for LSD, when Huxley took psilocybin with Timothy Leary at Harvard he was alarmed by Leary's ideas about the wider use of psychedelic drugs. He thought Leary was an 'ass' and felt that LSD, if it were to be widely tried at all, should be given to the cultural élite—to artists, psychologists, philosophers and writers. It was important that psychedelic drugs be used seriously, primarily as aids to contemplation. Certainly they changed nothing in the world, being 'incompatible with action and even with the will to action.' Huxley was especially nervous about the aphrodisiac qualities of LSD and wrote to Leary: 'I strongly urge you not to let the sexual cat out of the bag. We've stirred up enough trouble suggesting that drugs can stimulate aesthetic and religious experience.'

But there was nothing Huxley could do to keep the 'cat' in the bag. In 1961 Leary gave LSD to Allen Ginsberg, who became convinced the drug contained the possibilities for political change. Four years later the Beatles met Ginsberg through Bob Dylan. At his own birthday party Ginsberg was naked apart from a pair of underpants on his head and a 'do not disturb' sign tied to his penis. Later, Lennon was to learn a lot from Ginsberg's style of self-exhibition as protest, but on this occasion he shrank from Ginsberg, saying: 'You don't do that in front of the birds!'

Throughout the second half of the 1960s the Beatles functioned as that rare but necessary and important channel, popularizers of esoteric ideas—about mysticism, about different forms of political involvement and about drugs. Many of these ideas originated with Huxley. The Beatles could seduce the world partly because of their innocence. They were, basically, good boys who became bad boys. And when they became bad boys, they took a lot of people with them.

Lennon claimed to have 'tripped' hundreds of times, and he was just the sort to become interested in unusual states of mind. LSD creates euphoria and suspends inhibition; it may make us aware of life's intense flavour. In the tripper's escalation of awareness, the memory is stimulated too. Lennon knew the source of his art was the past, and his acid songs were full of melancholy, self-examination and regret. It's no surprise that *Sergeant Pepper*, which at one time was to include 'Strawberry Fields' and 'Penny Lane', was originally intended to be an album of songs about Lennon and McCartney's Liverpool childhood.

Soon the Beatles started to wear clothes designed to be read by people who were stoned. God knows how much 'is-ness' Huxley would have felt had he seen John Lennon in 1967, when he was reportedly wearing a green flower-patterned shirt, red cord trousers, yellow socks and a sporran in which he carried his loose change and keys. These weren't the cheap but hip adaptations of work clothes that young males had worn since the late 1940s—Levi jackets and jeans, sneakers, work boots or DMs, baseball caps, leather jackets —democratic styles practical for work. The Beatles had rejected this conception of work. Like Baudelairean dandies they could afford to dress ironically and effeminately, for each other, for fun, beyond the constraints of the ordinary. Stepping out into that struggling post-war world steeped in memories of recent devastation and fear—the war was closer to them than *Sergeant Pepper* is to me today— wearing shimmering bandsman's outfits, crushed velvet, peach-coloured silk and long hair, their clothes were gloriously non-functional, identifying their creativity and the pleasures of drug-taking.

By 1966 the Beatles behaved as if they spoke directly to the whole world. This was not a mistake: they were at the centre of life for millions of young people in the West. And certainly they're the only mere pop group you could remove from history and suggest that culturally, without them, things would have been significantly different. All this meant that what they did was influential and important. At this time, before people were aware of the power of the media, the social changes the Beatles sanctioned had happened practically before anyone noticed. Musicians have always been involved with drugs, but the Beatles were the first to parade their particular drug-use—marijuana and LSD—publicly and without shame. They never claimed, as musicians do now—when found out—that drugs were a 'problem' for them. And unlike the Rolling Stones, they were never humiliated for drug-taking or turned into outlaws. There's a story that at a bust at Keith Richards's house in 1967, before the police went in they waited for George Harrison to leave. The Beatles made taking drugs seem an enjoyable, fashionable and liberating experience: like them, you would see and feel in ways you hadn't imagined possible. Their endorsement, far more than that of any other group or individual, removed drugs from their sub-cultural, avant-garde and generally squalid associations, making them part of mainstream youth activity. Since then, illegal drugs have accompanied music, fashion and dance as part of what it is to be young in the West.

Allen Ginsberg called the Beatles 'the paradigm of the age,' and they were indeed condemned to live out their period in all its foolishness, extremity and commendable idealism. Countless preoccupations of the time were expressed through the Fabs. Even Apple Corps was a characteristic 1960s notion: an attempt to run a business venture in an informal, creative and non-materialistic way.

Whatever they did and however it went wrong, the Beatles were always on top of things musically, and perhaps it is this, paradoxically, that made their end inevitable. The loss of control that psychedelic drugs can involve, the political anger of the 1960s and its anti-authoritarian violence, the foolishness and inauthenticity of being pop stars at all, rarely violates the highly finished surface of their music. Songs like 'Revolution' and 'Helter Skelter' attempt to express unstructured or deeply felt passions, but the Beatles are too controlled to let their music fray. It never felt as though the band was going to disintegrate through sheer force of feeling, as with Hendrix, the Who or the Velvet Underground. Their ability was so extensive that all madness could be contained within a song. Even 'Strawberry Fields' and 'I Am the Walrus' are finally engineered and controlled. The exception is 'Revolution No. 9', which Lennon had to fight to keep on the *White Album*; he wanted to smash through the organization and accomplished form of his pop music. But Lennon had to leave the Beatles to continue in that direction and it wasn't until his first solo album that he was able to strip away the Beatle frippery for the raw feeling he was after.

At least, Lennon wanted to do this. In the 1970s, the liberation tendencies of the 1960s bifurcated into two streams—hedonism, self-aggrandizement and decay, represented by the Stones; and serious politics and self-exploration, represented by Lennon. He continued to be actively involved in the obsessions of the time, both as initiate and leader, which is what makes him the central cultural figure of the age, as Brecht was, for instance, in the 1930s and 1940s.

But to continue to develop, Lennon had to leave the containment of the Beatles and move to America. He had to break up the Beatles to lead an interesting life.

I heard a tape the other day of a John Lennon interview. What struck me, what took me back irresistibly, was realizing how much I loved his voice and how inextricably bound up it was with my own growing up. It was a voice I must have heard almost every day for years, on television, radio or record. It was more exceptional then than it is now, not being the voice of the BBC or of southern England, or of a politician; it was neither emollient nor instructing, it was direct and very hip. It pleased without trying to. Lennon's voice continues to intrigue me, and not just for nostalgic reasons, perhaps because of the range of what it says. It's a strong but cruel and harsh voice; not one you'd want to hear putting you down. It's naughty, vastly melancholic and knowing too, full of self-doubt, self-confidence and humour. It's expressive, charming and sensual; there's little concealment in it, as there is in George Harrison's voice, for example. It is aggressive and combative but the violence in it is attractive since it seems to emerge out of a passionate involvement with the world. It's the voice of someone who is alive in both feeling and mind; it comes from someone who has understood his own experience and knows his value.

The only other public voice I know that represents so much, that seems to have spoken relentlessly to me for years, bringing with it a whole view of life—though from the dark side—is that of Margaret Thatcher. When she made her 'St Francis of Assisi' speech outside 10 Downing Street after winning the 1979 General Election, I laughed aloud at the voice alone. It was impenetrable to me that anyone could have voted for a sound that was so cold, so pompous, so clearly insincere, ridiculous and generally absurd.

In this same voice, and speaking of her childhood, Thatcher once said that she felt that 'To pursue pleasure for its own sake was wrong.'

In retrospect it isn't surprising that the 1980s *mélange* of liberal economics and Thatcher's pre-war Methodist priggishness would embody a reaction to the pleasure-seeking of the 1960s and 1970s, as if people felt ashamed, guilty and angry about having gone too far, as if they'd enjoyed themselves too much. The greatest surprise was had by the Left—the ideological left rather than the pragmatic Labour Party—which believed it had, during the 1970s, made immeasurable progress since *Sergeant Pepper*, penetrating the media and the Labour Party, the universities and the law, fanning out and reinforcing itself in various organizations like the gay, black and women's movements. The 1960s was a romantic period and Lennon a great romantic hero, both as poet and political icon. Few thought that what he represented would all end so quickly and easily, that the Left would simply hand over the moral advantage and its established positions in the country as if it hadn't fought for them initially.

Thatcher's trope against feeling was a resurrection of control, a repudiation of the sensual, of self-indulgence in any form, self-exploration and the messiness of non-productive creativity, often specifically targeted against the 'permissive' 1960s. Thatcher's colleague Norman Tebbit characterized this suburban view of the Beatle period with excellent vehemence, calling it: 'The insufferable, smug, sanctimonious, naïve, guilt-ridden, wet, pink orthodoxy of that sunset home of that third-rate decade, the sixties.'

The amusing thing is that Thatcher's attempt to convert Britain to an American-style business-based society has failed. It is not something that could possibly have taken in such a complacent and divided land, especially one lacking a self-help culture. Only the immigrants in Britain have it: they have much to fight for and much to gain through being entrepreneurial. But it's as if no one else can be bothered—they're too mature to fall for such ideas.

Ironically, the glory, or, let us say, the substantial achievement of Britain in its ungracious decline, has been its art. There is here a tradition of culture dissent (or argument or cussedness) caused by the disaffections and resentments endemic in a class-bound society, which fed the best fiction of the 1960s, the theatre of the 1960s and 1970s and the cinema of the early 1980s. But principally and more prolifically, reaching a world-wide audience and being innovative and challenging, there is the production of pop music—the richest cultural form of post-war Britain. Ryszard Kapuściński in *Shah of Shahs* quotes a Tehran carpet salesman: 'What have we given the world? We have given poetry, the miniature and carpets. As you can see, these are all useless things from the productive viewpoint. But it is through such things that we have expressed our true selves.'

The Beatles are the godhead of British pop, the hallmark of excellence in song-writing and, as importantly, in the interweaving of music and life. They set the agenda for what was possible in pop music after them. And Lennon, especially, in refusing to be a career pop star and dissociating himself from the politics of his time, saw, in the 1970s, pop becoming explicitly involved in social issues. In 1976 Eric Clapton interrupted a concert he was giving in Birmingham to make a speech in support of Enoch Powell. The incident led to the setting up of Rock Against Racism. Using pop music as an instrument of solidarity, as resistance and propaganda, it was an effective movement against the National Front at a time when official politics—the Labour Party—were incapable of taking direct action around immediate street issues. And punk too, of course, emerged partly out of the unemployment, enervation and directionlessness of the mid-1970s.

During the 1980s, Thatcherism discredited such disinterested and unprofitable professions as teaching, and yet failed, as I've said, to implant a forging culture of self-help. Today, as then, few British people believe that nothing will be denied them if only they work hard enough, as many Americans, for instance, appear to believe. Most British know for a fact that, whatever they do, they can't crash through the constraints of the class system and all the prejudices and instincts for exclusion that it contains. But pop music is the one area in which this belief in mobility, reward and opportunity does exist.

Fortunately the British school system can be incompetent, liberal and so lacking in self-belief that it lacks the conviction to crush the creativity of young people, which does, therefore, continue to flourish in the interstices of authority, in the school corridor and after four o'clock, as it were. The crucial thing is to have education that doesn't stamp out the desire to learn, that attempts to educate while the instincts of young people—which desire to be stimulated but in very particular things, like sport, pop music and television—flower in spite of the teacher's requirement to educate. The sort of education that Thatcherism needed as a base—hard-line, conformist, medicinal, providing soldiers for the trenches of business wars and not education for its own sake—is actually against the tone or feeling of an England that is not naturally competitive, not being desperate enough, though desperate conditions were beginning to be created.

Since Hogg first played 'She's Leaving Home', the media has expanded unimaginably, but pop music remains one area accessible to all, both to spectators and, especially, to participants. The cinema is too expensive, the novel too refined and exclusive, the theatre too poor and middle-class and television too complicated and rigid. Music is simpler to get into. And pop musicians never have to ask themselves—in the way that writers, for instance, constantly have to—who is my audience, who am I writing for and what am I trying to say? It is art for their own sakes, and art which connects with a substantial audience hungry for a new product, an audience which is, by now, soaked in the history of pop music and is sophisticated, responsive and knowledgeable.

And so there has been in Britain since the mid-1960s a stream of fantastically accomplished music, encompassing punk and new wave, northern soul, reggae, hip-hop, rap, acid jazz and house. The Left, in its puritanical way, has frequently dismissed pop as capitalist pap, preferring folk and other 'traditional' music. But it is pop that has spoken of ordinary experience with far more precision, real knowledge and wit than, say, British fiction of the equivalent period. And you can't dance to fiction.

In the 1980s, during Thatcher's 'permanent revolution', there was much talk of identity, race, nationality, history and, naturally, culture. But pop music, which has bound young people together more than anything else, was usually left out. But this tradition of joyous and lively music created by young people from state schools, kids from whom little was expected, has made a form of self-awareness, entertainment and effective criticism that deserves to be acknowledged and applauded but never institutionalized. But then that is up to the bands and doesn't look like happening, pop music being a rebellious form in itself if it is to be any good. And the Beatles, the most likely candidates ever for institutionalization, finally repudiated that particular death through the good sense of John Lennon, who gave back his MBE, climbed inside a white bag and wrote 'Cold Turkey'.

GRANTA

# ADAM LIVELY
## LETTERS FROM WELLFLEET

Wellfleet
25 September 2064

Dear Sister,

I promised you an account of the town's musical life. Well, I
have met the town's musical life—his name is Monsieur Grenier.
Have you heard of Grenier? I suppose not. He had his flash of
fame some twenty years ago, and then the flame went out. He
has lived here ever since. His music is thoughtful, teasing,
physical, but all in a very French kind of a way. Scrape the
surface and you'll hear Boulez, even Debussy. Like all those
Frenchmen, he has munched on the Orient like an old cow.
Wisps of raga and gamelan dangle from his sensual lips. Now he
ruminates, not in an attic—I was disappointed to discover—but
in a spacious and dusty room in a house at the vent-end of the
Old Town, half a mile from the sea.

The house, which stands in a dignified position at the top of
the East Hill, is owned by one Clifford Patrick, an hairy man
whose brightest attribute is a beautiful young wife. The couple,
who are going up in the world, moved into this villa a couple of
years ago. And soon after they moved in, in a notable act of
patronage, they gave over one of their best rooms, together with
the sea view it affords, to this musical celebrity, rescuing him
thereby from the dingy digs where he'd been rotting.

I went there a few days after my arrival, on a muggy

**Adam Lively** was born in Swansea in 1961. He went up to
Cambridge with the ambition of becoming a professional
violinist. He completed a post-doctoral fellowship in philosophy
at Yale, where he 'majored in bar-room pool and solitude,' and
began his first book, *Blue Fruit*, a novel about alienation and
jazz. It was published in 1988 and was followed by *The Burnt
House* and *The Snail*. He has also published a pamphlet in the
Counterblast series, *Parliament: The Great British Democracy
Swindle*.

'Letters from Wellfleet' is taken from his new novel, *Sing
the Body Electric*, which will be published in June by Chatto &
Windus.

171

afternoon, and was greeted at the door by Madeleine Patrick. She led me with due reverence up the stairs and into his august presence. Monsieur Grenier is enjoying his Indian summer. He met me in a batik shirt, undone to his cavernous navel, looking for all the world like a colonial Balzac. To my relief, he had not the least notion who I was, but ushered me in anyway and served me with some green tea while Mrs Patrick withdrew. The tea had leaves floating in it, as large as lily-pads.

When I said that poor Grenier's flame had gone out, I was referring merely to the flame of fortune and fame, not the spark of creativity. Grenier still composes. A large table was littered with the evidence of numerous projects. He has recently completed a series of piano miniatures—'Vapours', I think they are called—and he did me the honour of playing me one of them. Unfortunately, his instrument was so excruciatingly out of tune, and the piece itself was so short—or perhaps I should say 'evanescent'—that it was difficult to form a judgement. Or perhaps Monsieur Grenier eschews the equal temperament and has his piano specially tuned to some obscure raga? Life is full of mysteries.

When he discovered that I too was a composer, Monsieur Grenier begged me to return the favour and play for him some of my own music. I replied that there was nothing I could play him, since I had never written anything for the piano alone. My music was all dramatic, and all written for large instrumental or vocal ensembles. And since it relied for its effect on shifting texture and coloration, nothing could be gained by my banging it out on a piano. Being a Frenchman—*timbre* is, after all, a French word —Monsieur Grenier was completely satisfied with my argument. From that moment, I think, he admitted me to his brotherhood.

It is, of course, an exaggeration to say that Monsieur Grenier alone constitutes the local musical life. Having tacitly admitted me to the brotherhood of composers, Monsieur Grenier complained to me at length—as composers will—about the musicians available to him. The town's Philharmonic Society, he announced, was a dinosaur, a lumbering, small-brained creature that would expire of its own inertia—and if that didn't happen, it should be swept out to sea by a deluge. (I suspect Monsieur Grenier had spent many happy hours elaborating this picturesque analogy for his own amusement.) As a respected *vieux de la vieille*, Monsieur Grenier had been commissioned on two occasions by the Society. On both of them, he told me, his delicate scores had (the dinosaur analogy marched on) 'been trampled by those idiotic musicians until there was nothing left of them but dust and fragments.' After the second occasion he had vowed never to have anything to do with the Philharmonic Society again.

But times were hard, royalties from his days of fame only trickled in—and after all, a man had to eat. (And Monsieur Grenier looked like one who had to more than most.) The 'vultures' of the Philharmonic Society had returned to him with a request for some dances and occasional pieces for their winter subscription series. What could he do but accept? Even now the vultures were circling around him, demanding the scores for rehearsal. It was insufferable. He hadn't spent his youth trekking through the jungles of Java, notebook in sweaty hand, to end up writing waltzes for Sunday afternoon tea dances! The task was so distasteful that he did anything to distract himself from it. Hence 'Vapours'.

Nothing in this tale of woe alarmed me, for I didn't come here in search of musical sophistication. Sophistication was what I was fleeing when I left New Venice. Sophistication was what was spoiling me. My operas oozed sophistication, which is what bought them popularity with that fashionably philistine audience. I have fled to the sea to find myself and my Art. It is only in Nature that one can find authenticity, and it is only in the midst of Nature that one can shed the shackles of sophistication and discover Nature and authenticity in oneself. If the local orchestra is made up of untutored musical peasants, then so much the better. I shall exalt them to stamp in rhythm. They want dances? Then dances it shall be. I'll make them dance till their tea tastes like gin.

But back to Monsieur Grenier, ruminating all the while on life's injustices. It was uncomfortably hot in his apartment, and the old man—to broach a delicate subject—was not without his own all too physical 'Vapours'. Perhaps this was the result of a lifetime's indulgence in green tea. At any rate, I asked him, as tactfully as I could, whether it would be possible to open one of the windows to let in some fresh air. His refusal was vehement. He never, he said, opened the windows. The noise from outside

173

disturbed his concentration. He had to have absolute silence, 'in order to hear the secret harmonies that lie hidden deep within my mind.' So the windows stayed shut. I smiled understandingly and sipped my hot green liquid, sweating in the fetid fug.

Since my meeting with Monsieur Grenier, the weather has turned fresh and windy again. Every day, at around noon, I go down to the beach and walk along the sea as far as the pier, opposite the New Town, then back again to the fishing beach. Everything here depends upon the rhythm of the tides; we could all happily throw our clocks into the sea. The boats can only be winched back on to the beach when the water is high, and it is at high tide, around the middle of each day, that they return from their fishing expeditions. The smaller boats have begun their trips before dawn. The larger ones set out at sunset and trawl through the night. On their return, there is a sense of relief. Wives and children come down to the beach to greet them, bringing food and bottles of the local beer. The atmosphere is one of carnival.

The men are tough, strong and weather-battered. They leap in and out of the boats in their heavy, thigh-length boots. They throw boxes of gutted, twitching fish to each other. They run up the beach from the sea, stamping the shingle, to secure the lines. They shout orders to each other, haul on ropes, toss a child on to their shoulders. Everywhere there is movement, yelling, laughter. I walk through it in a kind of daze, as happy a man as has ever lived.

With love,
Paul


Wellfleet
5 October 2064

Dear Sister,

Lately I have been thinking more and more about Berlioz, 'caressed by the wild, sweet breeze of fancy,' sailing out over the horizon 'to reach the enchanted isle where the temple of pure art stands alone under a clear sky.' I join hands with him across the centuries and dance—but not to the music of time. For what do true artists do if they do not defy time and thump their drums in defiance, drowning out the measured tread of the years? Already I have in mind a kind of 'Sea Symphony'. No seagulls (muted trumpets, string *glissandi* etc.), but a unified, *spiritual* expression of the feelings aroused in me by this marvellous place. When I was in New Venice turning out operas, music was something ready-to-hand, close to me, to be *used*. Now it feels much further away—over the horizon, something to be *attained*. This symphony that I talk about—this summation of all that I feel about the pounding waves, the slippery shingle, the spray dazzling in the morning—I feel it to be something *beyond me*, in the sense of something transcendent. Perhaps, also, in the sense of something I will never be able to do.

Now to my main news. I have had my first encounter with the Philharmonic Society. It was not a happy meeting, and I fear our relationship is to be that of two mountain beasts hurling themselves headlong at each other. One of us must tumble into the abyss.

I had seen posters around town advertising 'A Rich Feast of Music. An Orchestral Extravaganza' in the Everyman Theatre, opposite the pier. I duly went to the box office and purchased a seat in the front row. I wanted to examine at close quarters these musicians with whom I would have to deal. The evening of the extravaganza arrived, and taking an early supper with my landlord, I left the house and made my way along the front towards the theatre. A gale was blowing. The flags and banners outside the smarter hotels on the front flapped and cracked. The moon lit the foaming white breakers that pounded the shingle. Beyond the breakers—beyond the pier, which lifts its skirts above the waves on stilts—there was an inky-black immensity. I stopped and gazed out at it, pondering the immeasurable depths of the darkness, the inhuman distances travelled by those waves that expended themselves on the beach below me. Ah! I would happily have spent the rest of the night listening to that merry music of nature—the sudden, whirling *crescendo* as a fresh gust whipped in off the sea; the grinding *lento* of the waves. Indeed, it might have been better for everyone if I had stayed outdoors.

The Everyman Theatre is built to a curious design: it is wide, flat and shallow rather than deep and tall. The whole place is heavily carpeted (in a virulent red), which makes the acoustic as rewarding as a cardboard box. A full house (the capacity is about five hundred) might have improved the sound, but in the event only about a quarter of the seats were occupied. The audience for this 'extravaganza' was scattered across the hall in small groups, complaining loudly about the weather, sniffing ostentatiously and taking coats off—then putting them on again, then taking them off and wrapping them around their shoulders, then arranging them over the empty seats in front. All wore expressions of frumpish dissatisfaction.

The musicians of the orchestra began to take their places, wandering on in ones and twos. They looked, if anything, even more disconsolate than their prospective victims. Frowning, they studied the meagre audience, then consoled each other with head-shakings and eye-rollings. They then set to work rubbing their hands to restore life to their flesh. The oboist blew down his instrument, producing a sound like an asthmatic goose, examined his reed for a few moments and shrugged his shoulders. I took my place in the front row, which was otherwise empty.

The posters around town had been singularly uninformative about the delicacies which would be served at the forthcoming feast. A single sheet of paper handed to us at the door was more helpful, though not much. The most substantial item on the programme was the first: Mozart's Overture to *The Magic Flute*. Thereafter the programme degenerated rapidly, with Duncan Ritchie's piano concerto 'From the Cairngorms'—the kind of Hibernian fog that was produced much earlier and more effectively by a German (Felix Mendelssohn-Bartholdy). The second half was made up of a dismal collection of popular tunes and medleys, concluding with 'Merrie Dances' by someone called Montgomery Hummingbird. It looked like being a long evening.

The conductor, a severe looking lady in her fifties, walked on to the platform and acknowledged the trickle of applause with a curt nod. I have always believed that, at least at the beginning of a concert, musicians should be encouraged in their labours. So I clapped vigorously and turned around to encourage my fellow members of the audience. The conductor gave me a baleful glance and opened the score. (That should have forewarned me; what self-respecting conductor needs a score for a masterwork like *The Magic Flute?*) I leaned forward in my seat, my chin resting on my cupped hands, and awaited the unfolding of Mozart's sublime drama.

It did not so much unfold as fall apart. Those majestic opening chords, so redolent of esoteric ritual, require the utmost precision and unity to gain their full effect. The approach adopted by the Philharmonic Society was, shall we say, rather more relaxed. The conductor waved her baton loftily in the air, as though she were pointing out some interesting feature of the theatre's interior decoration. The orchestra, taken aback by this gesture, scrambled to get aboard the first chord. First on deck was the second horn, little more than a schoolboy, who had been watching the conductor nervously ever since she had walked on to the platform. As soon as her hand moved, he blew down his instrument with all his might, producing a loud approximation to an E flat. Violins, flutes, violas, clarinets, cellos and all the rest clattered aboard after him. The conductor evidently found this grotesque cacophony entirely satisfactory, for she repeated her vague wafting motion for the two pairs of mighty chords that follow. The results were broadly similar. This leaky tub was launched.

After the third pair of chords, as you may know, Mozart's music dissolves into sublime mystery. Beneath the stirrings of the violins, the cellos and basses heave gently, while the winds interject with blasts that echo the opening fanfare. The Philharmonic Society had a novel interpretation: they opted for syrupy muddle instead of sublime mystery. There was an old fellow in the second violins whose favourite key, I suspect, is G major. At any rate, he was clearly struggling with Mozart's perverse requirement that all the musicians play in three flats. In order, perhaps, to disguise his difficulties, he employed a lavish, wailing vibrato and such a generous use of audible slides between notes that it seemed as though he might be playing the entire part with a single, greased finger. None of this would have mattered too much if he had not also played extremely loudly. Fixing his part with a determined look, he dug his bow deep into the strings, as though the music were a particularly obstinate mollusc that he was trying to prise from its shell.

Mozart's slow introduction ends, as you know, with the music sinking down and dying away, until the violins break out, *piano*, with the bustling main theme. On this occasion the introduction did not so much die away as peter out. The conductor, disdainfully dismissing the last chord, turned on the violins and began thrashing the air impatiently with her baton. The violins, surprised by this turn of events, responded by sticking their heads further into their parts and pushing their bows backwards and forwards in a vigorous, businesslike manner. The aural effect was that of a bunch of alley cats scampering from some evil-minded pursuer. The conductor, clearly feeling that they were not scampering fast enough, glared at them and thrashed the air even more impatiently. The music gathered pace, like a boulder building momentum as it rolls downhill—except that a boulder would suggest something clear-edged and well-defined. This was more a ball of soft, ill-defined stuff—an enormous ball of fluff, perhaps, with bits hanging off and trailing behind. By the time of the bassoon's entry—that bold *cantus firmus* that upholds Mozart's edifice—the music was going at a headlong, reckless gallop. The poor bassoonist's eyes looked fit to pop out with exertion and alarm. By now, the whole orchestra was a seething mass of frantic, meaningless activity, like one of those ugly nests of insects you find when you lift a stone.

Now I can look back on all this with some wry detachment. But at the time I myself was seething with pity and rage—pity for the memory of that great genius, and rage at the insult that was being inflicted on him. But there was worse to come. Technical incompetence and sloppy musicianship I can just about stomach, if at least an honest attempt is made to stay faithful to the score. But what I have never, and will never, tolerate is the practice of 'improving' a score by cutting it or altering some aspect of its instrumentation. As though anybody could 'improve' upon what Mozart had written! The orchestra stumbled through the rest of the exposition, botched the Masonic wind chords that echo the opening, and then launched on the development. Here Mozart bends the fugal theme through a succession of rapid modulations, perhaps intending to suggest the symbolic journey of initiatory trials that Tamino and Pamina undergo in the opera proper. Here, also, the orchestra was at its execrable worst. If E flat major presented insurmountable obstacles for my old fellow in the violins, B flat minor was an impenetrable mystery. He glared at the music ever harder, attacked his instrument ever more fiercely. But he might as well have been trying to interpret a manuscript in Mandarin Chinese.

All this, as I have said, I was prepared to forgive. But at the *stretto*—where the fugue is tightened, the home key reached and the triumphant re-exposition prepared for—an unforgivable crime was committed. With a flourish of her baton, the conductor introduced a gratuitous roll on the timpani. This grotesque addition was presumably intended to provide some dramatic 'colour'. As though Mozart needed lessons in drama or colour! This was too much. I had reached breaking point. As soon as I heard the offending noise, I got to my feet and—half-turning to the audience behind me—I said in a loud voice: 'That drum-roll is not in Mozart's score.' Then I sat down again.

As you can imagine, this intervention had a galvanizing effect on the proceedings. All eyes were upon me. Muttered conversations erupted. The music chugged on in a distracted, mechanical kind of way, but the musicians were looking down at me with various expressions of horror, annoyance and amusement. The conductor had her back to me but I could see that her ears had turned a livid red colour—whether from anger or understandable shame, I could not tell. For myself, I was sitting quite impassively, content to have registered my protest and listening attentively now for any other artistic abominations. And what an abomination there was to come! Even now I can hardly believe it, can hardly credit even the most reckless of musical vandals with such a piece of aesthetic nihilism. *They had added cymbal clashes to the final chords.* Even as he did the disgusting deed, I glared at the miserable individual assigned this task of butchery, and thought I detected in the glance that he returned me a look of hang-dog apology. When the last chord died away, a deathly hush fell on the theatre. The conductor

179

remained facing the orchestra. It was almost as though they expected me to say something else. I was in no mood to disappoint them. I stood up and, addressing the conductor and orchestra, said in a loud voice: 'Those cymbal clashes are not in Mozart's score. You have insulted the memory of a great artist.' With that I turned on my heel and marched out of the theatre. Behind me I left only an awful silence.

So, dear sister, do not imagine that life is dull for me here.

Your loving brother,
Paul

GRANTA

# ADAM MARS-JONES
# NEIGHBOURS

Terry and I entertained hundreds of couples over the years, and I don't think we were unusual. Most of them were gay, of course, but there were some straights in there too. Some of them may even have been married, though I don't particularly remember. It takes all sorts, doesn't it?

Some of the straight couples were colleagues of Terry's. There are quite a few heterosexuals in the airline business, mainly in administration. I'm always surprised by how many straights there are, and in all walks of life, not just in the obvious professions.

If I'd had to rely entirely on Terry's colleagues for entertainment and social life I think I'd have gone mad. There's a limit to the number of times you can magic your lips into a smile when someone tells what passes for an amusing anecdote among airline folk. Example: a unit—that's a passenger—presents her ticket at the check-in counter. She's asked if she'd like a window seat. She replies, 'Are you mad? Can't you see I've just had my hair done?' How we laughed.

But most of our dinner guests, thank God, were our neighbours at various addresses, as we unhurriedly improved our standing in the housing market, in the years when money had momentum.

Not all of our neighbours, of course, were the sort you ask to dinner. Some of them wouldn't have come even if they'd been asked. One very sporty neighbour used to acknowledge us on his morning or evening runs, gasping out, 'Good . . . mor . . . ning,'

**Adam Mars-Jones** was born in London in 1954 and was educated at Westminster School and Cambridge before studying and then teaching creative writing at the University of Virginia between 1978 and 1981.

His first book was a collection of short stories called *Lantern Lecture*, which won the Somerset Maugham Award in 1982. His second collection, *Monopolies of Loss*, was published last year. 'Neighbours' is taken from *The Waters of Thirst*, which will be published by Faber & Faber later this year.

Adam Mars-Jones lives in London and is a film critic on the *Independent*.

183

or 'Good . . . eve . . . ning,' as evenly as his overstretched lungs would allow. Then there came a time when he would only nod, and we understood that he had grasped, or been told, the nature of our relationship. It was only a small indication, and by itself it wouldn't have been conclusive, but I spotted a piece of circumstantial evidence that pretty much clinched it.

Up to that point, he and his girlfriend (they weren't married) would hang up their washing to dry on a sort of carousel in the yard, visible from our kitchen window. Now I noticed that though she was as unselfconscious as ever in what she hung out to dry, he had started to censor the laundry bag. He had, well, privatized one particular area of the wash. He still yielded up his running shorts and Y-fronts, boxer shorts and even quite skimpy knickers to the public gaze. But he no longer trusted us to see his athletic supports—let's face it, his *jockstraps*.

It wasn't particularly that I scrutinized his contribution to the drying-carousel—I didn't use field-glasses or anything—but the colour spectrum of a straight man's wash is normally so narrow that even quite mildly daring choices stand out as if they were caught in actual beams of black light. I don't remember anything more flagrant than an item in battleship grey, possibly another in dark purple. Nothing so *very* compromising.

I don't know how he solved the problem he set himself by withdrawing from the public domain the manly pouches that would have inflamed our deviant eyes. Perhaps he made arrangements to send them out to be laundered. I prefer to think that he put them in the washer as before, but hung them indoors to dry. I like to imagine the living space festooned with strings of jockstraps, like Christmas decorations. Elasticated garlands out of season.

Perhaps after we moved on up the mortgage ladder, which in those days seemed to go up into the skies like Jack's beanstalk, this sensitive athlete went back to his old habits right away. Or perhaps he waited for a month or two to satisfy himself that the new residents were of good moral standing, a probationary period, before he ran up on to the clothes-line once more the shy bunting of his intimate sportswear.

Other neighbours down the years would have jumped at the chance of seeing inside the house—only they were never going to be invited. There was one woman I remember, at one of our addresses, who more or less ambushed the postman if he'd rung our doorbell and waited as much as five seconds. She couldn't wait to sign for parcels and packets, wanting to shake them or X-ray them or just hold them up to a strong light. She was always sweeping the pavement outside her front door. Then she started sweeping outside our place, too, 'just to be neighbourly' as she put it, but really so she could scan our windows for goings-on and be sure of catching the postman. Still, she was a fearless cleaner when she got to work, whatever her reasons for laying claim to our stretch of pavement. She'd even tackle dogshit.

She turned out to be a Jehovah's Witness, and sometimes she wouldn't wait for the postman, she'd play postie herself. She'd pop leaflets through our letter box off her own bat, with copious annotations. 'True,' she'd write against many passages, and sometimes a fuller comment, like *The POPE is WRONG as EVER,* or *unclean=hated of God.*

She was harmless. It was no different, from her point of view, from us neglecting the garden. Then she would have given us tips on borders and hardy annuals. She would have slipped seed packets through the door. She would have rung the bell shyly and offered us the use of her mower, her rake or her secateurs.

It just so happened that the garden she saw running to seed was our souls, mine and Terry's, and none of her business. All she wanted was for us to be completely different from the way we were, and then she'd have lost interest, found another hobby or another challenge for conversion. Apart from that, she was all right.

After we moved, she didn't give up, she just took to mailing us her homilies and annotations instead of delivering them herself. They followed us through several changes of address. We never did work out how she kept track of us for so long. Perhaps there are Jehovah's Witness moles in high street estate agents. I even almost missed the leaflets when they finally stopped coming. Actually, I found myself thinking, Wonder what happened to her?

With two incomes and a willingness to anticipate fashion in your choice of area, it's surprising how quickly you can afford a bit of garden, the double garage that was a virtual necessity for us, and some mildly ambitious remodelling. Now the bottom has fallen out of the housing market, too, of course, but for a while back there the going was good. I think Terry and I got the same sort of pleasure from seeing the potential of a dowdy suburb as we did from serving Chilean Cabernet Sauvignon, when our friends were only just summoning up the courage to risk Bulgarian.

On the subject of drink, I do think your duty to entertain your guests' palates extends beyond food. Sometimes, I have to say our various guests weren't exactly discriminating. I remember a couple who were our neighbours at one stage, Jenny and James, who knocked it back so freely that for once in my life I had to serve some white at room temperature. For some reason you can get away with exact calculation about food portions, and people understand it's not practical to ask for more, but if you hesitate to open another bottle you're dicing with death socially. An empty plate says nothing, it makes no statement, but an empty glass is always a hint or an accusation.

All the same, I was grudgingly liberal with the booze on the evening Jenny and James came to dinner. They were an odd couple, but I suppose it takes one to know one. Perhaps there are only odd couples. Certainly an *even* couple is a distinctly sinister-sounding idea.

I remember Jenny saying she was surprised when James took a romantic interest in her, because they'd been pals for a long time without any apparent tension. More than once he'd put her into a taxi after a party, or even accompanied her home if she had passed out and put her chastely to bed. Once he'd even cleaned her up after a vomit.

Jenny had warned me when I made the invitation that James had high blood pressure and had been warned to live more healthily, to cut down on saturated fat and so on. The two of them worked for the same brokerage firm, but in fact she seemed to be the higher flier, and it wasn't doing her blood pressure any harm at all. It seemed absurd that James should be so stressed at barely thirty, but of course I didn't know the background then. I told Jenny that I could at least promise that the dinner would be as low-sodium as James wanted it to be, since I never cooked with salt.

Jenny also asked me, rather disconcertingly considering I hardly knew her, if I thought she should be 'taking precautions' —I could hear the inverted commas in her voice. I suppose I was her only gay friend, and that's why she asked me, but I was slow on the uptake. I said of course she should take precautions, unless she was planning on a family. Then I realized what she was trying to say. The end of the world had been widely preached by then, in the leisure centre, at the dry cleaners. Everybody knew something, but I suppose in another way nobody knew anything, and it can't have been easy knowing who to ask.

I had to tell her that I was the last person on earth to give her advice. I've never worn a condom in my life, that was what I told her. I'm not about to start now. What I actually said was, 'My dear Jenny, the closest I've come to putting on a condom was when I made my own sausages—and *that* wasn't worth the trouble.'

Anyway, I'd taken Jenny's hint about the menu, and I had looked through all my cookbooks for something rich and healthy, complex in the mouth but bland in the belly and the bloodstream. If you know anything about it, you'll understand that's the culinary equivalent of squaring the circle, but finally I managed to work it out. I found an elaborate fish recipe with plenty of taste and no fat, only olive oil, and clove after clove of heart-soothing garlic. Good old Jane Grigson.

I was feeling lighthearted when I carried the finished and rather spectacular dish into the dining-room—I always get a lift when the garnish is scattered at last and there's nothing more to be done—and I couldn't resist a little gentle teasing of this odd couple, this couple as odd as we were ourselves. As I carried in the serving-dish, I said, 'We only ever serve the female monkfish in this house. It's one of our little rules.'

'Oh, and why is that?' asked James, with a now-you've-done-it look in Jenny's direction, as if she was bound to have something to say about that.

'Yes, why is that?' Jenny put in, squaring her shoulders for a set to.

'Well . . .' I explained, 'the male monkfish is only two inches long, you see, so they tend to slip through the nets,' and Jenny laughed so hard she choked on the last olive from the canapé tray. She said something I didn't quite catch, about throwing back the little ones.

After that, I thought James was a little truculent, which may just have been the gin and then the wine. I don't even think he noticed that the *entrée* was chosen with his needs in mind. It was like a savoury compliment flamed with brandy. Of course I know that not everybody sees entertaining the way I do, every plate piled high with sociability and commitment, but you'd think Jenny would nudge him under the table—kick him, even—to get him to be more gracious.

It was a good long while before we were invited over to their house, and I couldn't help feeling, when I realized that there would be ten of us at table, that this was one of those oh-god-who-do-we-owe occasions, where you pay off your social debts wholesale without really expecting your guests to get on. I felt that our hospitality was being repaid in a diluted form, somehow, without being appreciated for what it was. There was plenty of drink on offer, of course, which didn't do me a lot of good. The dinner itself was almost defiantly convenience food, top-of-the-line supermarket product, admittedly, but still hundreds of miles away from the real thing.

I've always been a better host than guest, even at my best, I suppose that's obvious, and I couldn't quite control my tongue. I'd planned to say, 'Delicious, you must give me the recipes,' with just a hint of sarcasm if Jenny cared to pick it up—she made no great claims for herself as a hostess, and she could be self-mocking—but then I found myself adding, quite clearly, ' . . . or the bar-codes, anyway,' which was going too far. Terry got us out of there in seconds flat. It was a classic display of a common social manoeuvre, the hurried marital retreat.

On that occasion, I noticed James was wearing a ponytail. It seemed such a badge of yuppie rank that it never occurred to me he had been sacked shortly before, while Jenny had kept her job in the same establishment. The ponytail was a little tassel of compensation for the privileges he had lost. It didn't suit him, but ponytails don't suit anybody, they're not meant to suit people, so that didn't signify. Jenny was trying to keep his spirits up—which may have been one of the reasons for the party—but from his point of view I suppose she was part of the problem, since every day she was commuting to what until recently had been his place of work also. With the loss of his salary he'd had to cut back on his cocaine habit more or less from one day to the next, which can't have helped. Jenny didn't approve of drugs and kept him on a tight rein as soon as she was in a position of power and could get away with it.

Then one evening he rang our doorbell. Terry answered the door to him. James explained that he had locked himself out, and asked if he could come inside to wait until Jenny came home. We brewed him some tea, but it was noticeable that he wouldn't come into the house proper. He was only happy in the hall. Perhaps he thought that gay men were certain to pounce on an unchaperoned male unless a line was drawn at the start. People have such funny ideas. But it may simply have been that the hall was where he felt he would be imposing on us least. All three of us ended up there, perched on chairs that weren't really for company, but for company's coats. James mentioned rather casually that the glaziers would be paying a call in the next day or two, since he had broken a window with his hand.

It should have occurred to us that the only way you are likely to break a window-pane with your hand is by giving it a good punch, but I have to say that it didn't. Still, we were only neighbours, and virtual strangers at that. By this time, though, Jenny couldn't afford to blind herself to the reality of James's mental state, and she arranged for him to visit a psychiatrist.

On the day fixed for his appointment, James went up to town instead. He went to a distinctly high-toned kitchen shop and bought a very beautiful meat cleaver, the finest and heaviest in the entire Sabatier range. Perhaps he had moved in his extremity beyond considerations of thrift and extravagance, or it may have been less dramatic than that. Perhaps he simply hadn't yet got into the habit of economy, even in the case of a purchase that would be used only once.

Back at the house, he made a serious attempt to cut his left wrist. He seems to have thought in terms of cutting the hand off, to judge by his choice of the cleaver and also, I gather, the action he used, closer to chopping than to slitting. He got as far as the tendons. Then his mind cleared in a remarkable way. He found that he was in great pain, and not at all depressed. There was no longer any fog in his head, but there was blood running down his arm.

He phoned the emergency services and told them what he had done. There happened to be an ambulance station just round the corner of the street where we all of us lived, but perhaps they were out on another job at the time. At any rate, his call wasn't answered with the speed he had expected. Perhaps his sense of urgency was only a hangover from the indomitable yuppie impatience. But he was also in steadily increasing pain and less depressed than ever. He ran out of the house to greet an ambulance that was nowhere to be seen, and the front door clicked shut behind him.

So it was that he rang our doorbell for the second time that week. He wasn't waving around his gashed wrist, which was a mercy, or Terry would have passed out. He had wrapped a tea-towel round it. He explained quite calmly what he had done, and asked if he could come inside to wait for the ambulance. Again he didn't want to come any further than the hall.

There was a ring of blood-stains round his mouth, and further staining of his neck and even his hair. It didn't seem a good time to ask if he had tried to drink his own blood. Perhaps he had only been hoping, unrealistically in the face of the damage he had done to himself, to stem the flow of blood or to hasten clotting with the mild coagulants in saliva.

Hospitality is how we make casual relationships sacred, but this was a challenge. Terry and I retreated to the kitchen and considered our options, talking in whispers. We knew better than to offer James anything to eat or drink, even though we both felt a powerful urge to do something that would endorse his choice of our hall as a place of refuge. It seemed important to find some way of acknowledging his gesture, however involuntary it was in reality. There were other doorbells in the street, and he had not passed us over in his need for shelter. He accepted us in this crisis, even if his feet had merely repeated a journey familiar to them from a few days before, when he had last locked himself out. No matter. He had accepted us, and we needed to show that we in our turn accepted him.

Eventually, whispering in our huddle, we decided we should give him another tea-towel for his hand. He had made mention of the hand in his hysterically calm speech when we had let him in, but had said nothing about the stains round his mouth. Best in the circumstances to pretend that we'd seen nothing, that there was nothing to see, though it would have been doing the ambulance men a favour if we'd cleaned James up a bit before they arrived. A tea-towel was the most tactful offering.

There followed a not very dignified wrangle, I'm afraid, about which tea-towel to offer. On that particular day, the only really clean tea-towel available was one from the National Trust for Scotland, not easily replaced. It seemed unlikely that something lent under these circumstances could be claimed back without giving offence.

I should say in our defence that it was the sort of emergency that is likely to find any household unprepared. In the end I went to the laundry basket and retrieved a tea-towel from there. It wasn't clean, obviously, or it wouldn't have been in the laundry basket, but it was no more than moderately soiled. It was a present from someone, and it had nothing more worth keeping printed on it than a recipe for Irish potato bread.

We took it in to James and wrapped it round his wrist over the towel that was already there—and which was by now pretty thoroughly stained. I wouldn't have let him unwrap his wound and put our dirty towel in contact with it. In any case, Terry would have fainted out if he had. He was already being tested to his limits by the marks round James's mouth, though strictly speaking what he minded wasn't actually blood but the wounded flesh that does the bleeding. I'm not squeamish myself.

It was only a few seconds after we had wrapped our symbolic welcome round James's arm that the ambulance came for him at last. I saw it arrive, flashing lights but not sounding its siren, and I ran out to tell the ambulance men that we were looking after their passenger. Again, James gave a calm and concise account of his attempt at self-mutilation, and they helped him into a wheelchair.

As they wheeled him out onto the street, I said I'd call Jenny and asked him for her phone number at work. He was in shock by this time and couldn't remember it, but he asked me to get his wallet from his back trouser-pocket. He stood up shakily, the ambulance men supporting him, and I fished for the wallet, while Terry watched from the porch. This was an intimacy that went beyond hospitality. I could feel the mortal shiver of his buttocks. James could have asked the ambulance men to find his wallet, and by asking me I felt that he was expressing his acknowledgement of the tea-towel and what it represented. But perhaps being in deep shock meant he was not in any condition to express nuances of acceptance and rejection. I was shocked myself at the time. But still I sensed a personal meaning in this request.

When I pulled out James's wallet from the sweat-drenched pocket, I thought I was looking for an address book or diary with Jenny's number in it. But of course they had been co-workers until recently, and what he wanted was one of his old business cards.

Only when James was standing shakily up in the wheelchair, and I was fishing through his trouser pockets for his wallet, did I realize what was different about him. Oh, of course he'd gone mad and he'd had a go at his wrist with a cleaver, and he'd smeared his face with blood like some voodoo priest of the suburbs, but I mean something different. At some time since I'd last seen him, James had cut off his little ponytail. A symbolic yuppie castration had preceded the more ambitious piece of self-inflicted damage—but he hadn't been satisfied for very long by the sacrifice of symbols.

I waited till the ambulance had left before I made the call. Terry came down from the porch into the street. It would have been crass for us to wave as James was taken away, but somehow it seemed necessary to stand there rooted, smiling faint encouraging smiles, as if we might in fact wave at any moment, until the ambulance moved off.

When I phoned Jenny, I listened carefully to how her voice sounded when she reacted to my news. She seemed not to be shocked, though I don't think she was actively expecting it either. I dare say what James did to himself was one of those things you realize after the event had been looming for some time. Most things are like that. I told Jenny which hospital James had been taken to, and she went there right away. I told her to stop in later for a cup of tea or a bite to eat. I thought she might need fortifying for what was waiting for her at home, but I underestimated her. She didn't look in on us. She coped on her own.

That was when I realized how strong she was, strong enough to visit her lover twice a day while he was in hospital (there was quite a bit of work to be done, they kept him there a week and a half), and then to cut him out of her life as quickly and cleanly as possible.

By the time James came out of hospital she had already accepted an offer for the house. Sometimes she must have come straight back from visiting him so as to show people round the house, though he wasn't to know that. In those days, of course, there was no need for the lures that vendors have been reduced to nowadays, the desperate aphrodisiacs of recession—the casual flowers everywhere, the fruit bowl overflowing just so, the handful of fresh herbs on the lifelike fire just before the doorbell rings—and she didn't suffer financially from selling up, even in a hurry.

We didn't see James again. He moved in with his parents for a time, that's all I know. But we did see Jenny. She who had passed her driving test only a little while before she moved into the area, and who would nose her car out on to the street with exemplary mousy caution, now hired a large van and did her own moving. She reversed the van up to the front door first time perfect, as if she'd been doing it all her life. She had become strong in a way that was almost frightening.

She must have been organizing the move for days, in all its details. Everything seemed to be in tea-chests that were numbered and even colour-coded. I went out to offer her a cup of tea, but she'd thought of that too. She'd stripped the kitchen, but she hadn't forgotten to make a great big thermos of tea before she packed the kettle.

She did accept a biscuit, for old times' sake, and that was when she told me what she had found, back at the house, on the day that James did what he did. It wasn't so bad, she said. The staining was almost all on a rug, which she threw away right there and then. There was the bloody great meat cleaver lying where James had dropped it, of course, when he realized that his depression had lifted, but there was also the bag from the Conran Shop nearby, with the receipt still in it. It would have been a shame to waste all that money. So she cleaned the blade with boiling water and took the cleaver back to the shop.

She exchanged it for things she wanted, for use in the smaller, neater kitchen that was already, I suppose, taking shape in her head while the stitches were still raw in James's wrist. A water filter, and one of those slow cookers that keep pace with your working day. You switch them on as you leave the house, and while you're away they very gradually reduce almost anything you care to throw inside them to a mush.

CANDIA MCWILLIAM
THE MANY COLOURS OF BLOOD

W e lived much of our life in the houses of others, and in our own house there lived with us most of the time people other than ourselves. My father worked for the National Trust for Scotland and had to travel all over the country. We stayed sometimes in green castles, sometimes in fish houses, sometimes bothies, while my father worked on the recording and saving of these buildings with their poetic names: Crathes, Culross, Tantallon, Pittenweem, Kirriemuir, Culzean, Craigievar.

My parents' house had been full of dry rot when they bought it in 1954, a modest grey sliver in a terraced Edinburgh crescent with steps up to the front and what is known as an 'area' beneath for storing coal, which came, as did milk, and beer for the pub at the end of the street, by drey. We gave the horses oats for their nosebags, and lump sugar; my mother collected their rotund droppings for the garden. Boys on their way to dig the allotments behind the crescent sometimes threw bangers under the hooves of a drey horse. The gunpowder in the firecrackers smelt more intoxicating than the heavy pall of fermenting hops from the Ushers Vaux brewery that set upon our part of town when there was no wind from the sea. All the time one smelt coal. The first brush Edinburgh children had with sex was a joke; in Edinburgh, sex is what you carry coal in.

In our basement was a large kitchen with an old range that must once have served the whole house. The range had to be fed by my parents with coal twice a day, and riddled more often to stir it into action, when it would produce a swelling, short and sulky heat that caused the laundry, hung above it on a pulley with curly wrought-iron brackets, to steam like a winded man in the cold. If the weather was fresh without the wetness of haar to it we hung the

**Candia McWilliam** was born in 1955 in Edinburgh, where she was educated until, at the age of thirteen, she went to school in England. She read English at Cambridge and then worked for *Vogue* and as an advertising copywriter. Her first novel, *A Case of Knives*, was published in 1988 and won a Betty Trask award; it was followed by *A Little Stranger* in 1989. Candia McWilliam lives with her husband and three children in Oxford, where she is at work on her third book, a novel about the sea.

washing in the garden on the line between spindly six-foot-long wooden props. We did the washing in two stone sinks, using a washboard whose surface was covered with a metal at once hard and soft that may have been zinc. Round her waist my mother wore a bag of pegs; a peg bag was an acceptable womanly gift at that time, and to be able to sew a peg bag was part of my education, so important that I was three times taught how to do it at my emphatically, Scottishly, academic school. The third time we sewed a peg bag we did it against time, as though the task were a competitive event in the race to domesticity.

The pegs themselves had a ruthless look like tribal jewellery. Around my middle I too had a peg bag, whose toy pegs were bright and fragile. These were stocked by Mr McDonald the newsagent, who kept a basket of crunchy cellophane sachets of toys priced around threepence and made in Hong Kong. Those seemed exotic words; I see them printed on cheap card, acid green lettering misaligned or incorporated in the moulding of a doll's pink neck, MADE IN HONG KONG, a declaration suggesting to me a glamour all the more vivid for its certainty of short life. The colours of these frail toys were harsh and tropical in Edinburgh, whose granite and sea mist and inhabitants' clothing hardly ever pushed beyond the seemlier shades. My mother and I took a bus to look at an avocado once, as Londoners at one time had visited the cameleopard, or giraffe. No one bought the green leather pear, and I am not sure if anyone knew how it might be opened.

My mother pined for colour in her short life. Sometimes she forced it into being, for which I as a native Scot found it hard to forgive her then. Towards the end of her life she began collecting me from school in wigs that were not intended to imitate reality. Her own fair hair was long; over it she might helm herself with her silver wig, or a strawberry blonde *coup sauvage* that gave her the look of an actress who has at short notice had to fill in for the man playing opposite her. She did not seem even to hope to convince. What she sought was, paradoxically, an inconspicuousness impossible for a woman of her appearance. She was held to be 'too friendly with tradesmen' and I was once told at school that the greengrocer 'had tried to kiss the Englishwoman among the greens';

it was Christmas time and the ceiling was all mistletoe in the bunch, so she was very likely kissing him in seasonal innocence. Her accent made her 'the Englishwoman'; she didn't have a gout of English blood, but a radio-drama quality of over-emphasis that was dated even then seems in my memory to mark her speech, as it does mine. It comes from my grandmother, who, as an actress and singer on stage from the age of five, spoke to carry, from the pit of her breath. My mother spoke Italian in Valvona & Crolla, the Italian grocer that was like an unofficial club for many war-exhausted people homesick for a Mediterranean they had not, or had only briefly, seen. Edinburgh is still full of Italians. Sweet teeth and a passion for starch married happily. The best fish and chips (Brattisani's) and the best ice cream (Lucca's of Musselburgh) and generations of handsome, double accented children are the issue.

It wasn't as though my mother had been transplanted from somewhere strange and fiery up to the north. The laurel and brick of her English childhood were actually less exotic than Edinburgh's silver and pearl and black and the river roaring along behind our garden, prone to flood, and all but classically named the Water of Leith. But the forms of eccentricity encouraged by Edinburgh's bracing traditions did not yet include her particular flavour, in which staginess combined as it often does with absence of vanity. Her energies were curiosity, inventiveness and an affectionate nature that did not understand how to tally, invest or calculate. In a city of thrift where things were made to last, the ephemeral was glorified by attendant disapproval. Neighbours watched for waste. A bit of income might have allowed her to be euphemized as bohemian; she had a way with rubbish, of turning what she had totted from street sales into something rare until the time of dusting and falling to dust. It might not tolerate much light and there were holes in everything and too many cats, but she deployed her flotsam like precious cargo.

Costume and making do seemed to be part of her, as they were of her mother. For her beauty my grandmother was married by my builder grandfather who was as Scots as harling. They had my mother only, with whom they were not invariably pleased. Her talents and dramatic appearance seemed to them wilful defiance of what they had worked for.

My mother's clothes came from a dress agency with a sad name such as the Scottish Ladies' Benevolent Frock Exchange. This discreet ossuary of fashions was known as 'The Dead Women's', with a long 'o' as in 'womb'—'The Dead Woo-men's'. My mother went through racks of coats that had represented thrift and respectability and regular attendance at the kirk with her eagle eye for something a bit off key, the off centre thing she hunted.

Occasionally we would go into a shop that sold things first hand. (Apart from food, I hardly recall her having anything first hand. It was a necessity that became a preference.) I had to be restrained in what might be called fresh shops from smelling the merchandise. Inserting myself in between crisp scented frocks on their big cartwheel rail, I would tread the circle like a drunken donkey, round and round in the stirring stuff with its nylon waft of blossom and insecticidal net. I was used to the smells of mothballs and cats from our hours among reeking mattresses, bargaining underground with old women who wore hats indoors. I did not dislike the junk shops but had a childish intolerance of kind overtures from the very old and the peculiar. I wanted the smoothness and flawless good humour of a life I saw on hoardings: 'You'll wonder where the yellow went/When you brush your teeth with Pepsodent.'

Both my parents, all their lives, fell easily into conversation with strangers. Neither of them liked to miss a story, and they were curious and not easy to embarrass—kinder to these strangers than to themselves or each other. A need for talk that began in her childhood was perhaps another reason for my mother's listening; she had no idea of when to stop, of how to preserve herself. My father's similar habits were to do with his anarchist's openness to life and a patience that could drive you mad. They could not resist drunks, tramps or beggars. Approached by such a person, whichever parent it was would listen to the story, even if it contradicted the one told two days before.

The Grassmarket was where the drunks with blue faces lived. They drank Blue Billy, a mix of meths and Brasso. They did not often wear shoes and had no understanding of cars, which occasionally blethered down the black sweep of setts, as the deep, orderly Edinburgh cobbles are called, granite dovetailed with the precision of igloo blocks. The drinkers would freeze when a car came as though at Medusa's passing. Most of the men had been at sea, in the war or on the fishing boats. Tears came to them, after so long being awash with the drink, with a tidal ease. My mother responded as though to romance, aware that politeness was too dim a mode for the drunk man's intense register. So surprising for those times was her appearance that perhaps they considered her one of them, in spite of the solid child at her side.

Such encounters could be alarming to a child. The worst was just after we got our first car, when my father was driving me and himself to England overnight on some business for the Trust, not then the plump institution it is now. We had an old, black Humber Snipe, with red leather seats, which was just as well.

Rain, the zippy repetitions of windscreen wipers and the for some hours certain presence of my elusive father composed a selfish bliss for me. I was six. We passed through the cooked-meat coloured town of Biggar. In the headlights was a man with a big head, waving astride the centre of the red metalled road. He had on a belted mackintosh. His shoulders and bent head seemed dark with the rain. He had the raw build of someone in the services, but new to it, not fully hardened to the life. We stopped and my father rolled down the window on my side, smiling his kind dog's smile, leaning over me.

The hitch-hiker lowered his head and looked down at us, a child and a friendly man. Before he spoke he put his hands in at the window. They were wet and red and in one of them was the top half of a bottle, which he did not brandish so much as flourish, loosely, as though offering tired flowers. His head and shoulders were bloody too. He was asking to be taken to a sea port, any one at all. He seemed indifferent to the pain that must accompany the blood, which seemed to be coming up out of the top of his head and spilling slowly down to be thinned by the rain. At the top of the head among the hair the blood was slow. It lay along his shorn red curls.

My father told him to hop in. The rest of the night was spent in stopping off to wash, feed and at last, when dawn came up over the chemists of the Borders, bandage this man, out of whose head came further bits of his, or someone's, bottle, that my father picked out. The reason for the fight was forgotten, and its subject, also its other participant or participants.

When the Biggar man had gone off to sleep, my father stopped the car and got out in order to rearrange him in the back so that he might be more comfortable. 'If he wakes up and sees a child, at least he won't be alarmed,' he said. 'You jump in next to him.'

Blood red is a newly terrible colour every time, worse when it is in the dark and temporarily black, the odd lasso of advancing and withdrawing headlights pulling tight to remind you of its unshaded redness. The man snored, with his head right back on the red leather, his broken pink lips and red eyelashes coming to colour slowly in the Lowland dawn.

When he woke up, he pleaded to be back in Biggar. Back we went. Can this be so? The order of events is sketchy to me now, but I remember the many colours of his blood. Perhaps he is always there at the roadside, each night, to tempt those who feel they can help things at all, a drunken sailor for all weathers.

With my mother, the victims were mainly women. Just as she would not allow mangled birds or shrews to perish in their absent tiny way without bringing them in for warmth and hopeless last rites, she picked up wrecks. One walk we took regularly was along the river down to a row of working men's houses called the Colonies. These were serried rows of terraced cottages, each with its small washing green. There was a stone staircase set sideways up the front of each, leading to a top storey front door, where the old might sit in the weather to grumble. Now favoured by middle-class couples with no children, these houses swarmed with families who gathered by the railings that dropped down to the river to gossip and play and chuck leftovers to the swans that begged there, braking in the water with their rubber feet. The water was clear and bright coppery brown and through it could be seen shards and remnants, bedsprings, broken tiles, bottle glass. I collected these treasures, using my minnow net, and watched them dry out, until like fish they lost their shine.

The walk was a short cut behind the big houses of Inverleith and the expanses of the Botanical Gardens (known as the Tanics to children thereabouts). It was called the Rocheid Path and it was dark and green and stank bitterly. A trembling bridge on chains led from the Rocheid Path over the river into the Colonies. So long fallen that the moss clipped it, a tree all but barred the mouth of the bridge, its branches gone for firewood. We would sit sometimes and make a picnic, spreading my mother's handkerchief and laying out a Pan Drop each. Squirrels came and once or twice she told my father that she had seen a red one, though I cannot remember ever doing so. Once in the country she said she saw a golden pheasant, one of those trailing glories with cadmium yellow earflaps, a neck thick with minute bevelled ruffles and a lorgnette-lifting gait.

Perhaps she did just want to see more colour than there was. But on a seemingly featureless field she would spy a hare standing among stalks in its own dry colour, and she saw spring flowers in the hours before they solidified into being open, so perhaps she was preternaturally sharp eyed.

We were on the bridge over the Water of Leith, looking back down the Rocheid Path, when there was suddenly a woman and the abrupt running departure of a man in blue. His hair was black and all in one shining piece as if he had just risen from a deep dive. I saw clearly because he moved at such speed that he compressed the attention. The woman had hair the sheepish gold of the chiropodist's wool my mother wound around her two broken toes so that she could wear winklepickers.

Not young, but busty, in an apron and a coat thrown over the shoulders, the woman turned her face to us, patting at her neck with her finger ends as though feeling in surprise for sudden rain.

The blood was coming down fresh from her face, from cuts you could not see but for the rising red, that seemed thin, like water or spirits. It stung to see the thin razor cuts.

My mother took off her own headscarf as though it was too formal and took the shorter, older woman in her arms.

I suppose the woman had done her washing, pinned it up and crossed the bridge over from her family life in the Colonies for that assignation in the dark leafy short cut, so certain of warmth that she had not even put her arms into the sleeves of her coat. I feel certain that the man was her lover, because she kept on saying, 'He done it for he was so young.' My mother was calm.

For all I knew, this might have been what happened as a rule when men and women met. We took the woman home. Her hands were freezing with shock and we each chafed one, I imitating my mother, who kept up a steady, encouraging flow of endearments that I recognized many years later as the words of exhortation used by midwives and other chance yet crucial helpmeets.

L iving in the basement of our house there were always lodgers who would invite me down the inside stone stairs to visit them. A curtain hung at the bottom of the stairs; through it I passed from one set of habits to another. I became fond of disappearing and of trying on different lives. The lodgers were often students, and 'thesis' became a word by whose constipated mystery I was early oppressed. I associated the disordered reams of notes with a kind of outlaw freedom that seemed to have fled by the time the thing appeared, caught and bound. The poet with his staring hair who lived at one point below us seemed to have a happier relation to paper, using it like birdlime, waiting for words to fly and settle in their order.

For my parents, the lodgers were sometimes a means of escape from each other. My father came down to draw in the basement whenever he and my mother fought. Taking his delicious alcohol-scented FloMaster pen, he would hesitate, cigarette in mouth, breathing with his inadequate lungs, then stab at the whitewashed wall, sweeping, whirling and cross-hatching with the black pen, not stopping until he had completed a man-sized pastiche of a nineteenth-century zoological drawing. A chameleon with a Vitruvian scroll of tongue looked down with its turreted eyes to where the egg of a monstrous lyre bird was hatching, the egg just burst to display a quivering tuning fork.

My mother increasingly complained about my father's absences, so it was also for company that she passed through the curtain on the stone stair. Of all the lodgers it was Mr Sapietis the Latvian who was the most comforting for her, not because he intended to be but because nothing could surpass what he had seen. He had no fingernails or toenails. They had been pulled from him. He was a handsome man with a thin profile and a blue jersey dingleberried with clay, a potter. When I played in our garden he would come and talk to me and sometimes he would cry as he watched me play with my invented companions. Perhaps he was amazed at my assumption that invisible presences might be benevolent. He touched things quite slowly, as though he felt them more sharply than nailed men. He would hold my fat face and look into its want of knowledge as though trying to get something through my blank trust.

But the lodgers I loved most were Bengali. The wife stood me on the table and wound me up in a green sari with a black mackerel zig-zag; she brushed and oiled and braided my dull brown hair and finished off its diminishing point with tassels threaded with silver. The rice she cooked rose high on the dish instead of sinking into a milk pudding. The husband was training to be a doctor; his wife was at home all day. They had left at least one child back at home with the wife's parents, so I suppose that it was in some ways pleasant to have me around. There must have been days when she wanted me to be gone, because I hung around staring at everything she did, rinsing and rinsing and rinsing the rice, the hair, the washing, and spreading her hair out down from her overturned head as she dried it in front of the pale cream range with its hardly glowing mica windows.

My mother and I were continually cold. The Bengali woman must have been cold to the bone. We gathered round one of two paraffin heaters that leaked a sick-making but reassuring smell. When it was bitter we used a squat heater that plugged in and made a noise like an old dog. Dust came off it like midges in the beams of its heat.

The Bengali husband I recall less pictorially although he was among the first men whose elegance I noticed, one evening as he worked by very little light and I saw a poised white shirt sitting up in a chair, folded and turned back over each hardly visible forearm. As the light withdrew the shirt's wearer was included in the gloom, leaving only the white mauve shape deepening at the table.

While these welcome strangers came and went, my father was away attending to the residences, abodes, castles, byres, doocots, follies, palaces, huntingtowers, keeps, but and bens and ruins of Scotland. The country then was full of houses lying open to its consuming rain, their roofs dynamited off by owners no longer wanting to pay rates.

The damp air and the salt of the sea ate into lath and plaster even where there was a roof. Mouldings got fat with moisture like fruit and, like fruit, fell. An Englishman of predominantly Irish blood who assumed a satirical manner when speaking of Scotland's smugger, frowstier, more snobbish self-delusions, my father developed a feeling for the country's rational yet eccentric architecture that came to rule his life, and my own and my mother's lives with his.

I grew up jealous of buildings. Buildings were inexhaustible, work and recreation. The matter of saving houses is associated now with styles of life and with an upholstered luxury that is as destructive as the death watch beetle. My father was suspicious of comfort; he preferred cigarettes to food. Tentative and ironic in speech, he mocked the gap between gloss and truth. He never went grey, but did not display a threatening boyishness because there was clearly no strength in his slimness; he was thin and never well, with a bad heart and dodgy lungs and a cough that pained its hearer. He trespassed everywhere (in Scotland there is no law of trespass, he said, and scaled a fence blaring with prohibitions) hunting the forgotten, the untraced, the deserted brides among houses. When involved with a house, he was dangerous. I do not remember often suspending a tension and concern for either of my parents. He climbed up ruins and along cracking beams, with more relish the higher and fainter the structure. Then he would forget his camera up there, so that he had to go back, past the willow herb and toads and lifting roof lead, or on his stomach along the splintering joists.

When I was lucky I went with him. It could be horrible, standing holding his T-square in rain while he sketched a neglected contemporary masterwork in Glenrothes, or when he rang the doorbell of a house whose entrance was grown over with giant hoary thistles and the reluctant interior footsteps began.

Once, we broached a house whose façade was a big classical dishface, curving in to a pediment yellow and crumbling as demerara sugar. A deer faced woman in many old garments answered. Prepared by my self-consciousness and by experience for someone deranged or very old, I wasn't expecting this alert character. My father asked about the house and whether he might come in, somehow making it clear he was not selling anything nor wanted to do more than share his enthusiasm for William Adam.

The lawn was full of groundsel and plantain. It was moving by entanglement over the gravel to the house.

'Go away, we fly to America tomorrow,' lied the I realized beautiful woman with spirit.

*Fly* to *America!* A place so other that it might be brandished in that way, to hold off the little man. The woman used the exotic name as a spell to keep the sleep on her house that was swooning into ochre dust.

My father, understanding but frustrated, got back into the car, and we spun and jarred our way back down the drive under the settling rookeries, pursued by a blue dog the height of the brambles, heavy mayoral fat on its walrus back.

Suddenly the dog fell back, recoiling on to its crupper as though pulled. We caught on a high stone between the wet ruts of the drive. Fists pummelled the back window and then, holding on to the car for a footing, the beautiful liar came round to my father's side window and put her hand flat up to it till the palm was pale. He wound down the window with a can-opening movement, and the woman's voice said, 'Come in for a drink. We think we like you.' Like another deer, her husband had been watching us from the wet roses beside the house.

In the drawing-room that was cold as a disused quarry the dog was the source of heat. Batons of Brussels sprout tops like green maces stuck out of a jug in the fireplace. Perhaps the deer couple cracked off some sprouts when it was time to dine, in a dining-room whose ceiling rested for the most part on its long, oxblood-red, plaster-dimmed table.

One of the best outings my father and I took, away from my mother's neglected and in consequence tarnishing dazzle, was by steamboat to the Cathedral of the Isles on Great Cumbrae, a green island in the mouth of the River Clyde. My mother had told me that God did not exist. The car deck was aseethe with sheep whose malicious eyes rolled at the forcible enclosure, noses upon each other's backs as though to browse sweeter air, restive hooves tittupping on the iron deck, perilous as the small shoes of fat women.

The minister of the cathedral met us and took my father and me to his house through a sunken field of hard cold green daffodils. There in his bare kitchen we had bottled coffee, tinned milk and cake like masonry, with a brown sugar crystal on a string that he dangled briskly in each cup before pulling it out like a mouse by the tail. No slices were separable from the cake, which remained a rich idea, solid with potential but unresolved by practicalities.

The creation of a single building in which might worship people living on islands separated by hundreds of miles of bad-tempered water was a notion as potentially rich and impractical as the indivisible cake.

Unlike all the many other churches I had been into, almost always visiting for secular reasons, this large grey building held no sense of small accumulated human gestures. There were no notices, no blush of heating, no flowers, no kneeling woman to one side or abandoned mitten by the stoop. It might as well have been full of seagulls.

Aged nine, I took this as impersonal truth and perpetual magnificent indifference made manifest. I was comforted by what I thought was a revelation that all pain was temporary, everything solved by distance. It was as though I were being swung through the lenses on a telescope until the planet I lived on became a grain in the pollen pocket at the knee of a bumble bee in some vast afternoon. It is a technique of painkilling that is unreliable but involuntary in the pessimistic adult mind, and I have been grateful more often than not that it came to me young.

The nervousness around my mother centred upon the absence of my father, and her thwarted glamour. It was probably I who thwarted it. Her impulse was to work and paint and draw. She was full of plans and had just begun to find a world under the chill, hard to lift, stone of Edinburgh. The Traverse Theatre used her, I think, as a cook. She and my father made and sold toys. Her art-school training was not used. Her desire to conform to an idea of wifehood led her into impersonations best not undertaken by an intelligent blonde of six foot two; she did not convince at coffee mornings. She was desperate to earn but over-educated for the jobs she could get, full of ideas and talk but stuck with me, to whom she talked as though I were her age. I knew too much.

My mother and I spent what turned out to be her last day on a farm where long-eared Nubian goats were reared. Their colours were those of driftwood and breakfast cereal and they would eat cigarettes as soon as apples. Their lips moved like surreptitious gossips' mouths on the flat of the hand, mouthing meanly, 'I wouldn't like to say, but . . . ' It was easy to imagine these goats snaffling a living in a dusty market under the Egyptian sun.

We had come to see some pups, pointers, liver and white, with breaks in the tail as definite and slight as breaks in a fount of type. The weight of a pup, picked up, fell to its lowest point; it was like holding living dough.

The long mother lay on her side in an army bed on a frame that twanged under the twelve lives lived on it. One pup, a bitch, was marked with sharp spatters like a carnation. My mother pulled it out repeatedly to set it on her hand and let it run inside her green knitted jacket from the Dead Women's. She held it on her lap while we spent far too much time on this farm with strangers up a lane. She talked to the dog as if to herself, with the least admissable emotion, self-pity, smuggling itself out of her.

Lying to herself and to me, she said, as we left the unforthcoming woman she had eventually charmed and made her friend, and the several matter-of-fact children who had suffered my uninvited urban presence all day, 'We'll come back tomorrow for the puppy.'

The very idea summed up normality and life above ground, a life I imagined most other children led. Seldom had I gone to sleep happier, sleeping out the last hours of my mother's life in dreams of a dog.

# Discover the Best New Fiction Published in America

Subscribe to STORY, the award-winning magazine that made literary history by discovering some of the best-known writing talents of this century.

STORY was created in 1931 with a commitment to publishing the best new fiction of the day, regardless of its commercial appeal. After a 22-year interim, STORY was revived in 1989, and was named *One of the 16 Best New Magazines* by *Library Journal.*

Today STORY maintains its tradition of recognizing fresh new writing talent. Each handsomely-bound collection will introduce you to brilliant new authors who promise to be the literary greats of tomorrow, just as it introduced the world to the first works of Salinger, Capote, Mailer, Cheever and others.

Be on hand for the next STORY discovery, and start your subscription to the most widely circulated literary magazine published in America.

*"STORY is one of the most attractive and consistently readable magazines of its kind. Its contents are wonderfully varied and scrupulously edited."* – Joyce Carol Oates

## STORY

# LAWRENCE NORFOLK
# A BOSNIAN ALPHABET

APOLOGY: A should be for Alphabet: the device I am resorting to in some desperation to structure my thoughts on this subject: my relations *vis-à-vis* two Yugoslavian wars. This is my fourth attempt at organizing the material, the deadline looms and the only virtue of this catch-all structure is its transparency. An ABC . . . ? You *know* the writer's in trouble. So, a pre-emptive strike on exaggerated expectations. A, in this instance, must be for Apology.

BAD FAITH: Primary sources for records of the second Austro-Turkic war of 1787–89 are only available in this country through the British Museum's Burney Collection. A badly catalogued selection of late eighteenth-century newspapers has been transferred to microfiche and is available to readers in a windowless room off the North Library Gallery. It is a vile working environment; neon-lit, unventilated and the heat from the projectors parches what air there is. A fortnight's digging gave me the details I needed to piece together a picture of the earlier war. I went to see the current conflict first-hand. So, with my impeccable credentials thus established . . . Except that this gambit—that I have knowledge, that you do not—will not wash. Yes, I have done the legwork, but the assumption of superiority based on this experience takes no account of the deracinating effects of the experience itself. Recrossing the River Drina to escape the present-day conflict, far from understanding it better, I felt I understood it worse. War is a special case; as a writer it makes you less capable,

---

**Lawrence Norfolk** was born in London in 1963 and lived in Iraq until his family was evacuated in 1967. He graduated from King's College London in 1986 and subsequently studied for a Ph.D, taught, wrote poetry reviews for the *Times Literary Supplement* and worked as a barman and on building sites. His first novel, *Lemprière's Dictionary,* tells, among many other things, the story of the East India Company in the seventeenth and eighteenth centuries. 'The whole idea' he says, 'was to get away from my own life.' It became a best-seller throughout Europe, though not in Britain. He is working on a new novel, *The Pope's Rhinoceros,* which Sinclair-Stevenson will publish next year. Lawrence Norfolk has recently moved to Chicago.

Photo: Barry Lewis

not more. Let B stand for Bad Faith, the general rubric for any account of a war that offers 'I was there' as a guarantee that 'this is how it was'.

COINCIDENCES: Extend the current conflict about 150 miles east, let Belgrade stand for Sarajevo, and you have the Austro-Turkic war of 1787–89. The same participants, the same hesitant foreign interventions, the same muddled aims, the same atrocities. I wrote about this war in my first novel which was completed three months before the present war began. A historical novelist rarely gets the chance to check his rendering against reality and, viewed from London, some of the parallels appeared striking enough—little villages and towns whose names I had unearthed and promptly forgotten were popping up in the conflict: Bosanski Brod, Gradiska, Dubica, Zvornik. I had researched and transcribed details of an ill-equipped refugee camp at Karlovac for instance, and the beating to death of a Muslim prisoner-column two days' march from there. Tjrnopolje, Omarska and Manjaca, where this act has latterly been repeated, are all within fifty miles of the current Red Cross camp at Karlovac. I was seeing events two centuries old on the Six O'Clock News.

DOUBTS: A sense that the war as I had written it, having now become available as an experience, was somehow inauthentic. The early reporting of the present conflict was necessarily fragmentary. Martin Bell's reports for the BBC in particular were always at pains to indicate the information that *wasn't* available. All this cast a great deal of retrospective suspicion on my own effort. I wanted what I thought I had before—the full story—but this was no longer true. What I had was the pieces of a war.

ESPRESSO: War is serious and this will seem too trivial to mention, but E is for Espresso. I met an Austrian war correspondent called Karl Wendl in November 1992 at a party in Vienna. We were both trying, unsuccessfully, to get some coffee. We were both extremely drunk. The previous night, Karl had had a dream. He was standing on a dock in Serbia. Below him in the water was a submarine. Karl was trying to hitch a lift to Venice to get an espresso. In the circumstances, it would have been more reasonable of me to pursue the espresso line of conversation (this was after all what had prompted this odd disclosure), or even the submarine. Instead, I asked him if he had ever been to Serbia.

FARCE: We spent the rest of the night drawing maps of Yugoslavia on paper napkins and comparing notes on the two-hundred-year-old war I had written about in my book and its modern equivalent, which he had then visited seven times. We never got our coffees. Instead, we planned a Serbian submarine-hunt. (They have, by most accounts, sixteen.) This is a stupid little story, and events would overtake our plan in any case, but it's quite true and, in as much as it was the first in a chain of events that would eventually have me dodging bullets in Sarajevo, I find its absurdity quite prophetic. F is for Farce, which like an off-colour joke at some supposedly momentous occasion, can also find its place in a war.

GUN: G, rather obviously, is for Gun. I have handled guns, am reasonably at ease with the idea of a device for firing projectiles. The guns in Bosnia are different. Their stocks have not been lovingly polished. Their barrels are unoiled. The metal they are made from is black and scarred with little nicks and scratches. Almost everyone I meet here carries a gun, but they are careless of them, waving them about, dumping them roughly on the ground. These are not treasured possessions and there is nothing iconic about them—they would look ridiculous hung above a fireplace. It is apparent at a glance that a Zastava Kalashnikov was never intended for pheasant. These guns are rough tools for the job of shooting people.

HEADS: On 12 March, 1788, the *Daily Universal Register* reported that the Ottoman (which is to say Muslim) forces, far from taking prisoners, were killing any Austrian solders unlucky enough to be captured and cutting off their heads. In April, the same paper (now renamed *The Times*) related that a group of headless bodies had been discovered in an overrun Turkish camp near Dubica, northern Bosnia. A codicil to this story was published on 27 May. Apparently a sackful of ears cut from the heads of the Austrian dead had been suspended from the gates of the seraglio in Constantinople. This is the story of a disappearance, or rather it is a story with its central fact missing—a bad story. In narrative terms it doesn't really work. Such deficiencies are, at one level, the reason I went to the latter-day version of this war. I went to find what I, the passages on war in my novel and this story in particular lacked. H is for the Heads.

ITINERARY: Karl Wendl, Riccardo Herrgott (our photographer) and I drove from Zvornik to Vlasenica, where we spent the night. The next day we reached Sarajevo, slept in the Serb barracks at Lukavica, and the following day spent some hours in Grbavica district in the centre of the city. Then we drove back to Zvornik, recrossing the Drina at ten-thirty that night.

JUSTIFICATION: Or the moral accounting for one's actions. All sides in the current war need to be seen to be in the right. The worse the atrocities the stronger the urge. Justification is having trouble keeping pace with events.

KOSOVO: An official working for the Serb Ministry of Information at Pale told me this story. On the eve of the battle of Kosovo in 1389, King Lazar Hrebelyanovic gathered his Serbian kinsmen and, looking forward to the coming battle, told them they must fight for the Kingdom of Heaven, not for the Kingdom of Earth. The battle of Kosovo was to be about more than territory. The next day, he and the best of his nobles were slaughtered by the Turks. The story is preserved in the song-cycles of the Serb *guslari*. Nationalism and poetry have always enjoyed a close alliance in Serbia (witness Dr Radovan Karadzic's lyric aspirations). In the Serbian historical consciousness, Kosovo might be seen as a signal realization: that a war could not be fought and won by aiming over the heads of the enemy. Henceforth their wars would be about earth, not heaven. The current war falls readily into this context: its talk is all of enclaves, havens, corridors, areas which are disputed or controlled or regained. Kosovo is presently being touted as where this war will happen next. Ask the Serbs why they are fighting and they will talk about a distant past or a spectral future. Kosovo, and all the other 'Kosovos', are a way of not talking about what is happening now—an amnesia of the present.

LOVE: L in an ABC is always for Love. In Vlasenica there is a graveyard for the victims of the current war, forty-three of them on 13 December 1992; undoubtedly more by now. Behind it, stretching up the hill, are graves dating from the war of 1939–45. There are more than four hundred of these. Hanging on a wall in the Serb Ministry of Information at Pale is a map showing mortality rates in Bosnia for 1939–45. The colours range from light to dark, from zero to one hundred per cent. About a fifth of this map is black. Vlasenica is a murky green colour, which the key tells me means sixty per cent. Even though (or perhaps because) it has killed so many of them, the Bosnians love their land—Serbs, Croats and Muslims alike.

MUJAHEDIN: Their presence in this war somehow persisted as a rumour long after it should have become a generally acknowledged fact. In July 1992, a group of mujahedin were captured by the Serbs in the region north of Banja Luka. They had travelled on Saudi Arabian passports to Vienna where they had acquired visas from the Croatian Embassy. One—his passport gave the name Saed al Garaf—had a camera. The Serbs developed the film in it and found heads. I was shown these photographs by the Serbs in Pale. The heads had been cut from the bodies of Serb fighters killed by Saed and his comrades. Some had their eyes gouged out, others looked strangely peaceful. I leafed through the prints and thought of a group of headless bodies found two hundred years before. And these mujahedin had been fighting around Travnik and Banja Luka, which is not so far from Dubica . . . Of course this line of thought is ludicrous, but putting Humpty together again is a strong novelistic instinct and I confess that I would very much like these gruesome holiday snaps to clear up my two hundred year mystery. Earlier wars are often used to justify later ones. Reports of headless bodies. Photographs of bodiless heads. I would at least

217

like to establish a correspondence. Trace a parallel or two.

NARRATIVE: War severs the relations between events. But paradoxically war's deep incoherence urges the necessity of these relations even more forcefully. What will happen next? The question has an obvious relevance if you are actually in this situation. The fact that you can never get an answer is what keeps you constantly at risk. This information is not being withheld: it actually doesn't exist. In its absence fabulous contortions result. Asked where the Bosnian Serbs got their oil supplies from, Radovan Karadzic explained that, by an extraordinary stroke of luck, an enormous cache, stored secretly during World War Two, had been discovered in a cave. Note the stock ingredients (cave, secret, cache) and the central role played by chance in this story. He was a little vague on the cave's exact location, too.

OUTRAGE: The instinct for psychic self-preservation flattens the peaks and troughs of your emotions. I anticipated, but never felt, outrage in Bosnia. Possibly, the 'out-' is instructive. In Geneva or the House of Commons or on Capitol Hill, outrage is invoked with some frequency. Being 'in', the '-rage' comes at a higher price.

PHOTOGRAPHY: A photograph enhances the prestige of its subject. A photograph steals your soul. Both attitudes are in evidence amongst the soldiery of Bosnia. Some pose. Some wave you away. Some pose and then rip the film from the camera. A baby-faced chetnik hung out the back of a lorry, carbine in one hand, cap in the other. A useless shot—he was smiling—but why not? Snap, snap, snap. The lorry pulls across us, his CO leaps out, demands the film. High drama! Babyface, apparently, has family in Sarajevo. The theory is that the Muslims in Sarajevo identify Serb families from newspaper photos of their relatives, then shoot them. Perhaps it's true. We test it. 'Sarajevo?' we ask solicitously of the waver-offers. They nod sadly. We commiserate. A few minutes of this and they pose mournfully with their machine-guns, resigned, it would seem, to the inevitable massacre of their families. The 'pose and rip' merchants remain problematic.

QUESTIONS: Karl interviewed General Gevero, commander of the Serb forces around Sarajevo. Karl asked, 'Do you think Sarajevo might one day be partitioned, as Berlin was in 1945?' Then, 'Dr Karadzic's plan [to offer safe-conduct out of the city to any who want it] is workable?' And lastly, 'Are any of the three sides capable of winning this war?' General Gevero spoke for over an hour and, according to the translator, was very impressed by Karl's questions. Most of his interviews come in well under five minutes. A few weeks before the outbreak of the Gulf War, Karl put the following to Saddam Hussein: 'Mister President, for decades the whole Arab world has searched for a leader strong enough to stand up to the West. I would like to ask you now,' a pause, 'are you that leader?'

RUMOUR: Here's some tittle-tattle from the Sarajevo rumour mill. Dr Karadzic's son Saskia is, naturally enough, a staunch supporter of the Serb cause in Bosnia, brave, upstanding, a devoted son, etc. Jusuf Brasnica, better known as Juka, is a petty gangster turned warlord on the Muslim side, wounded three times, famed for a series of daring raids, drives a BMW 7-series. He commands a militia of several hundred men based on Mount Igman. Saskia and Juka have been friends since childhood. Saskia regularly sneaks through the lines to meet with Juka. They drink, talk, laugh. Perhaps they are in love. That's the rumour.

SOURCES: Headless bodies again: the reports in the *Daily Universal Register* cited above would have been compiled from second-hand gleanings originating from 'briefings' given by the Imperial Ambassadors in London and Brussels. The ambassadors' information came from the Office of Correspondence in Vienna (essentially an organ of censorship, though not fabrication) which derived it in turn from dispatches sent back by the army. The provenance of this information does not inspire trust and I suspect that the whole story was recycled from some earlier incident, possibly belonging to another war entirely.

The heads are more firmly documented. There are the photographs. There is also, I was told, some particularly nasty video footage. I saw lists of names and passport numbers. With the indictments piling up against their own militias, the Serbs are naturally keen for this evidence to be accepted. Their motives are bad but the heads, I think, are for real.

TRUTH: Traditionally the first casualty of war, in present-day Bosnia it suffers something more analogous to death by a thousand cuts. In its place there are degrees of probability, increasing or decreasing likelihoods, hard and soft information, conflicting versions. Three days before we arrived in Sarajevo, several news agencies had reported that the Serbs had closed the road from the airport. This act, it is generally agreed, will be the first move if the Serbs mount an all-out assault on the city. Unfortunately, the report was false. So clear-cut a case is rare. It is more usual for the presented reality to bend obliquely from the truth. 'Alija Izetbegovic is President of Bosnia' seems incontrovertible, until you stop to wonder what 'Bosnia' is.

UNIFORMS: Uniforms, in a war, are intended to distinguish the combatants. In Bosnia, however, all sides wear the same uniform —that of the former Yugoslavian Army. The correspondent Kate Adie tells a story about having to ask one group of soldiers the identity of the soldiers they were firing on, then having to ask the identity of those doing the firing. The real distinction is between degrees of uniform. Full uniform implies a professional soldier under command; someone unlikely to shoot you without good reason. Part-uniform suggests a militiaman—something of an unknown quantity and thus more frightening. No uniform is very bad. But worst of all, for some reason, are people wearing tracksuits.

VICTIMS: Before the war, Slavko Milanovic used to be the director of the Kamerni Theatar '55, an avant-garde theatre in Sarajevo. Now he works for the Serbian Ministry of Information. He is quiet, urbane, very literate, a leading member of the Sarajevo intelligentsia when such a thing existed. At first I had Slavko pegged for a victim of this war; not an obvious one, but still someone whose life had been transformed utterly and would never be the same again. Through the noise of the shelling, we talked about productions of Buñuel and Jarry who, I couldn't help thinking, would have approved of this scene.

WOODSMOKE: Everyone in Bosnia smells faintly of stale woodsmoke. This is easy enough to explain. Although the army is supplied with oil by Serbia (we saw the freight containers lined up in a siding at Zvornik) the rest of the country has very little or none. Even the Serb barracks at Lukavica only run their generators for five hours a night. If you want to be warm, you burn wood. In the Muslim areas of Sarajevo, trees beyond sniper range have been cut down to stumps, and the stumps themselves hacked out with hand-axes. The temperature in December rarely rises above five degrees and can fall to twenty below. Not to smell of woodsmoke is to be at best very cold and at worst frozen to death. I associate this smell, reasonably enough, with life.

To write about causes and objectives suggests that there is a passage from one to the other, that the war follows it and this is the 'story'. Unfortunately this is nowhere discernible from within the war. When I smell stale woodsmoke my mind does not leap to the Vance–Owen plan. And the converse: thinking in strategic terms misses the essence of war, its irresolution and sloppiness, its inconsistency and refusal to assign fixed meanings to anything. The pot does not stop the water boiling over. In fact in as much as the removal of these trees opens up new lines of fire for the snipers, you could say that they are the fire under the pot. You can smell of stale woodsmoke and still get killed.

X : The first village we reached was Drinjaca. There were houses with gardens, a cow or two out the back, chicken runs and pigsties. Then, in the midst of these, there would be a house gutted by fire, its windows out and roof missing. A few more occupied houses—kids in the garden, Mum putting out the washing—then another fire-blackened wreck. Sometimes there would be a terrace of four or five dwellings with one destroyed in the middle. The others would be untouched, as though some low-tech surgical strike had taken place. Underneath the soot it was possible to see the sign used to mark these houses out: a circle, and within it an X. We saw this sign in every village we passed through.

221

YESTERDAY: A stretch of road, three hundred metres at most, somewhere between the town of Vlasenica and a little village called Han Piejsak. The sky is cloudless and if this ridge lay below five thousand feet the temperature would probably be above freezing. The road lies in a shallow crease: the land balloons up gently on either side, then flattens out and extends to the treeline a hundred metres or so distant. The men who work this land live with their families in the loose collection of little houses about half a mile behind us. It's been snowing, so the fields are white. A ridge of snow has collected in the middle of the road, but preceding vehicles have worn a pair of tramlines which we can follow. This is a good metalled road, well maintained, easy driving.

Yesterday, at the checkpoint we are now approaching, we were prodded back into our car at gunpoint, the film ripped from the cameras, and directed into a firefight by the irregulars manning it. Today we have just passed five corpses lying face down in one of the fields I have just described. So, we are on this road, within these events, and it would be reasonable to ask at this point '*What happens next?*'

There is something intensely human in this question, and something telling in the fact that war rubs it out. We reach the checkpoint and see faces familiar from yesterday. They wave us through with a smile. Yesterday may as well not have happened.

ZVORNIK: We have just been shot at, but now we are almost at Zvornik, where the bridge crosses the Drina, war ends and peace begins. A trade-off at the checkpoint will result in us giving a lift to a soldier who lives on the other side of the river. He has a little English, mostly the titles of Beatles' songs, and starts to sing, '*We all live in a yellow submarine, a yellow submarine, a yellow submarine . . .*'

Writing this now, I have only just realized how apt it is. We never did find our Serbian submarines. Karl makes a stab at singing along. The soldier knows the whole song. He is, by some margin, the most cheerful soldier we have met. We can't wait to get rid of him.

# BEN OKRI
# A BIZARRE COURTSHIP

One morning, more golden than yellow, I went outside to our housefront and saw that the beggars had gone. I scoured the street and asked everyone I met. I went to Madame Koto's bar-front. I searched for them along the edges of the forest, where they scavenged for food and slept in unfinished houses, but I simply couldn't find them.

Late in the afternoon when Dad returned from work, reeking of the bags of fish he had been carrying on his head all day, I told him that the beggars had gone.

'Gone?' he asked incredulously. 'How can they go? I'm going to build them a school. I've even started asking about the cost of a plot of land. They haven't really gone, have they?'

'They have,' I said.

Stinking of fish, his forehead glistening with iridescent scales, his boots thick with mud, he bustled out into the street and went looking for the beggars. He didn't even stop to change from his work clothes. I hurried out with him. Great energies swirled around Dad. His spirit was fiery. He walked with enormous strides, and I tried to keep up with him as he erupted into a torrent of fantastical ideas and schemes. He was going to build a unique school for beggars. He was going to supervise the education of all poor and illiterate people. He said they needed education the most.

'That is how the powerful people keep us down,' he maintained. 'They keep us illiterate and then they deceive us and treat us like children.'

He swore that he was going to teach the beggars

**Ben Okri** was born in 1959 in Minna, Nigeria. He published his first novel, *Flowers and Shadows*, in 1980 and his second, *The Landscapes Within*, in 1982, while studying comparative literature at Essex University. He has worked as a broadcaster for the BBC World Service and was poetry editor of *West Africa* magazine for seven years. His novel *The Famished Road* won the Booker Prize in 1991. He has also written a volume of short stories, *Stars of the New Curfew*, and a collection of poetry, *An African Elegy*. 'A Bizarre Courtship' is an extract from his new novel *Songs of Enchantment* which was published in March by Jonathan Cape.

mathematics, accountancy, law and history. He said I would teach them how to read. He talked of turning all the ghettos into special secret service universities where the most effective knowledge in the world would be made available.

We went up the street and got to the main road. Crowds of people all over the place were talking about politics. They talked about the forthcoming rally and the famous musicians who would be performing. And they also talked about those who had died in the political violence. We happened to notice a few beggars up the road and Dad went and talked to them as if they were old friends. I heard him asking one of them about Helen, a beautiful beggar girl with a bad eye. I heard him pleading with them to come back to our street and help with the building of the school. He was so fervent and earnest that he must have struck everyone as being quite mad. The beggars were frightened by him and they fled. Dad went after them, pleading, and they kept running: they must have thought that he was trying to steal what little money they had. Exasperated, Dad turned to me and said: 'What's wrong with them? Why are they afraid of me, eh?'

'They are not the same beggars.'

'Not the same beggars?'

'These are different beggars. They are not the ones from our street.'

Dad glared at them. Then he said: 'Let's go back.'

We pushed through the crowds, past bicyclists ringing their bells, cart-pullers groaning with their loads of garri and cement, past the tight throng of traders and market women. At the arena where the great rally was going to be staged carpenters were constructing a mighty dais with a zinc roof. Hundreds of artisans were working at the site, hammering away, sawing up wood, climbing up ladders, carrying thick planks, singing, shouting and arguing. Petty traders sat around selling soft drinks and ready-made food. Dad met some of his fellow load-carriers and engaged them in lengthy political disputations. And when we got back to our street we were astonished to find our beggars sitting round the broken vehicle, as if they had been there all along, and as if we had just re-entered their alien reality. Helen wasn't with them.

The beggars looked at us with dull eyes. They didn't move

from their positions and their faces didn't light up at the sight of Dad. It was clear that they had reached a decision. Dad felt excluded from the closed circle of their resolution and he tried to regain their trust and inspire them with his lofty schemes. But they had heard his promises a thousand times and their faces registered no response. He joked, and laughed at his own jokes, but they remained sullen. He asked about Helen, but they made no reply. He became unaccountably desperate.

'Where has she gone? Has someone touched her? Did she run away? Has she deserted our cause?'

The beggars were silent. Dad stared at them for a long time, apparently confused. Then, muttering something, he hurried back to the house. I went after him. When I got to the room he was taking off his boots. He told me to polish them till they shone. He went and had a bath and washed the fish smells off him.

While he bathed, Mum returned from her day-long hawking of cheap wares. She seemed leaner, her eyes dulled by the yellow dust, her face darkened by the fiery marigold sunlight. After dropping her basin of provisions on the cupboard, she sat on the bed. She did not move. She did not speak. She stank of profound exhaustion.

When Dad came in from the bathroom he did not seem particularly happy to see Mum. In fact, he ignored her altogether. He sat on his chair and proceeded to anoint himself with coconut oil. He combed and parted his hair. Then he put on his safari suit, which used to be white but which had turned brownish with age. He applied cheap perfume to his face. Something odd had happened to Dad after his great dream: he had become more susceptible to invisible presences in the air. It was as if holes had opened up in his spirit through which wisps of malevolence could enter.

When he saw that his boots had not been cleaned or polished, he exploded into a short burst of rage. He chased me twice round the room with a thick belt in his hand. He caught me at the door, dragged me in and was about to lash me when Mum—in a deadly voice—said: 'If you touch my son, you will have to kill me.'

Dad lowered his belt and sat in his chair. He retreated into the barely contained whirlwind of his fury. He poured himself a generous quantity of ogogoro, lit a cigarette and, in between smoking, proceeded to decrust his boots. While he cleaned his boots his spirit boiled, and I watched as a strange demon in the form of a beautiful girl with green eyes entered him. The demon-girl moved into Dad's spirit and sat comfortably, and then I couldn't see it any more. As he cleaned his boots with fiery vigour, smoking his cigarette with a grim intensity, his spirit rising and swirling, Dad lashed us with accusations. Sweating through his suit, his temper seemed to burn around him. His forehead became an agitation of wrinkles. Mum sat very still, listening. While Dad was shouting at us an evil spirit went right through our room, on its way to the preparations for the great political rally. The evil spirit, passing through our spaces, made all of us edgy. It awakened deep irrational passions in Dad's brain. Fuming, he scraped the dried mud off his boots angrily. His face swelling, his chest heaving, his big muscles bristling, he accused us of betraying him, of not caring enough for his ideals. Mum, he said, only cared for herself. He complained that we had no respect for him, that we didn't even see the importance of carrying on his schemes while he recovered from his fight.

He harangued us as if we were failed members of a government cabinet. He was angry about the fact that we had not supervised the beggars, had not encouraged them, had not fed them, and had not looked after Helen the beggar girl, whom he said was a princess from a distant and devastated kingdom. He rounded on me because I had stopped spying at Madame Koto's bar. He rounded on Mum because she had not been keeping in touch with political developments and had done nothing to recruit women to his political party. And he turned on both of us for failing to keep alive his dream of a university for beggars and the poor.

Mum said: 'You spend all your time talking about this university for beggars, but what about us, eh? Are we not beggars? Don't you hear how cracked my voice is? From morning till night I walked this ungodly city, hawking my provisions, crying out, while you slept like a goat for seven days.'

Leaping to his feet, Dad vented his full fury at Mum. Blindly he hurled his boots at the cupboard. The cupboard door flew open, revealing the pots empty of food. Cockroaches were sent scampering everywhere. Stamping his feet, lashing the air with his big fists, he went quite beserk with shouting. He said Mum was entirely devoid of vision and spent all her energy counting her wretched profits, while he tried to improve the condition of the people.

'Improve our condition first,' Mum replied.

Dad was momentarily stunned at the boldness of Mum's interruption. She continued.

'Where will you get the money to build a school for mosquitoes, talk less of beggars, eh? Will you steal, eh? Do you think money falls out of dreams, eh?'

Dad stopped in the beginnings of an antagonistic gesture.

'But what about all the money I won?' he asked, staring at us in utter disbelief, his bewilderment tinged with rage.

We were silent. We had completely forgotten the huge amount of money due to Dad for winning the fight with the warrior from the land of Battling Ghosts. Worried about his injuries, awestruck by his fabulous sleep and distracted by his recuperations, we had not remembered that Sami, the betting-shop man, owed us what amounted to a sizeable fortune.

'WHAT ABOUT MY MONEY?' Dad cried again.

'We forgot,' I said.

Mum shot me a furious glance. Dad sat on his chair and kept staring at us alternately, as if we had committed acts of unbelievable criminality.

'Do you mean to tell me,' he said, pressing such menace into every word, 'that you people haven't YET collected my money, eh?'

We dug deeper into our silence. Mum started to fidget. Then Dad, jumping up, sending the three-legged chair flying from underneath him, truly unleashed his mistral rage.

'You are not on my side,' he bellowed at Mum. 'You are clearly my enemy! You want me to fail! You want me to be destroyed by the world! You go around in dirty clothes and ugly shoes and a disgusting wig of a he-goat, when I have hundreds of pounds sitting just across the street! You starve me, you starve

229

my son, you obviously feed yourself in secret and meanwhile you don't even bother to secure my investments! I carry loads that would break the neck of Hercules. I fight with giants and monsters and thugs. Yes, I fight and get beaten and manage to win—and I win only because of you two—and yet, through all this agony, you don't even bother to look after the fruits of my victory?'

Dad paused. Then he drew a deep breath and, thrusting his raw face at Mum, he shouted: 'GET OUT OF MY HOUSE, YOU USELESS WOMAN WITH YOUR STUPID WIG! GET OUT! Go and sell your stupid provisions from morning till night! YOU ENJOY SUFFERING—YOU ENJOY POVERTY! Fine! GO and enjoy your poverty somewhere else and DON'T COME BACK! I will not kill myself for an UNGRATEFUL WIFE!'

Mum bore his tirade in a dangerous and stiff-necked silence. When Dad had exhausted himself, Mum stood up. With the movements of one who was enacting a decision she had reached long ago, she began to bundle her possessions. She gathered her faded wrappers, her moth-eaten wig, her undergarments, her old blouses, her slippers, her cheap jewellery, her tin-can of money, and dumped them all into an ancient box. Having almost reached the end of her forbearance, she took Dad's words extremely seriously.

'Where are you going?' I asked.

She screamed at me, deafening me with the full volume of her life-long frustration. Dad stamped on his boots, downed a shot of ogogoro, and stormed out of the room. I followed him, but I kept a careful distance between us. The demon-girl was growing in him, becoming more luminous and ecstatic.

Outside, green moths were thickening in the air. No one seemed to notice. Dad was striding furiously to Sami's betting shop when he saw Helen. Her beauty was more hypnotic than ever. Her blind eye was darker, her good one more jewelled and she was sitting on the bonnet of the burnt political vehicle, surrounded by the moths.

As if magnetized by the force of her astonishing serenity, Dad changed direction and ran over to her. He was about to speak when she turned her strange eyes to him and said: 'It's time for us to go.'

'Why?' Dad said.

'When the time is right we will be back,' she replied, turning away from him.

Dad pleaded with her to stay. The more he pleaded, the less interested she seemed. After a while she jumped down from the bonnet. The other beggars appeared mysteriously with rotting corn-cobs and mouldy bread in their hands. They gathered round Helen, awaiting her command. The moths had concentrated about them as if their poverty and their wretchedness were a unique kind of light. Without uttering another word Helen led the beggars up the road. The moths went with them, their clattering wings sounded oddly metallic.

Dad stood still for a long moment, watching the beggars leave. His face was disconsolate and it seemed his dreams were deserting him. The beggars had gone a short distance when Dad broke the trance of his abandonment and ran after them. The street watched us. The moths clicked in our faces. Thickly gathered around the beggars, they seemed a kind of shield. Was I the only one who saw the moths? Dad didn't seem to, for he had launched into an impassioned plea directed at the beggar girl. Staring deep into her gem-like eye, he begged her to give him one last chance to fulfil his promise. He blamed his neglect on his recuperation, on me and Mum; and swore that he was going to build a school for them as soon as he had collected his money from the betting shop man.

'I will prove it to you,' he kept saying.

But the beggar girl, deaf to his entreaties, carried on walking. Glowing in a new delirium, Dad began to praise her beauty and her elegance, her face of a yellow moon, her limbs of a blue gazelle, her eyes of a sad and sacred antelope. He completely amazed me with his declaration of fearless love. In a burning voice, robust and insane, he said: 'I dream of you every day, my princess from a strange kingdom. Everyone else sees you as a beggar, but I know you belong to a golden throne. You are so beautiful that even these butterflies . . . '

'Moths,' I corrected.

231

Dad glared at me, tapped me on the head and proceeded with his bizarre, passionate courtship.

'. . . that even these butterflies cling to you as if you are honey. You have the head of a spaceship, your eyes are like those of the wonderful maidens of Atlantis, you belong to the angelic kingdoms beneath the sea. You are a moon-woman come to brighten the earth. Your skin looks like flowers from another planet. You are the mistress of beauty, princess of grace, queen of the road. Let the flowers of the earth see you and weep . . .'

Dad went on and on, pouring out a stream of contradictory praises. The beggars ate their mould-encrusted bread and laughed at Dad's ridiculous words. Helen remained indifferent. Unable to bear her indifference, his face twitching under the assault of the moths, Dad finally blocked her path, just before we got to Madame Koto's bar-front. He astounded me by saying: 'I want you to be my second wife. Stay and marry me. I will take care of your people.'

The beggar girl went on as if she hadn't heard anything. Then Dad—his spirit swirling in the new yellow delirium—boldly declared his intention to honour his promises. He said Helen should come with him to Sami's betting shop, and if all he was saying wasn't true, if he didn't have the money to build them a school, to feed and cater for them, then she was free to go. He made a solemn oath, loudly and with dramatic gestures.

For the first time Helen acknowledged his persistence. She stopped. Dad's face broke into a triumphant smile. Turning to the rest of the beggars, he told them to wait for him. Then he seized Helen's hand and set off with her towards Sami's shop. Pestered by the moths, he strode defiantly through the rumour-making stares of the street.

Just as we were going past our house, Mum emerged with her tattered wig on and her ancient box under her arm. Dad didn't notice her. She looked so unlike herself, so wretched and haggard, as if she were a tramp, or as if she were fleeing the compound in shame, that even I nearly didn't recognize her. She followed us a short way and then, loud enough for the whole street to hear, she shouted: 'So you want me to go, eh? So you are throwing me out because of that stinking beggar girl with a goat's eye, eh?'

Dad looked back, saw her through the eyes of the demon sitting comfortably inside him, made a dismissive irritated movement of his hand and carried on, dragging the unwilling but mesmerized beggar girl with him. The demon that had entered my father had moved in for good. The occupation was complete. I could see his spirit whirling with grand dreams of love. For as he went, oblivious to the terrible changes he was bringing into our lives, I realized how much Dad was brimming over with love, possessed by its secret madness, bursting with love for everything, a wild unholy indiscriminate love, a love so powerful that it made him feel like a god, so vast that he didn't know how to contain it or express it. The love in him had become a double demon and it propelled him towards chaos.

Mum began weeping bitterly, cursing all the years of her privation and suffering; cursing the day she set eyes on Dad in the village, during the most beautiful years of her life; swearing at Dad for having drained the life out of her in so profitless a marriage. And between them both I didn't know who to choose. Mum went off, wailing, in the direction of Madame Koto's fabulous bar. Dad marched on to Sami's place, unmindful of the destruction he was sowing behind him. I started after Mum, but she screamed at me, as if she perceived that I was in alliance with Dad. And it may have been because of the moths (which I alone saw as moths), because of Helen and her tattered yellow dress, her emerald eye; or because of Dad's polished boots and his bristling demonic love, or because I didn't really believe Mum would disappear from our lives, that I chose to go after Dad—for with his mad passion lay the greater magnetic adventure, the curiosity and the rage.

And so, watching Mum grow smaller in the distance, a slouching figure, wailing and renting her wig, I reluctantly stuck with Dad's story, and suffered the choice I made for many nights to come.

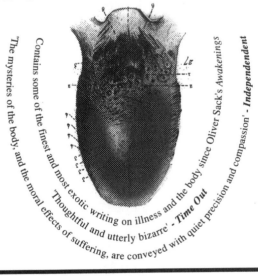

GRANTA

CARYL PHILLIPS
WEST

Curling herself into a tight fist against the cold, Martha huddled in the doorway and wondered if tonight she might see snow. Beautiful. Lifting her eyes without lifting up her head, she stared at the wide black sky that would once more be her companion. White snow, come quickly. A tall man in a long overcoat, and with a freshly trimmed beard, chin tucked into his chest, looked down at her as she walked by. For a moment she worried that he might spit, but he did not. So this was Colorado Territory, a place she had crossed prairie and desert to reach. Hoping to pass through it quickly, not believing that she would fall over foolish like a lame mule. Old woman. They had set her down and continued on to California. She hacked violently. Through some atavistic mist, Martha peered back east, beyond Kansas, back beyond her motherhood, her teen years, her arrival in Virginia, to a smooth white beach where a trembling girl waited with two boys and a man. Standing off, a ship. Her journey had been a long one. But now the sun had set. Her course was run. *Father, why hast thou forsaken me?*

Lucy would be waiting for her in California, for it was she who had persuaded Martha Randolph that there were colored folks living on both sides of the mountains now. Living. According to Lucy, colored folks of all ages and backgrounds, of all classes and colors, were looking to the coast. Lucy's man had told her, and Lucy in turn had told Martha. Girl, you sure? Apparently, these days colored folks were not heading west prospecting for no gold, they were just prospecting for a new life without having to pay no heed to the white man and his ways.

**Caryl Phillips** was born in St Kitts, West Indies in 1958. Later that same year his family emigrated to England. He grew up near Leeds and was educated at Oxford. He has written numerous scripts for film, theatre, radio and television. His books include *The Final Passage*, winner of the Malcolm X Award and *The European Tribes*, which was awarded the 1987 Martin Luther King Memorial Prize. 'West' is excerpted from his new book, *Crossing the River*, which Bloomsbury publish in May. He divides his time between West London, St Kitts and Massachusetts, where he is a Professor of English at Amherst College.

Photo: Barry Lewis

Prospecting for a place where things were a little better than bad, and where you weren't always looking over your shoulder and wondering when somebody was going to do you wrong. Prospecting for a place where your name wasn't 'boy' or 'aunty', and where you could be part of this country without feeling like you wasn't really a part. Lucy had left behind a letter for her long-term friend, practically begging her to come out west and join her and her man in San Francisco. It would make the both of us happy. And although Martha still had some trouble figuring out words and such, she could make out the sense in Lucy's letter, and she reckoned that's just what she was going to do. Pioneer. She was going to stop her scrubbing and washing. Age was getting the better of her now, and arthritis had a stern hand on all parts of her body. She would pioneer west. Martha pulled her knees up towards her and stretched out a hand to adjust the rags around her feet. She blocked up the holes where the wind was whistling through. Stop. The doorway protected her on three sides, and she felt sure that she should be able to sleep here without disturbing anyone. Just leave me be. But she felt strangely beyond sleep. As though her body was sliding carelessly towards a kind of sleep. Like when she lost Eliza Mae. Moma. Moma.

Martha unglued her eyes and stared up into the woman's face. 'Do you have any folks?' It had started to snow now. Early snow, huge, soft snowflakes spinning down out of the clear, black sky. 'You must be cold.' It was dark and, the woman aside, there was nobody else in sight. When they had set her down here, they had told her this was Main Street, as though this information freed them of any responsibility. But she did not blame them. A few saloons, a restaurant, a blacksmith, a rooming house or two, indeed this was Main Street. 'I have a small cabin where you can stay the night.' Martha looked again at the woman who stood before her in a black coat, with a thick shawl thrown idly across her shoulders and a hat fastened tightly to her head. Perhaps this woman had bought her daughter? Was Eliza Mae living here in Colorado Territory? There was no reason to go clear to California if Eliza Mae were here in Colorado Territory. Eliza Mae returned to her? 'Can you get up?' The woman stretched out her gloved hand and Martha stared hard at it. Eliza Mae was gone. This hand could no more lead her back to her daughter than it could lead Martha back to her own youthful self. A small cabin. This woman was offering her some place with a roof, and maybe even a little heating. Martha closed her eyes. After countless years of journeying, the hand was both insult and salvation, but the woman was not to know this. 'Please take my hand. I'm not here to harm you. I just want to help. Truly.' Martha uncurled her fingers and set them against the woman's hidebound hand. The woman felt neither warm nor cold. 'Can you stand by yourself?' Inside of herself, Martha laughed. Can this woman not see that they abandoned me? At least they had shown some charity and not discarded her on the plains. But stand by herself? Martha Randolph. Squatting like a filthy bag of bones. Watching the snow. Don't know nobody in these parts. Barely recognizing herself. No ma'am, she thought. I doubt if I'll ever be able to stand by myself again. But no matter. I done enough standing by myself to last most folks three or four lifetimes. Ain't nothing shameful in resting now. No ma'am, nothing shameful at all. She squeezed. The woman's hand squeezed back. 'Can you stand by yourself?' Martha shook her head.

I look into his eyes, but his stare is constant and frightens me. He shows no emotion. 'Lucas?' He turns from me and scrapes the wooden chair across the floor. He sits heavily upon it. He lifts his hands to his head and buries his face in his cupped and calloused palms. Eliza Mae runs to me and clutches the hem of my dress. The light in the lamp jumps and the room sways, first one way and then the next. I pull Eliza Mae towards me and hide her small body in the folds of my dress. Lucas looks up. He opens his mouth to speak. His face is tired, older than his thirty-five years. The weight of yet another day in the field sits heavily upon him. But not just this. I run my hand across Eliza Mae's matted hair. On Sunday I will pull the comb through the knots and she will scream. Outside, I can hear the crickets, their shrill voices snapping, like twigs being broken from a tree. 'Master dead.' Eliza Mae looks from me to her father, then back to me.

239

Poor child, she does not understand. 'Lucas, we going to be sold?' Lucas lowers his eyes.

The sun is at its highest point. The overseer is looking across at me, so again I bend down and start to pick. Already I have the hands of a woman twice my age, the skin beaten, bloodied and bruised, like worn out leather. The overseer rides his horse towards me, its legs stepping high, prancing, almost dancing. He looks down at me, the sun behind him, framing his head, forming a halo. He raises his whip and brings it down on my arm. I don't hear the words that fall from his mouth. I simply think, Master dead. What now? I bend down and again I start to pick. I can still feel his eyes upon me. And the sun. And now the horse is turning. It dances away from me.

I stand with the rest of the Virginia property. Master's nephew, a banker from Washington, is now our new master. He has no interest in plantation life. He holds a handkerchief to his face and looks on with detachment. Everything must be sold. The lawyer grabs the iron-throated bell and summons the people to attention. Then the auctioneer slaps his gavel against a block of wood. I fall to my knees and take Eliza Mae in my arms. I did not suckle this child at the breast, nor did I cradle her in my arms, and shower her with what love I have, to see her taken away from me. As the auctioneer begins to bellow, I look into Eliza Mae's face. He is calling out the date, the place, the time. Master would never have sold any of us. I tell this to my terrified child. Slaves. Farm animals. Household furniture. Farm tools. We are to be sold in this order. I watch as Lucas soaks a cloth in cold water. He comforts me and places it first on my forehead, and then on that of his child. Last night he came to me, his eyes grown red with drink. He confessed that death would be easier. This way we are always going to be wondering. Always worrying. His voice broke and he choked back the remaining words. Then he took me in the circle of his arms and laid me down. Until the old horn blew to mark the start of a new day.

Farmers have come from all over the county. A fun-seeking crowd, ready for haggling, but amongst them I see the lean-faced men. The traders, with their trigger-happy minds, their mouths tight and bitter. I try not to look into anybody's eyes. The

auctioneer is dressed formally. Dark vest, colorful cutaway coat.
He continues to yell. Now, as he does so, he motions towards us
with his gavel. Then he slaps this instrument against the wooden
block with a thud. Now again he gestures towards us. My throat
is dry. Eliza Mae moves restlessly, so I take her hand. She cries. I
pinch her to quiet her. I am sorry, but it is for her own good. The
auctioneer beckons forward the traders. They look firstly at the
men. A trader prods Lucas's biceps with a stick. If a trader buys
a man, it is down the river. To die. That much we all know. The
families in need of domestics, or the farmers in need of breeding
wenches, they look across at us and wait their turn. I am too old
for breeding. They do not know that I would also disappoint. My
Eliza Mae holds on to me, but it will be to no avail. She will be a
prime purchase. And on her own she stands a better chance of a
fine family. I want to tell her this, to encourage her to let go, but
I have not the heart. I look on. The auctioneer cries to the
heavens. A band strikes up. A troupe of minstrels begin to dance.
Soon the bidding will begin. 'Moma.' Eliza Mae whispers the
word over and over again, as though this were the only word she
possessed. This one word. This word only.

Martha leaned against the woman and peered into the
small, dark room. Still cold. Through the half-light, she
saw the single bed, the mattress rolled back and
revealing an ugly grid of rusty wire. Then she felt the woman's
gentle touch guiding her across the room and into a hard-backed
wooden chair. Like a child. Martha sat and watched as the
woman firstly lit the lamp and then quickly made up the bed,
stretching a clean sheet tight like a drumskin across its length and
breadth. Having done so, she helped Martha the two paces across
the room and set her down to rest upon the corner of the bed.
Martha's right eye was clouding over, but she could make out the
woman's motions as she now attempted to fire some life into the
pot-bellied stove. She failed, and bestowed a sad smile upon
Martha. Girl, don't worry. Don't worry yourself. The woman
reached for the pitcher and poured a glass of water. 'Here, take it
and drink. Are you cold?' Martha dragged her tongue around her
swollen lips. Then she took the water and held the glass between

241

both hands. She swallowed deeply, and as she did so the woman knelt and began to remove the wet rags that swaddled Martha's feet. No. Please. Martha closed her eyes.

She could only once remember being this cold. That was on that miserable December day that she had crossed the Missouri, riding in the back of the Hoffmans' open wagon. When they arrived on the western shore, Martha, by now gaunt and tired, having travelled clear from Virginia with only the briefest of stops, stepped down into the iciness that was a Kansas winter. Did they buy me to kill me? All her belongings dangled in a bundle that she held in one hand. She no longer possessed either a husband or a daughter, but her memory of their loss was clear. She remembered the disdainful posture of Master's nephew, and the booming voice of the auctioneer. She remembered the southern ladies in their white cotton sun-bonnets and long-sleeved dresses, and the poorer farmers who hoped to find a bargain, their bony mules hitched to lame carriages. The trader who had prodded Lucas with a stick bought him for a princely sum, but Martha held on to some hope, for Lucas was a man who never failed to make friends with dogs. He charmed them with his dark, gentle voice. Lucas was not a man to let his body fetch up in flinty, lonely ground. Eliza Mae was sold after Martha. The Hoffmans could no doubt detect in their purchase a powerful feeling towards this girl, so they had bundled Martha into their wagon and left quickly. They had made their transaction, and the festivities would run their natural course without them. Goodbye, everybody. Once they had passed out of sight, the woman offered Martha a lace handkerchief, which Martha ignored.

Within the year, the Hoffmans had decided to sell up and leave Virginia. They had decided to settle outside of the city of Kansas, in a part of the country which was young and promising for pioneers. Good roads provided easy access to the back country, and new arrivants were permitted to purchase land from the United States government at a cost of two dollars an acre. Mr Eugene Hoffman intended to do a little farming on his five acre homestead, and he had ambitions of building up a herd of forty cattle and a dozen or so hogs. Cleo Hoffman, her training having prepared her for a life of teaching music, mainly the piano, was equally optimistic. Deeply religious people, they were sadly without children. In this Kansas, Martha sometimes heard voices. Perhaps there was a God. Perhaps not. She found herself assaulted by loneliness, and drifting into middle age without a family. Voices from the past. Some she recognized. Some she did not. But, nevertheless, she listened. Recognizing her despair, Mr and Mrs Hoffman took Martha with them to a four-day revival by the river, where a dedicated young circuit rider named Wilson attempted to cast light in on Martha's dark soul. Satan be gone. The young evangelist preached with all his might, but Martha could find no solace in religion, and was unable to sympathize with the sufferings of the son of God when set against her own private misery. She stared at the Kansas sky. The shield of the moon shone brightly. Still she heard voices. Never again would the Hoffmans mention their God to Martha.

And then one morning, Mr Hoffman called the greying Martha to him. She knew this would eventually happen, for the crops were not selling, and once again the cattle had come back from market. A merciful market where nothing would sell. Martha had overheard them arguing with each other at the dinner table. Mr Hoffman looked at Martha, and then down at his hands which were folded in front of him. 'We have to go west, Martha. To where there is work for us. Kansas is still too young.' He paused. 'We are going to California, but we shall have to sell you back across the river in order that we can make this journey.' Martha's heart fell like a stone. No. 'We shall do all that we can to ensure that you are rewarded with good Christian owners.' No. He continued to speak, but Martha did not hear a word he uttered. Across the river to Hell. Eventually she asked, 'When?' She was unable to tell whether she had cut him off by speaking. Mr Hoffman cleared his throat. 'Next week, Martha.' He paused and looked up at her. 'I'm sorry.' This appeared to be his way of apologizing and dismissing her at the same time. It was possible that he was sorry. For himself. Martha was not sure if she should or could leave. Then Mr Hoffman climbed to his feet. 'You can leave, Martha.'

That night, Martha packed her bundle and left the house.

For where, she was not sure (don't care where), being concerned only with heading west (going west), away from the big river (away from Hell), and avoiding nigger traders who would gladly sell her back over the border and into Missouri. The dark night spread before her, but behind the drifting clouds she knew the sky was heavy with stars. (Feeling good.) And then Martha heard the barking of dogs, and she tumbled into a ditch. (Lord, give me Lucas's voice.) She waited but heard nothing, only silence. (Thank you.) Eventually, Martha climbed to her feet and began to run. (Like the wind, girl.) Never again would she stand on an auction block. (Never.) Never again would she be renamed. (Never.) Never again would she belong to anybody. (No sir, never.) Martha looked over her shoulders as she ran. (Like the wind, girl.) And then, later, she saw dawn announcing its bold self, and a breathless Martha stopped to rest beneath a huge willow tree. (Don't nobody own me now.) She looked up, and through the thicket of branches she saw the morning star throbbing in the sky. As though recklessly attempting to preserve its life into the heart of a new day.

The woman poured Martha another glass of water, which Martha held tightly, as though trying to pull some heat from the wet glass. Still cold. She stared at Martha, who noticed now that this woman had the defensive, watchful eyes of a person who had never lost control of herself. The woman loosened her shawl, revealing a gold necklace at her throat. Still cold. 'Should I leave you now?' Beneath the hat, Martha could detect a shock of grey hair, but she was unclear as to whether or not the woman was trying to conceal it. Then somebody moved outside, their shadow darkening the line of light at the bottom of the closed door, their weight firing the floorboards. No. Martha's breath ran backwards into her body. For a moment, she was unsure if she would ever have the power to expel it and then, against her will, she burst in a quiet sigh. Eliza Mae. Come back for her? 'Shall I leave you now?' 'No.' Martha released the word, without quite understanding why she had done so. Then, as the woman sat on the edge of the bed, and Martha felt the bed lurch beneath her, she regretted the generosity of her invitation. The woman was making herself at home.

I put down the plates in front of these men and stand back. They do not take their eyes from me. 'Thank you, ma'am.' The one with the blue eyes speaks quietly. The other two are in his shadow. They all dress alike in fancy attire; silver spurs, buckskin pants, and hats trimmed with rattlesnake skin. These three unshaven men, who sit uncomfortably in my restaurant. My other customers have left. They have driven away my customers. The truth is, there was only one other customer. These days, I am lucky to set eyes on more than six or seven a day. Colored men don't appear to be riding the trail like they used to. Coming in here with their kidneys and lungs all ruined, spitting blood, arms and legs broken over and over. Even the toughest of them lasted only a few years, but now it looks like their day is done. 'Anything else I can get you?' They still haven't touched their food. 'When's he due back, ma'am?' I run my hands down the front of my dress. They are more worn than ever, not just from the cooking, but from the washing and cleaning. It is almost ten years now since I arrived in Dodge and set up laundering clothes, then cooking some, then doing both when Lucy agreed to come in and help me out. 'He'll be back at dusk.' My mind turns to Lucy in the back. Waiting for me. Needing my help. We have a large order of washing needs finishing up before morning. 'Dusk?' He lets the word fall gently from his lips, as though he were the first man to coin such a term. I nod.

There used to be four of them when they last came up the trail. I don't remember the fourth man, but I know that there used to be a fourth. They arrived as four, but left as three. This time they have arrived as three and will leave as three. They tried to cheat Chester while playing poker in the saloon bar, but Chester, in his gentle manner, sneaked a little piece of chewing tobacco into his mouth and pointed up their ways. According to the sheriff, the fourth man, the scoundrel amongst them, he drew the first gun. The sheriff let Chester go. Gunplay is second nature to Chester. Their food is getting cold. One man picks up his fork and chases the potatoes through the gravy and around the plate a little. I know he wants to eat. He is waiting for the signal with mounting hunger. I tell the man that I have to go out back now, but he simply stares at me with those blue eyes. I tell him that I

245

have clothes to wash. I offer him this information almost as a gift. He looks across at his friends, who can barely restrain themselves. They want to eat. He waves a dismissive hand in my face. Then, as though it is not important, he reaches into his pocket and throws a few bills onto the table-top. He tells me that they will leave when they have finished. That they will wait out front for Chester.

I lift the dripping pile of clothes out of the boiler and drop them into the tub. I feel Lucy's eyes upon me, but I will not turn to face her. I am hot. I wipe my brow with the sleeve of my dress, and then again I bend over and try to squeeze more water from the shirts. She puts her hand on my shoulder, this woman who has been both friend and sister to me. She puts her hand on my shoulder and presses. She says nothing, and I still do not turn around. I continue to knead the clothes between my tired fingers. 'Martha,' she begins. 'Martha, child.' I turn to look at her. I drop the clothes and wrap my wet arms around her, and she pulls me close. I begin to sob. She says, 'You must go to Chester and warn him.' I listen to her, but we both know that it is too late. Even as she insists that I should leave now, she clasps me tighter.

I stand in the street. I see him in the distance, the dust clouding slowly around him as his horse, frame bent, head low, ambles out of the sunset and into the shadow that marks the beginning of the street. And they see him too. All three of them. They jump down from the rail. Lucy stands in the open doorway and looks on. I had only been in Dodge a few weeks when he came to me with his clothes to be laundered. He came back every Tuesday afternoon, as regular as sunset, but he barely spoke. Tipped his hat, always called me 'ma'am', never asked me for no money, or no credit, or no nothing. And then one day he told me that his name was Chester, that he was a wrangler on a ranch just outside of Dodge, that nobody could *top off* a bad horse like him, that he could smell loneliness like a buffalo could smell water. I told him, I didn't need no help, I just needed some companionship, that's all. He looked at me with a broad, knowing look, a look that could charm the gold out of a man's teeth, and asked if I wanted to move in with him into his store. I asked him what he sold, and he told me that he didn't sell a 'damn thing,' but there was plenty of room if I wanted to open up a business. He said that if we were going to prospect for happiness together, then he figured we ought to try and make a little money, too. I told Chester that I didn't think I could make him no babies no more. He smiled and said, 'I got babies some place that I ain't been no kind of father to. Figure it's best if I don't bother with no more baby-making.' He paused. 'I guess you noticed I ain't one to dress to impress the local belles.' Then he laughed some, till the tears streamed down his sweet chocolate face. That same afternoon, I pulled off my apron, pulled on a clean, calico dress, pinned down my hair with a bandanna, and moved everything to Chester's place, which turned out to be a proper store. Chester said he won it in a card game from a storekeeper who had headed south to Mexico with everything he owned in his pockets. He claimed that, to begin with, some folks didn't take to the idea of a colored owning decent property, but by and by people let him be. He sat among the lumber stores, merchants, watchmakers, carpenters, blacksmiths, mechanics, medical men, and lawyers, trading nothing.

I soon set up in business concocting stews and soups for weary, half-starved colored men who had long since spent their trail rations. Vegetables and livestock, grown and raised in and around Dodge, appeared on the market. Beans, potatoes, and onions at twenty-five cents a pound, beef at quarter the price, and large, plump turkeys at less than two dollars a piece. War came and war went and, almost unnoticed, the Union toppled. For a week or so, all lines were forgotten as Dodge toasted the victors in liquor until most folks could no longer hold a glass. I was free now, but it was difficult to tell what difference being free was making to my life. I was just doing the same things like before, only I was more contented, not on account of no emancipation proclamation, but on account of my Chester. I look down the street and see him coming yet closer, his shoulders square, his head held high. For ten long years, this man has made me happy. For ten long years, this man has made me forget—and that's a gift from above. I never thought anybody could give me so much love, even without trying, without appearing to make any effort, without raising no dust about it. Just steering and roping, and whatever manner of business he felt like seeing to in the days, watching the sunset at dusk, and a little whiskey and cards at night. Always there when I needed him. I glance at Lucy, whose face is a picture of fear. I want to tell her, 'Don't worry, Lucy.' And then the shots ring out and Chester slumps from the saddle, but his foot gets caught up in the stirrup. His horse stops and lets Chester fall respectfully to the ground. Three brave men with pistols smoking, and Lucy screaming.

Lucy brings the candle to my room and sits on a wicker chair. She has not yet stopped crying. I have not begun. 'We can go up to Leavenworth,' she says. 'I hear that the colored troops in the Fort are always looking for somebody to wash and clean for them. And plenty of colored folks still figuring to come across the Missouri and into Kansas.' I stare back at her, but say nothing. 'We can't stay here, Martha.' I know this. I know that I will never again be happy in fast-loving, high-speeding, Dodge. Not without Chester. And the restaurant. 'We can take our business to Leavenworth, establish a laundry.' I nod in agreement. Then I ask her. 'Lucy,' I say, 'Did I ever tell you that I had a daughter?' She looks back at me in astonishment.

Again she asked Martha if she was cold, and this time Martha could not hold back the sad confession that, despite this woman's efforts, her body remained numb. Too late. The woman smiled, then stood and stoked at the stove, but her gesture was one of idle hope. Too late. On top of the stove sat a great iron kettle which reminded Martha of the one back east, twenty-five years ago, in Virginia, which rang like a bell when you struck it. And if you put the tips of your fingers against it, you could feel the black metal still humming long after the kettle had ceased its song. Martha used to catch rainwater in it, the same rainwater with which she would wash Eliza Mae's matted hair. Keep still, girl. Such misery in one life. She looked at the palms of her hands where the darker skin had now bled into the lighter, and she wondered if freedom was more important than love, and indeed if love was at all possible without somebody taking it from her. Her tired mind swelled and surged with these difficult thoughts, until it pained her to think.

The woman finally stopped her stoking. Martha could feel the tears welling up behind her eyes. 'Can I help?' No, you must go. 'Are you alright?' No. Please go. 'I'm sorry about the stove.' No. No. No. Martha stifled a sob.

It seemed another age now, although in truth it was only two months ago that Lucy, her hair in a wrap, had come to her in the small, two-roomed cabin that they shared, and broken the news of her impending marriage. It had been a dark night, the solitary light from a candle teasing the two friends with the twin possibilities of both warmth and security. Not that Lucy's news came as any surprise to Martha, for she had long been aware of her friend's feelings for the colored man from the dry goods store. Tubs and boilers no longer had a hold on Lucy's mind, and now she would be escaping them by marrying this man who had built himself a storey and a half house from the profits of selling that boom town, sure-fire, money-maker at a dollar a pound; nails. Martha took Lucy's hands in her own, and told her that she was pleased, and that Lucy must not, under any circumstances, worry over her. With this said, she encouraged Lucy to begin packing if she was going to leave, as planned, in the morning. Lucy levered herself out of the chair and began to address herself to the tasks at hand, while an ailing Martha sat basking in the glow of the candle and watched her. These days, Martha's old body was overburdened, and seldom did she pass an afternoon without a few cat-naps. By evening her feet and ankles were so swollen that she had to use both hands to pull off her shoes, and her undergarments now grew strangely tight during the days, her underskirt band often cutting into her waist. She desperately needed to rest, but she had determined that Lucy must never see the evidence of her malaise. And certainly not now. Lucy was to leave with a clear conscience, but not before Martha had herded her into the picture-making man's studio and ordered her to sit still. She watched her friend as she continued to gather up her few belongings, and Martha began to laugh quietly to herself.

A week later, the man came into the cabin outhouse, his arms burdened down with a bundle of heavy flannel shirts and coarse pants that needed laundering. Such visits were becoming

249

less common, for either men seemed to be getting accustomed to giving their own garments the soap and water treatment, or Martha had serious competition from some place that she had not, as yet, heard about. The conversation that he struck up with Martha was a generous one, in that he desired to know if she could possibly manage this load by herself. Well, excuse me, mister. Was there anybody else in town to whom he might turn? Feigning ignorance of what he might be implying, Martha took the clothes and assured him that they would be ready for him whenever he needed them. This was just as well, he said, for he would soon be leaving for California with a group of colored pioneers. He informed her of this fact as though it were something that one ought to be proud of, and with this announcement delivered, he tipped his hat and wished her good day. After he left, Martha thought long and hard about her own prospects. The many years of her life with Lucy in this two-roomed cabin were now at an end, and although this Leavenworth had suited her, despite its numerous saloons, billiard parlors, and houses of joy, Martha felt that she must leave. Not that Leavenworth was either violent or dangerous. In fact, the townsmen had established a liking for law and order, and introduced codes that were rigidly enforced by deputies and marshals, which meant that in this town the fast gun was not the law. But although Leavenworth was free of the turbulence of Dodge, and in spite of the fact that her years here had been peaceful, if somewhat lonely, Martha had a strange notion that she, too, must become a part of the colored exodus that was heading west. Lucy had left behind a letter, not so much inviting Martha to come out and join her and her future husband in San Francisco, but begging her to do so. Martha unfolded the square of paper and decided to look it over one more time. Then, when she had finished, she blew out the lamp and sat quietly in the dark. Eliza Mae was once again back in her mind, not that her lost child had ever truly vanished. Perhaps her girl-child had pioneered west?

When, some days later, he returned for his clean and well-ironed garments, Martha eyeballed the man directly and announced that she, too, would be coming along. She deliberately did not ask, but he, with equal deliberation, did not respond. So once again, Martha informed him of her decision, and only now did he put down the clothes and begin to explain why this would not be possible. He advised Martha that this was to be a long and difficult journey, with at least twenty wagons, and they would have to cope with what the Indians called 'crazy weather', both blizzards and heat. Martha simply stared back at the man, forcing him to continue. 'We'll be following stream beds most of the way, but you never know.' He shrugged his shoulders. 'And we'll likely be called upon to walk, for the wagons will use every ounce of space for food, water, tools, and so on.' Martha found herself borrowing courage from this conversation, the way she had seen some men do from tequila. 'My role will be to cook for you,' she said. 'I won't be a burden, but I don't have no savings.' She went on, assuring him that she knew about wild and dangerous country, and had many times seen horses and oxen shot that had broken their legs, and watched as the trailriders made soup out of their hide and bones. She claimed that she had been aboard wagons that had fallen clean apart, that she knew sagebrush and sidewinders like they were her kin, and the shifting sands and whirling dust of the cactus-shrouded world would suit her just dandy. 'I'm afraid of nothing,' said Martha, 'least of all Indians or hard times. Colored folks generally got to be obligated to white folks to get clear to California, but you colored pioneers are offering me a chance. You let me work my fare out and I'll cook, wash clothes, and powerfully nurse to the sick and ailing. And I ain't fussy about sleeping on no bare ground. I done it plenty of times before, had the beaten hardness of the earth for a bed and the sky for covering.' The man looked blankly at her, but Martha, anxious that she should not be fooled, pressed on and asked after him when they proposed leaving. 'The day after tomorrow,' he said, his voice low, his expression now one of confusion. 'I'll be ready,' said Martha, tearing at her apron. 'And you just tell your people that you done found a cook.' He smiled weakly, then turned and left, his arms laden with clean laundry. My daughter. The energy of youth once more stirred within her. I know I'm going to find my child in California.

But the woman who now stood above Martha, casting pitiful

glances, was not her daughter. Eliza Mae? 'I'll leave you now,' she said. 'But you must expect to receive me in the morning.' You must expect to receive me? Did she mean by this to suggest that Martha had some choice over their arrangement? That she could, if she so wished, choose not to receive her in the morning? Martha watched the woman back slowly out of the cold room. Thank you. She left Martha alone. Sickness had descended upon her and she was unable to respond. Martha felt the sadness of not possessing a faith that could reassure her that, having served her apportioned span, she would now be ushered to a place of reunion. She looked through the cracked window pane. Dawn was some hours off, back east, approaching slowly. To be reunited. The town of Denver was mantled in a deep snow, the arms of the trees sheathed in a thin frost, the same thin frost that enveloped Martha's faithless heart.

The evening sky is streaked with red and yellow. I watch as the sun prepares to go down beneath the horizon. To my left, there is panic. Voices begin to climb. A pioneer has broken an ox by driving it too hard. It has to be slaughtered, but at least there will be fresh meat. He ignores this commotion and stands before me with frustration written across his face. I know that I have slowed down their progress. It is this that he wishes to talk with me about. He rolls a cigarette, his fingers clammy and stiff, and then he gestures me to rest upon the hide-bottom chair. He is a man who speaks as much with his hands as his voice. I had noticed this when he first came in with his bundle of flannel shirts and coarse pants. 'Well?' This is his beginning. I know what will follow. I look beyond him. A storm is working its way across the land. My old ears can still hear the dull rumbling of thunder.

Six weeks ago we set out across the open prairie, dust clouds rising, the noonday sun at full strength, a party of seventy colored people walking to the side of our wagons. The wagons are drawn by six oxen trained to work in pairs, animals which have a tendency to skittishness, and as such they initially frightened me. The first and rear wagons are attended to by experienced drivers, but the rest are handled by we pioneers. The idea is that I should cook for all those without family, mainly bullwhackers, all men, and this I have tried to do, rustling up bacon and salt pork and any game or beast that the men might happen to shoot along the way. I have made sure each wagon had ample amounts of flour, sugar, coffee, and rice, and a plentiful supply of ten gallon water kegs. Other provisions and equipment in my charge include vinegar, soap, matches, cooking utensils and field stoves. But it is never easy. Before dawn, the freezing wind rips through our clothing and right into the marrow. At noon, and early in the afternoon, the sun often causes us serious discomforts, made worse by the type of clothing that we wear. Heavy pants and flannel shirts for the men, and high-necked, long-sleeved, dark dresses that don't show the dirt for the women. At night, we draw the wagons into a circle, and camp-fires are built, meals cooked, and tales told of white expeditions where cruelties are often inflicted upon colored men and women.

The wagon train soon settled into a routine where one difficult day seemed much like the next, and where there was no discernible change to the uniform landscape. However, I felt myself growing weaker, and I tried in vain to disguise my ailments. Some days, we covered ten miles across the dry grass, some days twelve or fifteen, depending upon repairs or the weather. We saw Indians, and I felt some sympathy with them, but the Indian bands kept their distance and watched, choosing not to make anything of their encounters with the dark white men. Except on one occasion, when a column of a dozen warriors, at their head a chief, rode out towards the train. Behind them came the squaws, some with papooses slung across their backs, and all around them yapped pitiful-looking dogs who would in time become food. The chief halted, as did the wagon train, and he dismounted. By means of facial expressions and gestures, he made it known that we could pass in peace. I watched as our leader rewarded him with sugar and tobacco, and he in turn was rewarded with grunts of approval. Our only other visitors are the dark, shaggy buffalo who move at such a slow pace that it is difficult to make out their progress. Our leader forbade the men, who were tiring of my pork, to stalk and hunt these monsters, informing them that should they be *spooked* and stampede, they would happily trample all before them. The occasional deer or game bird is the only alternative to that which we carry aboard the wagons.

Ten days ago, the river source began to dwindle to a mere trickle, and water was severely rationed. I watched the oxen pulling the enormous loads with heroism, and I witnessed the equally impressive bravery of the pioneers who, dehydrated as they were, energy flowing back and forth, still managed to pursue the torture. My own state became perilous, racked as I was with exhaustion, but still I managed to keep my misery to myself. Until yesterday. When it became clear that I was unable to prepare any more meals. I had long since been relieved of laundry duties, owing to the water rationing, and I had occasionally begged a ride on a wagon while all others walked. But then, this final humiliation. Yesterday morning, under the dazzling, intense blue of the Colorado sky, the foothills of the Rockies in the distance, this frustrated man sat before me with a stern face and shared with me his water ration. Suddenly, and without warning, his face softened and he spoke. 'Today and tomorrow you will rest, Martha. Ride in Jacob's wagon on the flour sacks. Tomorrow evening we shall speak again.' He took my hand with what I imagined to be real affection.

'Well?' This is his beginning. I know what will follow. 'You must find some shelter, for you will never survive the journey to California.' I say nothing. The sun finally disappears beneath the horizon. I look across to the large fire where they are preparing the evening meal. Six weeks ago, I was one of them. But times have changed. Still, I cherish these brave people—these colored pioneers—among whom I travel. They took upon themselves this old, colored woman and chose not to put her down like a useless load. Until now. 'Tomorrow, Martha.' I nod, unable to find the words to convince him that he must not feel guilty. None of them should. I am grateful. That is all. I am simply grateful. I smile at this man who is young enough to be my son. 'Thank you,' he says. He turns away before one of us discovers words that are best left undisturbed.

At dawn, they bear me like a slaughtered hog up and into

the back of a wagon. But first they have cleared out some supplies to make room for me. Other wagons will bear the burden of carrying these provisions. He approaches and tells me that I will be taken to Denver, which lies some miles off their course. If I leave now, I may reach by sunset, which will give the wagon a chance to rejoin the group within two days. It is still cold. He offers me an extra blanket, which I take. We are to peel off from the main group, myself and two men, and strike out alone. He tells me that I have nothing to be afraid of. God willing, he hopes to one day find me in California. I thank him. All about me the pioneers stir. Sunken-eyed, still tired. I nursed and fed many of them through the first trying days, forcing food and water down their throats, and rallying them to their feet in order that they might trudge ten more miles towards their beloved California. Once there, they all dream of tasting true freedom, of learning important skills, of establishing themselves as a sober and respectable class of people. This is their dream. My weakness will delay them no longer. I hear the snap of a whip, and the driver yelling a sharp, impatient phrase to his oxen. As we move off, the tears begin to course down my old face.

We pass into a town on whose outskirts stand log-cabins, some finished, some unfinished, but clearly being attended to. The town is growing. As we journey on, I see stores, rooming houses and saloons. But I see only two people. Indians. I remember the day the colored troops of Leavenworth paraded Indian scalps, fingers with rings attached, and ears that had been pulled clean off. They behaved like the men whose uniforms they wore. And now the Indians disappear from view. Up here in the Rockies, my breath is short and I gasp for air. I lay back down, but cannot re-discover my previous position. And then the wagon shudders to a halt, and one of my fellow pioneers appears before me. 'This is Main Street, Miss Martha.' I look at him as he pulls his collar tight up under his chin. Behind him the wind is rising, and the sky is beginning to darken. 'We're under instructions to set you down right here and high-tail it back to the others.'

Caryl Phillips

In the pre-dawn hours of an icy February morning, Martha opened her eyes. Outside it was still dark, and the snow continued to spin. A dream began to wash through her mind. Martha dreamt that she had travelled on west to California, by herself, and clutching her bundle of clothing. Once there she was met by Eliza Mae, who was now a tall, sturdy colored woman of some social standing. Together, they tip-toed their way through the mire of the streets to Eliza Mae's residence, which stood on a fine, broad avenue. They were greeted by Eliza Mae's schoolteacher husband and the three children, who were all dressed in their Sunday best, even though this was not Sunday. A dumbstruck Martha touched their faces. Eliza Mae insisted that her mother should stay and live with them, but Martha was reluctant. All was not right. There was still no news of Lucas, and her Eliza Mae now called herself Cleo. Martha refused to call her daughter by this name, and insisted on calling her a name that her children and husband found puzzling. Soon it was time for Martha to leave, but her daughter simply forbade her mother to return east. Martha, feeling old and tired, sat down and wept openly, and in front of her grandchildren. She would not be going anyplace. She would never again head east. To Kansas. To Virginia. Or to beyond. She had a westward soul which had found its natural-born home in the bosom of her daughter.

Martha Randolph won't be taking any washing today. No tubs, no ironing. No cooking, either. Martha will simply sleep through the day. The woman, her cold body wrapped in her black coat, left the Denver streets which were now clad in thick snow. She opened the door and looked in upon the small colored woman, who stared back at her with wide eyes. The unsuccessful fire in the pot-bellied stove was dead. The woman gently closed in the door. Martha won't be taking any washing today. And the woman wondered who or what this woman was. They would have to choose a name for her if she was going to receive a Christian burial.

GRANTA

# WILL SELF
# SCALE

Some people lose their sense of proportion; I've lost my sense of scale.

Arriving home from London, late last night, I found myself unable to judge the distance from the last exit sign for Junction 2 to the slip-road itself. Granted it was foggy and the bright headlights of oncoming vehicles burnt expanding aureoles into my view, but there was a sequence of three oblong signs arranged to help me: the first sign had three oblique bars; the second had two; and then the third had one. The three signs were like the run-in strip to the beginning of the film; or the flying fingers of the pit crew boss as he counts down Nigel Mansell; or the decline in rank (from sergeant, to lance corporal, to corporal) that indicates your demotion from the motorway. Recognizing their sequence and reducing your speed, the needles falling on the warmly glowing instrument panel of the car, you are meant, intuitively, to apprehend three different scales at once (time, speed, distance) and merge effortlessly into the virtual reality that is motorway driving.

But for some obscure reason the Ministry had slipped up here. At Junction 2, the Beaconsfield exit, there was a gap between the last sign and the start of the slip-road that was far too long. I fell into this gap and lost my sense of scale. It occurred to me, when at last I gained the roundabout, and the homey green sign (Beaconsfield 4) heaved into view, that this gap, this lacuna, was— in terms of my projected thesis (*No Services: Reflex Ritualism and Modern Motorway Signs [with special reference to the M40]*)—an aspect of what the French call *delire*. I almost crashed.

By the time I reached home (a modest bungalow set hard against the model village which is Beaconsfield's principle visitor attraction), I had just about stopped shaking. I went straight to the kitchen.

---

**Will Self** was born in London in 1961. His parents—a professor and a publisher—were 'crashingly literate: I grew up reading Dostoevsky, Stendhal and Kafka.' He began to write fiction seriously when he was twenty-seven, after working for six years as a cartoonist for *The New Statesman* and *City Limits*. He has written a collection of stories, *The Quantity Theory of Insanity,* and a pair of linked novellas, *Cock and Bull*. He is currently working on a book of essays about drug addiction.

Photo: Barry Lewis

I had left a baking tray in the oven that morning and by now it should have become a miniature Death Valley of hard-baked morphine granules. I opened the oven door to find a dark brown ruckled surface, gratifyingly broken here and there into regular patterns of scales, like the skin of some moribund lizard. I used a steel spatula to scrape the material up and placed it carefully in a small plastic bowl (the one decorated with a sequence of leaping bunny rabbits; after the divorce, my wife divided the chattels: she took the adult-sized plates and cutlery, leaving me with our children's diminutive ware).

Although I've had no formal training in chemistry, I have, by a process of hit and miss, developed a method that allows me to precipitate a soluble tartrate from raw morphine granules. But there's a problem. Because I obtain my morphine supplies from bottles of kaolin purchased in sundry chemists (if the bottles sit for long enough most of the morphine rises to the top), the stuff still contains an appreciable amount of chalk. Months of injecting have given my body an odd aspect. With every shot, more chalk has been deposited along the walls of my veins, much in the manner of earth being piled up to form an embankment or a cutting around a roadway, mapping out the history of my addiction. Having methodically worked my way through the veins in my arms and legs, turning them the tan colour of drover's paths, then the darker brown of cart tracks, until eventually they've become macadamized, blackened, by my abuse. I can now stand on my broken bathroom scales and see a network of calcified conduits radiating from my groin. Some have been scored into my flesh like underpasses; others are raised up on hardened revetments of flesh: bloody flyovers.

I have been driven to using huge five millilitre barrels, each one fitted with the long, blue-collared needles necessary for hitting the arteries. Should I miss, the consequences for my circulatory system could be disastrous. I might lose a limb; there could be tailbacks. I wonder sometimes if I may be losing my incident room.

And can you blame me? There is, moreover, the matter of the thesis. Not only is the subject obscure (some might say risible), but I have no grant or commission. Why am I doing it? It would be all right if I were some dilettante, privately endowed, who could afford to toy with such things, but I am not. Rather, I have both myself to support and the maintenance to keep up. If the maintenance isn't kept up my ex-wife will become as obdurate as any consulting civil engineer. She has it within her power to arrange bollards around me, even to insist on tolls. There could be questions in the bungalow—something I cannot abide.

But last night none of this troubled me. I was lost in the arms of Morphia. Around I swept, pinned by g-force into the tight circularity of history. In my reverie I saw the M40 as it will be (still no services; all six carriageways and the hard shoulder are grassed over; only shallow depressions visible from the air), perhaps some twenty thousand years from now, when the second neolithic age has dawned over Europe.

# Relative

'Can I pay for these?'

'Whassat?'

'Can I pay for these—these de-scalers?' Time is standing still in the hardware store. It is dark and scented with nails and resinous timber. I had no idea that the transaction was going to prove so gruelling. The proprietor is looking at me the same way that the pharmacist does when I go to buy my kaolin.

'Why d'you want three?' Is it my imagination, or does his voice really have an edge of suspicion?

'I've got an incredible amount of scale in my kettle, that's why.' I muster an insouciance I don't feel. Since I have been accused, I know that I am guilty. I know that I lure young children away from the precincts of the model village and subject them to appalling, brutal, intercrural sex. I abrade their armpits, their knee pits, the juncture of their thighs, with my spun mini-rolls of wire. That's why I need three.

Guilt dogs me as I struggle to ascend the High Street. Guilt about my children. Ever since my loss of sense of scale, I have found it difficult to relate to my children. They no longer feel comfortable visiting me here in Beaconsfield. They say they would rather stay with their mother. The model village, which used to

261

entrance them, now bores them.

It was the boy who blew the whistle on me, grassed me up to his mother. At seven, he is old enough to know the difference between the smell of tobacco and the smell that comes from my pipe. Naturally he told his mother, and she realized immediately that I was back on the M.

In a way I don't blame him—it is a filthy habit. And the business of siphoning off the morphine from the bottles and then baking it in the oven until it forms a smokable paste—well, I mean, it's pathetic, this DIY addiction. No wonder that there are no pleasure domes for me, in my briccolage reverie. Instead I see twice five yards of fertile ground, with sheds and raspberry canes girded round. In a word: an allotment.

When my father died he subdivided his allotment and left a fifth of it to each of his children. The Association wouldn't allow it. They said that allotments were only leased rather than owned. It's a great pity, because what with the subsidies available and the new intensive agricultural methods, I could have probably made a reasonable living out of my fifth. I can see myself: making hay with a kitchen fork; spreading silage with a tea spoon; bringing in the harvest with a wheelbarrow; ploughing with a trowel tied to a two-by-four. Bonsai cattle wend o'er the lee of the compost heap as I recline in the pet cemetery . . .

It was not to be.

Returning home from High Wycombe, I add the contents of my two, new bottles of kaolin and morphine to the plant. Other people have ginger beer plants; I have a morphine plant. I made my morphine plant out of a plastic sterilizing unit. It would be a nice irony, this transmogrification of taboo, were it not for the fact that every time I clap eyes on the thing I remember with startling accuracy what it looked like, full of teats and bottles, when the children were babies and I was a happier man.

I mentioned the dividing of chattels following the divorce. This explains why I ended up, here in Beaconsfield, with the decorative Tupperware, the baby bouncer, sundry activity centres and the aforementioned sterilizing unit. Whereas my ex-wife resides in St John's Wood, reclining on an emperor-sized *bateau-lit*; my vessel, when I cast off and head out on to the sea of sleep, is a plastic changing mat, decorated with a regular pattern of Fred Flintstones and Barney Rubbles.

It's fortunate that the five 'police procedurals' that I wrote during my marriage are still selling well. Without the royalties I don't think I would be able to keep the members of my ex-family in the manner to which they have become accustomed. I cannot imagine that the book I am currently working on, *Murder on the Median Strip*, will do a fraction as well. (I say that confidently but what fraction do I mean? Certainly not a half or a quarter, but why not a two hundredth or a four hundredth? This is certainly conceivable. I must try and be more accurate with my figures of speech. I must use them as steel rulers to delimit thought. Wooliness will be my undoing.)

In *Murder on the Median Strip* (or *M on the MS* as I refer to it), a young woman is raped, murdered and buried on the median strip of the M40, in between Junction 2 (Beaconsfield) and Junction 3 (High Wycombe): a howdunnit, rather than a whodunnit. The murder occurs late on a Friday evening when the motorway is still crowded with ex-urbanites heading for home. The police are patrolling, looking for speeders. Indeed, they have set up a radar trap between the two principal bridges on this section of road. And yet no one notices a thing.

When the shallow, bitumen-encrusted grave is discovered, the police, indulging in their penchant for overkill, decide to reconstruct the entire incident. They put out a call on *Crimewatch UK* for all those who were on the motorway in that place, at that time, to re-assemble at Junction 2. The public response is overwhelming and by virtue of careful interviewing—the recollection of number-plates, makes of car, children making faces and so forth—they establish that they have managed to net all the cars and drivers that could have been there. The logistics are immensely complicated, but eventually, by dint of computer-aided visualizations, the police are able to re-enact the whole incident. The cars set off at staggered intervals; the police hover overhead in helicopters; patrol cars and officers on foot question any passers-by. But, horror of horrors, while the reconstruction is actually taking place, the killer strikes again. This time between Junction 6 (Watlington) and Junction 7 (Thame). Once more his victim is a young woman, who he sexually assaults, strangles and then crudely inters beneath the static, steel fender of the crash barrier.

That's as far as I've got with *M on the MS*. Sometimes, contemplating the MS, I begin to feel that I've painted myself into a corner with this convoluted plot. I realize that I may have tried to stretch the credulity of my potential readers too far.

In a way the difficulties of the plot mirror my own difficulties as a writer. In creating such an unworkable and fantastic scenario I have managed, at least, to fulfil my father's expectations of my craft.

'There's no sense of scale in your books,' he said to me, shortly before he died. At that time I had only written two procedurals, both featuring Inspector Archimedes, my idiosyncratic Greek Cypriot detective. 'You can have a limited success,' he went on, 'chipping away like this at the edges of society, chiselling off microscopic fragments of observation. But really important writing provides some sense of the relation between individual psychology and social change, of the scale of things in general. You can see that if you look at the great nineteenth-century novels.' He puffed on his pipe as he spoke; observing his wrinkled, scaly hide, his red lips and the yellow teeth masticating the black stem, I was reminded of a basking lizard, sticking its tongue out at the world.

A letter arrived this morning from the Municipality, demanding payment of their head tax. When I first moved here a man came from the borough valuer's to assess the rateable value of the property. By dint of quick work with the trellises, I managed to make it look as if Number 50, Crendon Road, was in fact one of the houses in the model village.

To begin with the official disputed the idea that I could possibly be living in this pocket-sized manse, but I managed to convince him that I was a doctoral student writing a thesis on 'The Apprehension of Scale in *Gulliver's Travels*, with special reference to Lilliput'; and that the operators of the model village had leased the house to me so that I could gain first-hand experience of Gulliver's state of mind. I even entered the house and adopted some attitudes—head on the kitchen table, left leg rammed through the french windows—in order to persuade him.

The result of this clever charade was that for two years my

rates were assessed on the basis of seven feet, eight inches square of living space. I had to pay eleven pounds fifty-nine pence per annum. Now, of course, I am subject to the full whack. Terribly unfair. And anyway, if the tax is determined by the individual rather than the property, what if that individual has a hazy or distorted sense of self? Shouldn't people with acute dissociation or multiple personalities be forced to pay more? I have resolved not to pay the tax until I receive a visit from the borough clinical psychologist.

# The Ascent

Some of my innovations in the new genre of 'Motorway Verse' have been poorly received by both the critics and the reading public. My claim, that my motorway verse represents a return to the very roots of *poetas*, an inspired attempt to link modish hermeneutics to the original function of oral literature, has been dismissed *sans* phrase.

I am disappointed. To me it seems self evident that the subconscious apprehension of signs by motorway drivers is exactly analogous to that act whereby the poets of primitive cultures give life, actually breathe reality, into the land.

Take the M40 as an example:

Jnc 1. Uxbridge. Jnc 1A. (M25) M4.
Jnc 2. Slough A365. No Services.
On M40 . . .

Is this not a very believable sample of such a 'singing up' of the country? Naturally, in order to understand the somewhat unusual scansion, it is necessary for readers imaginatively to place themselves in a figurative car driving up the aforementioned motorway. Metrical feet are, therefore, determined as much by the rhythm of the words themselves as by feeling the shift from macadamized to concrete surfaces or by hearing the susurration produced by alterations in the height and material construction of crash barriers.

Furthermore, a motorway verse that attempts to describe the ascent of the Chiltern scarp from the Oxfordshire side will, necessarily, be different from one that chronicles the descent from

Junction 5 (Stokenchurch) to Junction 6 (Watlington). For instance:

> Crawling, crawling, crawling. Crawler Lane.
> Slow-slow O'Lorry-o. Lewknor. 50 mph max.
> 11T! Narrow lanes, narrowing, narr-o-wing, na-ro-
> wing.

As opposed to:

F'tum. F'tum. F'tum. Kerchunk, kerchunk (Wat? [lingam] ton) . . .

On bad days, I console myself with the thought that there may be some grand conspiracy, taking in critics, publishers, editors and the executives in charge of giant type-founders such as Monotype, to stop my verse from gaining any success. Is it any wonder that I look for consolation; partly in draughts of sickly morphine syrup (drunk straight off the top of bottles of kaolin and morphine); and partly in hard, dedicated work on my 'Motorway Saga', entitled *From Birmingham to London and Back Again Delivering Office Equipment, with Nary a Service Centre to Break the Monotony?*

You can also see why I have come to view my opiate addiction as a source of literary inspiration. When I am beginning a new habit, my hypnogogia are intricate processions of visions that I can summon and manipulate at will. But when I am withdrawing I am frequently plunged into startling nightmares.

Last night's dream was classic. In it, I found myself leaving the bungalow and entering the precincts of the model village. I wandered around the forty-foot-long village green, admiring the precision and attention to detail which the model makers had lavished on their creation. I peeked first into the model butcher's shop. Lilliputian rashers of bacon were laid out on plastic trays, together with sausages, perfect in every respect, but the size of mouse droppings. Then I sauntered over to the post office. On the eight-inch-high counter sat an envelope the size of a postage stamp. Wonder of wonders I could even read the address on the envelope. It was a poll tax demand, destined for me.

Straightening up abruptly, I caught sight of a model building that I was unfamiliar with. It appeared to be my own bungalow. I couldn't be certain of this—it is after all not that remarkable an edifice—until I had looked in through the kitchen window. There, under the dirty cream Melamine work surface that surrounded the aluminium sink, I could see hundreds of little kaolin and morphine bottles, serried in dusty ranks. That settled it.

As soon as I had clapped eyes on them, I found myself miraculously reduced in size and able to enter the model bungalow. I wandered from room to room, more than a little discomfited at my phantasamagoric absorption into Beaconsfield's premier visitor attraction. Stepping on to the sun porch, I found another model. As it were: a model model. Also of the bungalow. Once again I was diminished and able to enter.

I must have gone through at least four more of these vertiginous descents in scale before I was able to stop and pause before yet another model bungalow. As it was, I knew that I must be standing on a sun porch for which a double-glazing estimate would have to be calculated in Angstroms. How to get back? That was the problem.

It took me three months to ascend, back up the six separate stages of scale, and reach home once more. Some of the pitches, especially those involving climbing down off the various tables the model bungalows were placed on, were, I would wager, the most extreme ever attempted by a solo climber. On many occasions I found myself dangling from the rope I had plaited out of strands of carpet underlay, with no apparent way of regaining the slick varnished face of the table leg or dropping to the checker board of lino—relative to my actual size—some six hundred feet below.

Oh, the stories I could tell! The sights I saw! It would need an epic to contain them. As it is I have restrained myself. Although, on awakening, I did write a letter to the Alpine Club on the ethics of climbers, finding themselves in such situations, utilizing paperclips as fixed crampons.

The final march across the 'true' model village to my bungalow was, of course, the most frightening. Here, out in the open, I was exposed to all the terrors of small scale adventuring: wasps the size of zeppelins, fluff the weight of an avalanche, mortar bomb explosions of plant spore, and so on and so forth.

My most acute anxiety was that I would be sighted by a human. I could not be much above the size of a sub-atomic particle, and as such subject to Heisenberg's Uncertainty Principle. Were I to be in any way observed I might not only find the direction of my journey irremediably altered, I could even cease to exist altogether!

# To the Bathroom

'Like, we're considering the historic present . . . ?'

'Yeah.'

'And David says, "I want to go to the bathroom."'

'Yeah.'

'So, like, we all accompany him there and stuff. 'Cos in his condition it wouldn't like be a . . . '

'Good idea for him to be alone?'

'Yeah, thassit. So we're standing there, right. All four of us, in the bathroom, and David's doing what he has to do. And we're still talking about it.'

'It?'

'The historic present. Because Diane—you know Diane?'

'Sort of.'

'Well, she says the historic present is like . . . err . . . like, more emotionally labile than other tenses. Yeah, thass what she says. Anyway, she's saying this and David is like, steaming, man . . . I mean to say he's really plummeting. It's like he's being de-cored or something. This is not just Montezuma's revenge, it's everyone's revenge. It's the revenge of every deracinated group of indigenes ever to have the misfortune to encounter the European. It's a sort of collective curse of David's colon. It's like his colon is being crucified or something.'

'He's anally labile.'

'Whadjewsay?'

'He's anally labile.'

Labile, labile. Labby lips. Libby-labby lips. This is the kind of drivel I've been reduced to. Imaginary dialogues between myself and a non-existent interlocutor. But is it any surprise? I mean to say, if you have a colon as spastic as mine it's bound to insinuate itself into every aspect of your thinking. I'm damned. If I don't drink vast quantities of kaolin and morphine I'm afflicted with terrifying bouts of diarrhoea. And if I do—drink a couple of bottles a day, that is—I'm subject to the appalling seismic colonic ructions. It doesn't really stop the shits either. I still get them; I just don't get caught short. Caught short on the hard shoulder, that's the killer.

Say you're driving up to High Wycombe, for example. Just out on a commonplace enough errand. Like going to buy a couple of bottles of K&M. And you're swooping down towards Junction 3, the six lanes of blacktop twisting away from you like some colossal wastepipe, through which the automative crap of the metropolis is being voided into the rural septic tank, when all of a sudden you're overcome. You pull over onto the hard shoulder, get out of the car and squat down. Hardly dignified. And not only that, destructive of the motorway itself. Destructive of the purity of one's recollection.

That's why I prefer to stay home in my kaolin-lined bungalow and summon up my memories of the motorway from the days before I was so afflicted: in the days when my vast *roman fleuve* was barely a trickle and my sense of scale was intact. Then distance was defined by regular increments, rather than the haphazard lurch from movement to movement.

This morning I was sitting, not really writing, just dabbling. I was hunkered down inside of myself, my ears unconsciously registering the whisper, whistle and whicker of the traffic on the M40, when I got that sinking feeling. I hied me to the bathroom, just in time to see a lanky youth disappearing out the window, with my bathroom scales tucked under his arm.

I grabbed a handful of his hip-length jacket and pulled him back into the room. He was a mangy specimen. His head was badly shaven, with spirals of ringworm on the pitted surface. The youth had had these embellished with crude tattoos, as if to dignify his repulsive skin condition. His attire was a loose amalgam of counter-cultural styles. The ragged chic of a redundant generation. His pupils were so dilated that the black

269

was getting on to his face. I instantly realized that I had nothing to fear from him. He didn't cry out or even attempt to struggle.

I had seen others like him. There's quite a posse of them, these 'model heads'. That's what they call themselves. They congregate around the model village, venerating it as a symbol of their anomie. It's as if, by becoming absorbed in the detail of this tiny world, they hope to diminish the scale of society's problems. In the winter they go abroad, settling near Legoland in Belgium.

'Right you,' I said, in householder tones. 'You might have thought that you would get away with nicking something as trivial as those bathroom scales, but it just so happens that they have a sentimental value for me.'

'Whadjergonna do then?' He was bemused—not belligerent.

'I'm going to put you on trial, that's what I'm going to do.'

'You're not gonna call the filth, are you?'

'No, no. No need. In Beaconsfield we have extended the whole principle of Neighbourhood Watch to include the idea of neighbourhood justice. I will sit in judgement on you myself. If you wish, my court will appoint a lawyer who will organize your defence.'

'Err . . . ' he had slumped down on top of the wicker laundry basket, which made him look even more like one of Ali Baba's anorectic confrères. 'Yeah, OK, whatever you say.'

'Good. I will represent you myself. Allow me, if you will, to assume my position on the bench.' We shuffled around one another in the confinement of tiles. I put the seat down, sat down and said, 'The court may be seated.'

For a while nothing happened. The two of us sat in silence. I thought about the day the court-appointed officer had come to deliver my decree nisi. He must have been reading the papers in the car as he drove up the motorway, because when I encountered him on the doorstep he was trying hard—but failing —to suppress a smirk of amusement.

I knew why. My wife had sued for divorce on the grounds of adultery. The co-respondent was known to her, and the place where the adultery had taken place was none other than these self same scales. The ones the model head had just attempted to steal. At that time they were still located in the bathroom of our

London house. After the decree absolute, my ex-wife sent them to me in Beaconsfield, together with a caustic note.

It was a hot summer afternoon in the bathroom. I was with a lithe young foreign woman, who was full of capricious lust. 'Come on,' she said, 'let's do it on the scales. It'll be fun, we'll look like some weird astrological symbol or a diagram from the Kama Sutra. She twisted out of her dress and pulled off her underwear. I stood on the scales. Even translated from metric to imperial measure, my body weight still looked unimpressive. She hooked her hands around my neck and jumped. The flanges of flesh on the inside of her thighs nearly fitted the notches above my bony hips. I grasped the fruit of her buttocks in my sweating palms. She braced herself, feet against the wall, toenails snagging on the Artex. Her panting smoked the mirror on the medicine cabinet. I moved inside of her. The coiled spring inside the scales squeaked and groaned. Eventually it broke altogether.

That's how my wife twigged. When she next went to weigh herself she found the scales jammed, the pointer registering 347 pounds. Exactly the combined weight of myself and the family au pair . . .

Oh, *mene, mene, tekel upharsin*! What a fool I was! Now fiery hands retributively mangle my innards! The demons play upon my sackbut and I am cast into the fiery furnace of evacuation. I am hooked there, a Toilet Duck, condemned forever to lick under the rim of life!

T he model head snapped me out of my fugue: 'You're a Libra,' he said, 'aren't you?'
'Whossat?'
'Your sign. It's Libra, innit?' He was regarding me with the preternatural stare of a madman or a seer.
'Well, yes, as a matter of fact it is.'
'I'm good at that. Guessing people's astrological signs. Libras are like, err . . . creative an' that.'
'I s'pose so.'
'But they also find it hard to come to decisions . . .'
'Are you challenging the authority of this court? I tried to sound magisterial, but realized that the figure I cut was ridiculous.

'Nah, nah. I wouldn't do that mate. It's just . . . like . . . I mean to say, wass the point, an' that?'

I couldn't help but agree with him, so I let him go. I even insisted that he take the bathroom scales with him. After all, what good are they to me now?

# Lizard

Epilogue. Many years later . . .

I am old and since the publication of the last volume of my magnum opus, *A History of the English Motorway Service Centre*, I have gained a modest eminence. People tell me that I am referred to as 'the Macaulay of the M40', a sobriquet which, I must confess, gives me no little pleasure. I feel vindicated by the verdict of posterity.

I spend most of my days out on the sun porch. Here I lie naked, for all the world like some moribund reptile, sopping up the rays. My skin has turned mahogany with age and melanoma. It's difficult for me to distinguish now, between the daub of cancerous sarcoma and the toughened wattle of my flesh. Be that as it may, I am not frightened of death. I feel no pain, despite having long since reduced my pernicious habituation to kaolin and morphine to a mere teaspoon every hour.

With age has come stoicism and repose. When I was younger I could not focus on anything or even apprehend a single thought without feeling driven to incorporate it into some architectonic, some Great Design. I was also plagued by lusts, both fleshly and demonic, which sent me into such dizzying spirals of self-negation, that I was compelled to narcosis.

But now even the contemplation of the most trivial things can provide enough sensual fodder to last me an entire morning. Today, for example, I became transfixed, staring into the kettle, by the three separate levels of scale therein. Firstly the tangible scale, capping the inverted cradle of the water's meniscus. Secondly, the crystalline accretions of scale that wreathed the element. And thirdly, of course, the very abstract notion of 'scale' itself, implied by my unreasoned observation. It's as if I were possessed of some kind of Escher-vision, allowing me constantly to perceive the dimensional conundrum that perception presents.

It is a delicious irony that although, when I first moved to Beaconsfield, the bungalow was regarded as tacky in the extreme, it has become a period piece. The aluminium-framed picture windows, the pebble-dashed façade, the corrugated perspex carport. All of these are now regarded as delightfully authentic and original features. Such is the queer humour of history.

And what of the M40 itself, the fount of my life's work? How stands it? Well, I must confess, that since the universal introduction of electric cars with a maximum speed of 15mph, the glamour of motorway driving seems entirely lost. Every so often I'll take the golf-buggy out and tootle up towards Junction 5 (Stokenchurch), but my motives are really rather morbid.

Morbid, for it is here that I am to be buried. Here, where the motorway plunges through a gunsight cutting, and the rolling plain of Oxfordshire spreads out into the blue distance. Just beyond the Chiltern scarp, where the M40 bisects the Ridgeway, that neolithic drovers' path which was the motorway of Stone Age Britain. It is here that the Nationalist Trust has given gracious permission for me to construct my mausoleum.

I have opted for a long, regular heap of layered stones, with corbelled walls rising to a slab roof. At one end, the burial mound will tastefully elide with the caisson of the bridge where the M40 spans the Ridgeway.

Will the similarities in construction between my tomb and the great chamber tombs of Ireland and the Orkneys lead future historians to posit a theory of a continuous motorway culture, lasting some seven thousand years? I hope so. It has always been my contention that phenomena such as Silbury Hill and the Avebury stone circle can best be understood as, respectively, an embankment and a roundabout.

And so it seems that it is only by taking this very, very long term view, that the answer to that pernicious riddle: 'Why are there no services on the M40?' will find an answer.

In conclusion then. It may be said of me that I have lost my sense of scale, but never that I have lost my sense of proportion.

GRANTA

# NICHOLAS SHAKESPEARE
# WAVERY'S LAST POST

A t five in the afternoon, the *Bahia de Abyla* sailed out of Algeciras. It was the last ferry of the day, and Thomas Wavery was on his way to Africa, having spent the morning in Gibraltar.

He stood on the upper deck, a tall silver-haired man in his late fifties. He had removed his tie, and the sleeves of his shirt were rolled up. The deck was empty. He lifted his bag on to a seat and walked to the rail.

The air smelled of grease from the lifeboat cables and engine oil from the funnel. Most of all, it smelled of the bay which rose and fell in the wind, a short fetch between the waves.

Gibraltar had been everything he hated about England—the Union Jack T-shirts and the early Christmas decorations, the chips and the beer and the career diplomats, reminding him of all he hoped to avoid and everything he had become.

He watched the battered hat of rock until the haze claimed it. When he could no longer see Gibraltar, he crossed the deck and looked into the grimy horizon for Abyla.

W avery had never requested Abyla. For nine years he had written down one preference only: Lisbon. In their inimitable, roundabout way Personnel Department had informed him that the post would be his.

There was a time when Lisbon had been the least of his ambitions. He might have hoped for Paris or an important governorship. He had been going a long way then. The future held out promise of a grand knighthood and Wavery Commissions into a wide assortment of vexed issues. Once upon

**Nicholas Shakespeare** was born in 1957 in Worcester. The son of an English Diplomat he grew up in Brazil, Cambodia, Portugal and Argentina. His story of his search for Abimael Guzmán in Peru appeared in *Granta* 23. He completed his first novel, *The Vision of Elena Silves*, in 1989, when he was Literary Editor of the *Daily Telegraph*. 'Wavery's Last Post' is taken from his second book, *High Flyer*, which Collins Harvill publish in the summer. He has recently returned from Patagonia where he has been conducting research for a biography of Bruce Chatwin.

Photo: Barry Lewis

a time he had been a high flyer.

'I realize I held you back, Tom.'

'Darling, please. Not even in jest.'

But Penny was right. In the end, it was no good having a wife who was more committed to the German Expressionists than the Queen's Birthday Party. When a choice had to be made, at some indefinable point an enormous number of years ago, he had chosen his wife. He had been faithful for all those years and deserved credit. But he did not deceive himself. If he had left her he would have been sunk anyway.

Penny wanted Lisbon above all. 'God, we were so *happy* then. Weren't we?'

They had met in Cambridge thirty-seven years before, at a dinner party in Barton Road. It was a time in Wavery's life when the party always seemed to be elsewhere. He noticed Penny sitting in the corner on a pile of reddish cushions. She sat with her long legs drawn into her side, tying the lace on a grey boot with severe concentration. She had dark agate eyes, fair hair she had forgotten to brush and a round white face. 'That is the girl I am going to marry,' he told himself.

He had been looking to make such a statement. He was twenty and a virgin. The capacity to love lay heavy inside him and he wished to discharge it full square, with maximum force, at the person with whom he would share his life.

She was studying art, the daughter of a Suffolk lawyer. He was a third-year Classicist, the only son of a professional historian—whose books, concerned with a seven-year period in the eighteenth century, he had never managed to finish.

Wavery was too inexperienced to know how we tell people we love them before we mean it, to create a space for love to move in. He recognized the distance between himself and the pretty art student. But with the confidence of a young Latin scholar he believed he might bridge it. When he realized he could not, he respected the distance—until, finally, it became a matter of acceptance.

The term ended and at Easter they met in London. Penny was working in a department store in Knightsbridge, behind the ceramics counter. He was studying for finals. One lunch hour they took a picnic to Hyde Park. She wore a new linen dress, white with narrow shoulder-straps, but was unable properly to flaunt it. The pollen was bad that year and she spent most of the lunch with a creased face, sneezing.

All afternoon his fingers felt the absence of her hand.

When he returned to his aunt's house in Holland Park he wrote to Penny, proposing. He wrote out the letter four times before he was satisfied with the words, after which he walked up Ladbroke Grove. He placed the envelope in the pillar box mouth. Arrested by doubts, he was on the point of snatching it back when he felt rain speckle the back of his hand. Rather than allow the rain to blur the ink in which he had painstakingly written her name and address, he posted the letter.

They were married in August. On returning from honeymoon in the Ardèche, Wavery learned he had been accepted into the Foreign Service. Six months later they arrived in Lisbon, occupying an apartment on the lower half of a palace in Lapa. The apartment's finest feature was a broad, blue-tiled terrace with a matchless view over the Tagus. On this terrace Penny painted in oils for the first time.

Their happiness was conventional. Both were delighted to fall into a mould. They were perpetuating a way of life and a class. If their love was not as passionate as love could be, this was because it had never been put to the test. They were accepted by society. And they were young.

Sometimes after work Wavery would rush home with flowers from a barrow in Estrela, tumbling upon Penny on the terrace where she sat in a thin grey slip, undressing her as she tried to smell the blooms through the tang of paint and turpentine. On Fridays they would drive south and weekend in the pine trees near Lagoa. At night they made love on the beach among the abandoned beach chairs, silently in case they were seen by an old lady walking her dachshund. 'Oh, Basualdo,' she breathed, licking his shoulder, calling him by the name of the make-believe lover she had been awarded in her Portuguese class. She kissed him and the sweat on her tongue was gritted with sand.

They were trying to have children too. When after two years

Penny had not conceived, she saw a doctor recommended by the Embassy. A preliminary examination found nothing untoward. 'He said he'd better check you before going further.' But the fault did not lie with Wavery. Three months later Penny made another appointment. Wavery was sitting on the terrace when she returned from the clinic.

She had not expected him to be there. He told her he was having drinks with a friend of theirs at the British Council. She had not prepared herself.

'Michael had to cancel,' he explained. 'He had to go to Evora.' He waited for her to speak. 'Well, darling? What did he say?'

But he could see the answer in her face. In the months afterwards Wavery realized it was not possible to overestimate the misery of childlessness. It became a source of profound insecurity in Penny. He had to perform daily feats of assurance, telling her it made no difference to his feelings. If he saw someone childless he learnt never to ask why they didn't have children. But when he did come into contact with children he was accidentally wonderful. Not having experience of them, he treated them like adults—which they adored.

For a while Penny's infertility bound them together, producing in her a fervour of creativity. On the Lisbon terrace she painted Wavery as he was then. Pale, black-haired—so black that others joked he used boot-polish. Intelligent. Efficient. But not vain.

'Penny, am I vain?'

'Totally.'

He was proud of his wife, although he could not pretend always to understand her paintings. Once, coming to wash her brushes, she found him alone, standing before a canvas. Becoming aware of her behind him, he turned. He began, 'I love it—but I don't see what's going on.'

'You don't have to.'

'There's something so—' And he said what he had meant to say, '—so *gloomy* there. You're not that gloomy, are you, darling?'

She touched his cheek with her brush. The paint had dried and the brush was harder than she knew. 'Thomas, when will you learn not to confuse me with my work?'

At art school Penny had experimented with gouache and aquatint. Then her most successful paintings had been conventional, blurrily delicate landscapes—trees reflected in the Cam near Granchester, cornfields with a patina of frost, some decently praised studies of Wistman's Wood. In Lisbon she discovered the influences which transformed these landscapes beyond all recognition.

The Museu Nacional de Arte Antigua below their terrace housed a *Temptation of St Anthony* by Bosch, a few unrestored canvases by Romney and Reynolds and a selection from the Portuguese School of the sixteenth century, well represented by unknown masters whose motifs—decapitated saints, mongoloid Christs, fish-shaped Satans—she found pertinent to the twentieth century. Late Picasso she would acknowledge as an influence; and a teacher whose lessons she attended at the Gulkbenkian, who advised her whenever she found herself blocked in the execution of a painting to turn it upside down. Wavery had no such recourse. In moments of depression it was something he envied his wife.

She began to give curious titles to her paintings. Time and again he could see no clearly established relationship between title and content. In *Danger, Mirror Ahead*, painted in tempera, she staged a mournful dialogue between an empty guitar case, a serpent of the underworld and a false moustache. 'I thought of calling it *Melusine on a Saturday*,' she told him, folding her arms. He thought she might have been teasing. He searched the canvas for clues. He had interrupted a gathering, the meaning of which was not in any way evident to him. He watched Penny type her preferred title on to a small white card, detailing the year in which it was painted, its size in centimetres and the materials used in its execution.

'Lovely, darling.'

Many galleries had given her exhibitions. These included the Galeria Lobo in Lisbon, the venue of her first show. When there was a reasonable chance Wavery might return to Lisbon as

281

ambassador, Penny was pleased—not merely for herself, intending to keep the owner of the Galeria Lobo to his long-held promise of a retrospective, but also for her husband, she being more ambitious for Wavery than he had become for himself.

Lisbon might also restore something that had gone underground between them.

When first he joined the Diplomatic Service, Wavery had been full of the great anticipations in life. He had intended to set fire to the sea. But in Lisbon his ambitions began their long, slow, guttering out. While at night, in sleep, he might dream of sitting again the Foreign Office exam, day greeted him with the miserable pettiness of diplomatic life, until one morning, fumbling with the combination on the bag-room lock in Phnom Penh, the realization came to him it was no longer Thomas Wavery who occupied the position of Second Secretary with commercial responsibility, but the position which occupied him.

After six years abroad, in Lisbon and Phnom Penh, Wavery was posted to London and discovered he represented a country he knew nothing about. He had been living out the middle-class manners of a generation that had vanished from the face of Britain. For six years he had been speaking for a people and a country that no longer existed. Like the boy in *Woyzeck*, he had glimpsed the moon and believed it was friendly. He had flown to the moon only to discover it was made of cheese. He had returned to earth. But the earth wasn't there any more. The earth was an upturned pot and he was quite alone.

Instead he saw its countries and its cities reduced to counters in a game to further a career. Budapest, Buenos Aires, Amman, Lima—these names didn't evoke real places inhabited by real people. They evoked a residence and a large staff.

Six years became thirty-six. He rested on his oars. He crossed his fingers behind his back, hoping no one suspected the truth about him, merely playing the role expected of an officer in the Administrative Stream, the part of a responsible, patriotic, intelligent, efficient and above all virtuous career diplomat. And no one did suspect. They might see he lacked the hunger for high office—and the day must have arrived when it was decided he would never be given Paris or Moscow after all—but they thought incredibly well of him, at any rate well enough for Lisbon, which was the only post he coveted anyway.

At fifty-eight, Wavery had a fine haggard look. He was not a handsome man feature for feature, but he exerted a definite presence. He had the aura of a wise man and people deferred to him. In conversation he never betrayed himself if he was bored or irritated. When he looked at you his gaze was not lazy but direct. You felt you could tell him anything and he would behave perfectly, inclining his head as he listened, never flicking his eyes towards someone more important, more exciting.

Women found him attractive because he exuded an air of safety, but it did not cross his mind to be unfaithful, as much out of support for Penny as from an incomplete sense of himself. Diplomatic life had been a continual party at which he could not be himself. After thirty-six years of not being himself, he was beginning to believe there was no self to be.

And in that limbo love had also died.

They had been married ten years when Penny said, 'Whatever happened to your hands?'

'My hands?'

She had been sitting back, contemplating him. 'I've just been thinking, you never wave them any more.'

He held out the offending hands and looked at them. 'Don't I?'

'You're tired, darling, aren't you?'

'I suppose.'

'Why?'

He dropped his arms. 'Well, that's it, isn't it? Because of that. There's nothing to tire me.'

She came forward and embraced him. 'Tom, I'm sorry,' she said, her closed eyes adding, 'Sorry for the fact I have been able to compensate myself. Sorry for not giving you children.'

Penny's paintings were the children they'd never had. She lavished on them what once she had lavished on him and over a period he came to miss the burnish of her attention which he received whenever he sat for her. Wavery, looking at his wife as

283

she painted him, would think: That palette knife is a scalpel. She is scraping herself into her work. She is giving to her art bits and pieces of herself which can never be retrieved. The better the work, the more its completion leaves her diminished, exhausted, brittle. The more it leaves us apart.

'No, don't move.' She was concentrating on his eyes, a pair of slanted, sad-happy things she was filling with crimson.

As Penny grew more successful as an artist, so Wavery made a conscious effort to create a landscape for himself. To his immense surprise and pleasure he discovered he possessed a natural talent for gardening. He may have been a childless, unfathering creature, but he was able to bring plants to life.

'Of course, it's very *akin* to being a painter,' Penny would tell visitors, more and more of whom tended to be fellow artists. 'He takes everything from his own palette. But instead of putting it into words or pictures, he makes a little spot of orange or a patch of blue. The only drawback is the place is so full of bees.'

He dreamed of the gardens he was forced to leave behind.

To himself he argued his heart was a robust thing. It would fill again like a magic cistern they visited near Petra, where water was a crop that ripened, oozing mysteriously from the rocky walls. But he felt unreplenished, until the time came when he told Penny he loved her and hearing the tone he employed to appreciate her paintings, she said, 'No, Thomas. You don't love me. You're just very, very fond of me.'

She was right. She had not called him Basualdo for many years. He longed to experience the passion he had lost. He thought, people never tell you about the end of sex, when the love you make is made to a sister. In the silted channels of his desire, he noticed each new hair on her breast, each scratchmark below her eye, and he hated his revulsion. He criticized Penny mercilessly to himself. He saw all her vulnerable parts and he exaggerated them. Because he loved her, loved her, loved her, he told himself. But it wasn't that. The sweet words he had used to preface their lovemaking, he now used later—usually following an argument.

Wavery was content to live with his unfulfilment. After all, it was he who had developed an ability to sit through painful situations without saying a word.

Penny was less content. She had been inflamed by his passion, loving things in him even he found repellent. When his passion subsided she continued to feel the scalds.

So they trotted along, enveloped in the pantomime horse of their marriage, towards an embassy in Lisbon, followed by compulsory retirement at sixty—'Just when you know what you're talking about!'—in a vaguely discussed cottage on the Sintra hills outside Lisbon, where he planned to lay out a garden modelled on Monserrate and look at the sea through olive trees.

One evening towards the end of his time in Lima, they were invited by the American *chargé d'affaires* to attend a buffet supper in celebration of his wife Rita's fortieth birthday, an occasion billed as 'Millstone or Milestone?'

'It's very informal,' said Penny. 'He won't be wearing a tie.'

Wavery had not wanted to go. The Tennyson's house was la-di-da gone mad and party games were promised. But Penny insisted. Rita was one of the few diplomatic wives Penny liked. Attractive to men, Rita reserved her fiercer sympathies for women.

Penny said, 'You can't pretend Denver's thrilling, because he isn't. He's a perky bore. But Rita does throw good parties—if you know what I mean.' Besides, Rita was the President of the *Damas Diplomaticas*. 'She's not your type, but she's doing a lot for the young wives.'

He returned home late. A bomb had exploded near the Pan-Americana, killing a policeman. The traffic thinned beyond the Gold Museum. Wavery turned right, past an empty playground from which the shouts of children woke him in the morning. He hooted twice at his gate. Antonio reached for his attaché case.

He said, 'Gin-tonic, Antonio.'

He tumbled on to the sofa an armful of week-old copies of *The Times*.

'Penny?'

He walked towards the bedroom, untying his tie. He jerked it from his neck. The diagonals of green and yellow made up the

285

rebellious colours of his old school croquet club. They conferred on its members, elected through a mysterious process which had little to do with the game, an importance he never again assumed. He opened the door.

'I'm ready.' She came into the bedroom from the bathroom. She was over-dressed. She wore her fair hair in curls, a treat she liked to give him. He preferred her hair long and unbrushed, but he had never summoned the courage to tell her. The curls bobbed against the earrings he had bought in Buenos Aires—her favourites, she claimed, overlooking their tendency to inflame her lobes.

'How's the office?' It was a duty question. Out of duty he answered. The Ambassador suspected two policemen guarding his residence of involvement in drugs trafficking. 'And there's a letter in my briefcase from Lawrence.'

'That's nice.'

Rather than talk about Penny's brother, he told her about the bomb.

She said, 'That's the fourth this week,' and opened a cupboard. She separated some dresses. The hangers grated as they grated every morning when she rose to paint and poked about for something to wear. Once, removing the pillow from his face, Wavery asked, 'Why not decide before going to bed?'

'Because I don't know if I'll wake up feeling fat or thin, ugly or pretty.'

She drew out a shawl of crimson alpaca. 'I hate this place.'

'Only three weeks now. Three weeks, Penny.'

'Why haven't we heard? I suppose you still haven't heard?'

Wavery shook his head. 'They have other things to think about.' There was the Gulf. There was South Africa. There were the French farmers. 'Lisbon's not that important.'

'The way they treat you.' She threw the metal hanger on to the bed and walked to the window. 'I look out at this fog and I wish I was in bed with a bear.'

He said, 'Have I time for a bath?'

'She wants us at eight.'

'Not even a small one?' But he didn't insist. He telephoned Antonio. 'Antonio, don't bother with that drink.' He changed into a pair of trousers folded on a chair beside her easel. In the cupboard he found a shirt and a jacket.

'You're not serious?' she said. 'That shirt. With that jacket?'

He felt stupid. 'Why not? The jacket's Harris tweed. And you gave me the shirt.'

'I may have bought it, but I didn't expect you to wear it with a jacket like that.' She left the room and Wavery dressed. He was not interested in clothes. All his work went into the initial purchase. Once he had made the effort to buy something good, he felt it had to look after itself on him, an attitude which annoyed Penny.

Her unhappiness tonight upset Wavery. He tried to conjure away the moment, hoping it was dust on the needle. But he knew it was more than dust. Never had the Bible intended two people to live so long together. The life expectancy envisaged by the ceremony in Clare College chapel was forty. Long before her fortieth birthday Penny had parted company with the young woman he had sat down beside on a Cambridge floor. Wavery was different too. In earlier days he would have insisted on his bath.

A fterwards Wavery told himself: had he insisted on his bath they would have left their house in Monterrico fifteen minutes later and the evening would not have differed from a thousand such evenings.

They would have walked through the Tennyson's door, Penny's back protected by his palm, suspended two inches above her shawl, and greeted Rita, a tall woman with a long neck and sharp elbows who was telling the Colombian Defence Attaché, a man with crumbs on his face, 'It's life isn't it, and life is people and if you don't invest in people . . . ', and Rita, catching sight of Penny, would say, 'Remember Tino?' who had taken the opportunity to vanish in pursuit of a tray, and Penny would say, 'Yes, he's frightfully nice,' and Rita would say, 'Thomas would like him,' and stick a piece of paper on their backs bearing the name of someone famous whom they had to guess by asking ten questions, yes or no answers, no cheating, mind, and why don't you start with Denver, he still doesn't know who he is, no, really he doesn't, and dutifully they would amble over to Denver, his back adorned by a large placard and the words KING KONG, and Denver who was a little hard of hearing so one was obliged to repeat oneself would smile fixedly and ask, 'Am I alive?' and tell Wavery that Rita always had such nice friends and this was their very good friend Mr Riding who'd just come from London on business, and Wavery would politely have enquired of the good-looking, florid-faced man with CLARK GABLE on his back how long he had been in the wine trade, and the waitress whose shoulders Mr Riding was squeezing would pause long enough for Penny to receive a tomato juice and Wavery would take a gin and tonic and two long swallows and, Will you excuse me?, cross the room to greet his ambassador, a man with a whim of steel who had written on the whiskered tern and kept black-necked geese in the residence garden, and they would talk about the political situation in a spiritless way, the ambassador blinking because he believed himself to be a security risk, and too distracted to ask Wavery a yes, no question, he would say he must go and speak with Denver who had a fairly good ear to the ground, and turning reveal himself as RONALD BIGGS which was possibly an error on Rita's part, and Wavery feeling very dull would move towards the buffet table where presently Penny would join him accompanied by a famous Peruvian gouache artist, a small man with a long grey beard and a dirty word in the art world because he'd overcleaned Lima's National Gallery, who was giving her some painterly advice he'd picked up from a most terrible woman, his mother, and Penny would tell him in her most earnest voice, 'I believe people who hate their mothers often get on very well in life,' and did he know her husband, they were chalk and cheese, which is so much better—if you have things in common, you only fight over them, to which the artist would reply holding Wavery's hand for several seconds longer than necessary, 'I have heard proof he is of our species,' and very shortly afterwards, to escape the German Cultural Attaché, a narcolept who fell asleep in mid-sentence, to escape the wife of the French Number Two, an attender of poetry readings, 'I'm coming to talk to you when I've done my stint with Denver!', to escape the cigarette smoke and the fly-plague of questions, am I dead? am I alive? am I a movie star? a politician? Jesus Christ? to escape for a moment this party and its brutal similarity to every other party he attended, Wavery would have walked out of the rage of the light and breathed a sigh of unrestrained relief because Rita's patio was empty, not a soul, just a chair for him to sit and count the shooting stars, because fifteen minutes earlier Catherine Riding would have escorted her husband back to their hotel in Miraflores, and Wavery's destiny would not have altered for ever.

GRANTA

# HELEN SIMPSON
# HEAVY WEATHER

'Y ou should never have married me.'
'I haven't regretted it for an instant.'
'Not *you*, you fool! *Me!* You shouldn't have got me to marry you if you loved me. Why *did* you, when you knew it would let me in for all *this*. It's not *fair!*'
'I didn't know. I know it's not. But what can I do about it?'
'I'm being mashed up and eaten alive.'
'I know. I'm sorry.'
'It's not your fault. But what can I do?'
'I don't know.'

So the conversation had gone last night in bed, followed by platonic embraces. They were on ice at the moment, so far as anything further was concerned. The smoothness and sweet smell of their children, the baby's densely packed pearly limbs, the freshness of the little girl's breath when she yawned, these combined to accentuate the grossness of their own bodies. They eyed each other's mooching bulk with mutual lack of enthusiasm, and fell asleep.

At four in the morning, the baby was punching and shouting in his Moses basket. Frances forced herself awake, lying for the first moments like a flattened boxer in the ring trying to rise while the count was made. She got up and fell over, got up again and scooped Matthew from the basket. He was huffing with eagerness, and scrabbled crazily at her breasts like a drowning man until she lay down with him. A few seconds more and he had abandoned himself to rhythmic gulping. She stroked his soft head and drifted off. When she woke again, it was six o'clock and Matthew was sleeping between her and Jonathan.

**Helen Simpson** was born in Bristol in 1957. She read English at Oxford and subsequently worked for five years as a staff writer at *Vogue* after winning its talent competition. Her collection of short fiction *Four Bare Legs in a Bed* won the Somerset Maugham Prize and the 1990 *Sunday Times* Young Writer of the Year award. Helen Simpson is also the author of *The Ritz Book of Afternoon Tea*, a 'scholarly little book with ur-recipes for the Victoria sponge.' She lives in south-west London with her husband and two young children.

Photo: Barry Lewis

For once, nobody was touching her. Like Holland she lay, aware of a heavy ocean at her sea wall, its weight poised to race across the low country.

The baby was now three months old, and she had not had more than half an hour alone since his birth in February. He was big and hungry and needed her there constantly on tap. Also, his two-year-old sister Lorna was, unwillingly, murderously jealous, which made everything much more difficult. This time round was harder, too, because when one was asleep the other would be awake and vice versa. If only she could get them to nap at the same time, Frances started fretting, then she might be able to sleep for some minutes during the day and that would get her through. But they wouldn't, and she couldn't. She had taken to muttering I can't bear it, I can't bear it, without realizing she was doing so until she heard Lorna chanting I can't bear it! I can't bear it! as she skipped along beside the pram, and this made her blush with shame at her own weediness.

In her next chunk of sleep came that recent nightmare, where men with knives and scissors advanced on the felled trunk which was her body.

'How would you like it?' she said to Jonathan. 'It's like a doctor saying, now we're just going to snip your scrotum in half, but don't worry, it mends very well down there, we'll stitch you up and you'll be fine.'

It was gone seven by now and Lorna was leaning on the bars of the cot like Farmer Giles, sucking her thumb in a ruminative pipe-smoking way. The room stank like a lion house. She beamed as her mother came in, and lifted her arms up. Frances hoisted her into the bath, stripped her down and detached the dense brown nappy from between her knees. Lorna carolled, 'I can sing a *rain*bow,' raising her faint fine eyebrows at the high note, graceful and perfect, as her mother sluiced her down with jugs of water.

'Why does everything take so long?' moaned Jonathan. 'It only takes *me* five minutes to get ready.'

Frances did not bother to answer. They were all four in Dorset on a week's holiday. She was sagging with the effortful boredom of assembling the paraphernalia needed for a morning out in the car. Juice. Beaker with screw-on lid. Flannels. Towels. Changes of clothes in case of car sickness. Nappies. Rattle. Clean muslins to catch Matthew's curdy regurgitations. There was more. What was it?

'Oh, come on, Jonathan, think,' she said. 'I'm fed up with having to plan it all.'

'What do you think I've been doing for the last hour?' he shouted. 'Who was it that changed Matthew's nappy just now? Eh?'

'Congratulations,' she said.

Lorna burst into tears.

'Why is everywhere always such a *mess*,' said Jonathan, picking up plastic spiders, dinosaurs, telephones, beads and bears, his grim scowl over the mound of primary colours like a traitor's head on a platter of fruit.

'I *want* dat spider, daddy!' screamed Lorna. 'Give it to me!'

During the ensuing struggle, Frances pondered her tiredness. Her muscles twitched as though they had been tenderized with a steak bat. There was a bar of iron in the back of her neck, and she felt unpleasantly weightless in the cranium, a gin-drinking side effect without the previous fun. The year following the arrival of the first baby had gone in pure astonishment at the loss of freedom, but second time round it was spinning away in exhaustion. Matthew woke at one and four, and Lorna at six-thirty. During the days, fatigue came at her in concentrated doses, like a series of time bombs.

'Are we ready at last?' said Jonathan, breathing heavily. 'Are we ready to go?'

'Um, nearly,' said Frances. 'Matthew's making noises. I think I'd better feed him, or else I'll end up doing it in a lay-by.'

'Right,' said Jonathan. 'Right.'

Frances picked up the baby. 'What a nice fat parcel you are,' she murmured in his delighted ear. 'Come on, my love.'

'Matthew's not your love,' said Lorna. '*I'm* your love. You say C'mon love to *me*.'

'You're *both* my loves,' said Frances.

The baby was shaking with eagerness, and pouted his mouth as she pulled her shirt up. Lorna sat down beside her, pulled up her own T-shirt and applied a teddy bear to her nipple. She grinned at her mother.

Frances looked down at Matthew's head, which was shaped like a brick or a small wholemeal loaf, and remembered again how it had come down through the middle of her. She was trying very hard to lose her awareness of this fact, but it would keep re-presenting itself.

'D'you know,' said Lorna, her free hand held palm upwards, her hyphen eyebrows lifting, 'D'you know, I was sucking my thumb when I was coming down stairs, mum, mum, then my foot slipped and my thumb came out of my mouth.'

'Well, that's very interesting, Lorna,' said Frances.

Two minutes later, Lorna caught the baby's head a ringing smack and ran off. Jonathan watched as Frances lunged clumsily after her, the baby jouncing at her breasts, her stained and crumpled shirt undone, her hair a bird's nest, her face craggy with fatigue, and found himself dubbing the tableau, Portrait of Rural Squalor in the manner of William Hogarth. He bent to put on his shoes, stuck his right foot in first then pulled it out as though bitten.

'What's *that*,' he said in tones of profound disgust. He held the shoe in front of Frances's face.

'It looks like baby sick,' she said. 'Don't look at me. It's not my fault.'

'It's all so bloody *basic*,' said Jonathan, breathing hard, hopping off towards the kitchen.

'If you think that's basic, try being me,' muttered Frances. 'You don't know what basic *means*.'

'Daddy put his foot in Matthew's sick,' commented Lorna, laughing heartily.

At Cerne Abbas they stood and stared across at the chalky white outline of the Iron Age giant cut into the green hill.

'Do you remember when we stood on it?' said Jonathan. 'Five years ago?'

'Of course,' said Frances. She saw the ghosts of their frisky former selves running round the giant's spreading limbs and up on to his phallus. Nostalgia filled her eyes and stabbed her smartly in the guts.

'"The woman riding high above with bright hair flapping free,"' quoted Jonathan. 'Will you be able to grow *your* hair again?'

'Yes, yes. Don't look at me like that, though. I know I look like hell.'

A month before Matthew was born, Frances had had her hair cut short. Her head had looked like a pea on a drum. It still did. With each year of pregnancy, her looks had hurtled five years on. She had started using sentences beginning, 'When I was young.' Ah, youth! Idleness! Sleep! How pleasant it had been to play the centre of her own stage. And how disorientating was this overnight demotion from Brünnehilde to spear-carrier.

'What's that,' said Lorna. 'That *thing*.'

'It's a giant,' said Frances.

'Like in Jacknabeanstork?'

'Yes.'

'But what's that *thing*. That thing on the giant.'

'It's the giant's thing.'

'Is it his stick thing?'

'Yes.'

'My baby budder's got a stick thing.'

'Yes.'

'But I haven't got a stick thing.'

'No.'

'Daddy's got a stick thing.'

'Yes.'

'But mummy hasn't got a stick thing. We're the same, mummy.'

She beamed and put her warm paw in Frances's.

'You can't see round without an appointment,' said the keeper of Hardy's cottage. 'You should have telephoned.'

'We did,' bluffed Jonathan. 'There was no answer.'

'When was that?'

'Twenty to ten this morning.'

'Humph. I was over sorting out some trouble at Cloud's

Hill. T. E. Lawrence's place. All right, you can go through. But keep them under control, won't you.'

They moved slowly through the low-ceilinged rooms, whispering to impress the importance of good behaviour on Lorna.

'This is the room where he was born,' said Jonathan, at the head of the stairs.

'Do you remember from when we visited last time?' said Frances slowly. 'It's coming back to me. He was his mother's first child, she nearly died in labour, then the doctor thought the baby was dead and threw him into a basket while he looked after the mother. But the midwife noticed he was breathing.'

'Then he carried on till he was eighty-seven,' said Jonathan.

They clattered across the old chestnut floorboards, on into another little bedroom with deep thick-walled window seats.

'Which one's your favourite now?' asked Frances.

'Oh, still *Jude the Obscure*, I think,' said Jonathan. 'The tragedy of unfulfilled aims. Same for anyone first generation at university.'

'Poor Jude, laid low by pregnancy,' said Frances. 'Another victim of biology as destiny.'

'Don't *talk*, you two,' said Lorna.

'At least Sue and Jude aimed for friendship as well as all the other stuff,' said Jonathan.

'Unfortunately, all the other stuff made friendship impossible, didn't it,' said Frances.

'Don't *talk*!' shouted Lorna.

'Don't shout!' said Jonathan. Lorna fixed him with a calculating blue eye and produced an ear-splitting scream. The baby jerked in his arms and started to howl.

'Hardy didn't have children, did he?' said Jonathan above the din. 'I'll take them outside. You stay up here a bit longer if you want to.'

Frances stood alone in the luxury of the empty room and shuddered. She moved around the furniture and thought fond savage thoughts of silence in the cloisters of a convent, a blessed place where all was monochrome and non-viscous. Sidling up unprepared to a mirror on the wall she gave a yelp at her reflection. The skin was the colour and texture of pumice stone, the grim jaw set like a lion's muzzle. And the eyes, the eyes far back in the skull were those of a herring three days dead.

Jonathan was sitting with the baby on his lap by a row of lupins and marigolds, reading to Lorna from a newly acquired guide-book.

'When Thomas was a little boy he knelt down one day in a field and began eating grass to see what it was like to be a sheep.'

'What the sheep say?' asked Lorna.

'The sheep said, er, so now you know.'

'And what else?'

'Nothing else.'

'Why?'

'What do you mean, why?'

'*Why?*'

'Look,' he said when he saw Frances. 'I've bought a copy of *Jude the Obscure* too, so we can read to each other when we've got a spare moment.'

'Spare moment!' said Frances. 'But how lovely you look with the children at your knees, the roses round the cottage door. How I would like to be the one coming back from work to find you all bathed and brushed, and a hot meal in the oven and me unwinding with a glass of beer in a hard-earned crusty glow of righteousness.'

'*I* don't get that,' Jonathan reminded her.

'That's because I can't do it properly yet,' said Frances. 'But, still, I wish it could be the other way round. Or at least half and half. And I was thinking, what a cheesy business Eng. Lit. is, all those old men peddling us lies about life and love. They never get as far as this bit, do they.'

'Thomas 1840, Mary 1842, Henry 1851, Kate 1856,' read Jonathan. 'Perhaps we could have two more.'

'I'd kill myself,' said Frances.

They found themselves corralled into a cement area at the back of the Smugglers' Arms, a separate space where young family pariahs could bicker over fish fingers. Waiting at the bar, Jonathan observed the comfortable tables inside, with their noisy laughing groups of the energetic elderly tucking into plates of gammon and plaice and profiteroles.

'Just look at them,' said the crumpled man beside him, who was paying for a trayload of Fanta and baked beans. 'Skipped the war. Nil unemployment, home in time for tea.' He took a great gulp of lager. 'Left us to scream in our prams, screwed us up good and proper. When our kids come along, what happens? You don't see the grandparents for dust, that's what happens. They're all off out enjoying themselves, kicking the prams out the way with their Hush Puppies, spending the money like there's no tomorrow.'

Jonathan grunted uneasily. He still could not get used to the way he found himself involved in intricate conversations with complete strangers, incisive, frank, frequently desperate, whenever he was out with Frances and the children. It used to be only women who talked like that, but now, among parents of young children, it seemed to have spread across the board.

Frances was trying to allow the baby to finish his recent interrupted feed as discreetly as she could, while watching Lorna move inquisitively among the various family groups. She saw her go up to a haggard woman changing a nappy beside a trough of geraniums.

'Your baby's got a stick thing like my baby budder.' Lorna's piercing voice soared above the babble. 'I haven't got a stick thing cos I'm a little gel. My mummy's got fur on her potim.'

Frances abandoned their table and made her way over to the geranium trough.

'Sorry if she's been getting in your way,' she said to the woman.

'Chatty, isn't she,' commented the woman unenthusiastically. 'How many have you got?'

'Two. I'm shattered.'

'The third's the killer.'

'Dat's my baby budder,' said Lorna, pointing at Matthew.

'He's a big boy,' said the woman. 'What did he weigh when he came out?'

'Ten pounds.'

'Just like a turkey,' she said, disgustingly, and added, 'Mine were whoppers too. They all had to be cut out of me, one way or the other.'

By the time they returned to the cottage, the air was weighing on them like blankets. Each little room was an envelope of pressure. Jonathan watched Frances collapse into a chair with children all over her. Before babies, they had been well matched. With the arrival of their first child, it had been a case of Woman Overboard. He'd watched, ineffectual but sympathetic, trying to keep her cheerful as she clung on to the edge of the raft, holding out weevil-free biscuits for her to nibble, and all the time she gazed at him with appalled eyes. Just as they had grown used to this state, difficult but tenable, and were even managing to start hauling her on board again an inch at a time, just as she had her elbows up on the raft and they were congratulating themselves with a kiss, well, along came the second baby in a great slap of a wave that drove her off the raft altogether. Now she was out there in the sea while he bobbed up and down, forlorn but more or less dry, and watched her face between its two satellites dwindling to the size of a fist, then to a plum, and at last to a mere speck of plankton. He dismissed it from his mind.

'I'll see if I can get the shopping before the rain starts,' he said, dashing out to thew car again, knee-deep in cow parsley. 'You really should keep an eye on how much bread we've got left,' he called earnestly as he unlocked the car. 'It won't be *my* fault if I'm struck by lightning.'

There was the crumpling noise of thunder, and silver cracked the sky. Frances stood in the doorway holding the baby, while Lorna clawed and clamoured at her to be held in her free arm.

'Oh, Lorna,' said Frances, hit by a wave of bone-aching fatigue. 'You're too heavy, my sweet.' She closed the cottage door as Lorna started to scream, and stood looking down at her with something like fear. She saw a miniature fee-fi-fo-fum creature working its way through a pack of adults, chewing them up and spitting their bones out.

'Come into the back room, Lorna, and I'll read you a book while I feed Matthew.'

'I don't want to.'

'Why don't you want to?'

'I just don't want to.'

'Can't you tell me why?'

'Do you know, I just don't WANT to!'

'All right, *dear*. I'll feed him on my own then.'

'NO!' screamed Lorna. 'PUT HIM IN DA BIN! HE'S RUBBISH!'

'Don't scream, you little beast,' said Frances hopelessly. The baby squared his mouth and joined in the noise.

Lorna turned the volume up and waited for her mother to crack. Frances walked off to the kitchen with the baby and quickly closed the door. Lorna gave a howl of rage from the other side and started to smash at it with fists and toys. There followed a punishing stint of ricochet work, where Frances let the baby cry while she comforted Lorna; let Lorna shriek while she soothed the baby; put Lorna down for her nap and was called back three times before she gave up and let her follow her destructively around; bathed the baby after he had sprayed himself, Lorna and the bathroom with urine during the nappy-changing process; sat on the closed lavatory seat and fed the baby while Lorna chattered in the bath which she had demanded in the wake of the baby's bath.

She stared at Lorna's slim silver body, exquisite in the water, graceful as a Renaissance statuette.

'Shall we see if you'd like a little nap after your bath?' she suggested hopelessly, for only if Lorna rested would she be able to rest, and then only if Matthew was asleep or at least not ready for a feed.

'No,' said Lorna, off-hand but firm.

'Oh, thank God,' said Frances as she heard the car door slam outside. Jonathan was back. It was like the arrival of the cavalry. She wrapped Lorna in a towel and they scrambled downstairs. Jonathan stood puffing on the doormat. Outside was a mid-afternoon twilight, the rain as thick as turf.

'You're wet, daddy,' said Lorna, fascinated.

'There were lumps of ice coming down like tennis balls,' he marvelled.

'Here, have this towel,' said Frances, and Lorna span off naked as a sprite from its folds to dance among the chairs and tables while thunder crashed in the sky with the cumbersomeness of heavy furniture falling down uncarpeted stairs.

'*S'il vous plaît*,' said Frances to Jonathan, '*Dansez, jouez avec le petit diable, cette fille. Il faut que je* get Matthew down for a nap, she just wouldn't let me. *Je suis tellement* shattered.'

'Mummymummymummy,' Lorna chanted as she caught some inkling of this, but Jonathan threw the towel over her and they started to play ghosts.

'My little fat boy,' she whispered at last, squeezing Matthew's strong thighs. '*Hey*, fatty boomboom, *sweet* sugar dumpling. It's not fair, is it? I'm never alone with you. You're getting the rough end of the stick just now, aren't you.'

She punctuated this speech with growling kisses, and his hands and feet waved like warm pink roses. She sat him up and stroked the fine duck tail of hair on his baby bull neck. Whenever she tried to fix his essence, he wriggled off into mixed metaphor. And so she clapped his cloud cheeks and revelled in his nest of smiles; she blew raspberries into the crease of his neck and on to his astounded hardening stomach, forcing lion-deep chuckles from him.

She was dismayed at how she had to treat him like some sort of fancy man to spare her daughter's feelings, affecting nonchalance when Lorna was around. She would fall on him for a quick mad embrace if the little girl left the room for a moment, only to spring away guiltily at the sound of the returning Startrites.

The baby was making the wrangling noise which led to unconsciousness. Then he fell asleep like a door closing. She carried him carefully to his basket, a limp solid parcel against her bosom, the lashes long and wet on his cheeks, lower lip out in a soft semi-circle. She put him down and he lay, limbs thrown wide, spatchcocked.

fter the holiday, Jonathan would be back at the office with his broad quiet desk and filter coffee while she, she would have to submit to a fate worse than death, drudging round the flat to Lorna's screams and the baby's regurgitations and her own sore eyes and body aching to the throb of next door's Heavy Metal. The trouble with prolonged sleep deprivation was that it produced the same coarsening side-effects as alcoholism. She was rotten with self-pity, swarming with irritability and despair.

When she heard Jonathan's step on the stairs, she realized that he must have coaxed Lorna to sleep at last. She looked forward to his face, but when he came into the room and she opened her mouth to speak, all that came out were toads and vipers.

'I'm smashed up,' she said. 'I'm never alone. The baby guzzles me and Lorna eats me up. I can't ever go out because I've always got to be there for the children, but you flit in and out like a humming bird. You need me to be always there, to peck at and pull at and answer the door. I even have to feed the cat.'

'I take them out for a walk on Sunday afternoons,' he protested.

'But it's like a favour, and it's only a couple of hours, and I can't use the time to read, I always have to change the sheets or make a meatloaf.'

'For pity's sake. I'm tired too.'

'Sorry,' she muttered. 'Sorry. Sorry. But I don't feel like me any more. I've turned into some sort of oven.'

They lay on the bed and held each other.

'Did you know what Hardy called *Jude the Obscure* to begin with?' he whispered in her ear. '*The Simpletons*. And the Bishop of Wakefield burnt it on a bonfire when it was published.'

'You've been reading!' said Frances accusingly. '*When* did you read!'

'I just pulled in by the side of the road for five minutes. Only for five minutes. It's such a good book. I'd completely forgotten that Jude had three children.'

'*Three?*' said Frances incredulously. 'Are you sure?'

'Don't you remember Jude's little boy who comes back from

Australia?' said Jonathan. 'Don't you remember little Father Time?'

'Yes,' said Frances. 'Something very nasty happens to him, doesn't it?'

She took the book and flicked through until she reached the page where Father Time and his siblings are discovered by their mother hanging from a hook inside a cupboard door, the note at their feet reading, 'Done because we are too menny.'

'What a wicked old man Hardy was!' she said, incredulous. 'How *dare* he!' She started to cry.

'You're too close to them,' murmured Jonathan. 'You should cut off from them a bit.'

'How *can* I?' sniffed Frances. '*Somebody's* got to be devoted to them. And it's not going to be you because you know I'll do it for you.'

'They're yours, though, aren't they, because of that,' said Jonathan. 'They'll love you best.'

'They're *not* mine. They belong to themselves. But I'm not allowed to belong to *my* self any more.'

'It's not easy for me either.'

'I know it isn't, sweetheart. But at least you're allowed to be your own man.'

They fell on each other's necks and mingled maudlin tears.

'It's so awful,' sniffed Frances. 'We may never have another.'

They fell asleep.

When they woke, the landscape was quite different. Not only had the rain stopped, but it had rinsed the air free of oppression. Drops of water hung like lively glass on every leaf and blade. On their way down to the beach, the path was hedged with wet hawthorn, the fiercely spiked branches glittering with green-white flowers.

The late sun was surprisingly strong. It turned the distant moving strokes of the waves to gold bars, and dried salt patterns on to the semi-precious stones which littered the shore. As Frances unbuckled Lorna's sandals, she pointed out to her translucent pieces of chrysophase and rose quartz in amongst the more ordinary pebbles. Then she kicked off her own shoes and walked wincingly to the water's edge. The sea was casting lacy white shawls on to the stones, and drawing them back with a sigh.

She looked behind her and saw Lorna building a pile of pebbles while Jonathan made the baby more comfortable in his pushchair. A little way ahead was a dinghy, and she could see the flickering gold veins on its white shell thrown up by the sun through moving sea water, and the man standing in it stripped to the waist. She walked towards it, then past it, and as she walked on, she looked out to sea and was aware of her eyeballs making internal adjustments to the new distance which was being demanded of them, as though they had forgotten how to focus on a long view. She felt an excited bubble of pleasure expanding her rib-cage, so that she had to take little sighs of breath, warm and fresh and salted, and prevent herself from laughing aloud.

After some while she reached the far end of the beach. Slowly she wheeled, like a hero on the cusp of anagnorisis, narrowing her eyes to make out the little group round the pushchair. Of course it was satisfying and delightful to see Jonathan—she supposed it *was* Jonathan?—lying with the fat mild baby on his stomach while their slender elf of a daughter skipped around him. It was part of it. But not the point of it. The concentrated delight was there to start with. She had not needed babies and their pleased-to-be-aliveness to tell her this.

She started to walk back, this time higher up the beach in the shade of cliffs which held prehistoric snails and traces of dinosaur. I've done it, she thought, and I'm still alive. She took her time, dawdling with deliberate pleasure, as though she were carrying a full glass of milk and might not spill a drop.

'I thought you'd done a Sergeant Troy,' said Jonathan. 'Disappeared out to sea and abandoned us.'

'Would I do a thing like that,' she said, and kissed him lightly beside his mouth.

Matthew reached up from his arms and tugged her hair.

'When I saw you over there by the rock pools you looked just as you used to,' said Jonathan. 'Just the same girl.'

'I am not just as I was, however,' said Frances. 'I am no longer the same girl.'

The sky, which had been growing more dramatic by the minute, was now a florid stagey empyrean, the sea a soundless blaze beneath it. Frances glanced at the baby, and saw how the sun made an electric fleece of the down on his head. She touched it lightly with the flat of her hand as though it might burn her.

'Isn't it mind-boggling,' said Jonathan, 'Isn't it impossible to take in that when we were last on this beach, these two were thin air. Or less. They're so solid now that I almost can't believe there was a time before them, and it's only been a couple of years.'

'What?' said Lorna. '*What* did you say?'

'Daddy was just commenting on the mystery of human existence,' said Frances, scooping her up and letting her perch on her hip. She felt the internal chassis, her skeleton and musculature, adjust to the extra weight with practised efficiency. To think, she marvelled routinely, that this great heavy child grew in the centre of my body. But the surprise of the idea had started to grow blunt, worn down by its own regular self-contemplation.

'Look, Lorna,' she said. 'Do you see how the sun is making our faces orange?'

In the flood of flame-coloured light their flesh turned to coral.

# SEAN FRENCH

## THE IMAGINARY MONKEY

## AN OUTRAGEOUS TALE OF AN OVERWEIGHT, UNWANTED UNDERPERFORMER AND HIS REMARKABLE TRANSFORMATION.

Hardcover   25 March   £12.99

For further information on Granta Books, please write to Granta Book Information, Freepost, 2-3 Hanover Yard, Noel Road, London N1 8BR, fax 071-704 0474, tel 071-704 9776

GRANTA BOOKS

GRANTA

# JEANETTE WINTERSON
# THE POETICS OF SEX

# Why do you sleep with girls?

My lover Picasso is going through her Blue Period. In the past her periods have always been red. Radish red, bull red, red like rose-hips bursting seed. Lava red when she was called Pompeii and in her Destructive Period. The stench of her, the brack of her, the rolling splitting cunt of her. Squat like a Sumo, ham thighs, loins of pork, beefy upper cuts and breasts of lamb. I can steal her heart like a bird's egg.

She rushes for me bull-subtle, butching at the gate as if she's come to stud. She bellows at the window, bloods the pavement with desire. She says, 'You don't need to be Rapunzel to let down your hair.' I know the game. I know enough to flick my hind-quarters and skip away. I'm not a flirt. She can smell the dirt on me and that makes her swell. That's what makes my lithe lover bull-rush-thin fat me. How she fats me. She plumps me, pats me, squeezes and feeds me. Feeds me up with lust till I'm as fat as she is. We're fat for each other we sapling girls. We neat clean branching girls get thick with sex. You are wide enough for my hips like roses, I will cover you with my petals, cover you with the scent of me. Cover girl wide for the weight of my cargo.

My bull-lover makes a matador out of me. She circles me and in her rough-made ring I am complete. I like the dressing up, the little jackets, the silk tights, I like her shiny hide, the deep

---

**Jeanette Winterson** was born in 1959. Her first book, *Oranges are not the only Fruit*, won a Whitbread Award in 1985. She has since written three more novels: *The Passion*, *Sexing the Cherry* and *Written on the Body*. Her feature film *Great Moments in Aviation* starring Jonathan Pryce, Vanessa Redgrave and John Hurt will be premièred later this year at the Cannes Film Festival. It is set on board a ship sailing from Grenada to England in 1954. 'It is,' she says, 'a journey physical and metaphysical, an enquiry into the nature of truth and the possibility of personal redemption. It is also very funny.'

'The Poetics of Sex' will appear in *The Penguin Book of Lesbian Short Stories*, edited by Margaret Reynolds, which will be published in September.

Photo: Barry Lewis

tanned leather of her. It is she who has given me the power of the sword. I used it once but when I cut at her it was my close fit flesh that frilled into a hem of blood. She lay beside me slender as a horn. Her little jacket and silk tights impeccable. In my broken ring I sweated muck and couldn't speak. We are quick change artists we girls.

# Which one of you is the man?

Picasso's veins are kingfisher blue and kingfisher shy. The first time I slept with her I couldn't see through the marble columns of her legs or beyond the opaque density of each arm. A sculptor by trade Picasso is her own model.

The blue that runs through her is sanguine. One stroke of the knife and she changes colour. Every month and she changes colour. Deep pools of blue silk drop from her. I know her by the lakes she leaves on the way to the bedroom. Her braces cascade over the stair-rail, she wears earrings of lapis lazuli which I have caught cup-handed, chasing her *déshabillé*.

When she sheds she sheds it all. Her skin comes away with her clothes. On those days I have been able to see the blood-depot of her heart. On those days it was possible to record the patience of her digestive juices and the relentlessness of her lungs. Her breath is blue in the cold air. She breathes into the blue winter like a Madonna of the Frost. I think it right to kneel and the view is good.

She does perform miracles but they are of the physical kind and ordered by her Rule of Thumb to the lower regions. She goes among the poor with every kind of salve unmindful of reward. She dresses in blue, she tells me, so that they will know she is a saint, and it is saintly to taste the waters of so many untried wells.

I have been jealous of course. I have punished her good deeds with some alms-giving of my own. It's not the answer, I can't catch her by copying her, I can't draw her with a borrowed stencil. She is all the things a lover should be and quite a few a lover should not. Pin her down? She's not a butterfly. I'm not a wrestler. She's not a target. I'm not a gun. Tell you what she is? She's not Lot no. 27 and I'm not one to brag.

We were by the sea yesterday and the sea was heavy with salt so that our hair was braided with it. There was salt on our hands and in our wounds where we'd been fighting. 'Don't hurt me,' I said and I unbuttoned my shirt so that she could look at my breasts if she wanted to. 'I'm no saint,' she said and that was true, true too that our feet are the same size. The rocks were reptile blue and the sky that balanced on the top of the cliffs was sheer blue. Picasso made me put on her jersey and drink dark tea from a fifties flask.

'It's winter,' she said. 'Let's go.'

We did go, leaving the summer behind, leaving a trail of footprints two by two in identical four. I don't know that anyone following could have told you which was which and if they had there would have been no trace by morning.

# What do lesbians do in bed?

Under cover of the sheets the tabloid world of lust and vice is useful only in so much as Picasso can wipe her brushes on it. Beneath the sheets we practise Montparnasse, that is Picasso offers to paint me but we have sex instead.

We met at art school on a shiny corridor. She came towards me so swiftly that the linoleum dissolved under her feet. I thought, 'A woman who can do that to an oil-cloth can certainly do something for me.' I made the first move. I took her by her pony tail the way a hero grabs a runaway horse. She was taken aback. When she turned round I kissed her ruby mouth and took a sample of her sea blue eyes. She was salty, well preserved, well made and curved like a wave. I thought, 'This is the place to go surfing.'

We went back to her studio, where naturally enough there was a small easel and a big bed. 'My work comes first,' she said, 'Would you mind?' And not waiting for an answer she mixed an ochre wash before taking me like a dog my breasts hanging over the pillow.

Not so fast Picasso, I too can rumple you like a farm hand,

313

roll you like good tobacco leaf against my thighs. I can take that arrogant throat and cut it with desire. I can make you dumb with longing, tease you like a doxy on a date.

Slowly now Picasso, where the falling light hits the floor. Lie with me in the bruised light that leaves dark patches on your chest. You look tubercular, so thin and mottled, quiescent now. I picked you up and carried you to the bed dusty with ill-use. I found a newspaper under the sheets advertising rationing.

The girl on the canvas was sulky. She hadn't come to be painted. I'd heard all about you my tearaway tiger, so fierce, so unruly. But the truth is other as truth always is. What holds the small space between my legs is not your artistic tongue nor any of the other parts you play at will but the universe we make together beneath the sheets.

We were in our igloo and it couldn't have been snugger. White on white on white on white. Sheet Picasso me sheet. Who was on top depends on where you're standing but as we were lying down it didn't matter.

What an Eskimo I am, breaking her seductive ice and putting in my hand for fish. How she wriggles, slithers, twists to resist me but I can bait her and I do. A fine catch, one in each hand and one in my mouth. Impressive for a winter afternoon and the stove gone out and the rent to pay. We were warm and rich and white. I had so much enjoyed my visit.

'Come again?' she asked. Yes tomorrow, under the sodium street lights, under the tick of the clock. Under my obligations, my history, my fears, this now. This fizzy, giddy, all-consuming now. I will not let time lie to me. I will not listen to dead voices or unborn pain. 'What if?' has no power against 'What if not?' The not of you is unbearable. I must have you. Let them laugh those scorn-eyed anti-romantics. Love is not the oil and I am not the machine. Love is you and here I am. Now.

# Were you born a lesbian?

Picasso was an unlikely mother but I owe myself to her. We are honour-bound, love-bound, bound by cords too robust for those healthy hospital scissors. She baptized me from her own font and said, 'I name thee Sappho.' People often ask if we are mother and child.

I could say yes, I could say no, both statements would be true, the way that lesbians are true, at least to one another if not to the world. I am no stranger to the truth but very uncomfortable about the lies that have dogged me since my birth. It is no surprise that we do not always remember our name.

I am proud to be Picasso's lover in spite of the queer looks we get when holding hands on busy streets. 'Mummy, why is that man staring at us?' I said when only one month old. 'Don't worry dear, he can't help it, he's got something wrong with his eyes.'

We need more Labradors. The world is full of blind people. They don't see Picasso and me dignified in our love. They see perverts, inverts, tribades, homosexuals. They see circus freaks and Satan worshippers, girl-catchers and porno turn-ons. Picasso says they don't know how to look at pictures either.

# Were you born a lesbian?

A fairy in a pink tutu came to Picasso and said, 'I bring you tidings of great joy. All by yourself with no one to help you, you will give birth to a sex toy who has a way with words. You will call her Sappho and she will be a pain in the ass to all men.'

'Can't you see I've got a picture to finish?' said Picasso.

'Take a break,' said the fairy. 'There's more to life than Art.'

'Where?' said Picasso whose first name wasn't Mary.

'Between your legs,' said Gabriel.

'Forget it. Don't you know I paint with my clit?'

'Here, try a brush,' said the fairy, offering her a fat one.

'I've had all the brushes I need,' said Picasso.

'Too late,' said the fairy. 'Here she comes.'

Picasso slammed the door on her studio and ran across to the art college where she had to give a class. She was angry so that her breath burnt the air. She was angry so that her feet dissolved the thin lino tiles already scuffed to ruin by generations of brogues. There was no one in the corridor, or if there was she was no one.

315

Picasso didn't recognize her, she had her eyes on the door and the door looked away. Picasso, running down the clean corridor, was suddenly trip-wired, badly thrown, her hair came away from her glorious head. She was being scalped. She was being mugged. She was detonated on a long fuse of sex. Her body was halfway out of the third floor window and there was a demon against her mouth. A poker-red pushing babe crying 'Feed me, Feed me now.'

Picasso took her home, what else could she do? She took her home to straighten her out and had her kinky side up. She mated with this creature she had borne and began to feel that maybe the Greek gods knew a thing or two. Flesh of her flesh she fucked her.

They were quiet then because Sappho hadn't learned a language. She was still two greedy hands and an open mouth. She throbbed like an outboard motor, she was as sophisticated as a ham sandwich. She had nothing to offer but herself, and Picasso, who thought she had seen it all before, smiled like a child, and fell in love.

# Why do you hate men?

Here comes Sappho, scorching the history books with tongues of flame. Never mind the poetry feel the erection. Oh yes, women get erect, today my body is stiff with sex. When I see a word held hostage to manhood I have to rescue it. Sweet trembling word, locked in a tower, tired of your prince coming and coming. I will scale you and discover that size is no object especially when we're talking inches.

I like to be a hero, like to come back to my island full of girls carrying a net of words forbidden them. Poor girls, they are locked outside their words just as the words are locked into meaning. Such a lot of locking up goes on on the Mainland but here on Lesbos our doors are always open.

Stay inside, don't walk the streets, bar the windows, keep your mouth shut, keep your legs together, strap your purse around your neck, don't wear valuables, don't look up, don't talk to strangers, don't risk it, don't try it. He means she but not when He means Men. Mainland is a private club.

That's all right boys, so is this. This delicious unacknowledged island where we are naked with each other. The boat that brings us here will crack beneath your weight. This is territory you cannot invade.

W e lay on the bed, Picasso and I, listening to the terrible bawling of Salami. Salami is a male artist who wants to be a Lesbian.

'I'll pay you twice the rent,' he cries, fingering his greasy wallet.

'I'll paint you for posterity. I love women, don't you know? Oh God I wish I was a woman, wafer-thin like you, I could circle you with one hand.' He belches.

Picasso is unimpressed. She says, 'The world is full of heterosexuals, go and find one, half a dozen, swallow them like oysters, but get out.'

'Oh whip me,' says Salami getting moist.

We know the pattern. In half an hour he'll be violent and when he's threatened us enough, he'll go to the sleaze pit and watch two girls for the price of a steak.

As soon as he left we forgot about him. Making love we made a dictionary of forbidden words. We are words, sentences, stories, books. You are my New Testament. We are a gospel to each other, I am your annunciation, revelation. You are my St Mark, winged lion at your feet. I'll have you, and the lion too, buck under you till you learn how to saddle me. Don't dig those spurs too deep. It's not so simple this lexographic love. When you have sunk me to the pit I'll mine you in return and we shall be husbands to each other as well as wives.

I'll tell you something Salami, a woman can get hard and keep it there all night and when she's not required to stand she knows how to roll. She can do it any way up and her lover always comes. There are no frigid lesbians, think of that.

On this island where we live, keeping what we do not tell, we have found the infinite variety of Woman. On the Mainland, Woman is largely extinct in all but a couple of obvious forms. She is still cultivated as a cash crop but is nowhere to be found growing wild.

Salami hates to hear us fuck. He bangs on the wall like a zealot at an orgy. 'Go home,' we say, but he doesn't. He'd rather lie against the skirting board complaining that we stop him painting. The real trouble is that we have rescued a word not allowed to our kind. He hears it pounding through the wall day and night. He smells it on our clothes and sees it smeared on our faces. We are happy Picasso and I. Happy.

# Don't you find there's something missing?

I thought I had lost Picasso. I thought the bright form that shapes my days had left me. I was loose at the edges, liquid with uncertainty. The taut lines of love slackened. I felt myself unravelling backwards, away from her. Would the thinning thread snap?

For seven years she and I had been in love. Love between lovers, love between mother and child. Love between man and wife. Love between friends. I had been all of those things to her and she had been all of those things to me. What we were we were in equal parts, and twin souls to one another. We like to play roles but we know who we are. You are beauty to me, Picasso. Not only sensuous beauty that pleases the eye but artistic beauty that challenges it. Sometimes you are ugly in your beauty, magnificently ugly and you frighten me for all the right reasons.

I did not tell you this yesterday or the day before. Habit had silenced me the way habit does. So used to a thing no need to speak it, so well known the action no need to describe it. But I know that speech is freedom which is not the same as freedom of speech. I have no right to say what I please when I please, but I have the gift of words with which to bless you. Bless you Picasso. Bless you for your straight body like a spire. You are the landmark that leads me through the streets of the everyday. You take me past the little houses towards the church where we worship. I do worship you because you are worthy of praise. Bless you Picasso for your able hands that carry the paint to the unbirthed canvas. Your fingers were red when you fucked me and my body striped with joy. I miss the weals of our passion just as

I miss the daily tenderness of choosing you. Choosing you above all others, my pearl of great price.

My feelings for you are Biblical; that is they are intense, reckless, arrogant, risky and unconcerned with the way of the world. I flaunt my bleeding wounds, madden with my certainty. The Kingdom of Heaven is within you Picasso. Bless you.

There is something missing and that is you. Your clothes were gone yesterday, your easel was packed flat and silent against the wall. When I got up and left our unmade bed there was the smell of coffee in the house but not the smell of you. I looked in the mirror and I knew who was to blame. Why take the perfect thing and smash it? Some goods are smashed that cannot be replaced.

It has been difficult this last year. Love is difficult. Love gets harder which is not the same as to say that it gets harder to love. You are not hard to love. You are hard to love well. Your standards are high, you won't settle for the quick way out which is why you made for the door. If I am honest I will admit that I have always wanted to avoid love. Yes give me romance, give me sex, give me fights, give me all the parts of love but not the simple single word which is so complex and demands the best of me this hour this minute this forever.

Picasso won't paint the same picture twice. She says develop or die. She won't let yesterday's love suffice for today. She makes it new, she remixes her colours and stretches her canvas until it sighs. My mother was glad when she heard we'd split up. She said, 'Now you can come back to the Mainland. I'll send Phaeon to pick you up.' Phaeon runs a little business called LESBIAN TOURS. He drives his motor boat round and round the island, just outside the one mile exclusion zone. He points out famous lesbians to sightseers who always say, 'But she's so attractive!' or 'She's so ugly!'.

'Yeah,' says Phaeon, 'And you know what? They're all in love with me.' One sightseer shakes his head like a collecting box for a good cause. 'Can't you just ask one of 'em?' he says.

'I can ask them anything,' says Phaeon who never waits to hear the answer.

# Why do you sleep with girls?

Picasso has loved me for fifty years and she loves me still. We got through the charcoal tunnel where the sun stopped rising. We no longer dress in grey.

On that day I told you about I took my coat and followed her footprints across the ice. As she walked the world froze up behind her. There was nothing for me to return to, if I failed, I failed alone. Despair made it too dark to see, I had to travel by radar, tracking her warmth in front of me. It's fashionable now to say that any mistake is made by both of you. That's not always true. One person can easily kill another.

Hang on me my darling like rubies round my neck. Slip on to my finger like a ring. Give me your rose for my buttonhole. Let me leaf through you before I read you out loud.

Picasso warms my freezing heart on the furnace of her belly. Her belly is stoked to blazing with love of me. I have learned to feed her every day, to feed her full of fuel that I gladly find. I have unlocked the storehouses of love. On the Mainland they teach you to save for a rainy day. The truth is that love needs no saving. It is fresh or not at all. We are fresh and plentiful. She is my harvest and I am hers. She seeds me and reaps me, we fall into one another's laps. Her seas are thick with fish for my rod. I have rodded her through and through.

She is painting today. The room is orange with effort. She is painting today and I have written this.